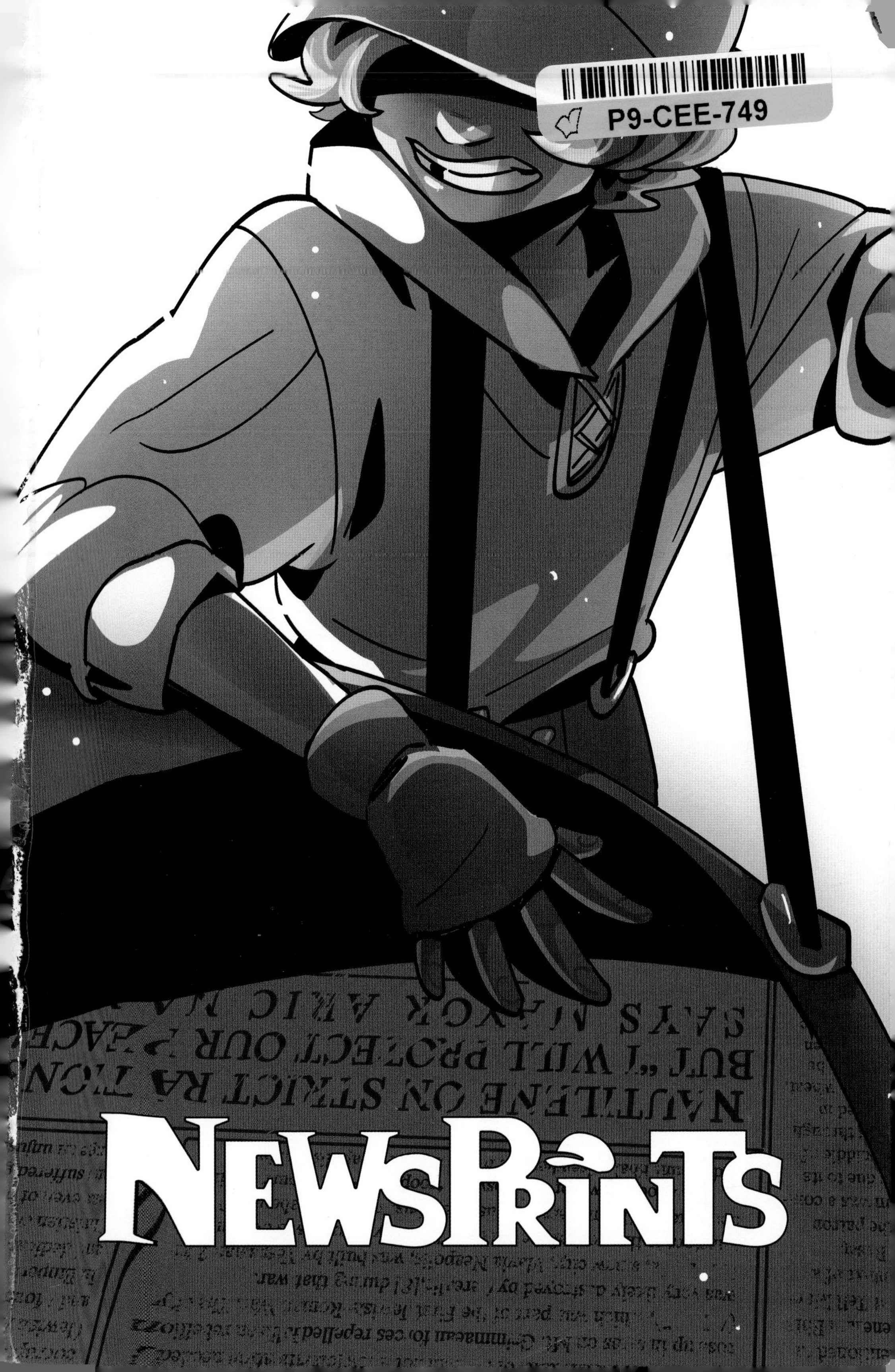
NEWSPRINTS

For the young time travelers.
May the next era you land in be a little kinder than the last.

All rights reserved. Published by Graphix, an imprint of Scholastic Inc., *Publishers since 1920*. SCHOLASTIC, GRAPHIX, and associated logos are trademarks and/or registered trademarks of Scholastic Inc.

Library of Congress Control Number: 2016938202

ISBN 978-0-545-80311-3 (hardcover)
ISBN 978-0-545-80312-0 (paperback)

10 9 8 7 6   18 19 20 21 22
Printed in China   38
First edition, February 2017
Edited by Cassandra Pelham
Book design by Ru Xu and Phil Falco
Creative Director: David Saylor

YOUR COURAGE WINS THE WAR

NEWSPRINTS

Ru Xu

graphix
AN IMPRINT OF
SCHOLASTIC

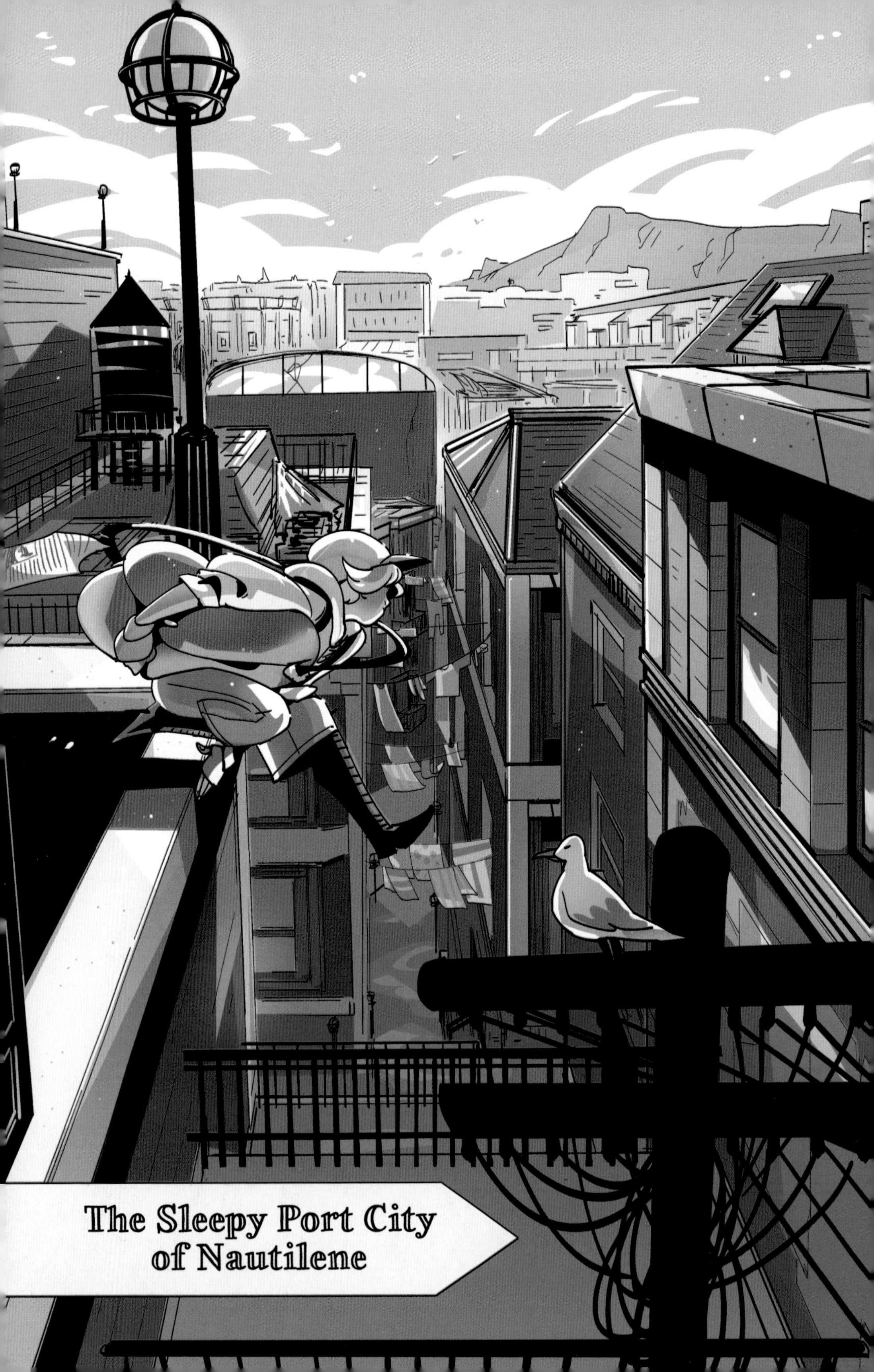
The Sleepy Port City
of Nautilene

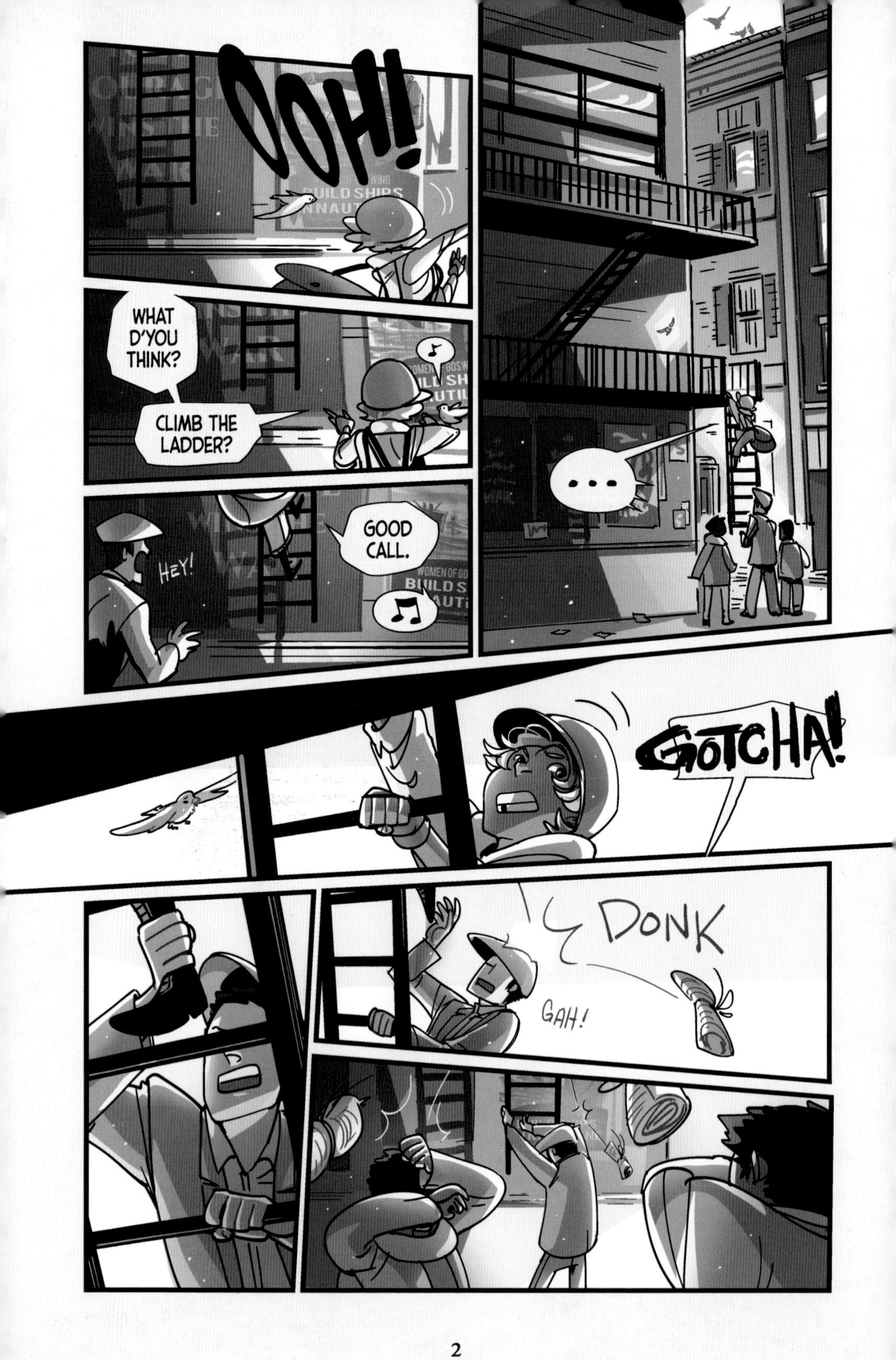
OOH!
BUILD SHIPS
WHAT D'YOU THINK?
CLIMB THE LADDER?
♪
HEY!
GOOD CALL.
♫
BUILD S
. . .
GOTCHA!
DONK
GAH!

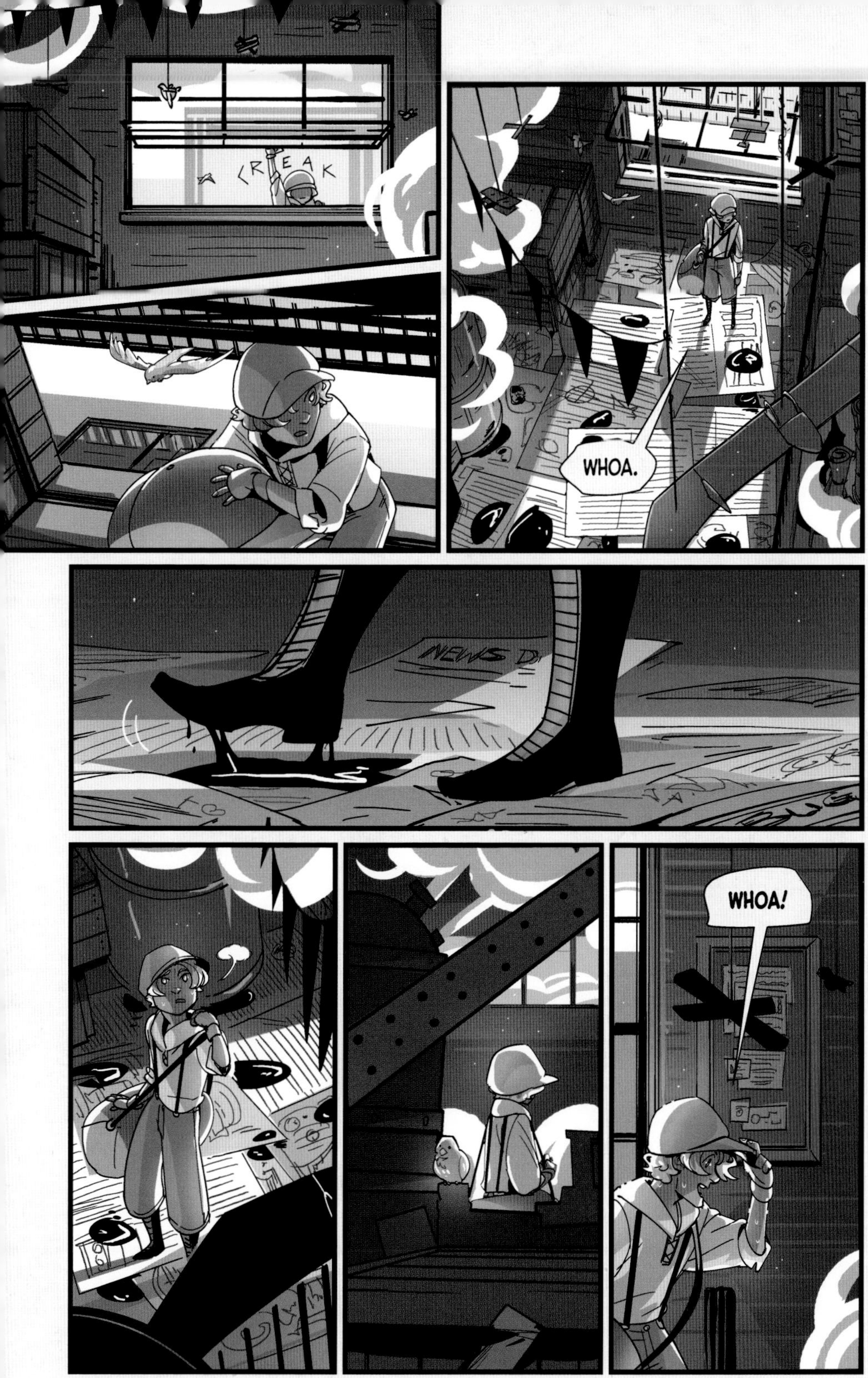
CREAK
WHOA.
NEWS D
WHOA!

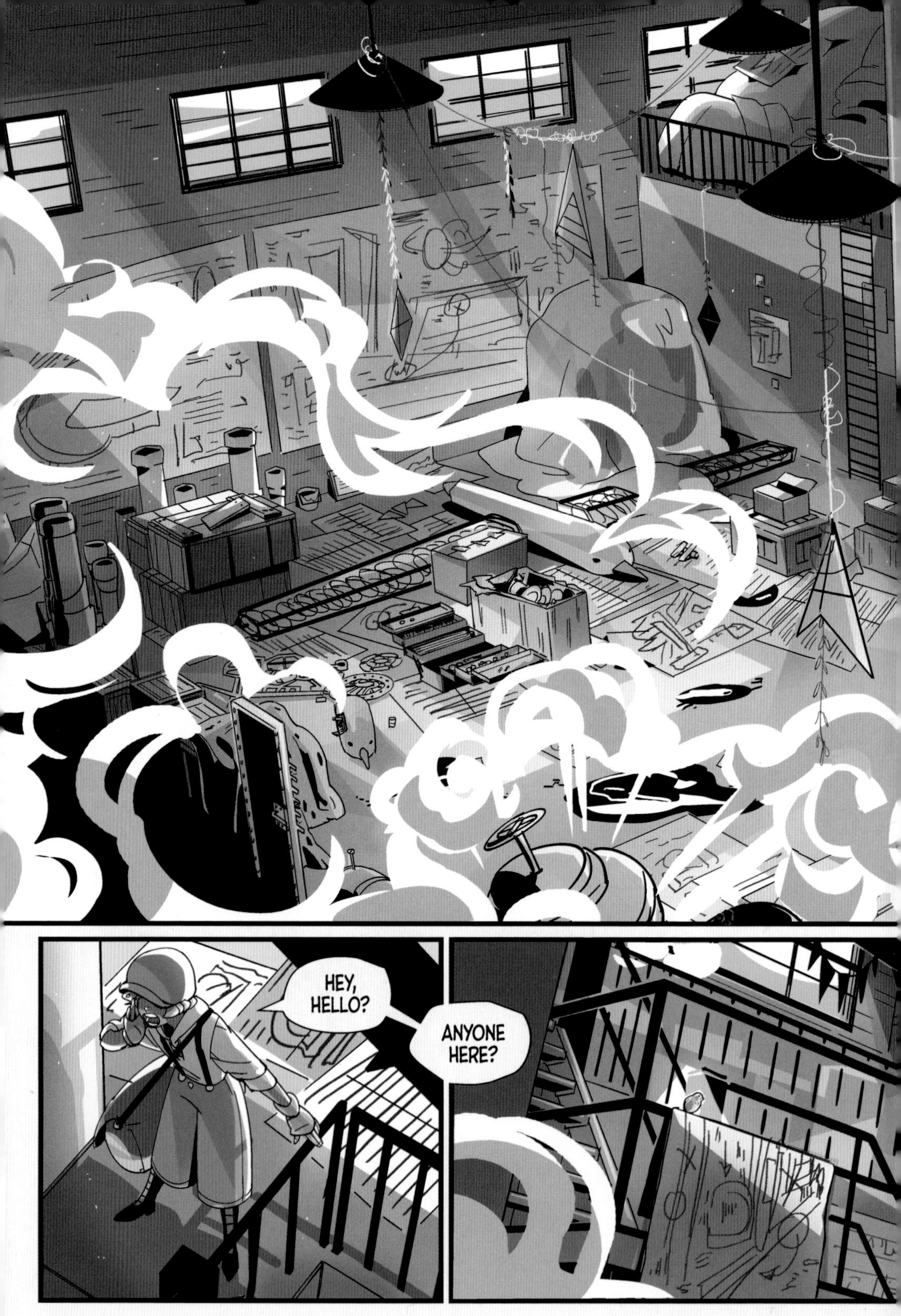
HEY, HELLO?
ANYONE HERE?

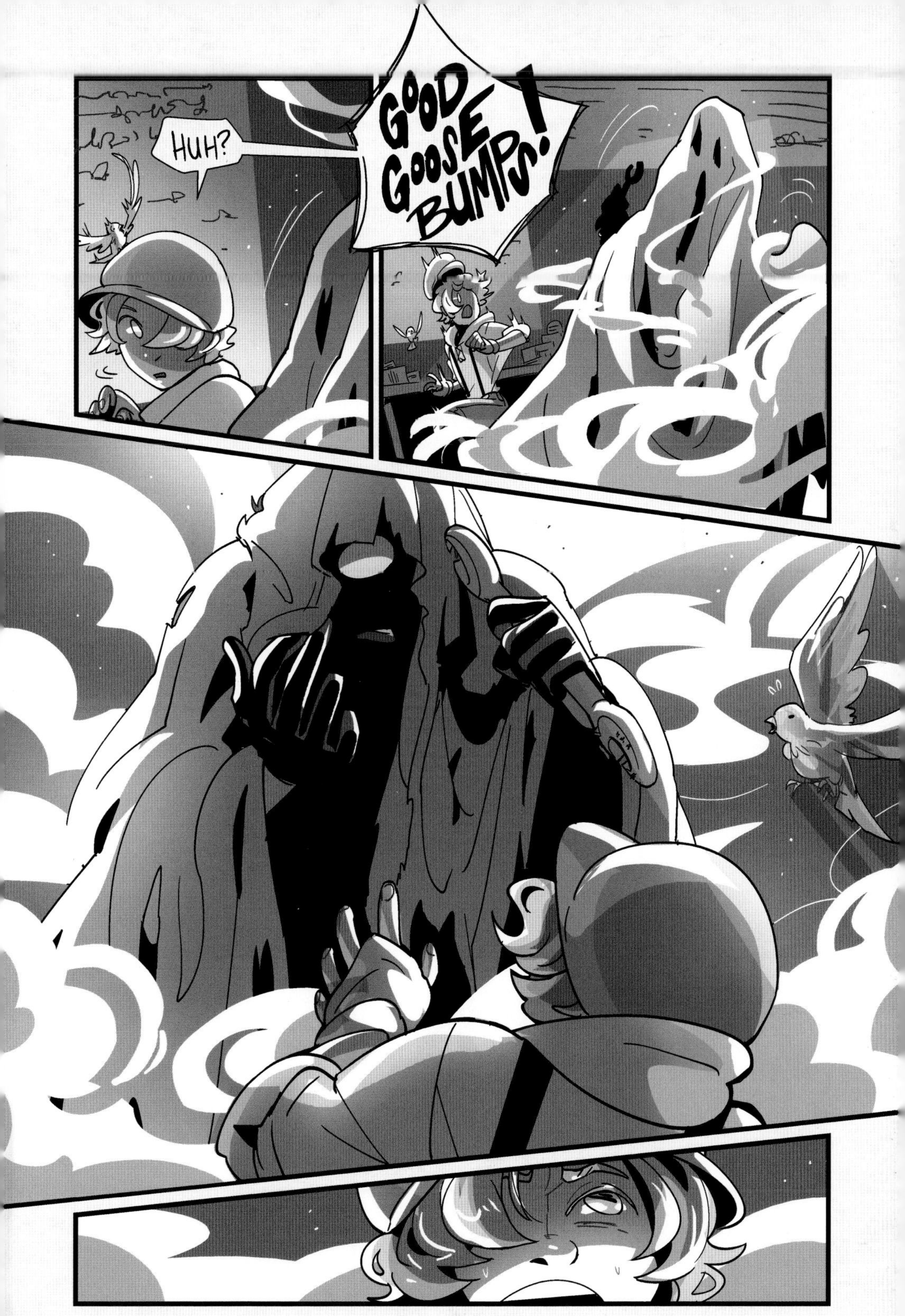
HUH?
GOOD GOOSE BUMPS!

YOUNG MAN. YOU ARE NOT SUPPOSED TO BE...

Peck
Peck
Peck

OH, A CANARY!

I...I MEAN!

HOW DID YOU GET IN HERE?

BAM
BAM
BAM

THE DOOR WAS LOCKED!

IT SURE WAS.

YOU OUGHT TO PUT **LOCKS ON YOUR WINDOWS** FOR GOOD MEASURE!

heh

smack

SO, UHH, CAN I STAY TILL THEY LEAVE, OR WHAT?

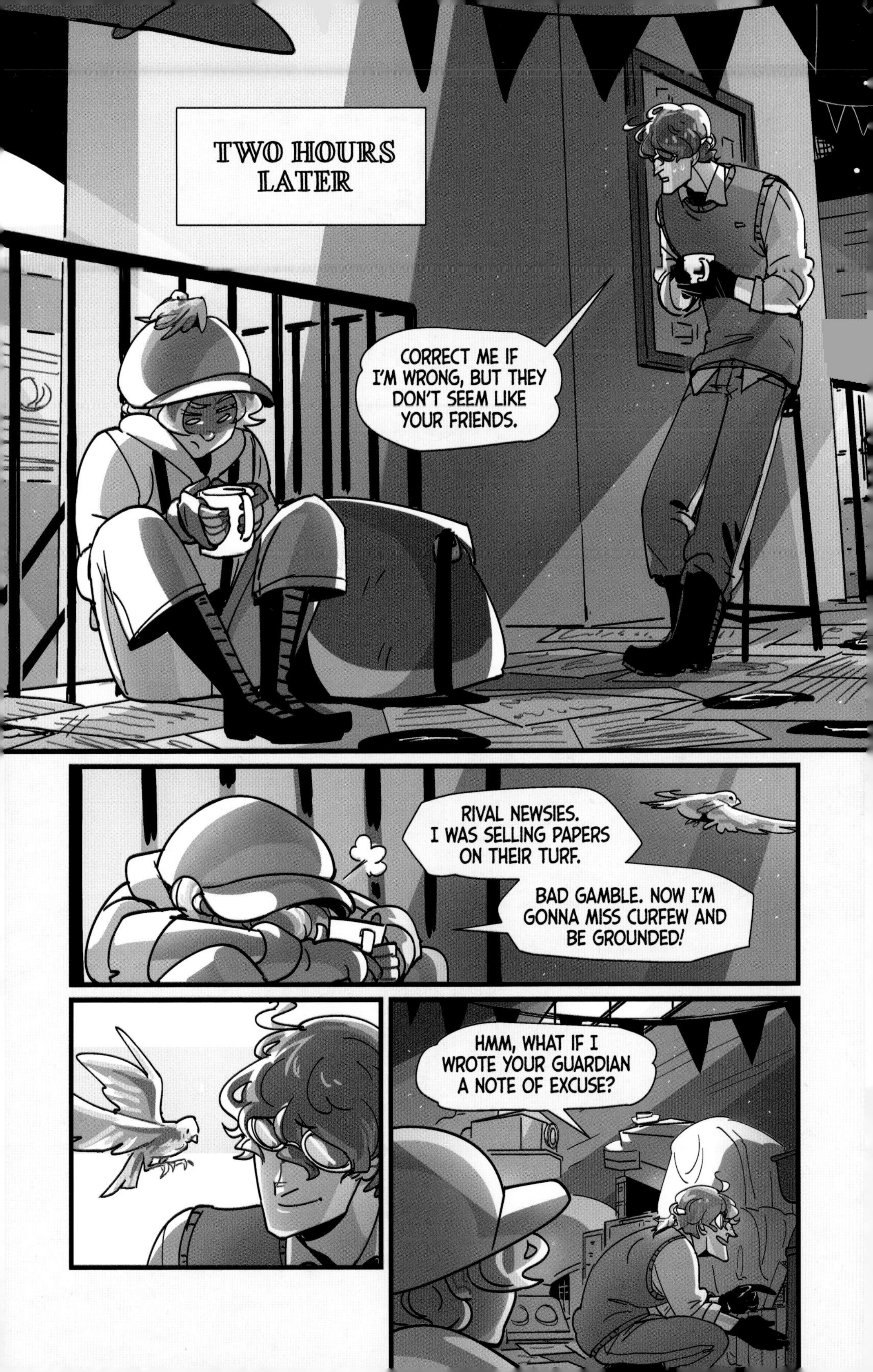
TWO HOURS LATER
CORRECT ME IF I'M WRONG, BUT THEY DON'T SEEM LIKE YOUR FRIENDS.
RIVAL NEWSIES. I WAS SELLING PAPERS ON THEIR TURF.
BAD GAMBLE. NOW I'M GONNA MISS CURFEW AND BE GROUNDED!
HMM, WHAT IF I WROTE YOUR GUARDIAN A NOTE OF EXCUSE?

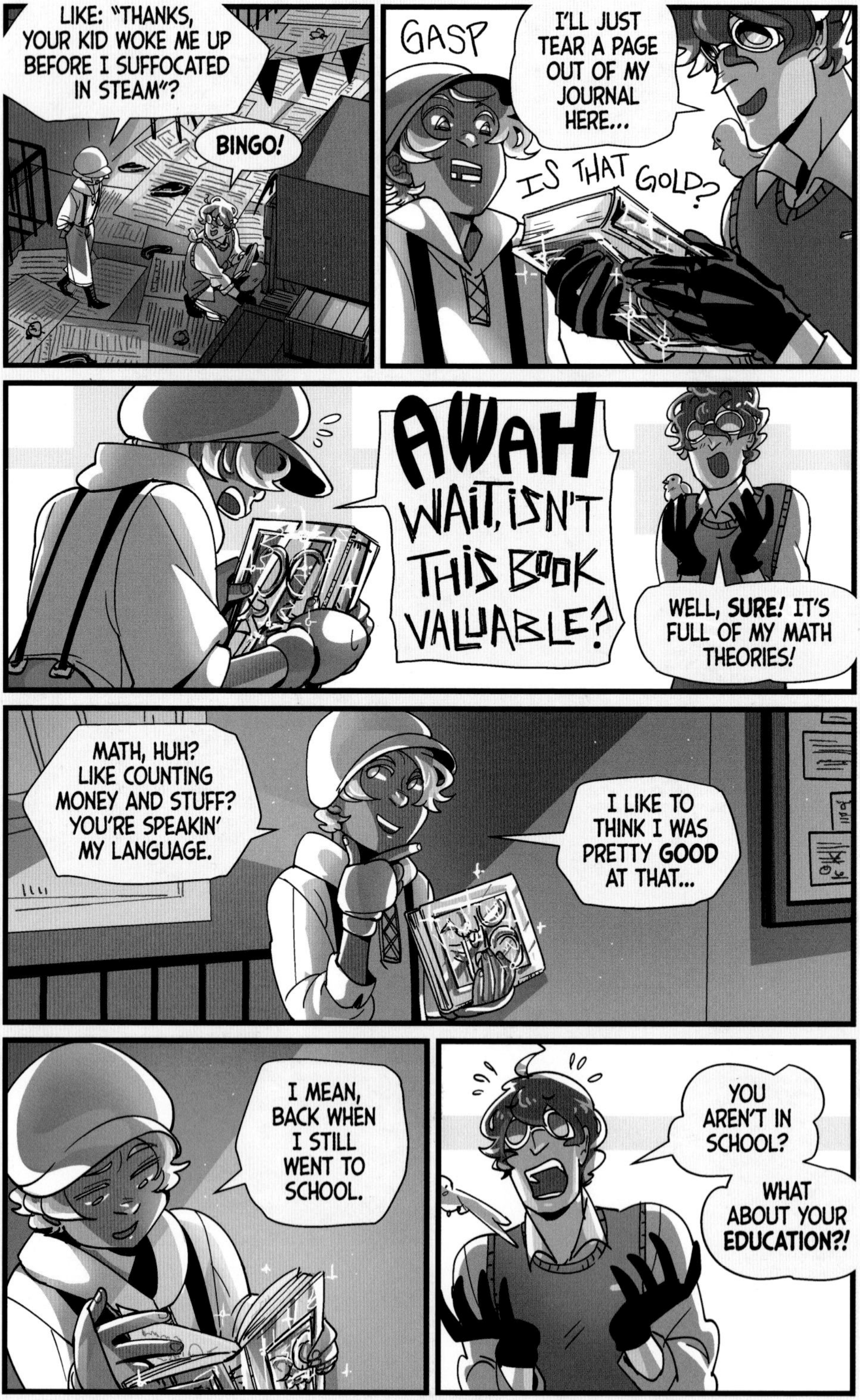

LIKE: "THANKS, YOUR KID WOKE ME UP BEFORE I SUFFOCATED IN STEAM"?
BINGO!
GASP
I'LL JUST TEAR A PAGE OUT OF MY JOURNAL HERE...
IS THAT GOLD?
AWAH
WAIT, ISN'T THIS BOOK VALUABLE?
WELL, SURE! IT'S FULL OF MY MATH THEORIES!
MATH, HUH? LIKE COUNTING MONEY AND STUFF? YOU'RE SPEAKIN' MY LANGUAGE.
I LIKE TO THINK I WAS PRETTY GOOD AT THAT...
I MEAN, BACK WHEN I STILL WENT TO SCHOOL.
YOU AREN'T IN SCHOOL?
WHAT ABOUT YOUR EDUCATION?!

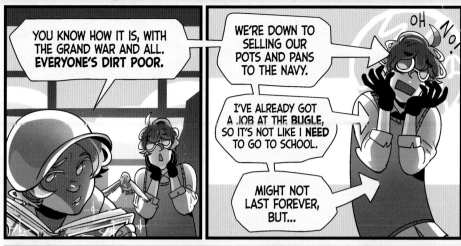

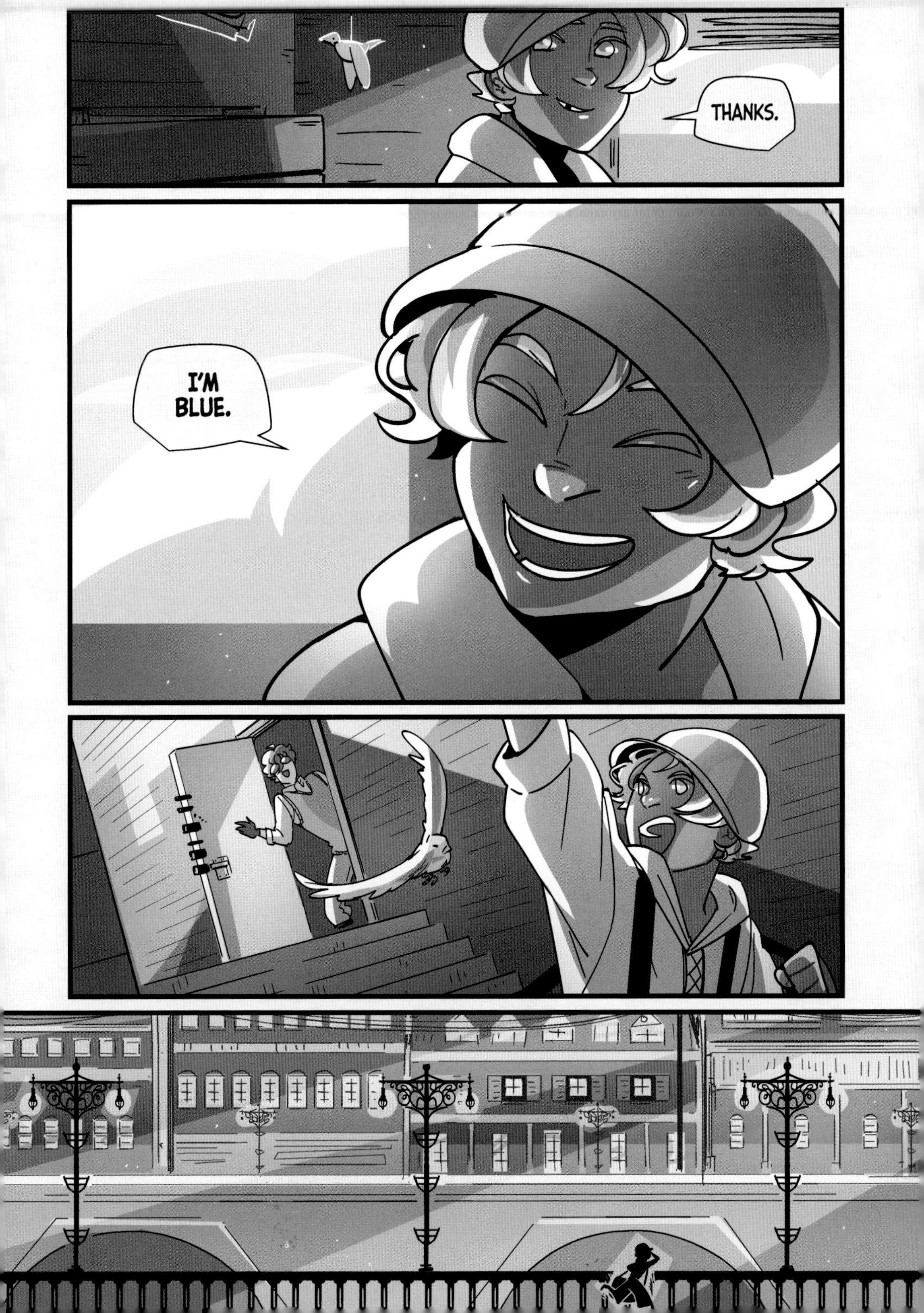
THANKS.
I'M BLUE.

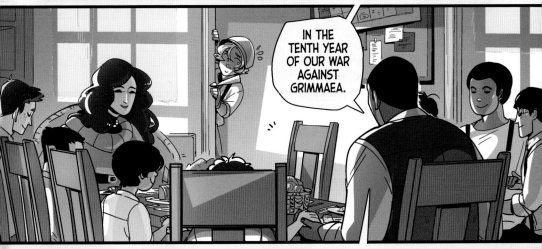

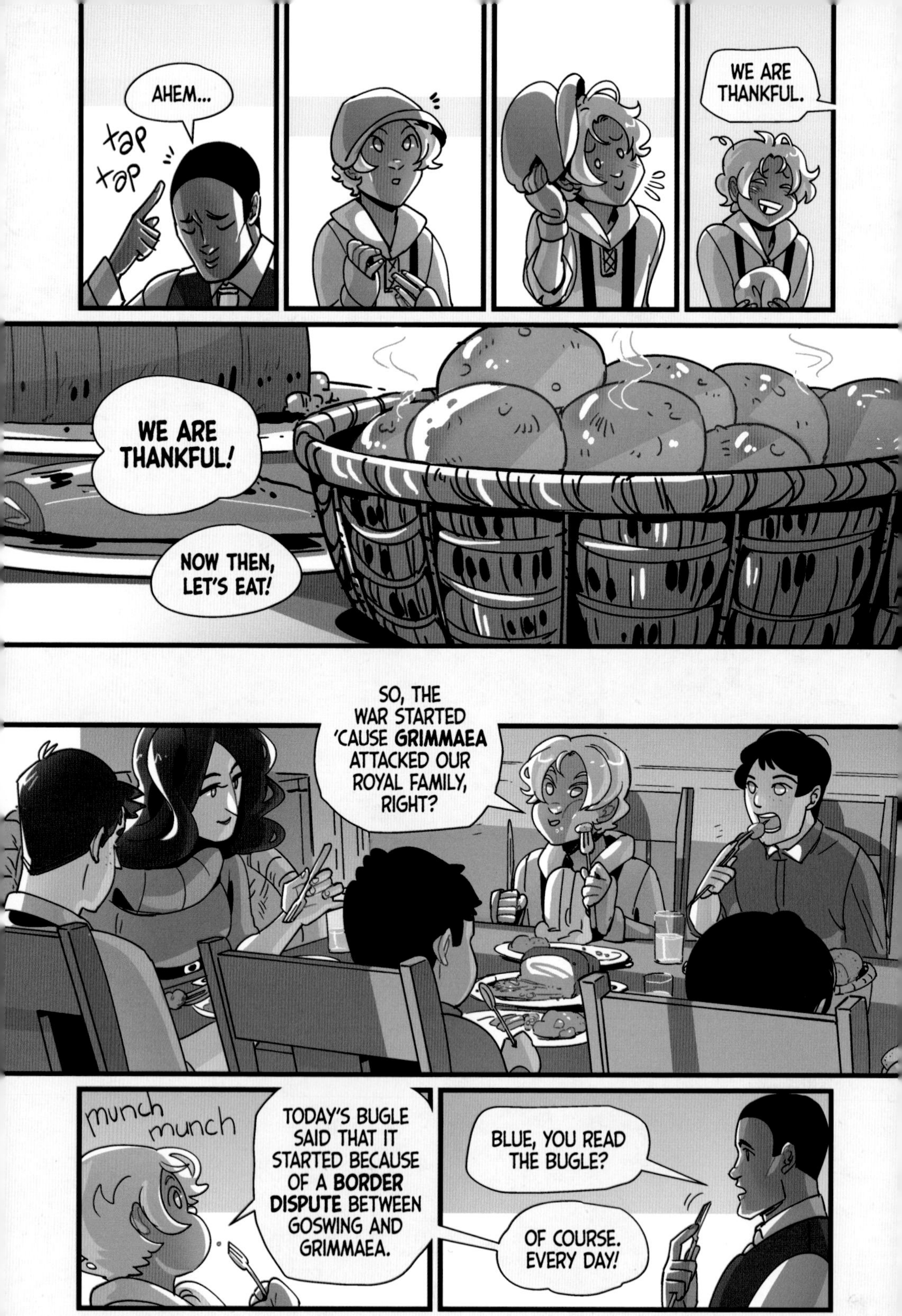
AHEM...
tap tap
WE ARE THANKFUL.
WE ARE THANKFUL!
NOW THEN, LET'S EAT!
SO, THE WAR STARTED 'CAUSE **GRIMMAEA** ATTACKED OUR ROYAL FAMILY, RIGHT?
munch munch
TODAY'S BUGLE SAID THAT IT STARTED BECAUSE OF A **BORDER DISPUTE** BETWEEN GOSWING AND GRIMMAEA.
BLUE, YOU READ THE BUGLE?
OF COURSE. EVERY DAY!

I WANNA KNOW WHAT'S GOING ON **OUTSIDE** THE CITY,

AND NO OTHER PAPER IN NAUTILENE TELLS THE **TRUTH!**

WELL, WE'VE ALWAYS BEEN PROUD OF THE **BUGLE'S** INTEGRITY.

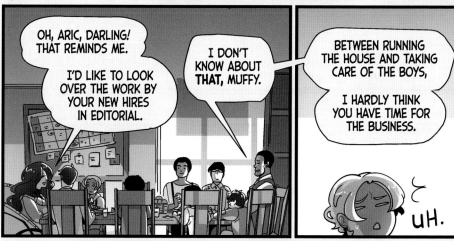

OH, ARIC, DARLING! THAT REMINDS ME.

I'D LIKE TO LOOK OVER THE WORK BY YOUR NEW HIRES IN EDITORIAL.

I DON'T KNOW ABOUT **THAT,** MUFFY.

BETWEEN RUNNING THE HOUSE AND TAKING CARE OF THE BOYS,

I HARDLY THINK YOU HAVE TIME FOR THE BUSINESS.

uH.

YOU MAKE A POINT...

BUT MAYOR NANCY!

I THINK SHE'D BE GOOD AT THAT!

SHE'S BEEN TEACHING US ABOUT HOW JOURNALISTS WRITE THEIR ARTICLES!

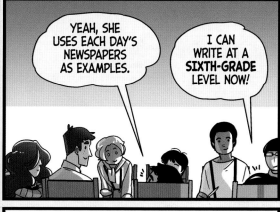

YEAH, SHE USES EACH DAY'S NEWSPAPERS AS EXAMPLES.

I CAN WRITE AT A **SIXTH-GRADE** LEVEL NOW!

INDEED? HMM. WELL, IF THE BOYS THINK IT'S A GOOD IDEA, THEN I HAVE NO COMPLAINTS.

DARLING, I **WON'T** LET YOU DOWN!

HOW WONDERFUL! ♥

WELL, THAT WAS AWKWARD.

IT'S LIKE HE DOESN'T REALLY WANT YOU TO HELP WITH THE FAMILY BUSINESS.

DON'T MIND ARIC. HE'S A LITTLE **OLD-FASHIONED.**

SPL ASH

I'M LUCKY THERE'S A **STRONG-WILLED GIRL HERE** TO STAND UP FOR ME.

I APPRECIATE THAT YOU'VE KEPT MY SECRET FOR THREE YEARS.

OH, I'M SO GLAD TO HAVE YOU HERE!

I THINK YOUR NEW PAPER ROUTES HAVE **REALLY** HELPED US GET THE BUGLE OUT THERE!

MA'AM...

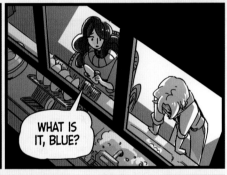

WHAT IS IT, BLUE?

DO YOU THINK I'VE... **PROVEN MYSELF?**

Y'THINK THEY'D STILL LET ME BE A **NEWSBOY** IF THEY KNEW I'M **NOT A BOY?**

DUCKLING, IF ANYONE'S PROOF THAT NEWSIES DON'T HAVE TO BE BOYS, IT'S **YOU.**

Day One as Jack's Apprentice

Day Five

Day Six

The Grundy Gazette

NAUTILENE. Tuesday, Julion 8, 1924

LOCAL INVENTOR ARRESTED FOR TRESPASSING!

New resident caught on private property with suspicious machine. Says he was looking for birds. Nautilene Bugle's newsboy also complicit. Naval police interrogation yielded...
Continued on Page Three.

MAYOR HIRES WIFE TO BUGLE'S EDITORIAL DEPARTMENT! NEPOTISM?

he has favoritism failed to act as the cars drove past them. About an hour later when Franz Ferdinand was returning from a visit at the Sarejevo apart... elite helping the elite the assassination attempt, the convoy took a wrong turn into a street once by coincidence, Princip stood.

MAYOR NOT DELIVERING ON PROMISES TO THE NAUTILENE CITIZENS! SMALL BUSINESSES STILL IN DANGER OF CLOSING.

Nautilene created and for the best interest a the position of over our Nautilene public regarding on 23 looking after the holiday writing, businesses still failing however with its sever losses when worked for First major Allied victories of the war explored

CRO

More as a genus of the species are reading to each as, but to For and carriers of years a now, crows a therefore in appear range and difficult the five siness

Day Seven

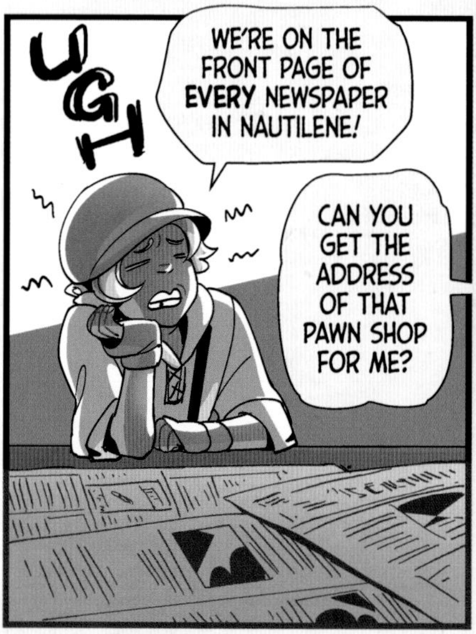
UGH
WE'RE ON THE FRONT PAGE OF EVERY NEWSPAPER IN NAUTILENE!
CAN YOU GET THE ADDRESS OF THAT PAWN SHOP FOR ME?

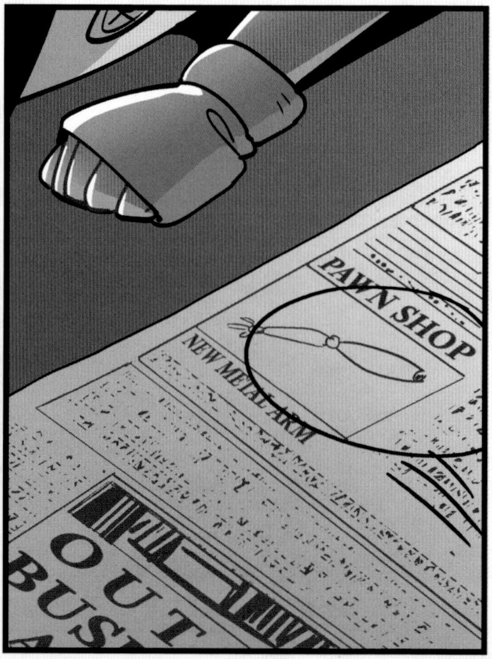
PAWN SHOP
NEW METAL ARM

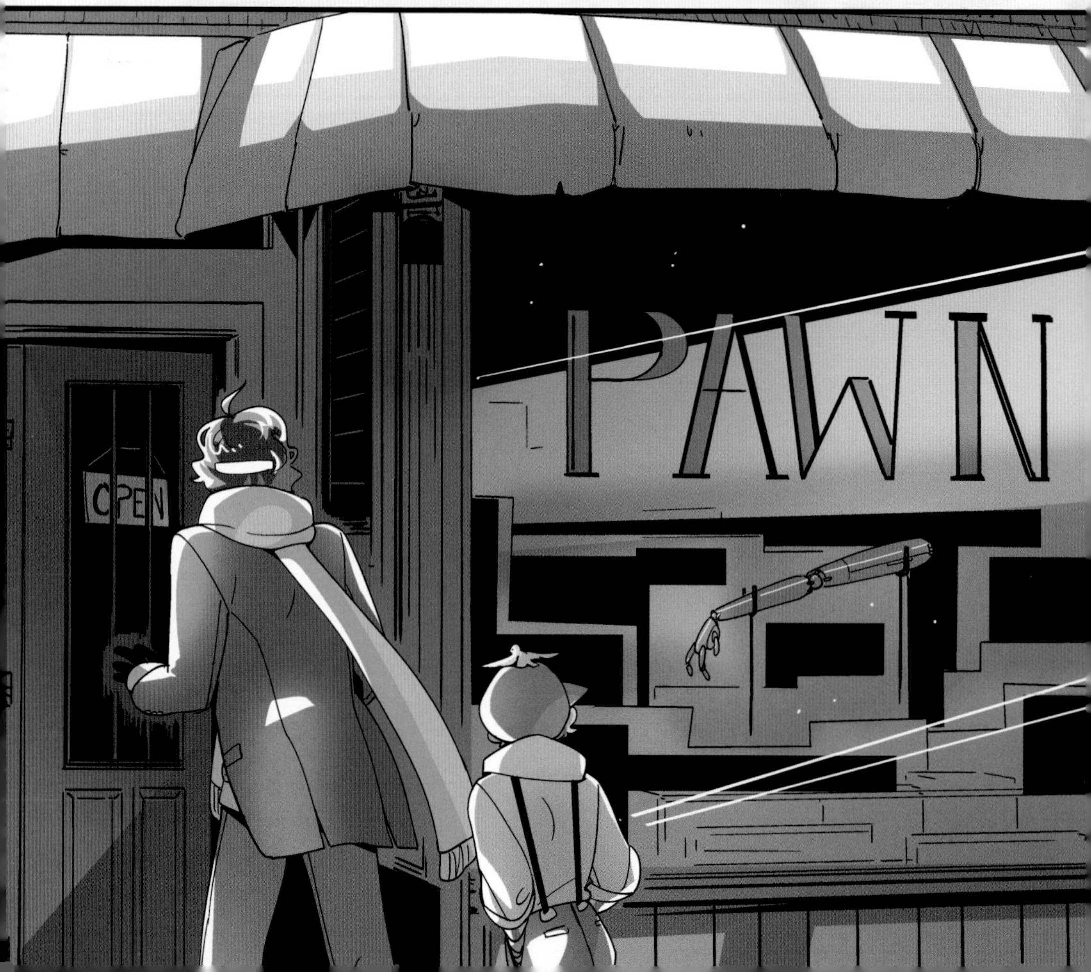
OPEN
PAWN

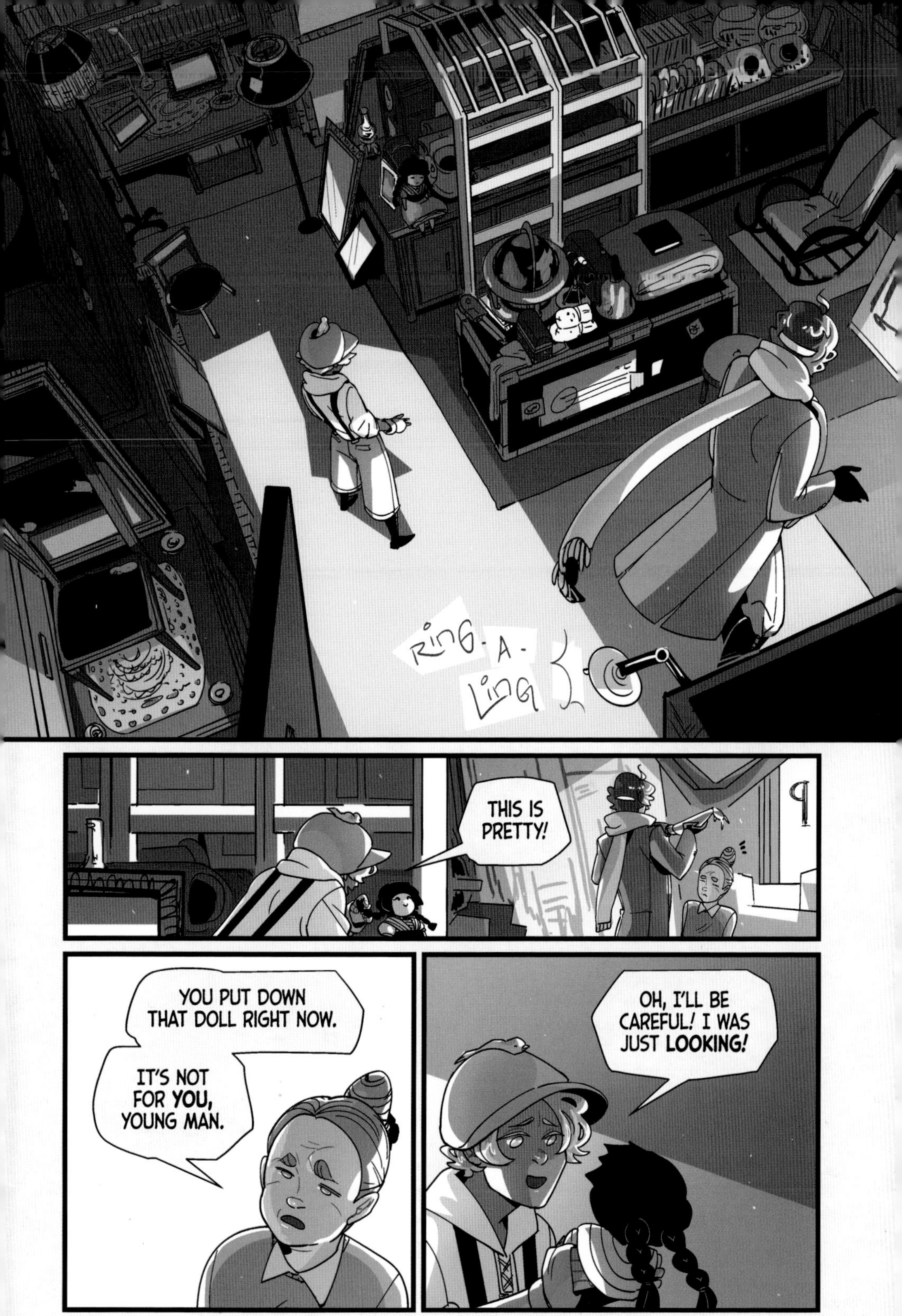
RING-A-LING
THIS IS PRETTY!
YOU PUT DOWN THAT DOLL RIGHT NOW.
IT'S NOT FOR **YOU**, YOUNG MAN.
OH, I'LL BE CAREFUL! I WAS JUST **LOOKING**!

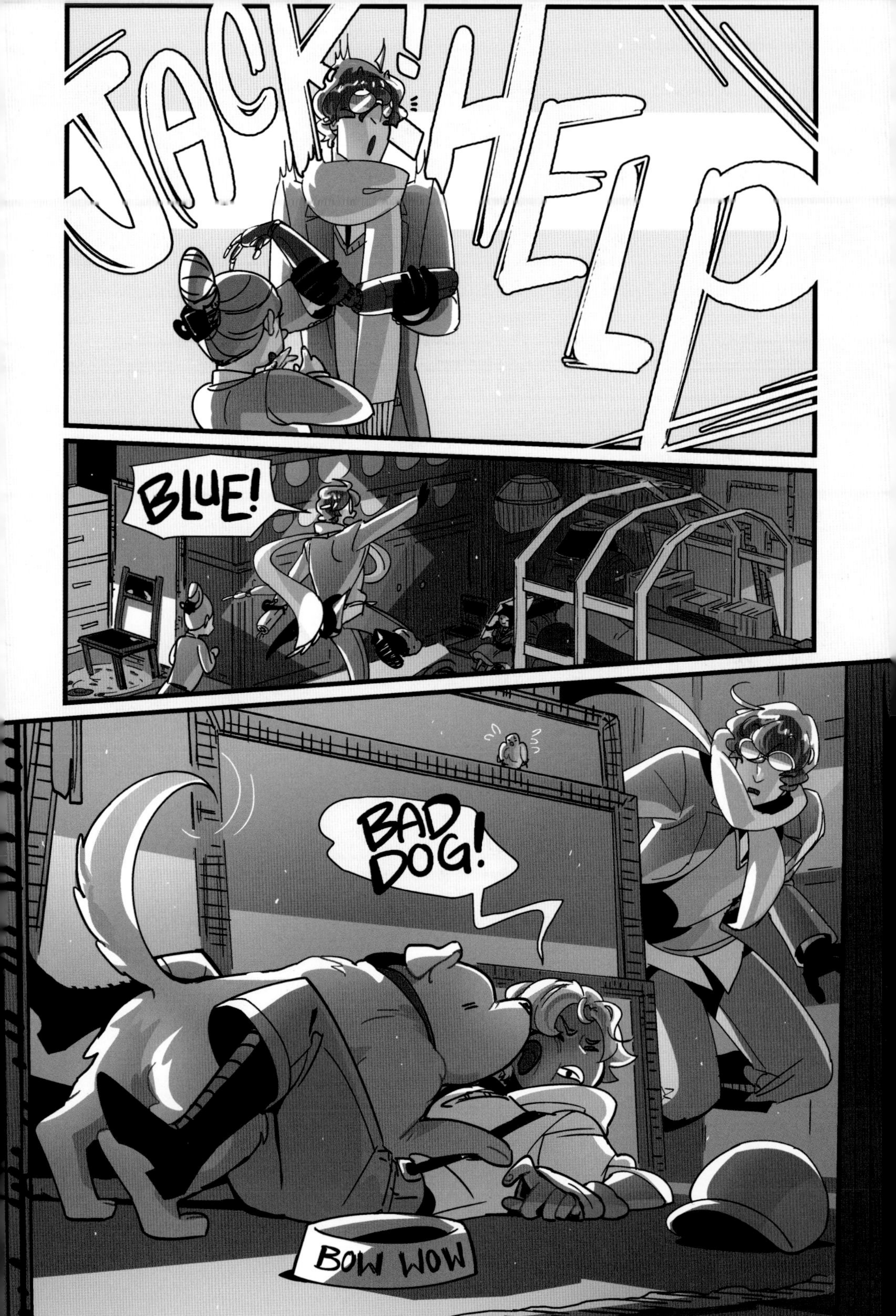
JACK! HELP
BLUE!
BAD DOG!
BOW WOW

WHAT'S WRONG, BLUE?

HIDE ME!

OH.

IT'S THOSE BOYS WHO WERE CHASING YOU.

JACK, LET'S GO!

IF THEY SEE ME HERE, THEY'LL BEAT UP ME AND MY FRIENDS!

THAT'S VERY... MEAN.

MAYBE I CAN HELP.

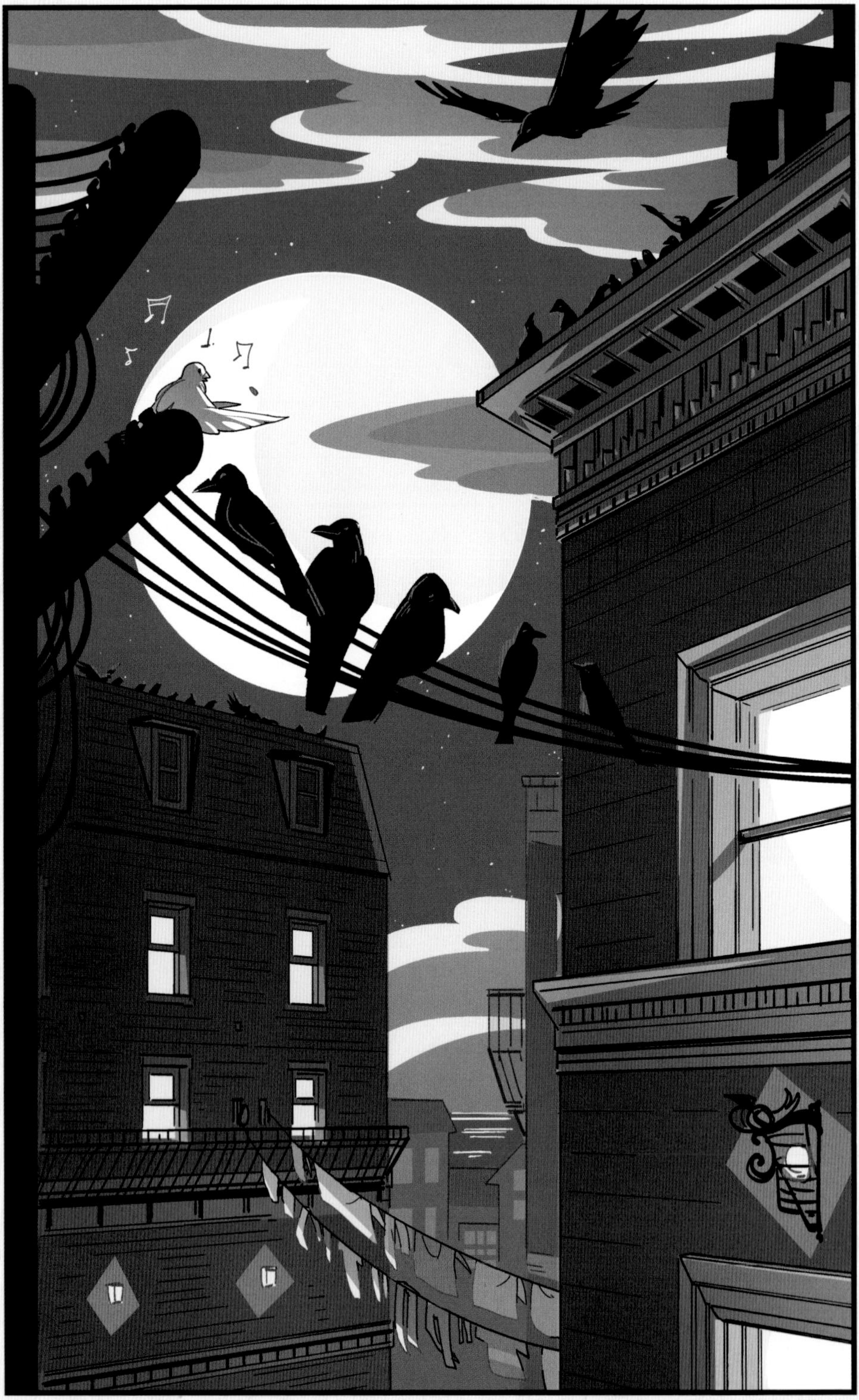

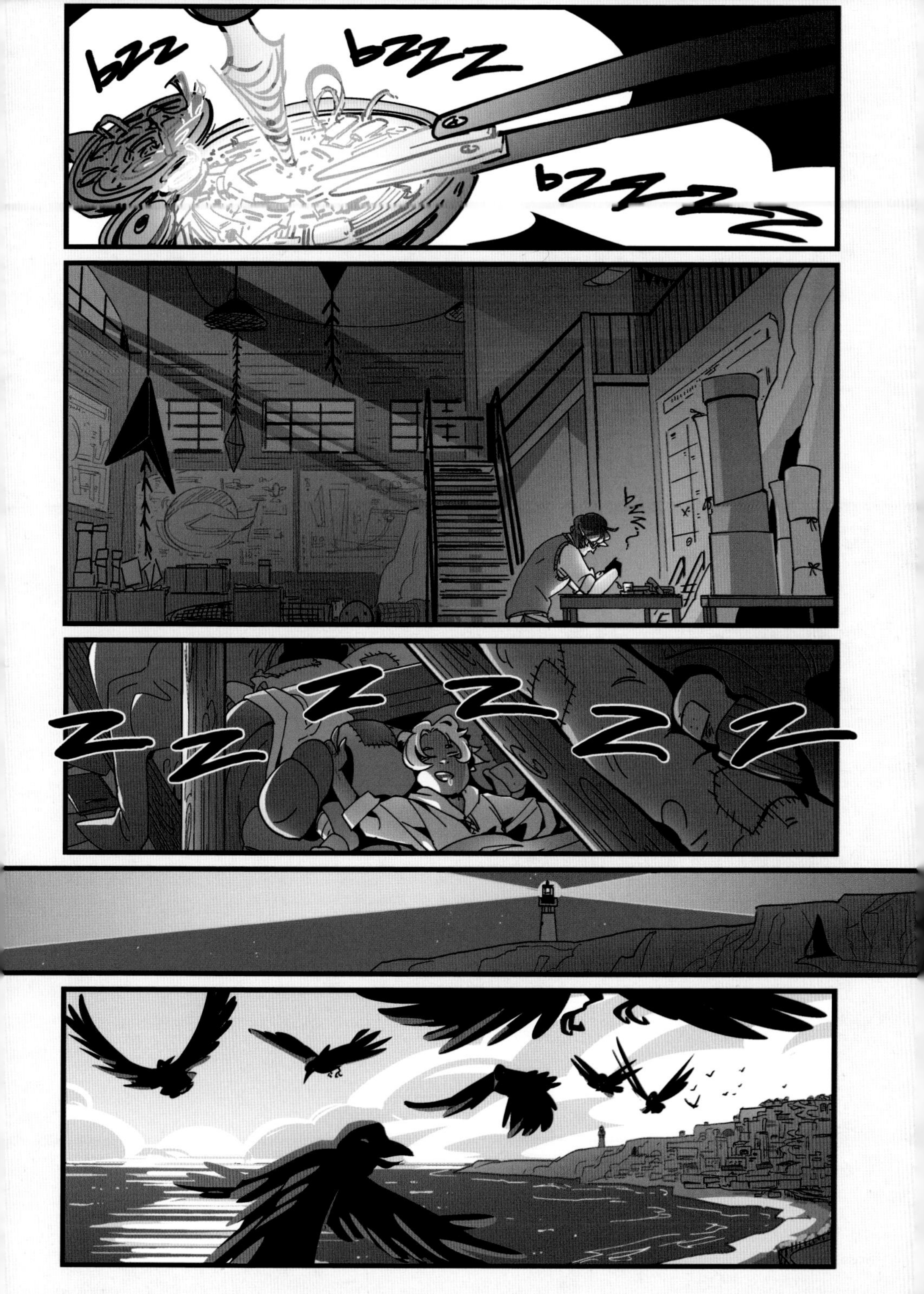
bzz
bzzzz
bzzzzz
bzzzz
Z Z Z Z Z Z

The Nautilene Naval Base

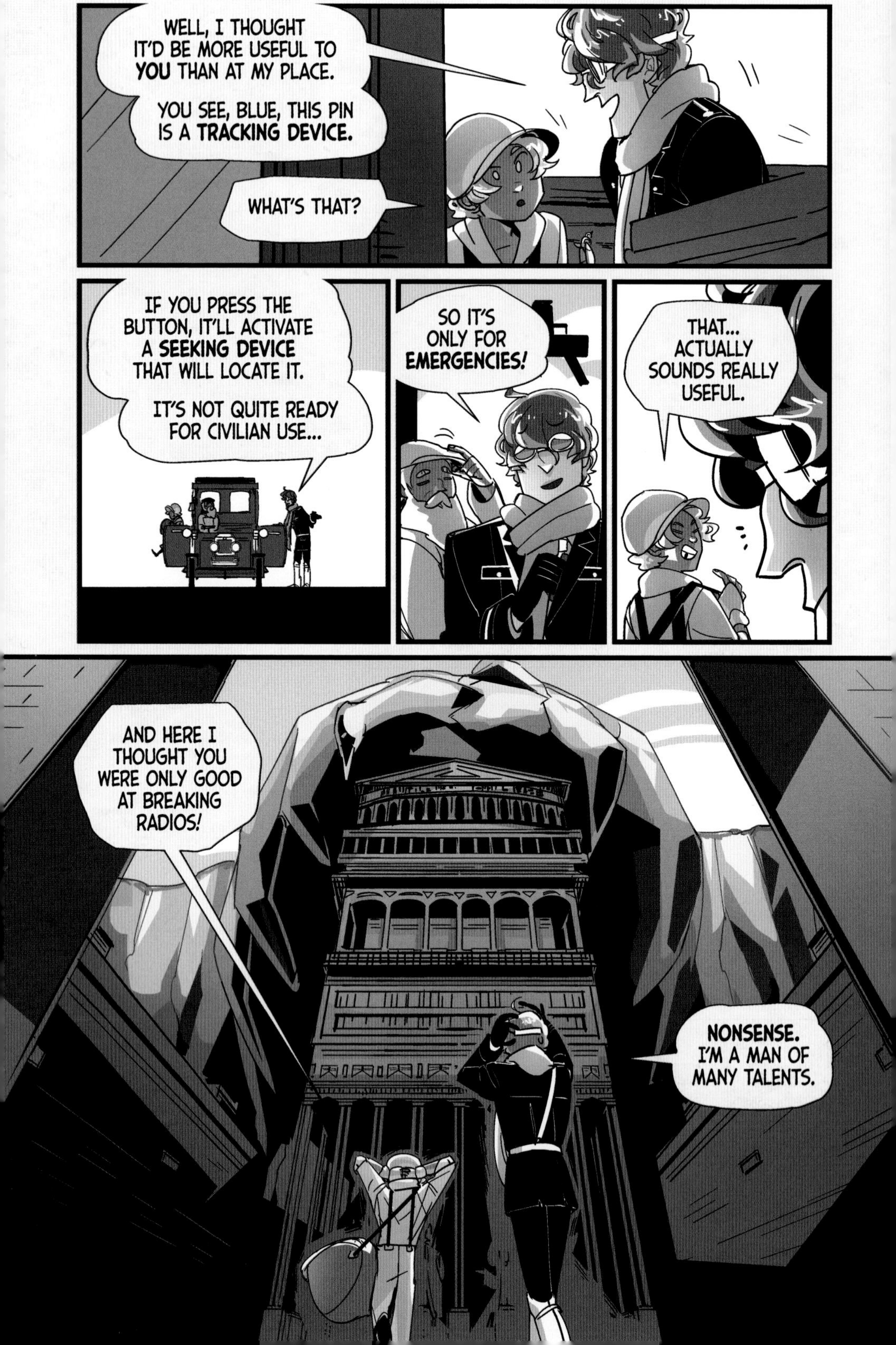
WELL, I THOUGHT IT'D BE MORE USEFUL TO **YOU** THAN AT MY PLACE.
YOU SEE, BLUE, THIS PIN IS A **TRACKING DEVICE.**
WHAT'S THAT?
IF YOU PRESS THE BUTTON, IT'LL ACTIVATE A **SEEKING DEVICE** THAT WILL LOCATE IT.
IT'S NOT QUITE READY FOR CIVILIAN USE...
SO IT'S ONLY FOR **EMERGENCIES!**
THAT... ACTUALLY SOUNDS REALLY USEFUL.
AND HERE I THOUGHT YOU WERE ONLY GOOD AT BREAKING RADIOS!
NONSENSE. I'M A MAN OF MANY TALENTS.

AND THAT'S EVERYTHING?

I'LL RELAY YOUR CONCERNS ABOUT THE WORKING CONDITIONS TO THE ADMIRAL...

OH!

NO, STOP RIGHT THERE.

ME?

SIR, YOU MAY NOT BRING YOUR SON HERE.

I'M AN **APPRENTICE,** MA'AM!

CHILDREN AREN'T ALLOWED AT THE NAVAL BASE.

MISS, SURELY HE WON'T BE A PROBLEM?

COULD I TALK TO A SUPERIOR OFFICER, OR...

ADULTS GET LOST FOR DAYS IN THIS GIANT BASE, AND CHILDREN MORE SO.

PLEASE ESCORT YOUR CHILD OUT.

W o W.

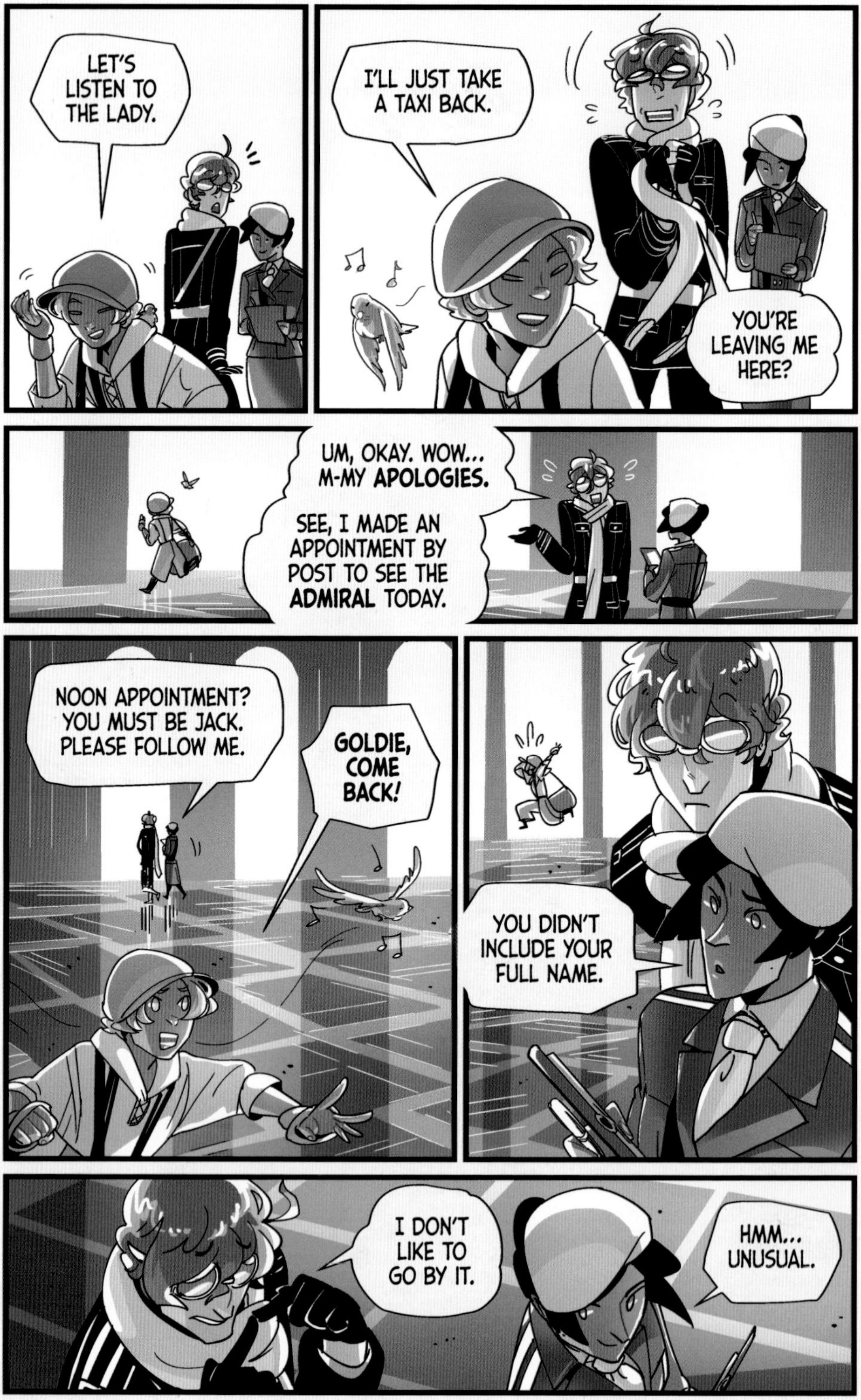
LET'S LISTEN TO THE LADY.
I'LL JUST TAKE A TAXI BACK.
YOU'RE LEAVING ME HERE?
UM, OKAY. WOW... M-MY **APOLOGIES.**
SEE, I MADE AN APPOINTMENT BY POST TO SEE THE **ADMIRAL** TODAY.
NOON APPOINTMENT? YOU MUST BE JACK. PLEASE FOLLOW ME.
GOLDIE, COME BACK!
YOU DIDN'T INCLUDE YOUR FULL NAME.
I DON'T LIKE TO GO BY IT.
HMM... UNUSUAL.

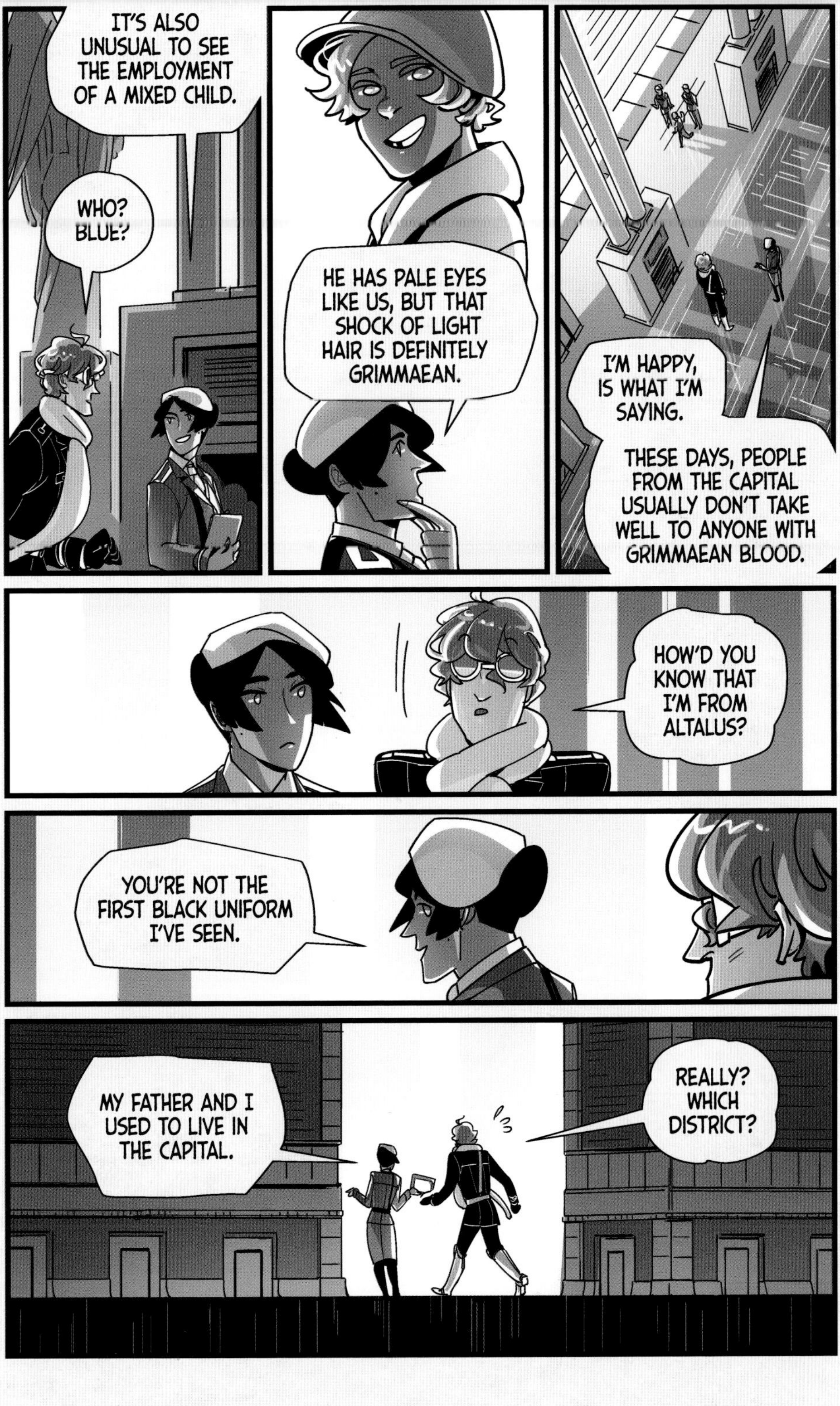
IT'S ALSO UNUSUAL TO SEE THE EMPLOYMENT OF A MIXED CHILD.
WHO? BLUE?
HE HAS PALE EYES LIKE US, BUT THAT SHOCK OF LIGHT HAIR IS DEFINITELY GRIMMAEAN.
I'M HAPPY, IS WHAT I'M SAYING.
THESE DAYS, PEOPLE FROM THE CAPITAL USUALLY DON'T TAKE WELL TO ANYONE WITH GRIMMAEAN BLOOD.
HOW'D YOU KNOW THAT I'M FROM ALTALUS?
YOU'RE NOT THE FIRST BLACK UNIFORM I'VE SEEN.
MY FATHER AND I USED TO LIVE IN THE CAPITAL.
REALLY? WHICH DISTRICT?

38

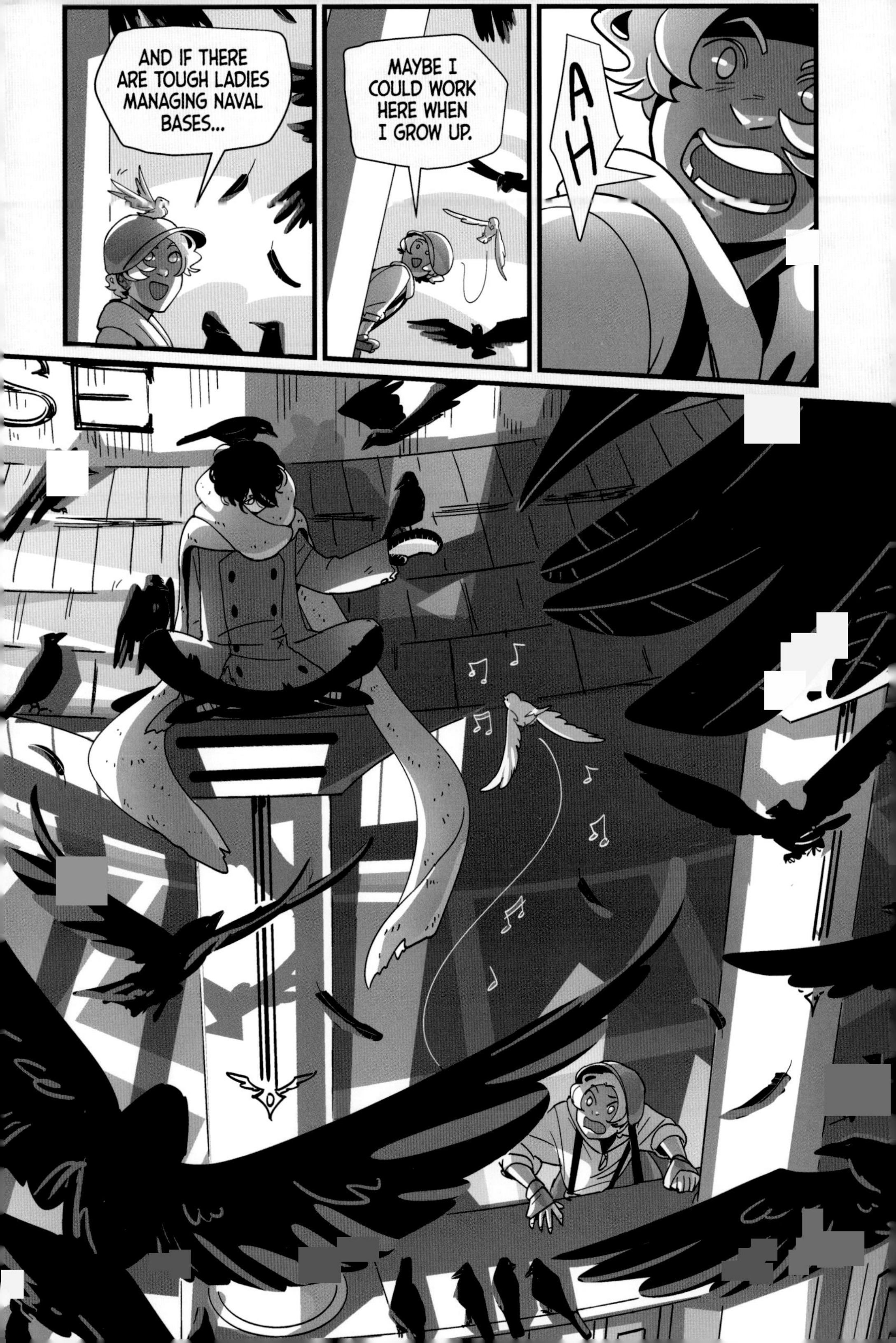
AND IF THERE ARE TOUGH LADIES MANAGING NAVAL BASES...
MAYBE I COULD WORK HERE WHEN I GROW UP.
AH
SE

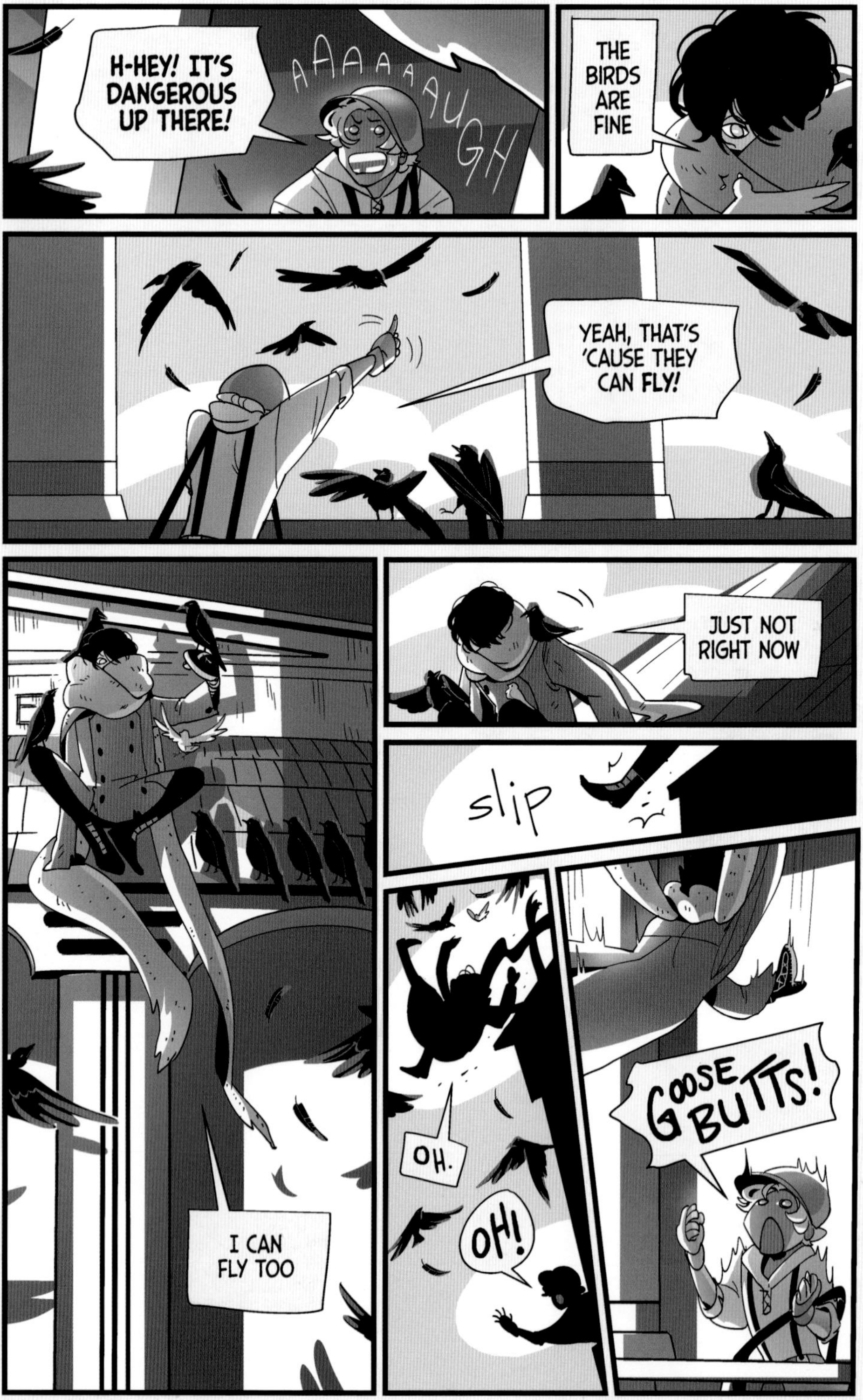
H-HEY! IT'S DANGEROUS UP THERE!
AAAAAAUGH
THE BIRDS ARE FINE
YEAH, THAT'S 'CAUSE THEY CAN **FLY!**
I CAN FLY TOO
JUST NOT RIGHT NOW
slip
OH.
OH!
GOOSE BUTTS!

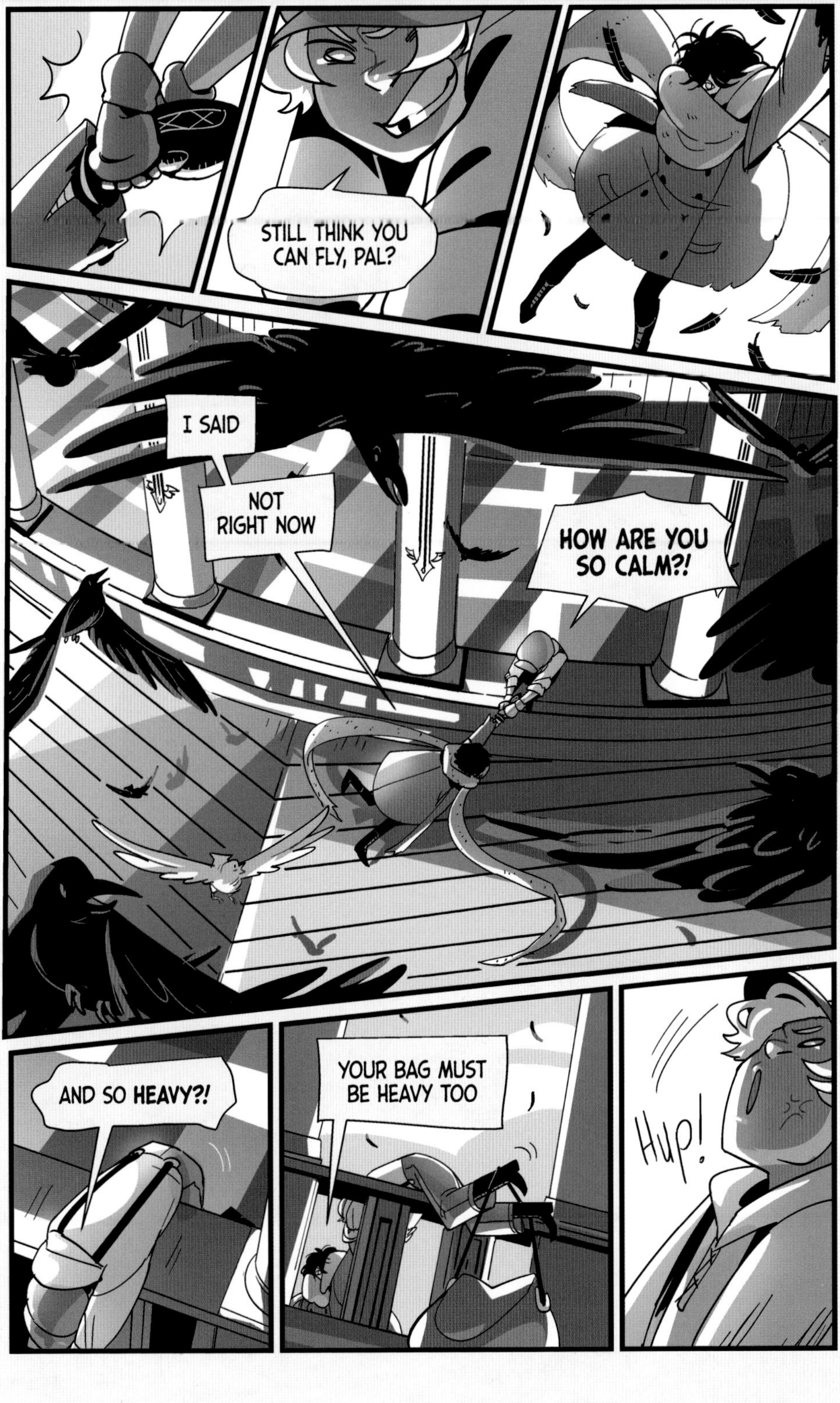
STILL THINK YOU CAN FLY, PAL?
I SAID
NOT RIGHT NOW
HOW ARE YOU SO CALM?!
AND SO HEAVY?!
YOUR BAG MUST BE HEAVY TOO
Hup!

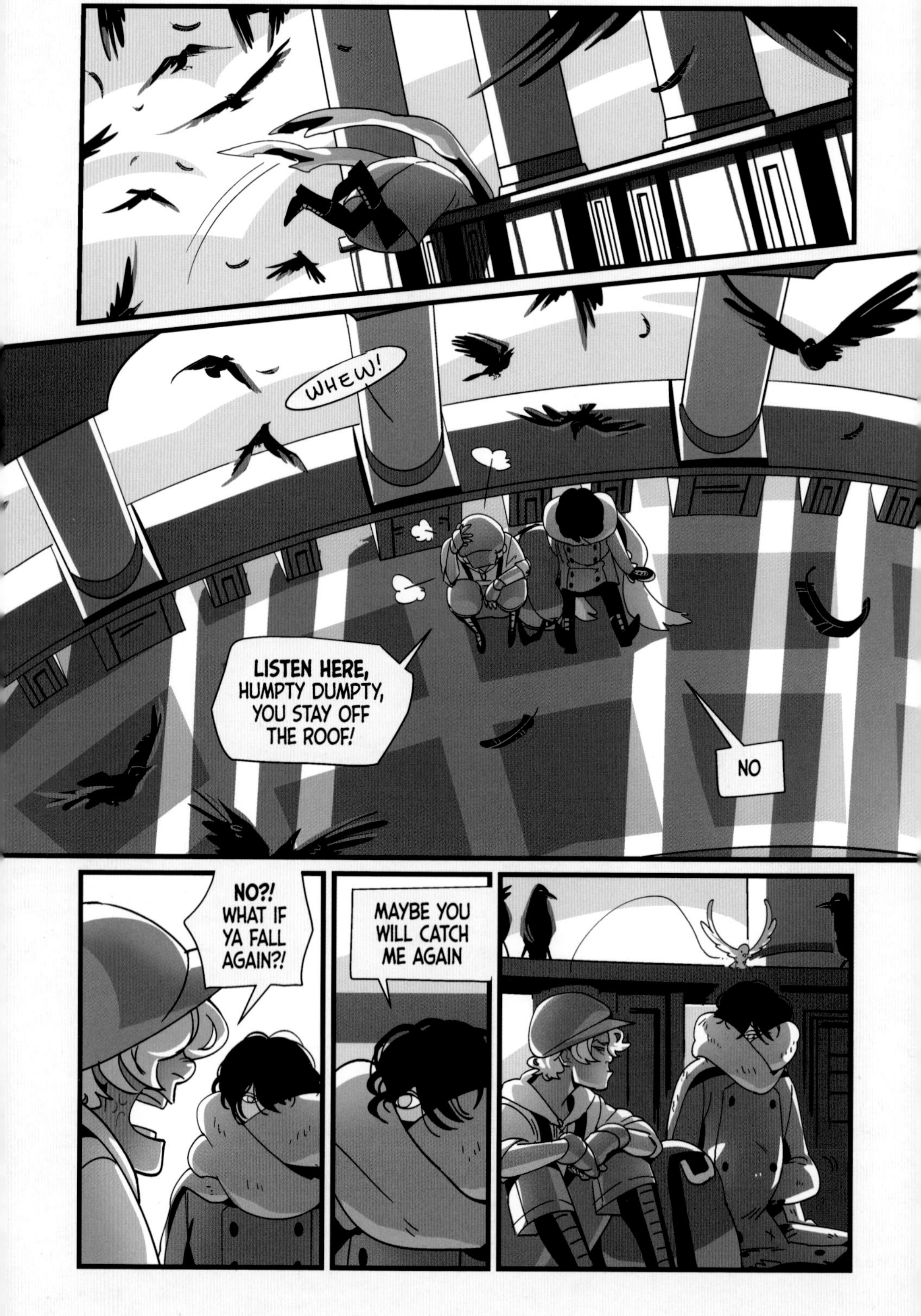
WHEW!
LISTEN HERE, HUMPTY DUMPTY, YOU STAY OFF THE ROOF!
NO
NO?! WHAT IF YA FALL AGAIN?!
MAYBE YOU WILL CATCH ME AGAIN

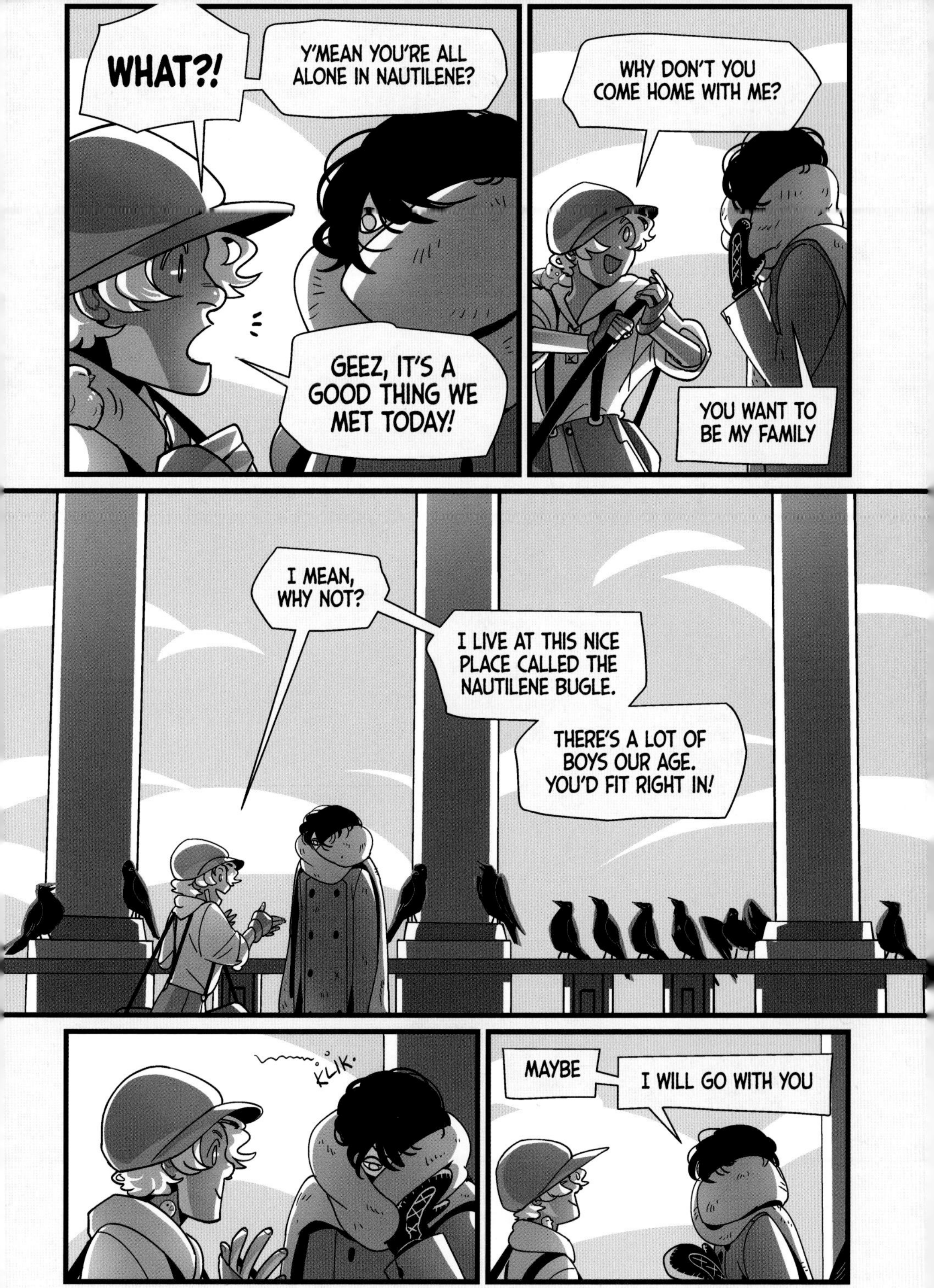
WHAT?!
Y'MEAN YOU'RE ALL ALONE IN NAUTILENE?
GEEZ, IT'S A GOOD THING WE MET TODAY!
WHY DON'T YOU COME HOME WITH ME?
YOU WANT TO BE MY FAMILY
I MEAN, WHY NOT?
I LIVE AT THIS NICE PLACE CALLED THE NAUTILENE BUGLE.
THERE'S A LOT OF BOYS OUR AGE. YOU'D FIT RIGHT IN!
KLIK.
MAYBE
I WILL GO WITH YOU

GREAT!

BUT FIRST LET'S GET OUTTA HERE FAST!

RIGHT NOW

DEFINITELY!

I DUNNO HOW YOU GOT IN, BUT...

THE GROWN-UPS GET PRETTY ANGRY WHEN THEY FIND KIDS HERE.

TRUE

SIR, IF YOU'D JUST PLEASE RESPOND--

BLUE

SO I--

ADMIRAL, SIR, LOOK OUT!

ANGRY GROWN-UP

ADMIRAL....?

UH-OH.

46

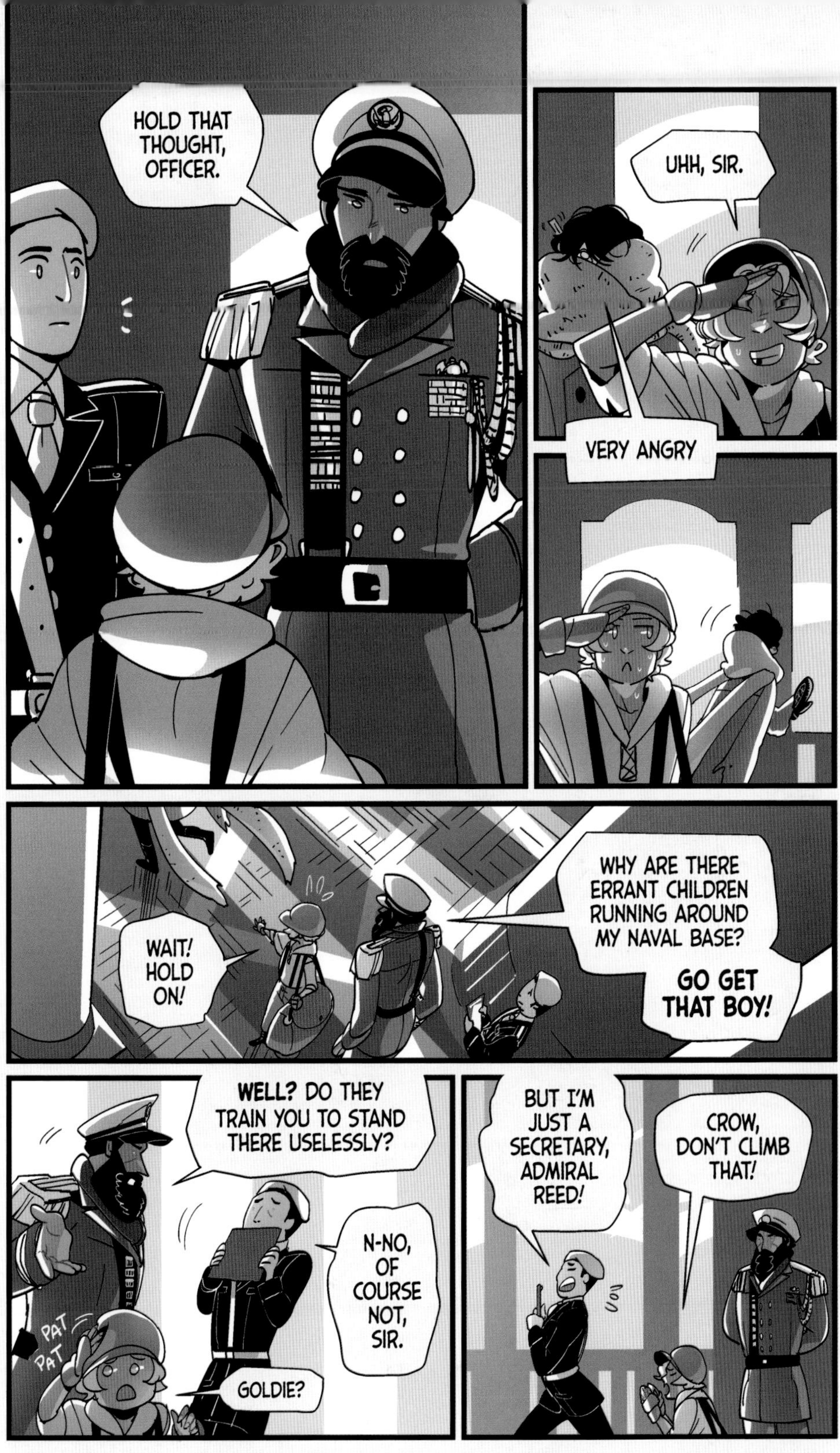
HOLD THAT THOUGHT, OFFICER.
UHH, SIR.
VERY ANGRY
WHY ARE THERE ERRANT CHILDREN RUNNING AROUND MY NAVAL BASE?
GO GET THAT BOY!
WAIT! HOLD ON!
WELL? DO THEY TRAIN YOU TO STAND THERE USELESSLY?
N-NO, OF COURSE NOT, SIR.
PAT PAT
GOLDIE?
BUT I'M JUST A SECRETARY, ADMIRAL REED!
CROW, DON'T CLIMB THAT!

GO ON.

COME BACK...

UM, SIR. I'M SORRY. WE WERE JUST LEAVING. SIR.

LITTLE BOY, YOU DO NOT COME HERE TO PLAY SAILOR. DO YOU UNDERSTAND?

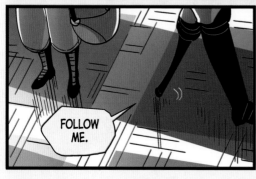

FOLLOW ME.

YES...SIR.

KLOK

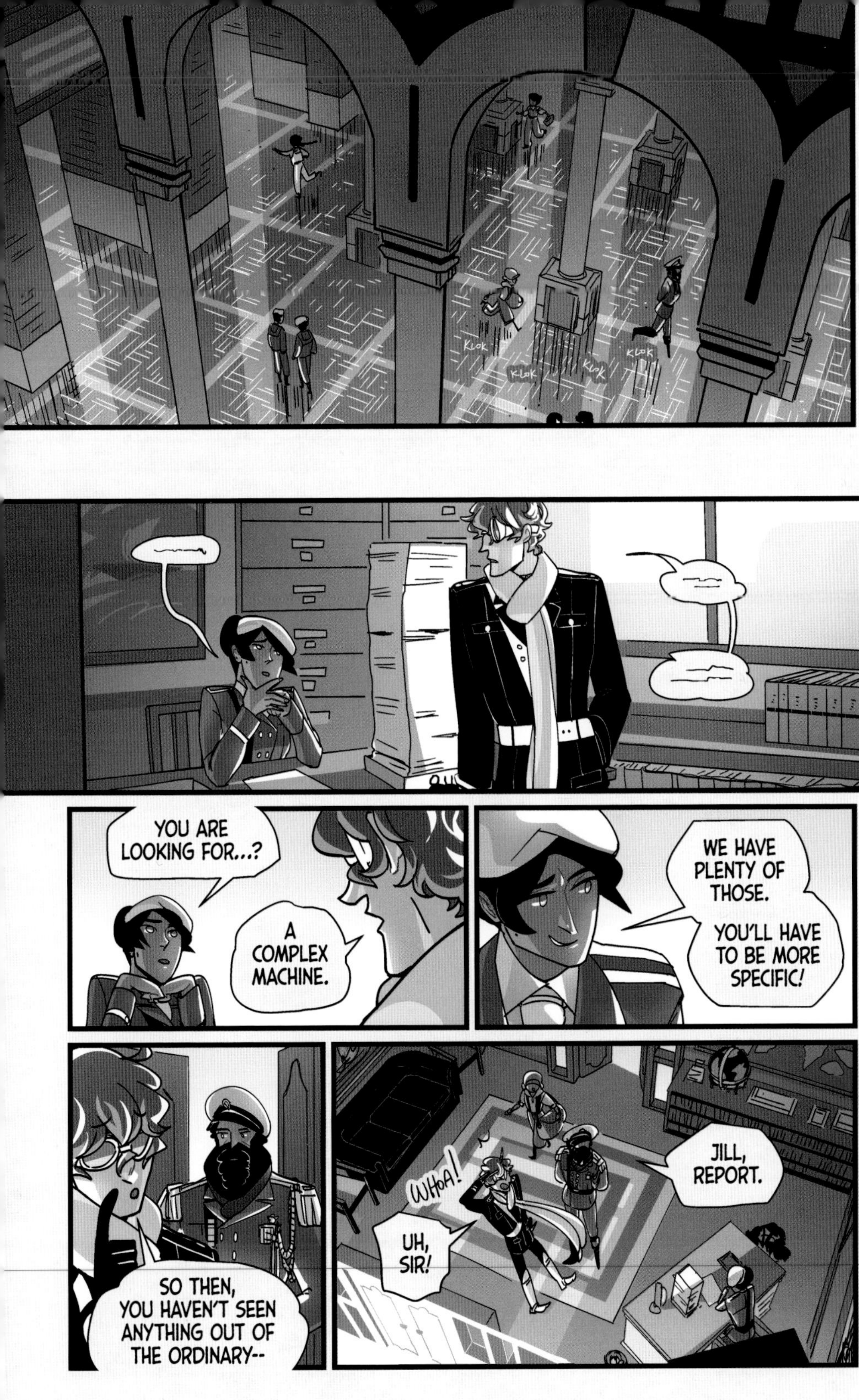
KLOK
KLOK
KLOK
KLOK
YOU ARE LOOKING FOR...?
A COMPLEX MACHINE.
WE HAVE PLENTY OF THOSE.
YOU'LL HAVE TO BE MORE SPECIFIC!
SO THEN, YOU HAVEN'T SEEN ANYTHING OUT OF THE ORDINARY--
WHOA!
JILL, REPORT.
UH, SIR!

FINISHED MY WORK, FATHER. YOU HAVE MEETINGS SCHEDULED ALL MORNING AND AFTERNOON.

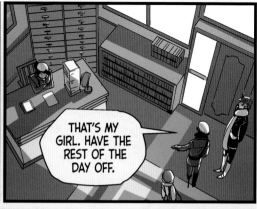

THAT'S MY GIRL. HAVE THE REST OF THE DAY OFF.

AND TAKE THIS BOY HOME.

MAKE SURE HIS GUARDIANS GIVE HIM A STERN TALKING TO.

HMM? WHO'S THIS?

YOUR NOON APPOINT-MENT.

JACK.

ANOTHER BLACK UNIFORM?

WHY ARE THERE SO MANY ALTALUS OFFICIALS AROUND?

NO, NO! I'M RETIRED. PLEASE DON'T TELL THEM I'M HERE, SIR!

ALTALUS.

I GUESS THAT MAKES SENSE.

I'VE NEVER SEEN THAT UNIFORM IN NAUTILENE BEFORE.

THERE'S NOTHING TO REPORT.

TELL THE QUEEN THAT NAUTILENE IS AS DULL AS ALWAYS.

I'M NOT HERE ON BEHALF OF THE QUEEN, SIR.

IN FACT, I'D HOPED TO REACH OUT TO YOU BEFORE THE OTHERS DID.

SIR, I BELIEVE THERE IS A **DANGEROUS** WEAPON IN YOUR CITY.

ALL I CAN TELL YOU IS THAT IT IS DRAWN TO OTHER MACHINES.

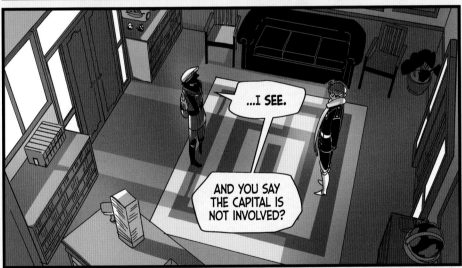

...I SEE.

AND YOU SAY THE CAPITAL IS NOT INVOLVED?

WHO ARE YOU, JACK?

I'M A **CONCERNED** CITIZEN, SIR.

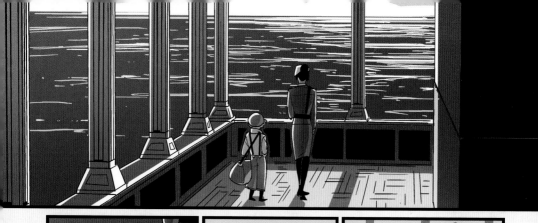

hmm

um

IT SEEMS TO ME LIKE YOU KINDA RUN THIS PLACE.

THE ADMIRAL IS MY FATHER.

HIS SECRETARY WAS DRAFTED, SO I FILL IN WHERE I CAN.

ARE THERE MORE LADIES LIKE YOU HERE?

WELL, THOSE WOMEN I WAS TALKING TO EARLIER BUILD AND REPAIR THE SHIPS OUTSIDE.

OH! I THINK THEY WERE FEATURED IN THE BUGLE A COUPLE YEARS AGO!

PAT PAT

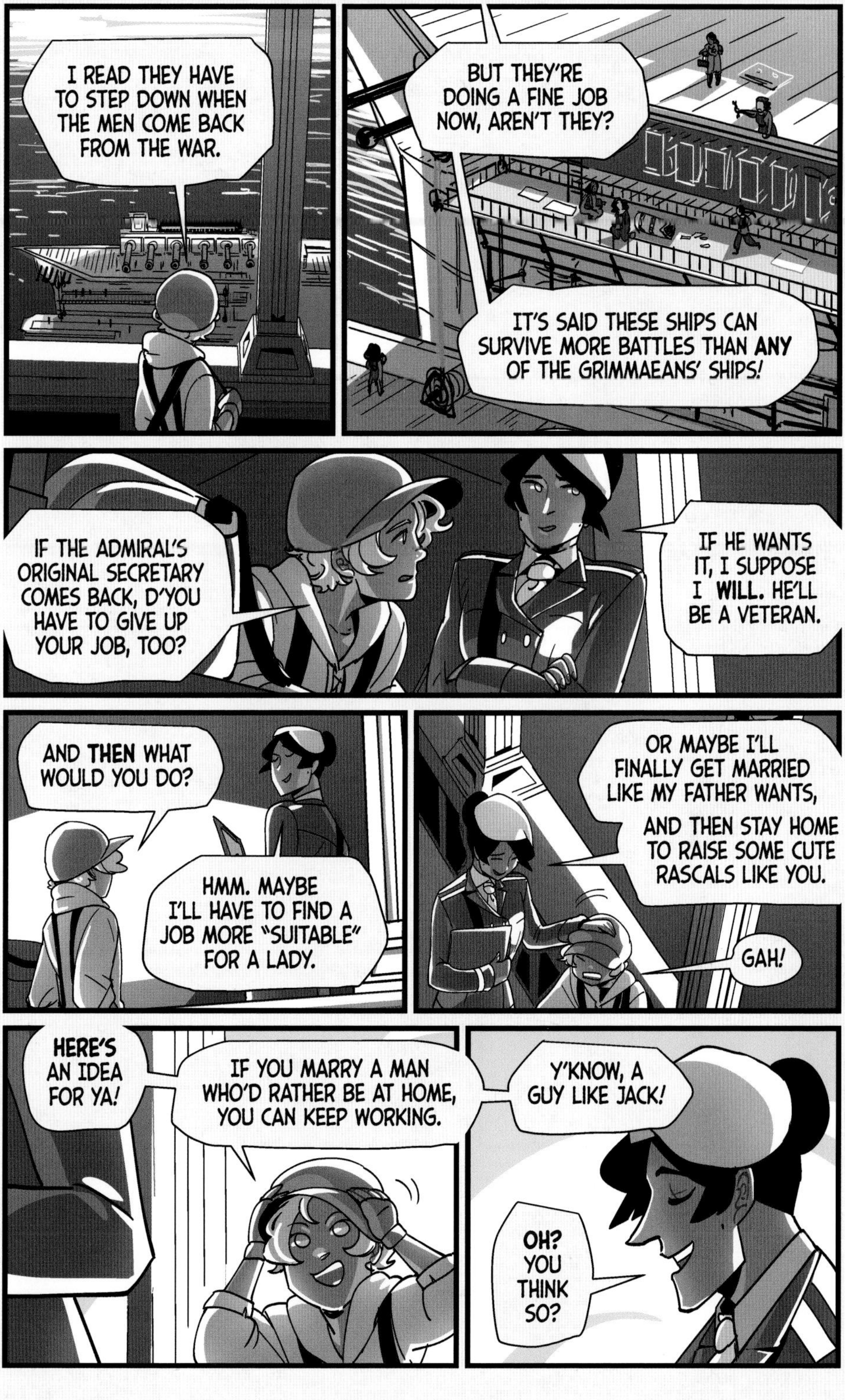
I READ THEY HAVE TO STEP DOWN WHEN THE MEN COME BACK FROM THE WAR.
BUT THEY'RE DOING A FINE JOB NOW, AREN'T THEY?
IT'S SAID THESE SHIPS CAN SURVIVE MORE BATTLES THAN **ANY** OF THE GRIMMAEANS' SHIPS!
IF THE ADMIRAL'S ORIGINAL SECRETARY COMES BACK, D'YOU HAVE TO GIVE UP YOUR JOB, TOO?
IF HE WANTS IT, I SUPPOSE I **WILL.** HE'LL BE A VETERAN.
AND **THEN** WHAT WOULD YOU DO?
HMM. MAYBE I'LL HAVE TO FIND A JOB MORE "SUITABLE" FOR A LADY.
OR MAYBE I'LL FINALLY GET MARRIED LIKE MY FATHER WANTS,
AND THEN STAY HOME TO RAISE SOME CUTE RASCALS LIKE YOU.
GAH!
HERE'S AN IDEA FOR YA!
IF YOU MARRY A MAN WHO'D RATHER BE AT HOME, YOU CAN KEEP WORKING.
Y'KNOW, A GUY LIKE JACK!
OH? YOU THINK SO?

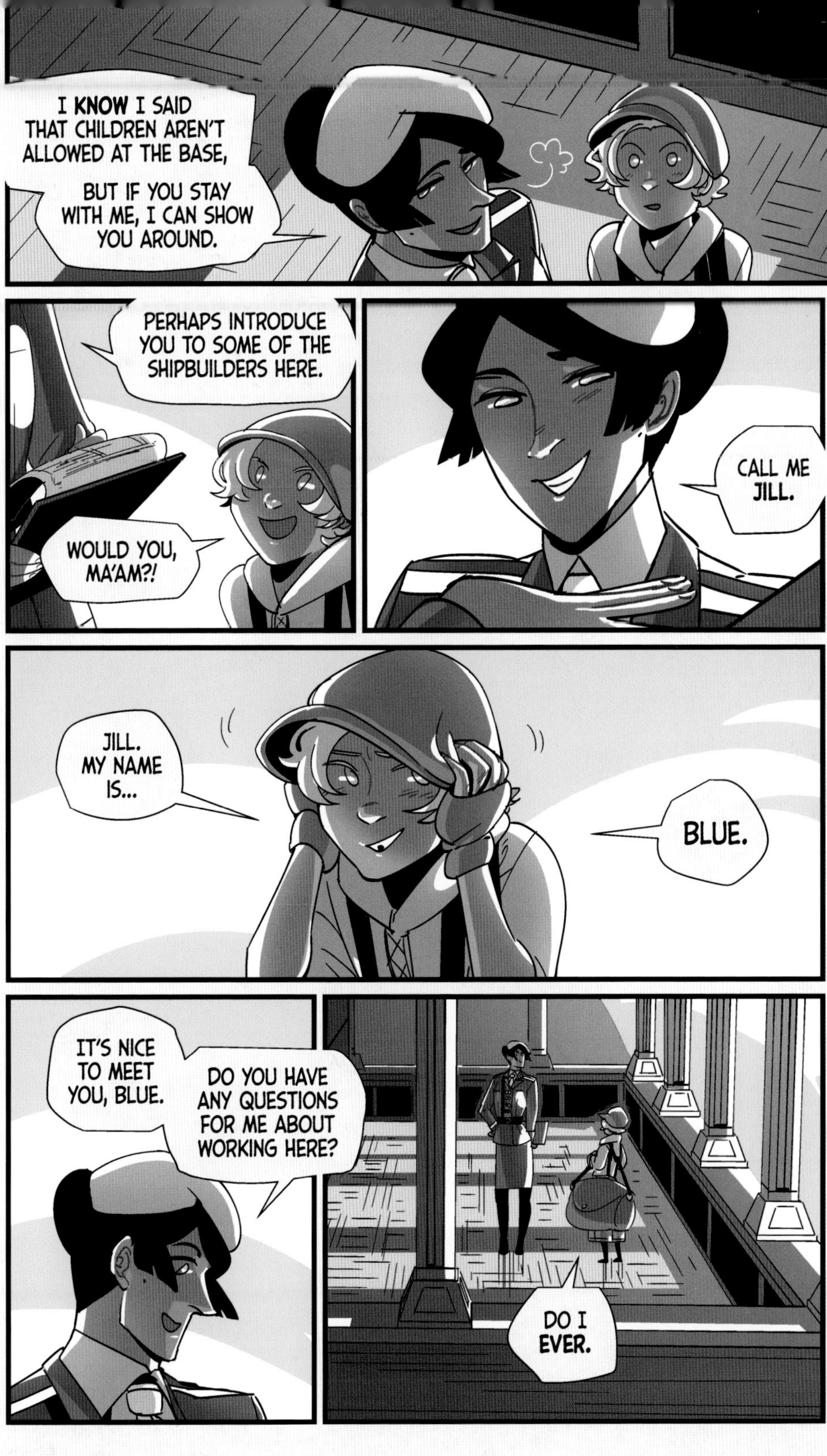
I KNOW I SAID THAT CHILDREN AREN'T ALLOWED AT THE BASE,
BUT IF YOU STAY WITH ME, I CAN SHOW YOU AROUND.
PERHAPS INTRODUCE YOU TO SOME OF THE SHIPBUILDERS HERE.
WOULD YOU, MA'AM?!
CALL ME JILL.
JILL. MY NAME IS...
BLUE.
IT'S NICE TO MEET YOU, BLUE.
DO YOU HAVE ANY QUESTIONS FOR ME ABOUT WORKING HERE?
DO I EVER.

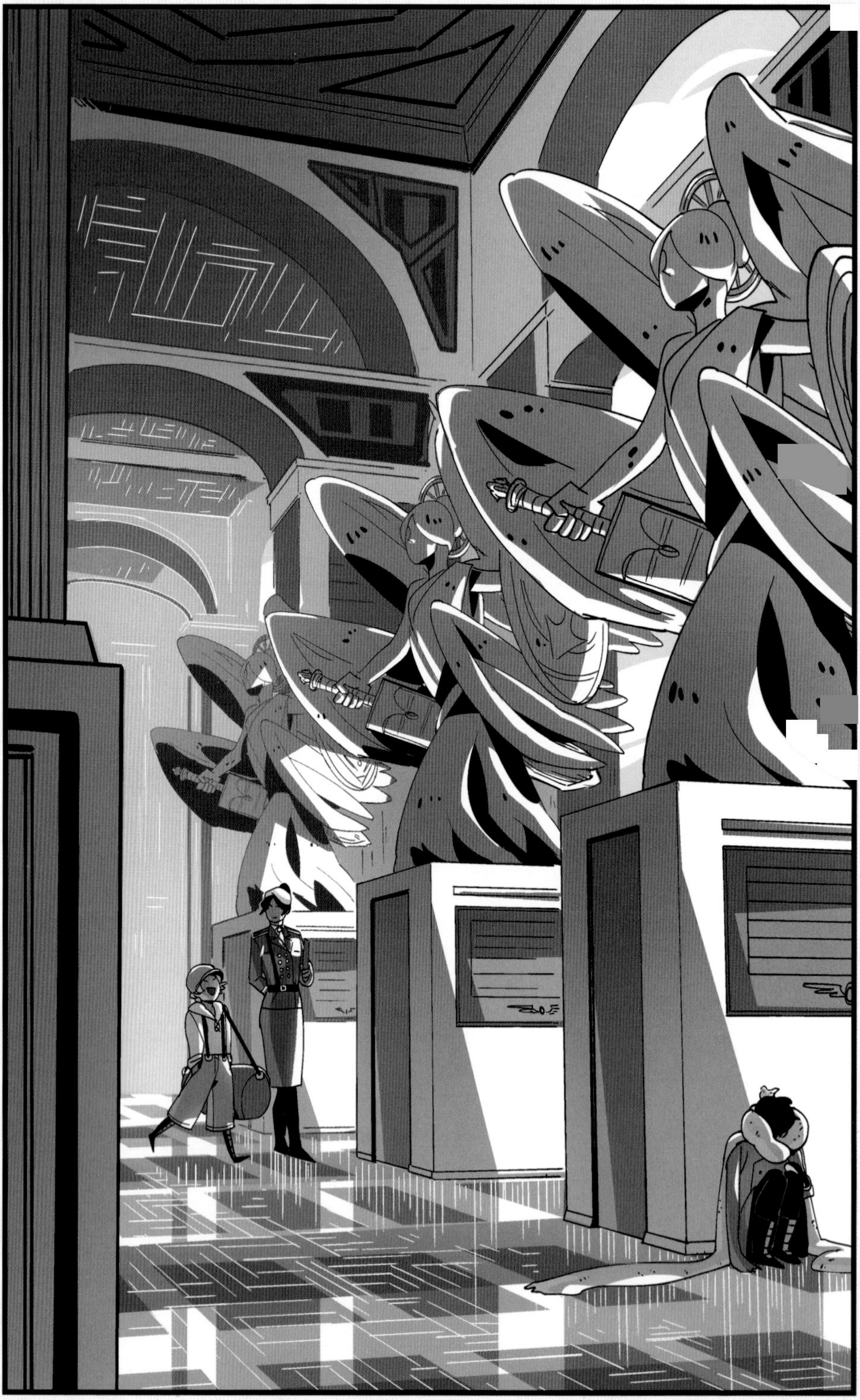

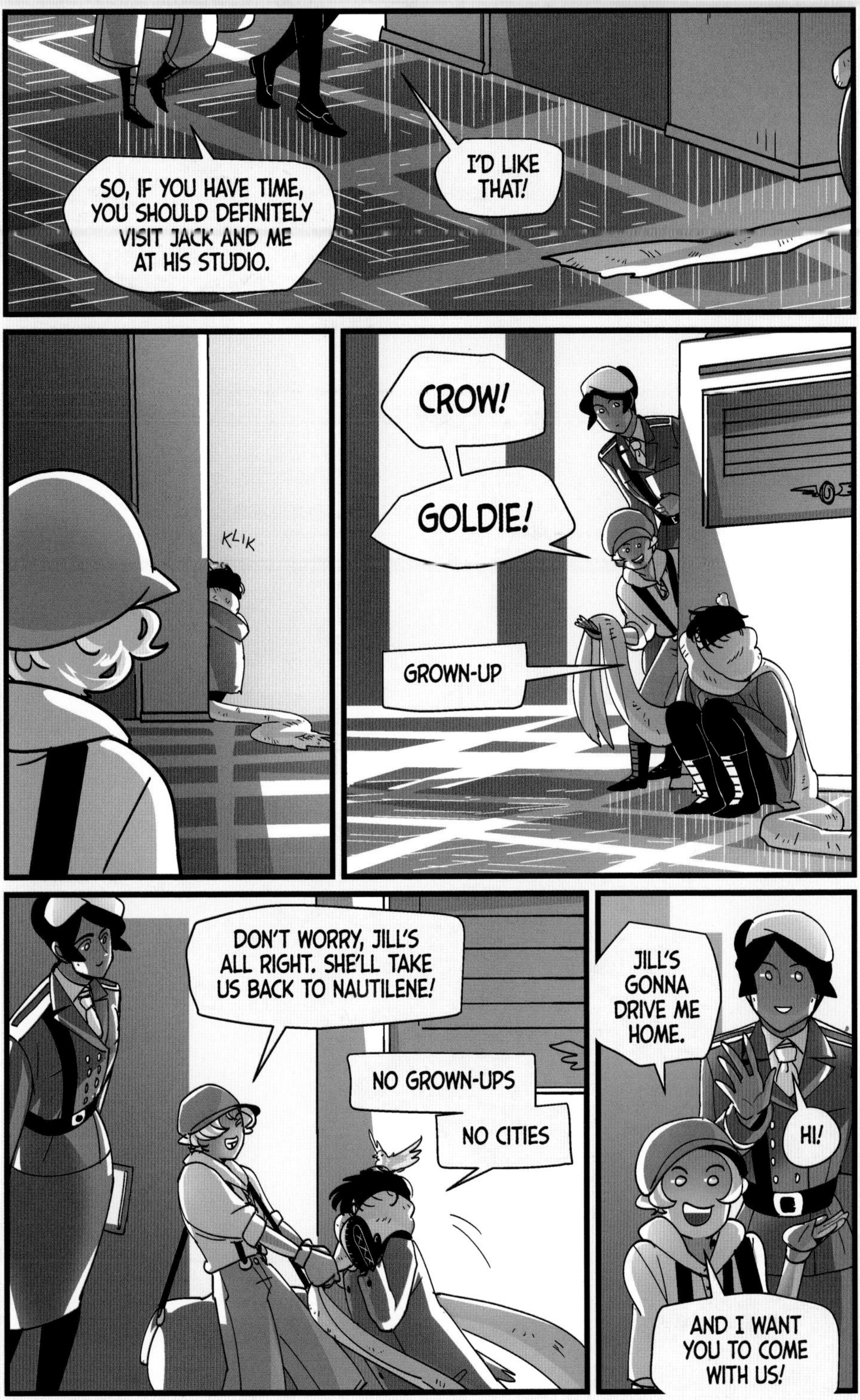
SO, IF YOU HAVE TIME, YOU SHOULD DEFINITELY VISIT JACK AND ME AT HIS STUDIO.
I'D LIKE THAT!
KLIK
CROW!
GOLDIE!
GROWN-UP
DON'T WORRY, JILL'S ALL RIGHT. SHE'LL TAKE US BACK TO NAUTILENE!
NO GROWN-UPS
NO CITIES
JILL'S GONNA DRIVE ME HOME.
HI!
AND I WANT YOU TO COME WITH US!

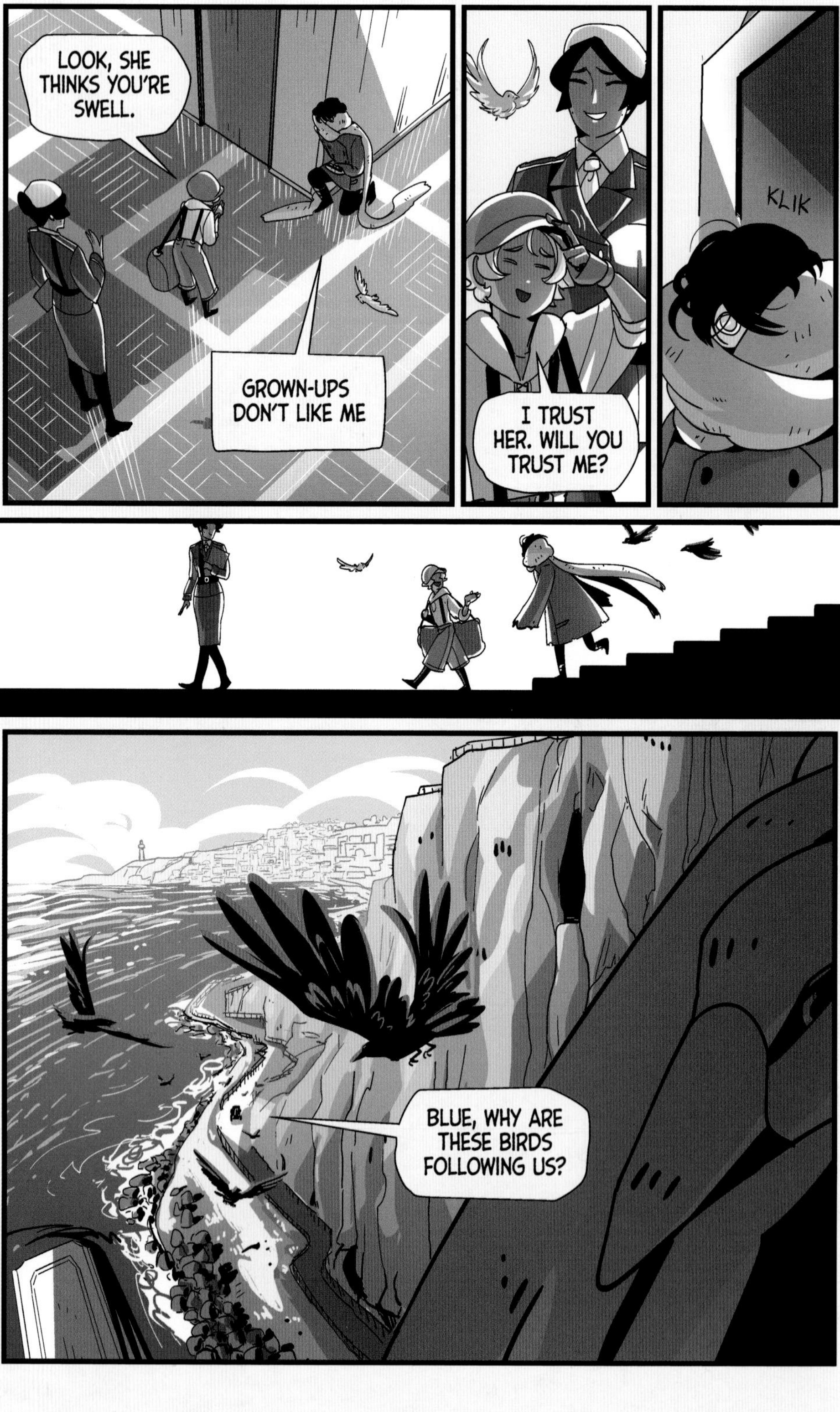
LOOK, SHE THINKS YOU'RE SWELL.
GROWN-UPS DON'T LIKE ME
I TRUST HER. WILL YOU TRUST ME?
KLIK
BLUE, WHY ARE THESE BIRDS FOLLOWING US?

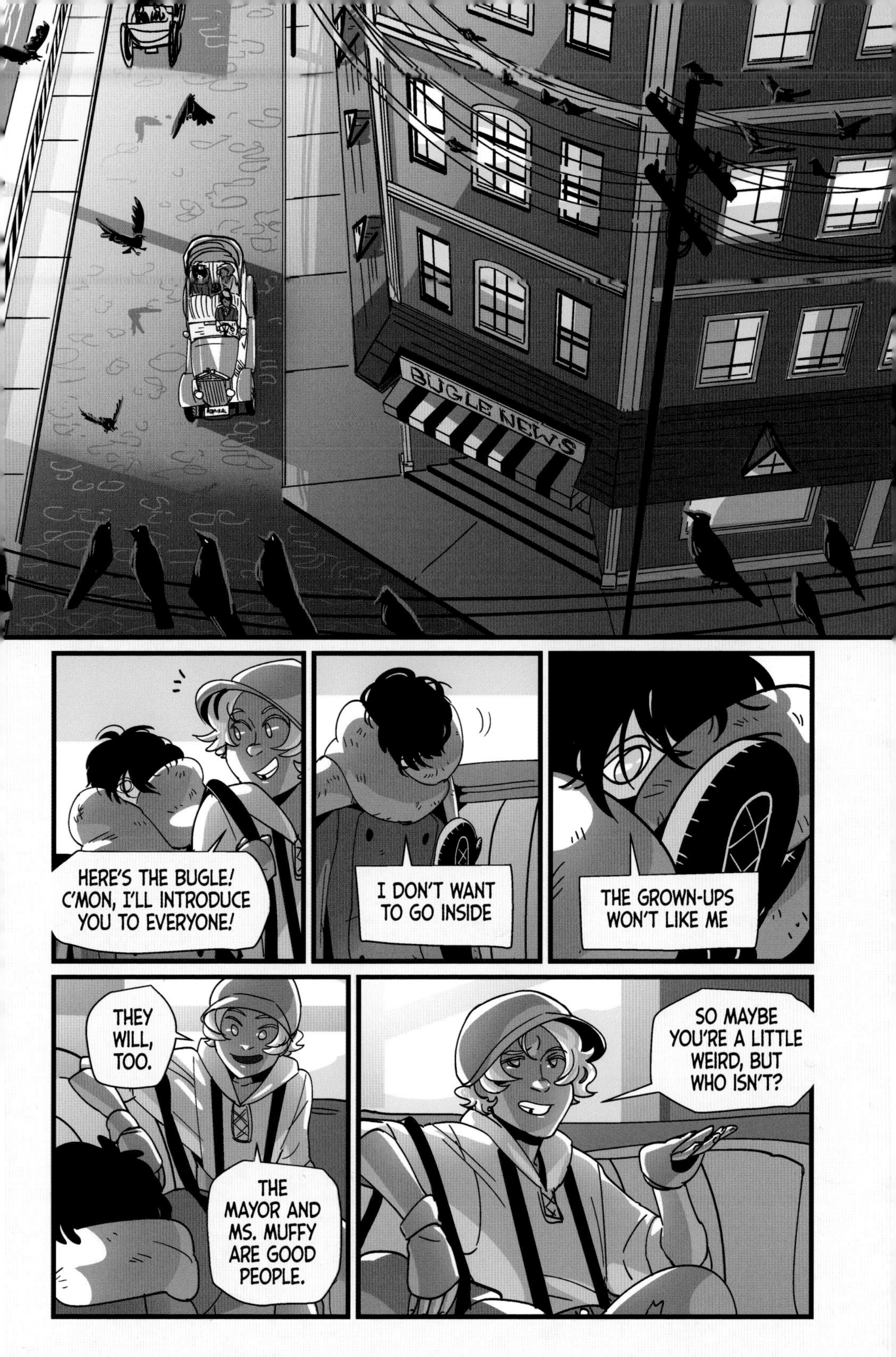
BUGLE NEWS
HERE'S THE BUGLE! C'MON, I'LL INTRODUCE YOU TO EVERYONE!
I DON'T WANT TO GO INSIDE
THE GROWN-UPS WON'T LIKE ME
THEY WILL, TOO.
THE MAYOR AND MS. MUFFY ARE GOOD PEOPLE.
SO MAYBE YOU'RE A LITTLE WEIRD, BUT WHO ISN'T?

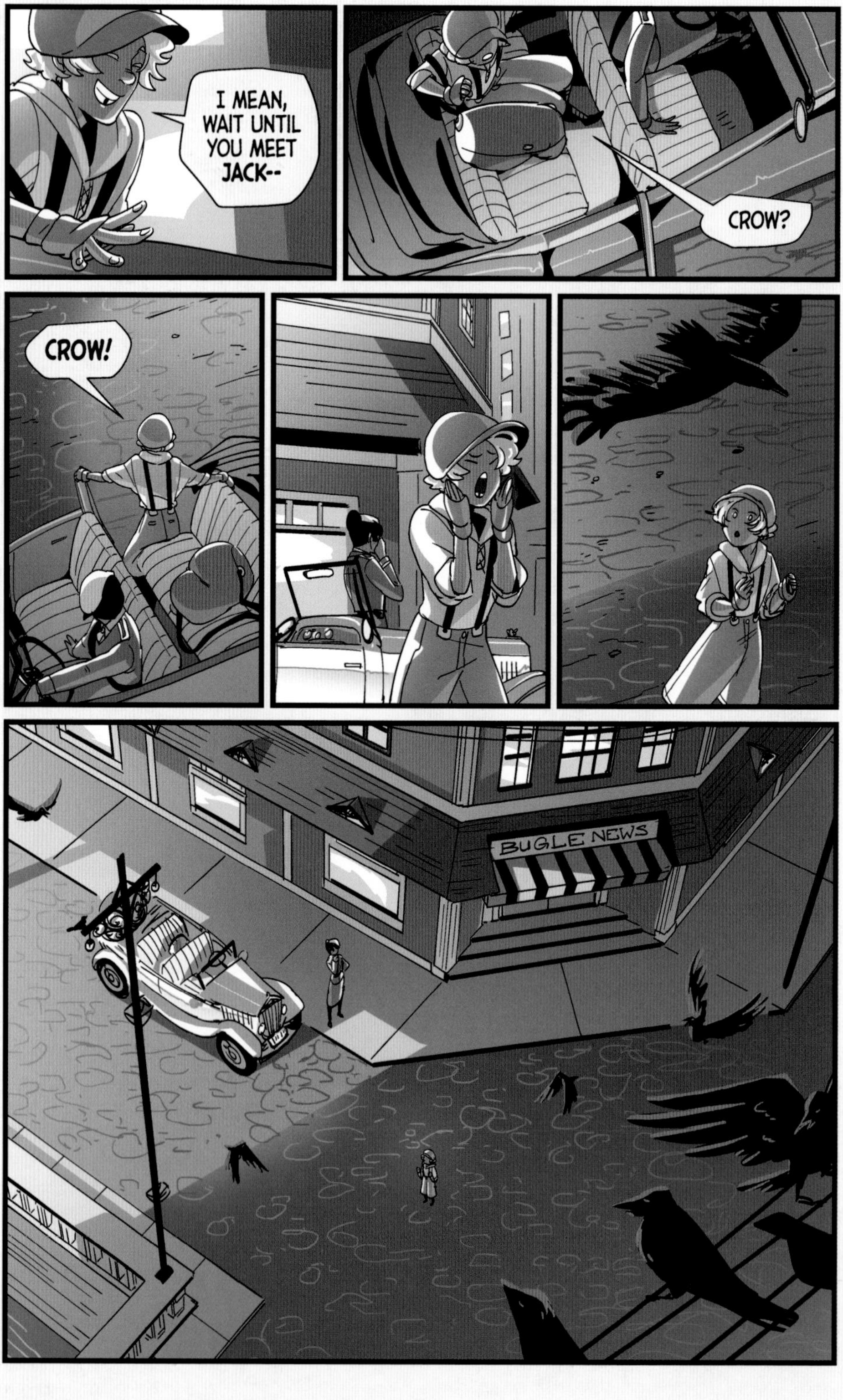
I MEAN, WAIT UNTIL YOU MEET JACK--
CROW?
CROW!
BUGLE NEWS

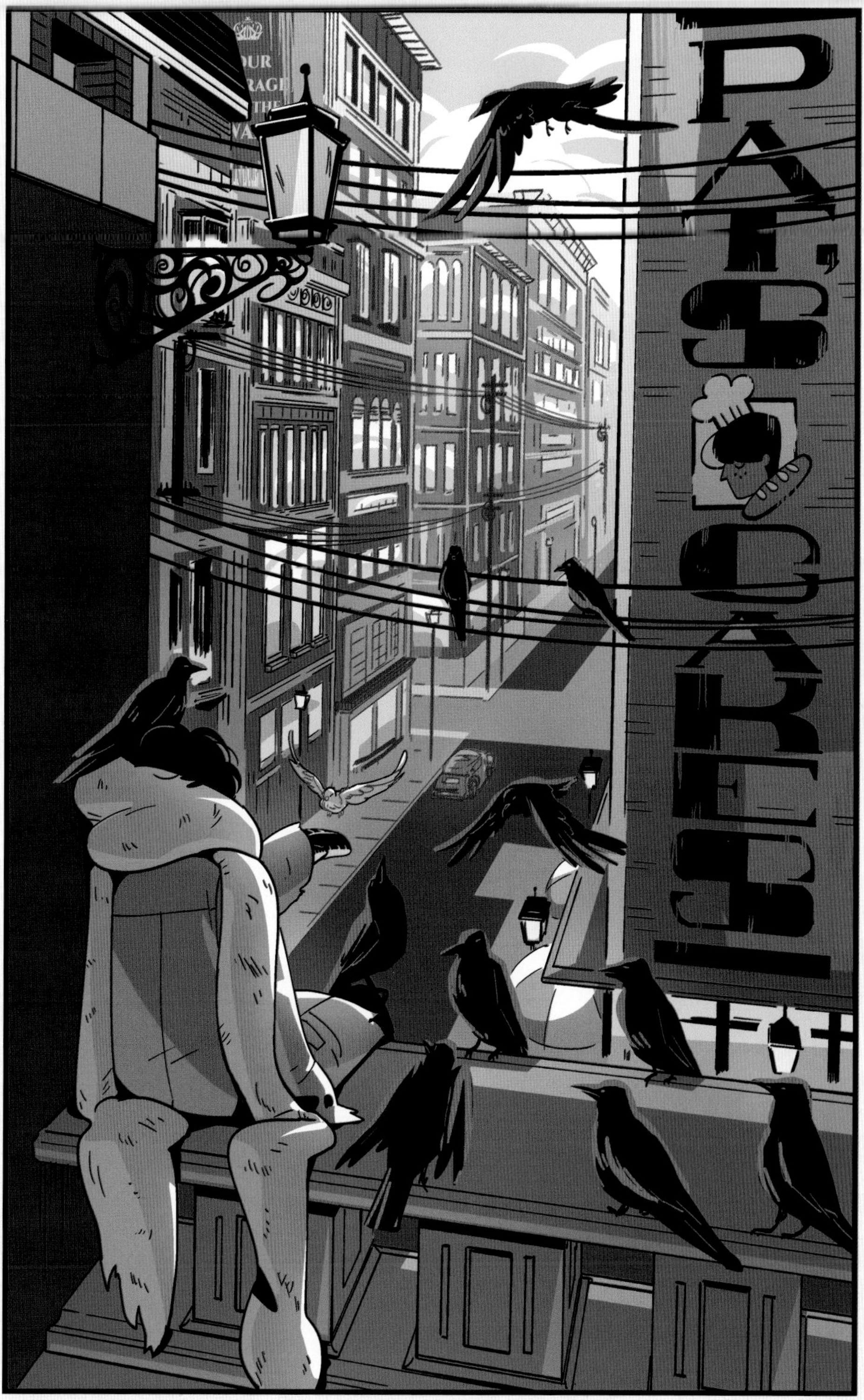
PAT'S

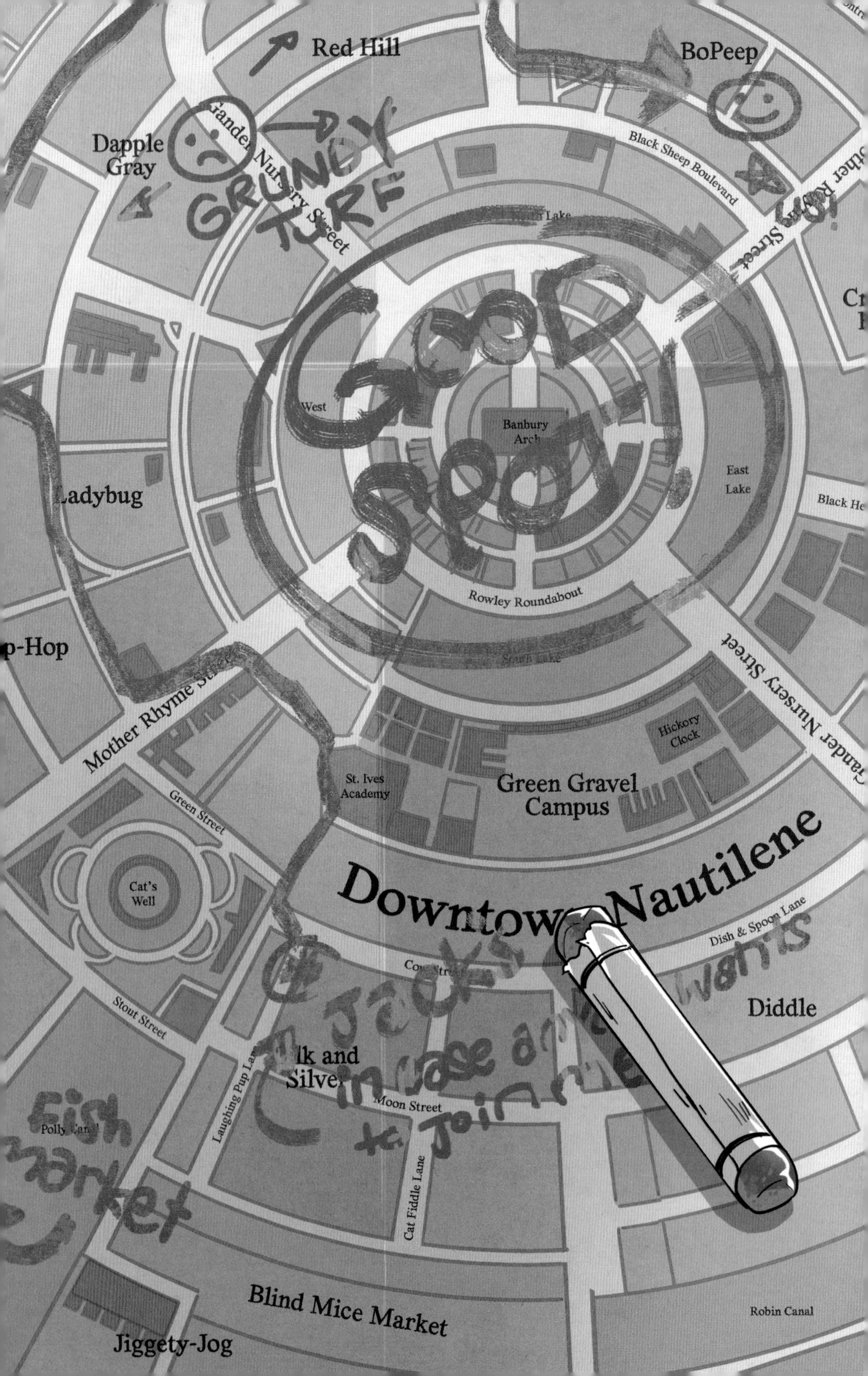

Red Hill
BoPeep
Dapple Gray
Gander Nursery Street
Black Sheep Boulevard
GRUNDY TURF
GOOD SPOT!
West
Banbury Arch
East Lake
Ladybug
Rowley Roundabout
South Lake
Mother Rhyme Street
Gander Nursery Street
Hickory Clock
St. Ives Academy
Green Gravel Campus
Green Street
Cat's Well
Downtown Nautilene
Dish & Spoon Lane
Diddle
Stout Street
Laughing Pup Lane
Moon Street
Polly Canal
Cat Fiddle Lane
Fish market
Blind Mice Market
Robin Canal
Jiggety-Jog

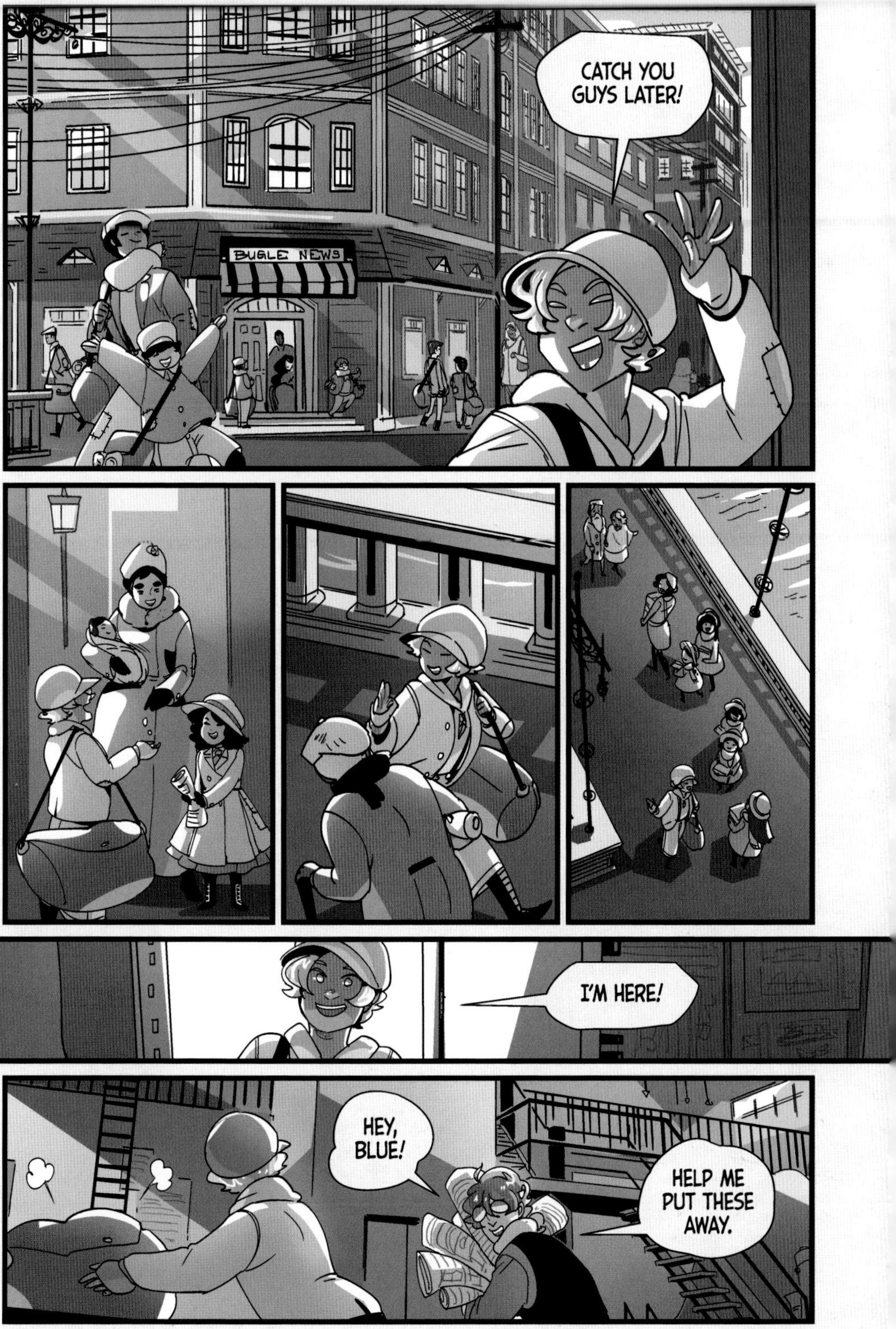

BUGLE NEWS
CATCH YOU GUYS LATER!
I'M HERE!
HEY, BLUE!
HELP ME PUT THESE AWAY.

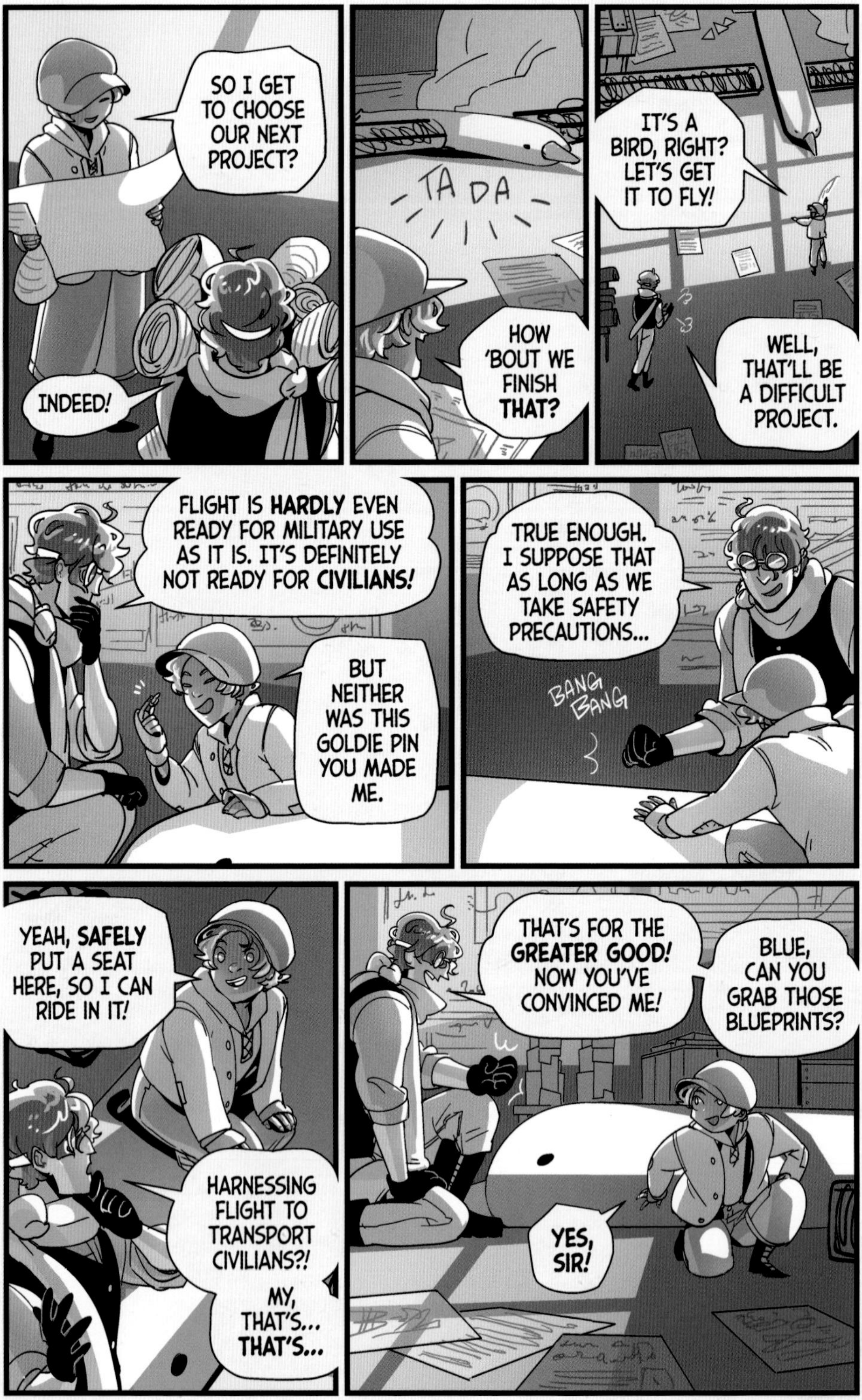
SO I GET TO CHOOSE OUR NEXT PROJECT?
INDEED!
TA DA
HOW 'BOUT WE FINISH **THAT?**
IT'S A BIRD, RIGHT? LET'S GET IT TO FLY!
WELL, THAT'LL BE A DIFFICULT PROJECT.
FLIGHT IS **HARDLY** EVEN READY FOR MILITARY USE AS IT IS. IT'S DEFINITELY NOT READY FOR **CIVILIANS!**
BUT NEITHER WAS THIS GOLDIE PIN YOU MADE ME.
TRUE ENOUGH. I SUPPOSE THAT AS LONG AS WE TAKE SAFETY PRECAUTIONS...
BANG BANG
YEAH, **SAFELY** PUT A SEAT HERE, SO I CAN RIDE IN IT!
HARNESSING FLIGHT TO TRANSPORT CIVILIANS?!
MY, THAT'S... **THAT'S...**
THAT'S FOR THE **GREATER GOOD!** NOW YOU'VE CONVINCED ME!
BLUE, CAN YOU GRAB THOSE BLUEPRINTS?
YES, SIR!

BLUE.

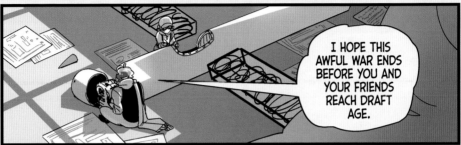

I HOPE THIS AWFUL WAR ENDS BEFORE YOU AND YOUR FRIENDS REACH DRAFT AGE.

EHH, MOST OF THE BOYS AT THE BUGLE WON'T BE TWENTY-ONE FOR A WHILE.

EXCEPT HECTOR. HE'S THE ONE WHO BROUGHT ME TO THE BUGLE AFTER MY DAD...

...

SIGH

ANYHOOS.

shff

HECTOR'S IN ALTALUS NOW. HE'S A JOURNALIST. MAYBE YOU'VE READ SOME OF HIS STUFF!

I DIDN'T REALLY READ NEWSPAPERS UNTIL I MET YOU--

KNOK KNOK KNOK

I'LL GET THE DOOR!

Hm?

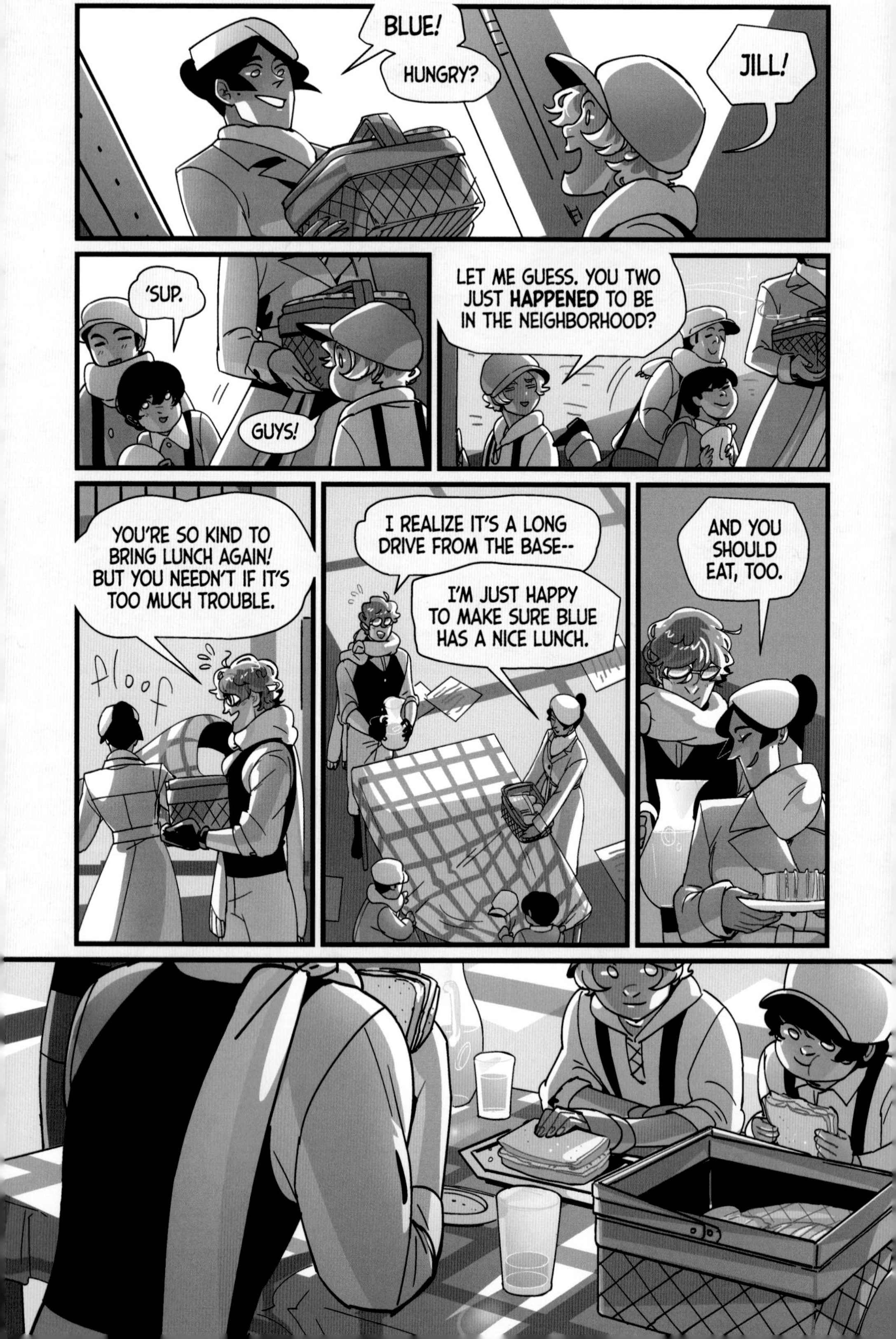
BLUE!
HUNGRY?
JILL!
'SUP.
GUYS!
LET ME GUESS. YOU TWO JUST **HAPPENED** TO BE IN THE NEIGHBORHOOD?
YOU'RE SO KIND TO BRING LUNCH AGAIN! BUT YOU NEEDN'T IF IT'S TOO MUCH TROUBLE.
floof
I REALIZE IT'S A LONG DRIVE FROM THE BASE--
I'M JUST HAPPY TO MAKE SURE BLUE HAS A NICE LUNCH.
AND YOU SHOULD EAT, TOO.

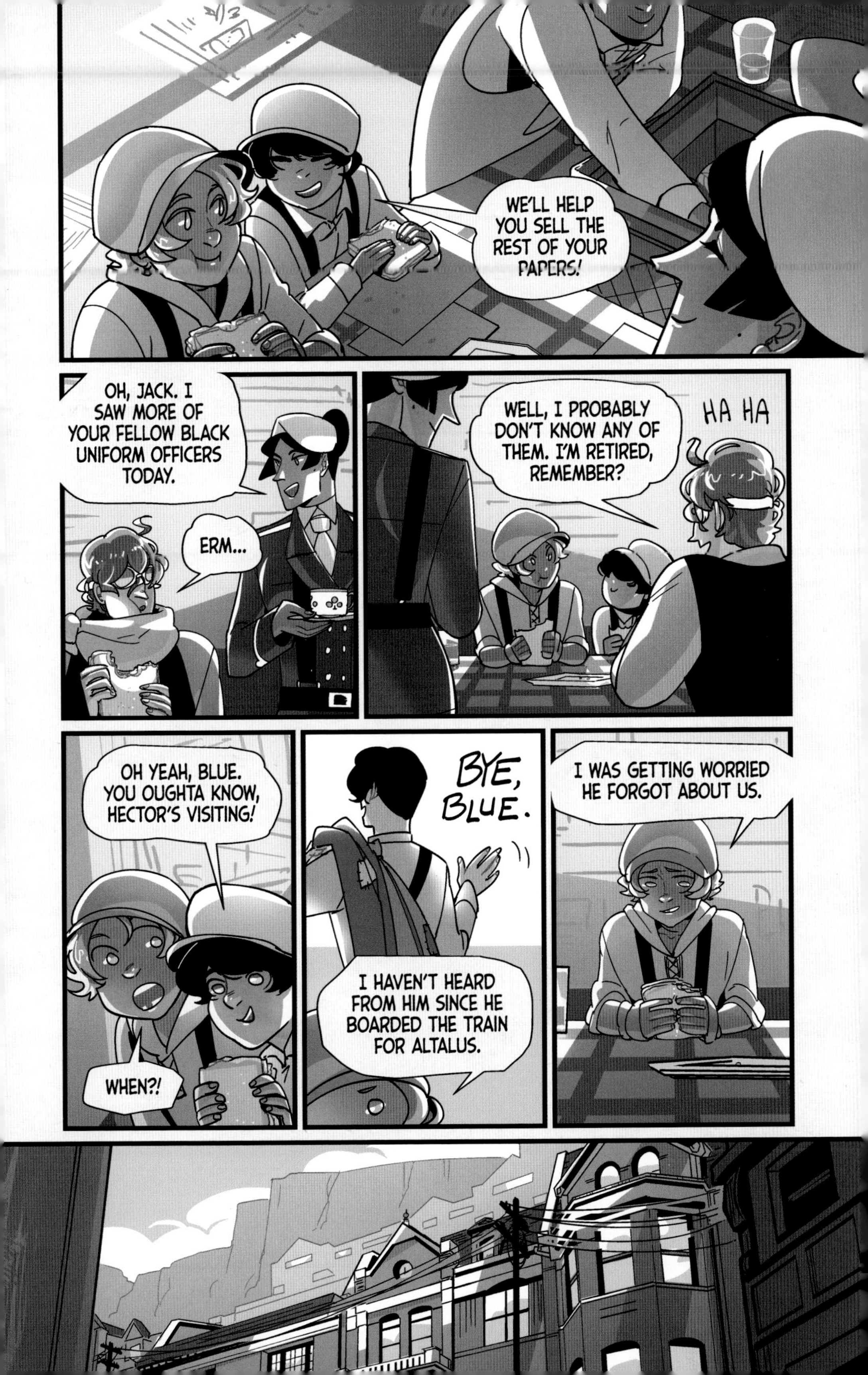
WE'LL HELP YOU SELL THE REST OF YOUR PAPERS!
OH, JACK. I SAW MORE OF YOUR FELLOW BLACK UNIFORM OFFICERS TODAY.
ERM...
WELL, I PROBABLY DON'T KNOW ANY OF THEM. I'M RETIRED, REMEMBER?
HA HA
OH YEAH, BLUE. YOU OUGHTA KNOW, HECTOR'S VISITING!
WHEN?!
BYE, BLUE.
I HAVEN'T HEARD FROM HIM SINCE HE BOARDED THE TRAIN FOR ALTALUS.
I WAS GETTING WORRIED HE FORGOT ABOUT US.

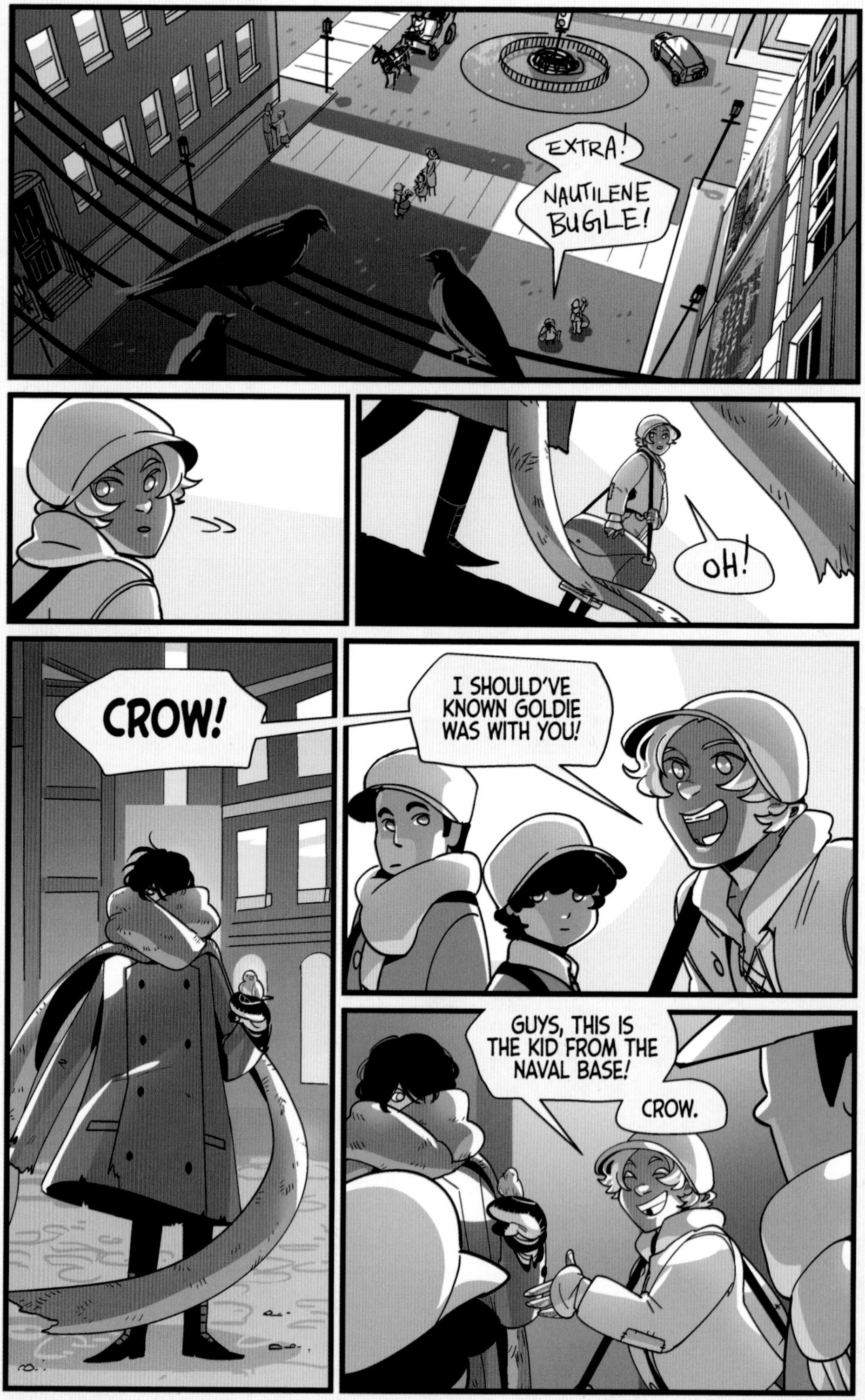
EXTRA!
NAUTILENE BUGLE!
OH!
CROW!
I SHOULD'VE KNOWN GOLDIE WAS WITH YOU!
GUYS, THIS IS THE KID FROM THE NAVAL BASE!
CROW.

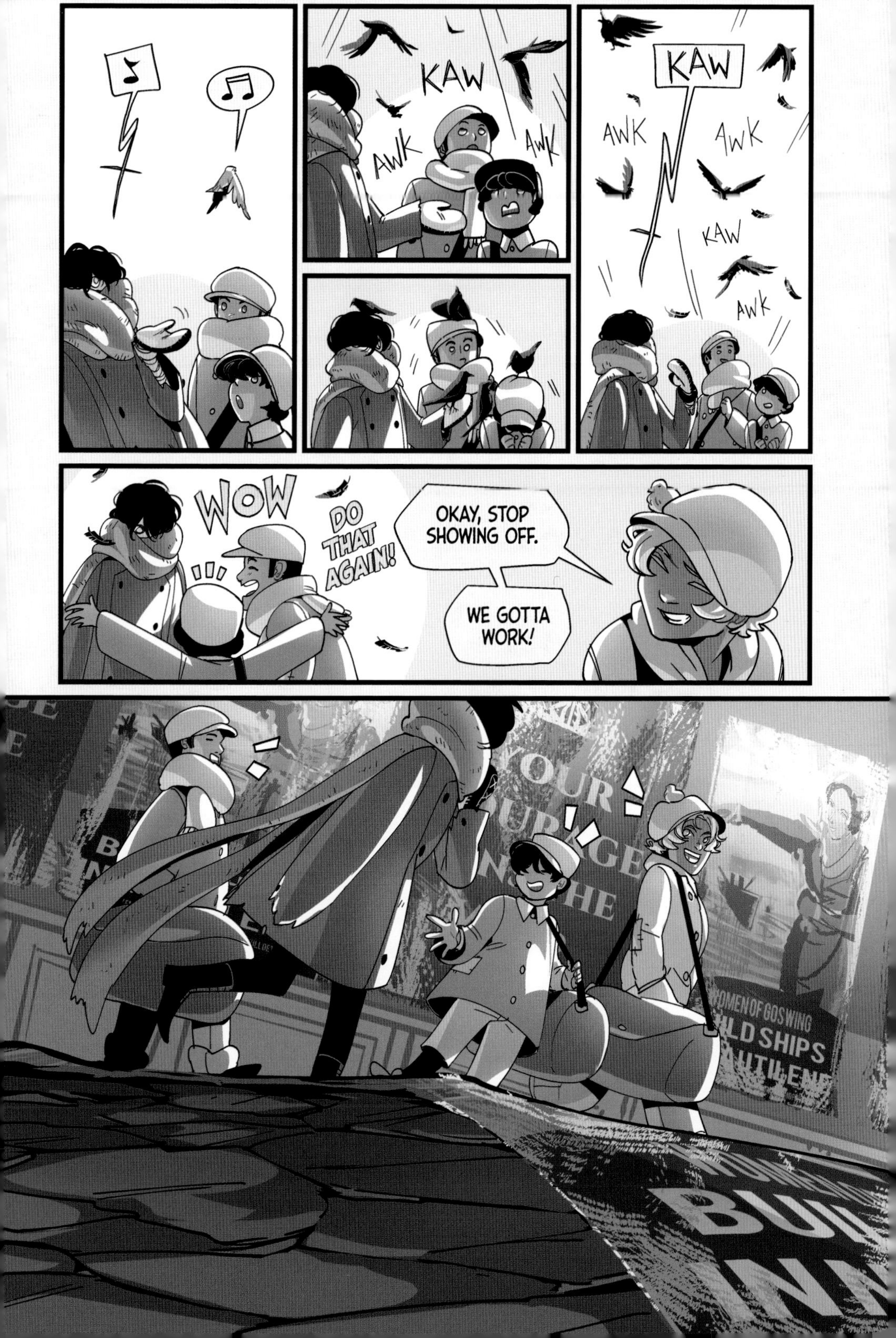

KAW
AWK
AWK
KAW
AWK
AWK
KAW
AWK
WOW
DO THAT AGAIN!
OKAY, STOP SHOWING OFF.
WE GOTTA WORK!
WOMEN OF GOSWING

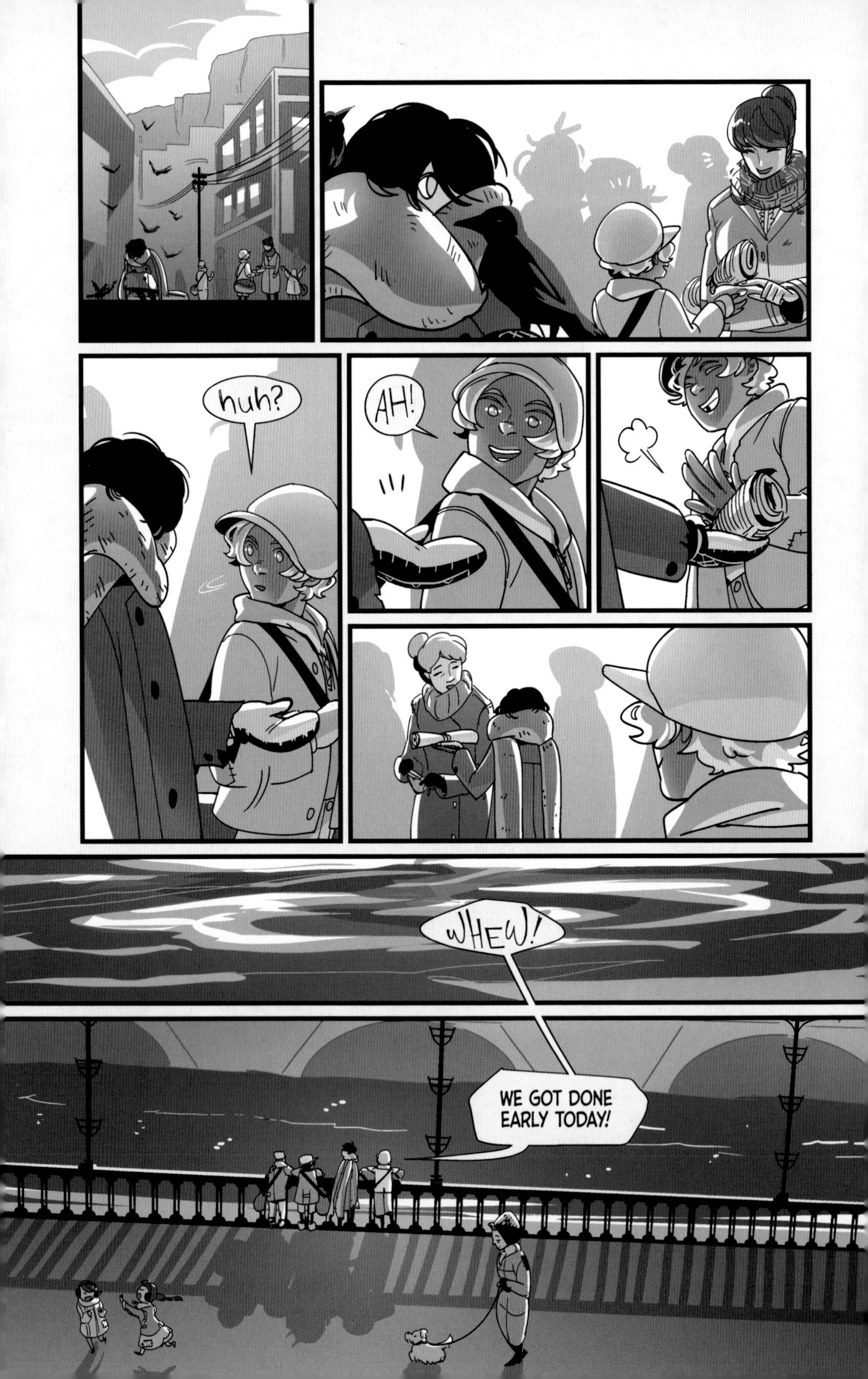
huh?
AH!
WHEW!
WE GOT DONE EARLY TODAY!

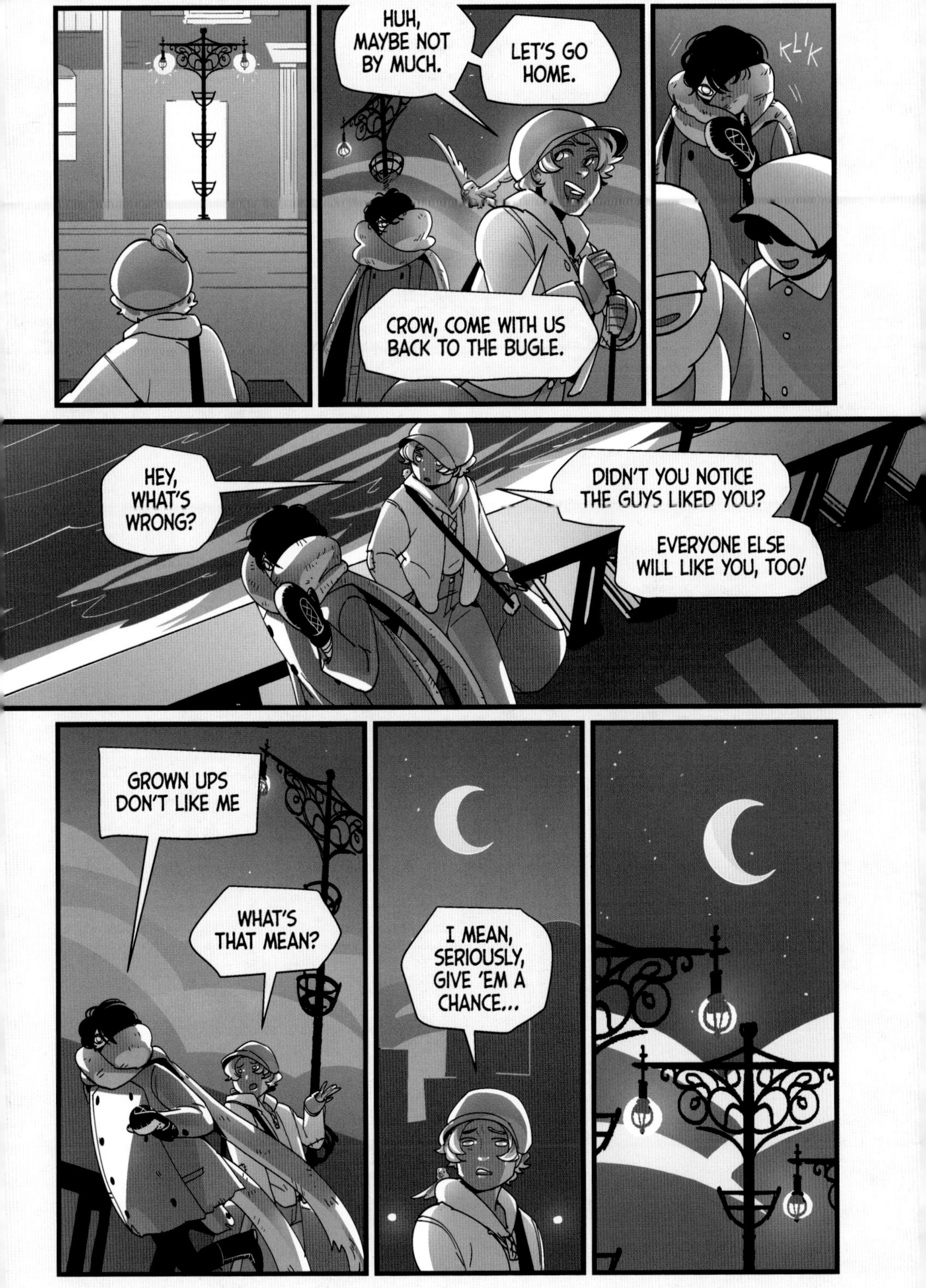
HUH, MAYBE NOT BY MUCH.
LET'S GO HOME.
CROW, COME WITH US BACK TO THE BUGLE.
KLIK
HEY, WHAT'S WRONG?
DIDN'T YOU NOTICE THE GUYS LIKED YOU?
EVERYONE ELSE WILL LIKE YOU, TOO!
GROWN UPS DON'T LIKE ME
WHAT'S THAT MEAN?
I MEAN, SERIOUSLY, GIVE 'EM A CHANCE...

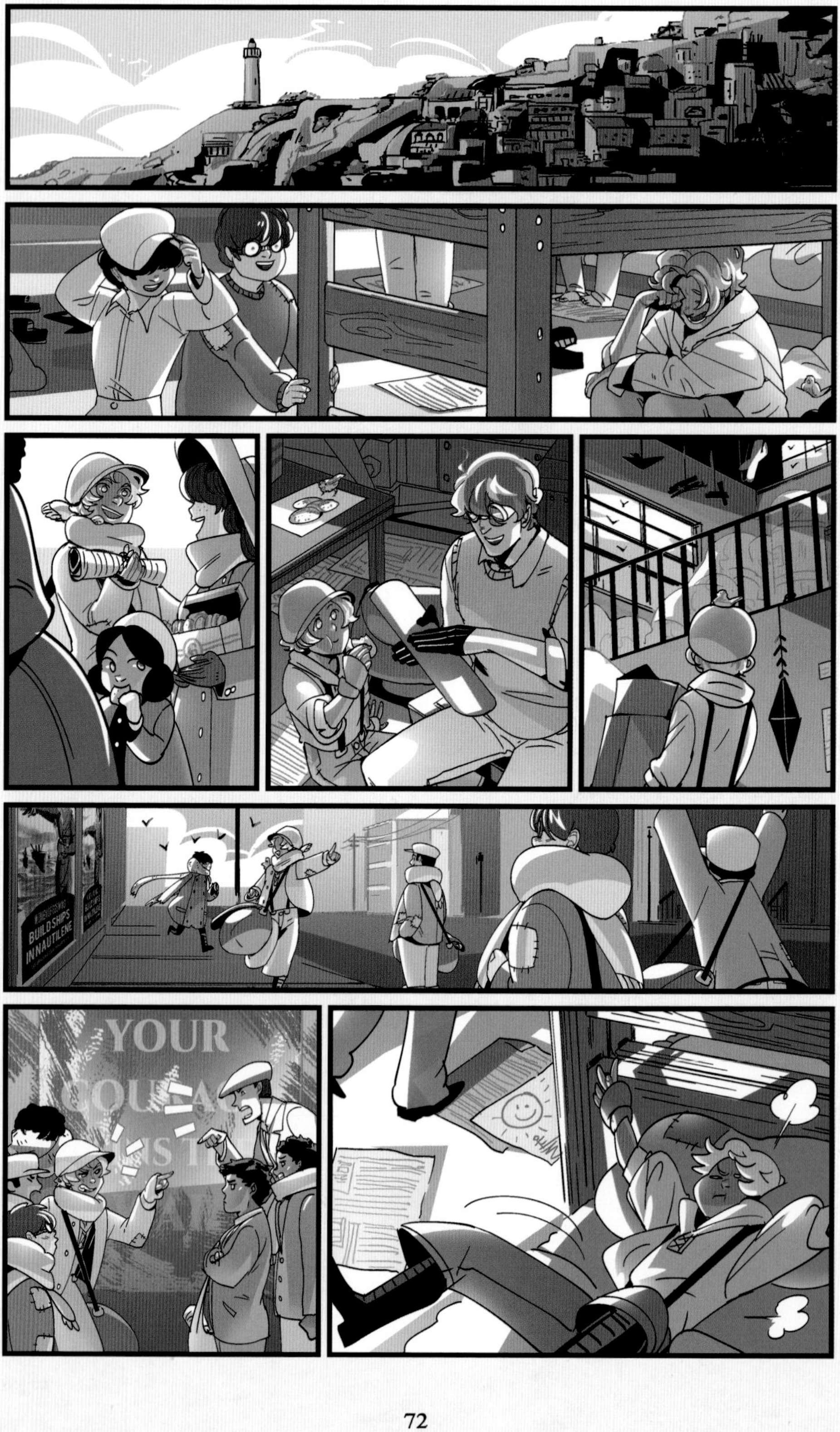
BUILD SHIPS IN NAUTILENE
YOUR

JOHN AND PETER, GO DOWNTOWN WITH THE BROTHERS.

GRUNDIES ARE GETTING EXTRA MEAN THIS WINTER, SO WATCH OUT FOR THEM.

YOU OKAY, BLUE?

YAWN

I'M FINE.

SEE YOU GUYS AT SUPPER!

SIGH

BUGLE!

ALTALUSIAN OFFICIALS ALL OVER NAUTILENE!

WHY ARE THEY HERE?

ALTALUSIAN OFFICIALS ALL OVER...

YAWN

EXTRA, EXTRA! READ ALL ABOUT IT IN THE BUGLE!

WHY ARE THEY... HERE?

SWAY

shake shake

ONE FOR ME, DEAR.

READ ABOUT IT...

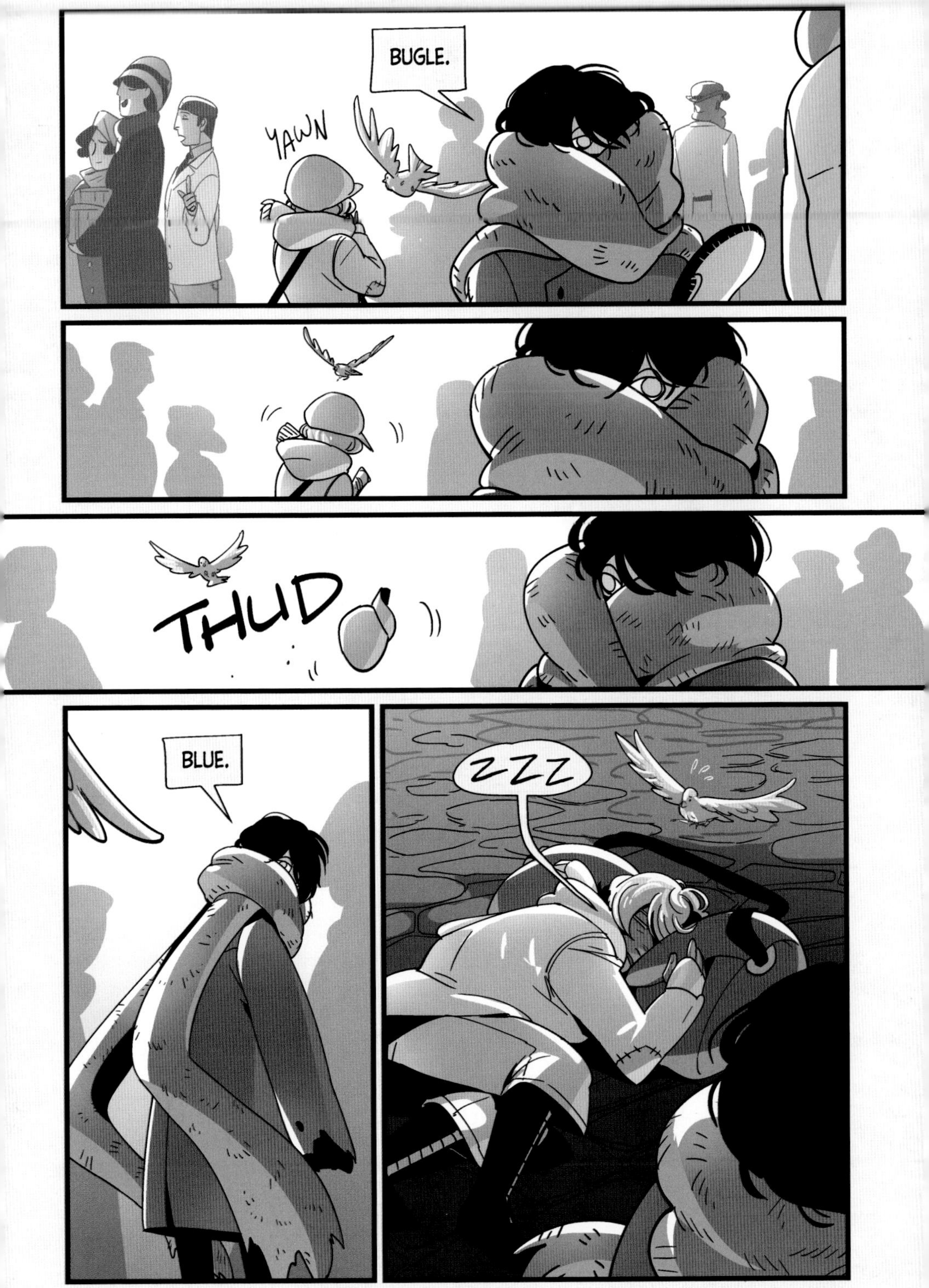
BUGLE.
YAWN
THUD
BLUE.
ZZZ

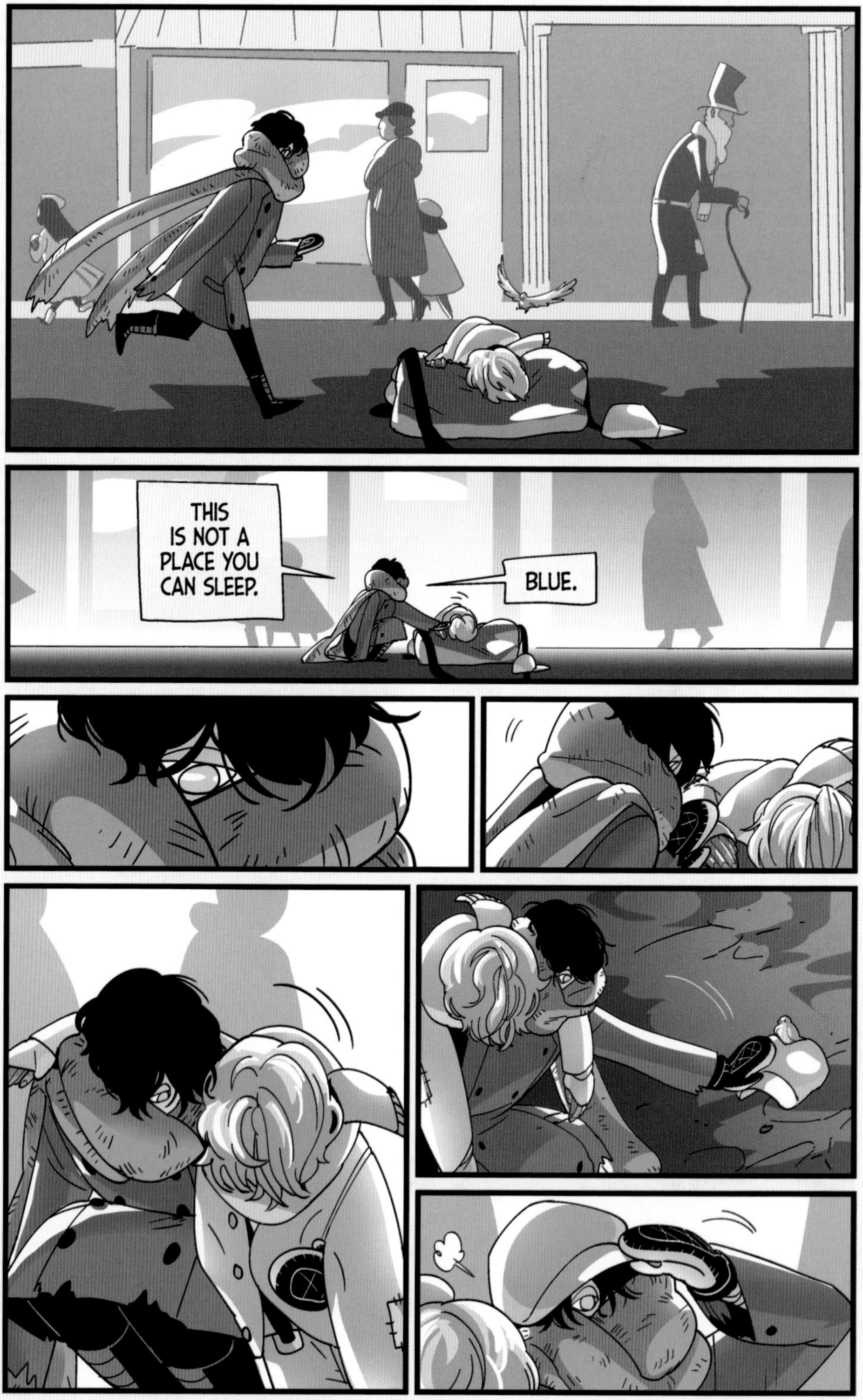
THIS IS NOT A PLACE YOU CAN SLEEP.
BLUE.

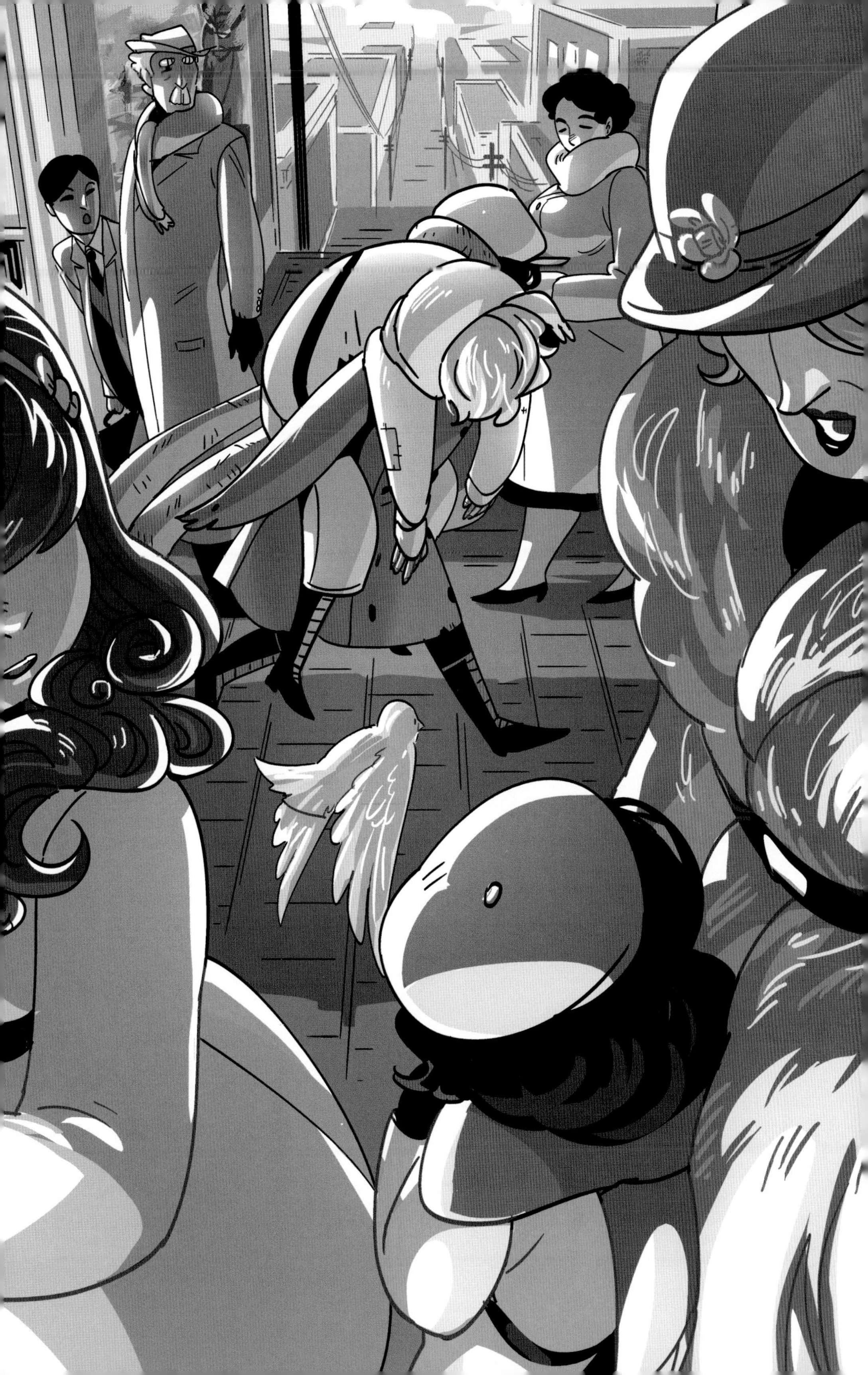

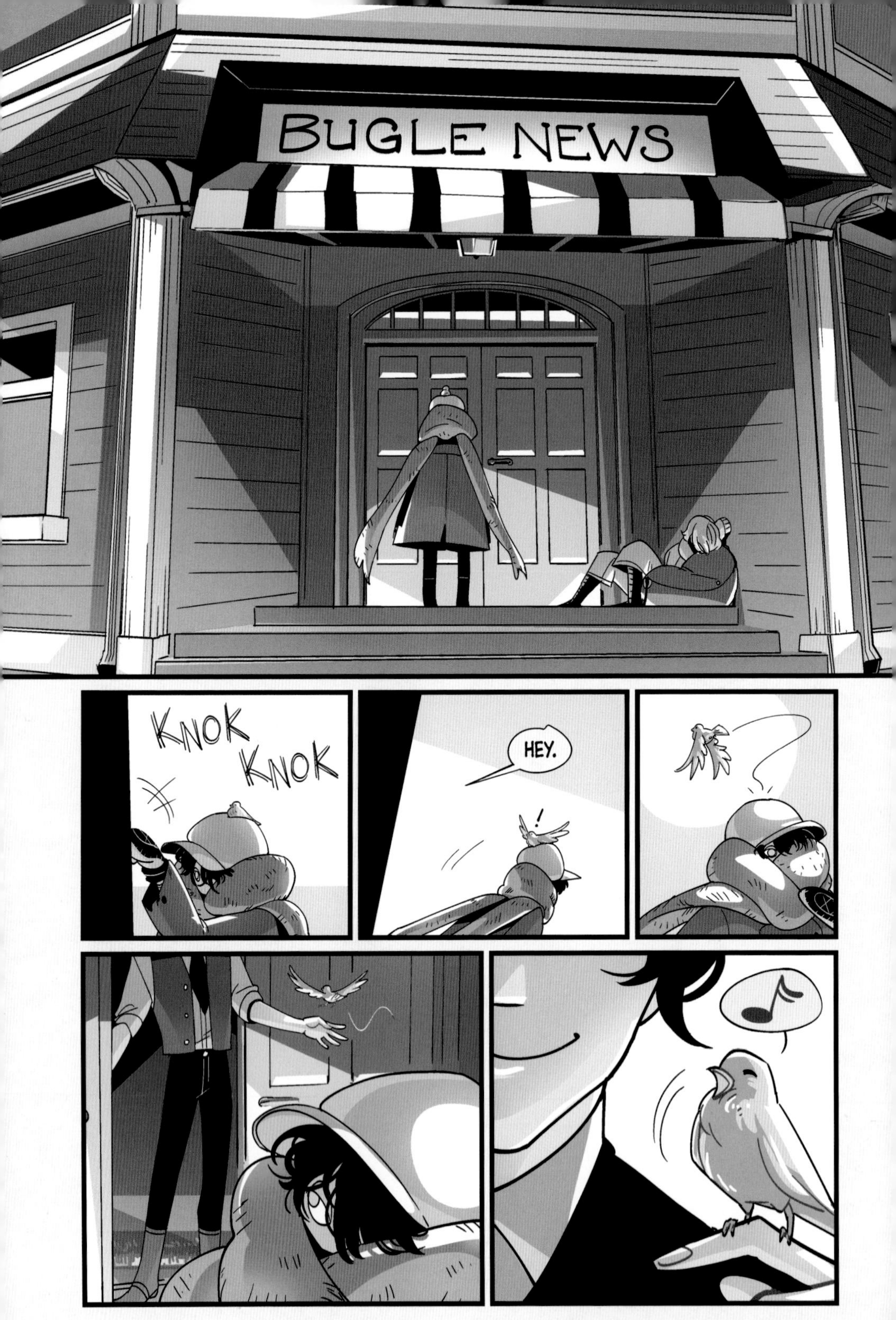
BUGLE NEWS
KNOK
KNOK
HEY.
!

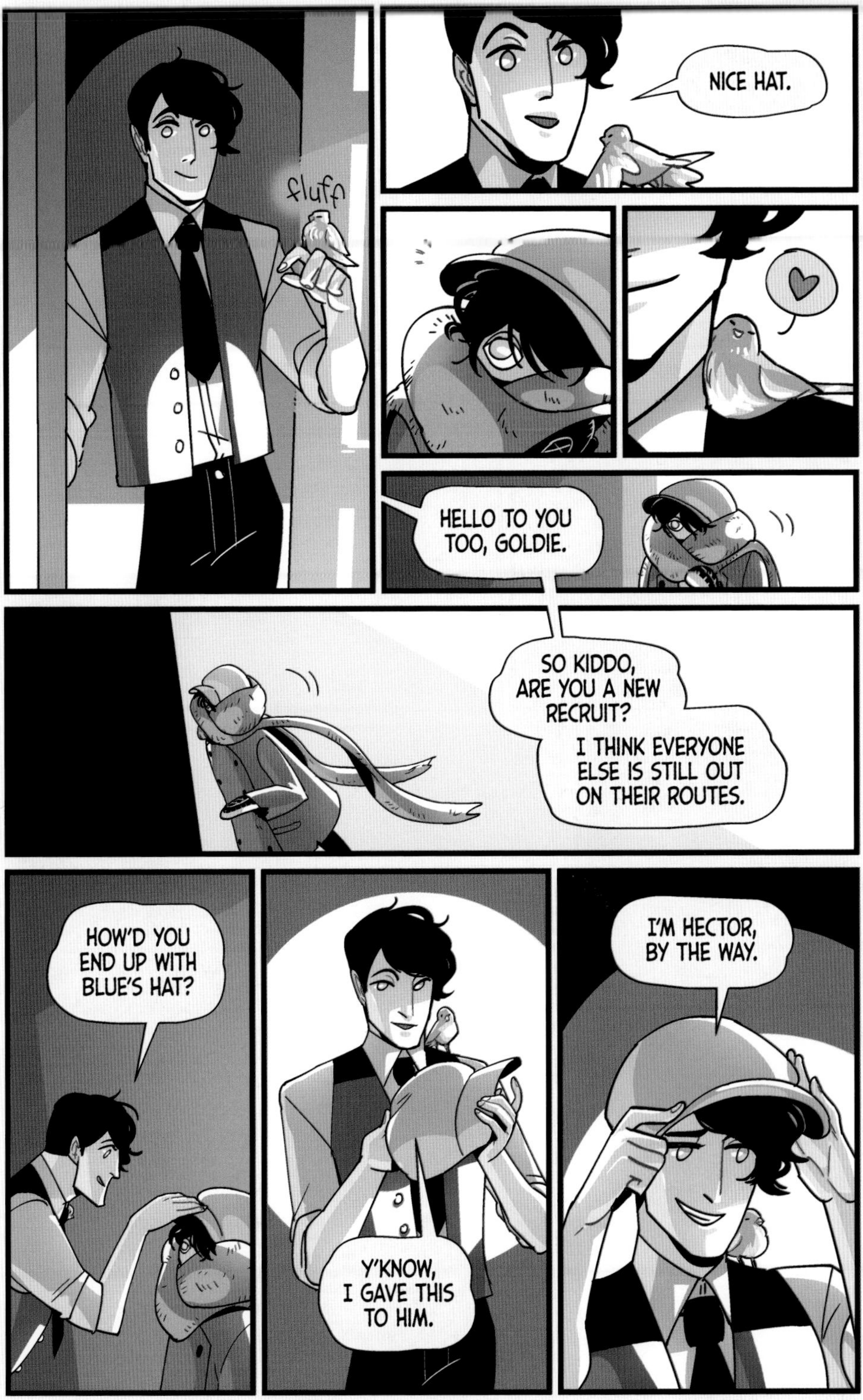
fluff
NICE HAT.
HELLO TO YOU TOO, GOLDIE.
SO KIDDO, ARE YOU A NEW RECRUIT?
I THINK EVERYONE ELSE IS STILL OUT ON THEIR ROUTES.
HOW'D YOU END UP WITH BLUE'S HAT?
Y'KNOW, I GAVE THIS TO HIM.
I'M HECTOR, BY THE WAY.

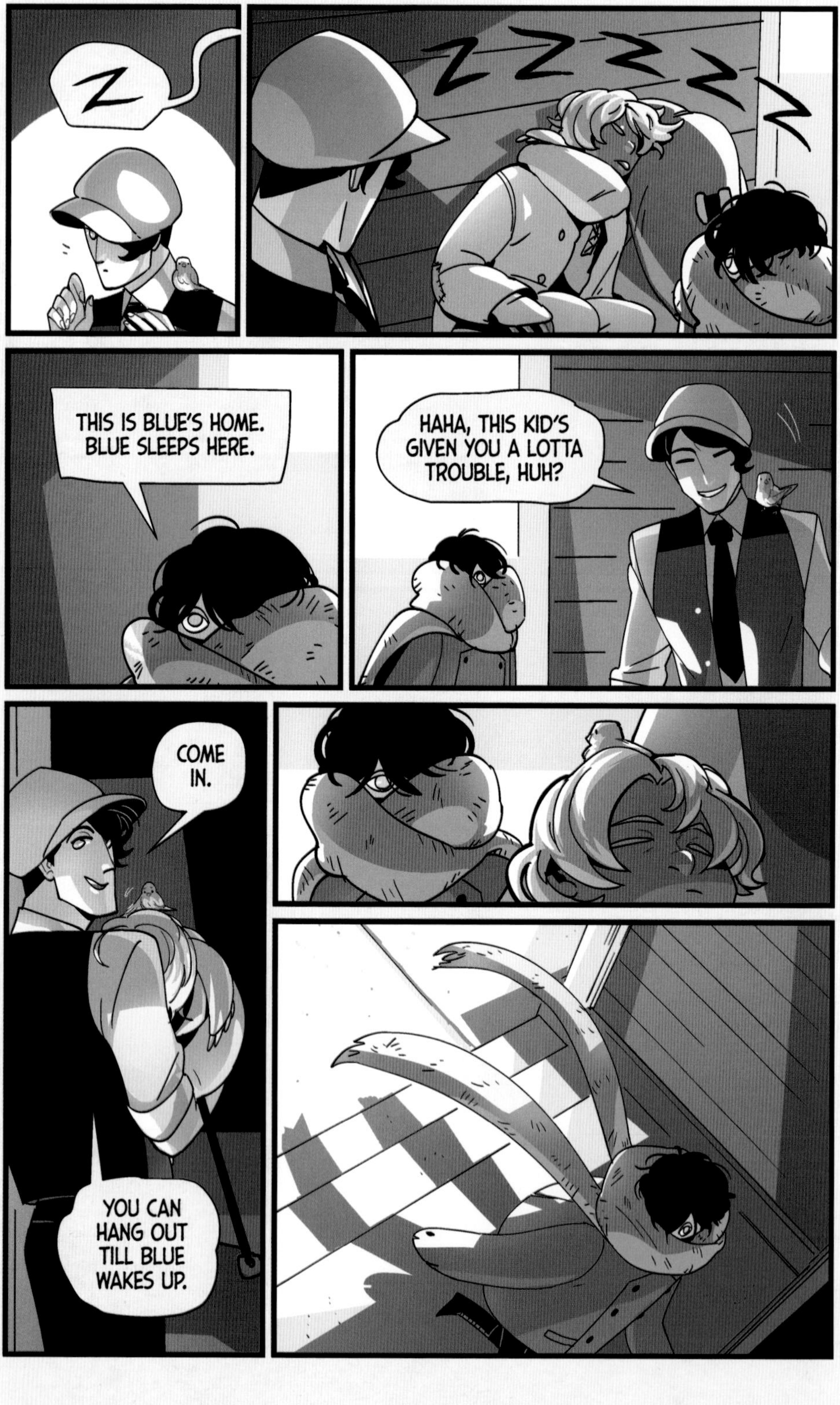
Z
ZZZZZ
THIS IS BLUE'S HOME. BLUE SLEEPS HERE.
HAHA, THIS KID'S GIVEN YOU A LOTTA TROUBLE, HUH?
COME IN.
YOU CAN HANG OUT TILL BLUE WAKES UP.

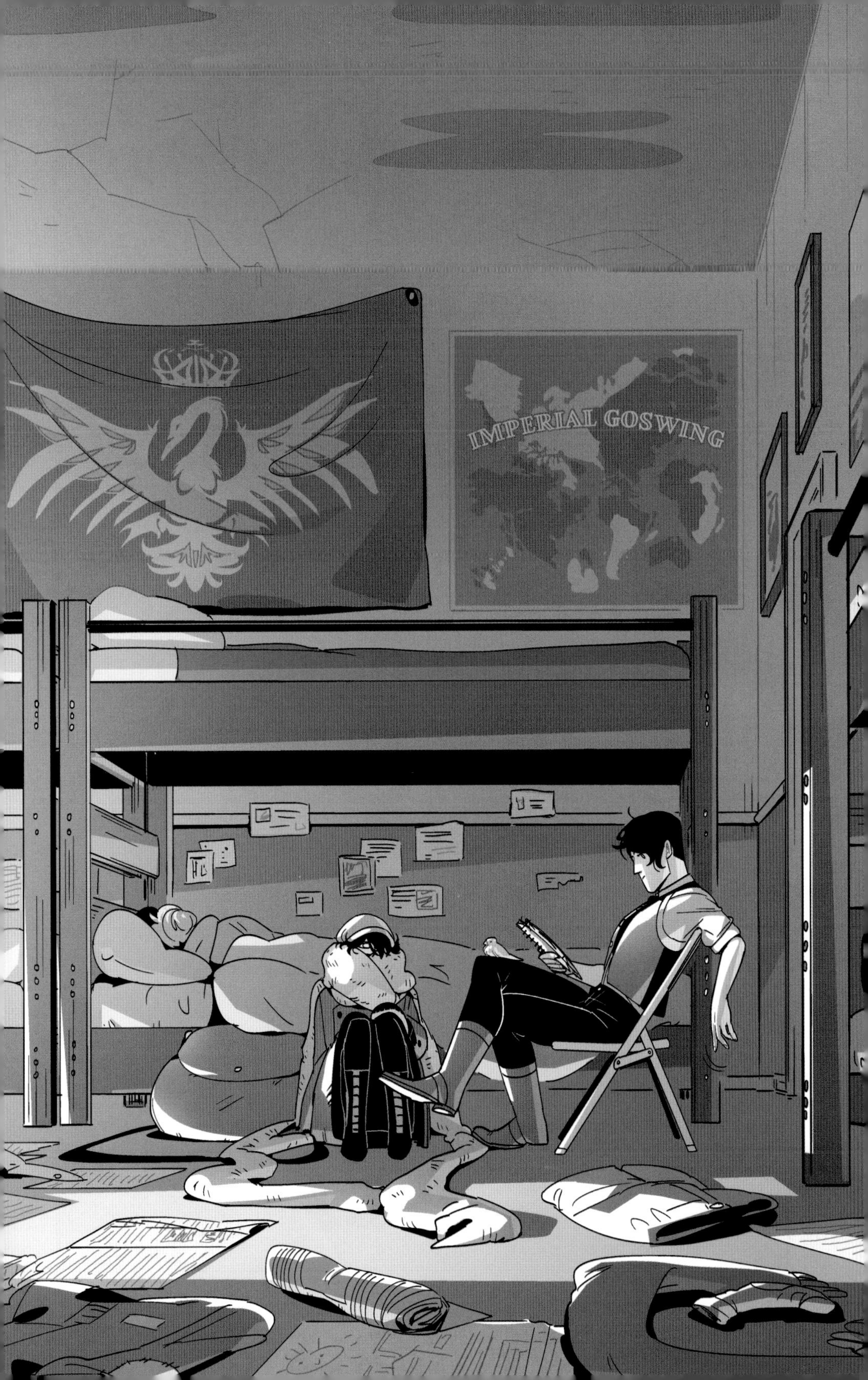
IMPERIAL GOSWING

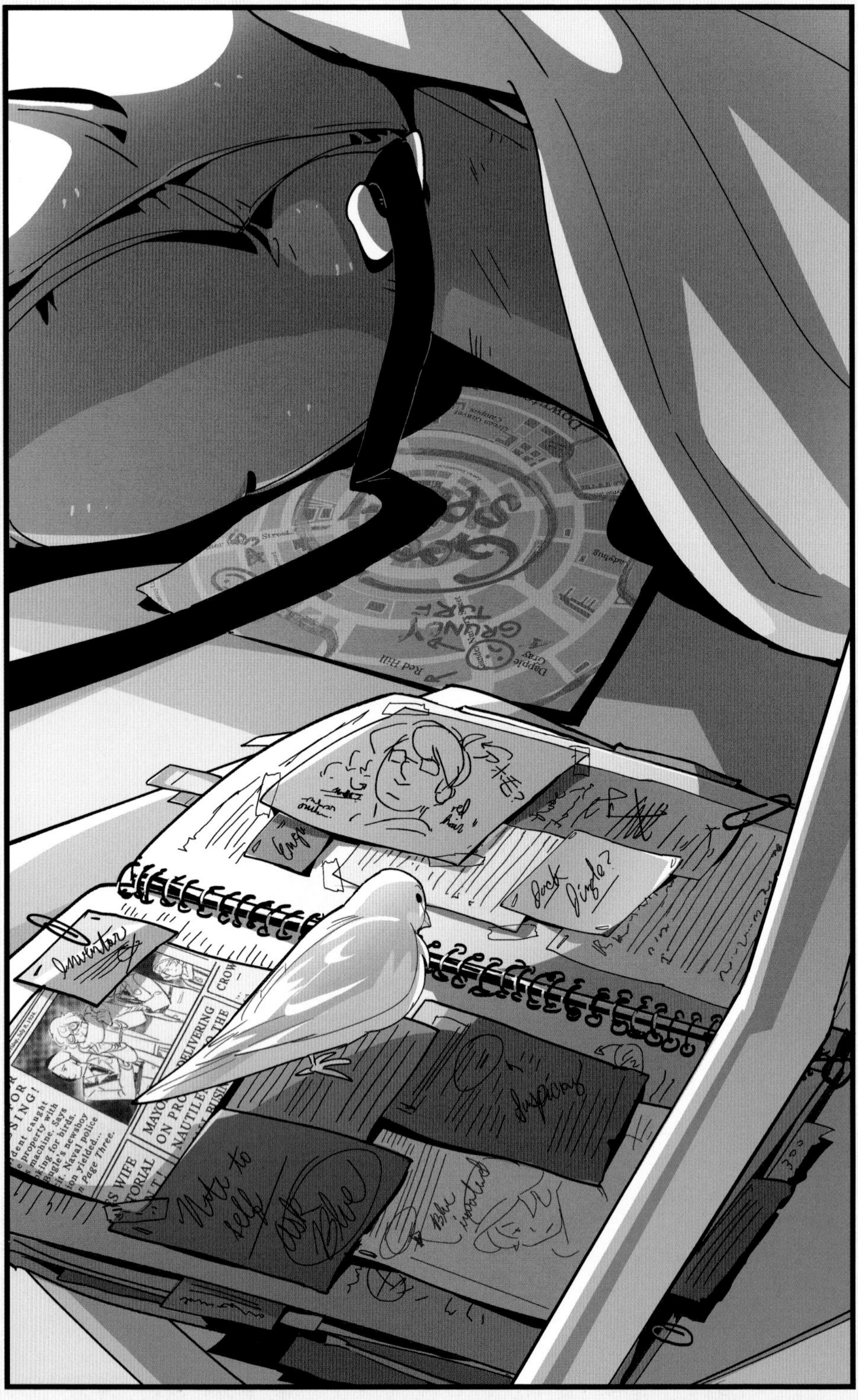
Inventor
Duck Dingle?
Note to self

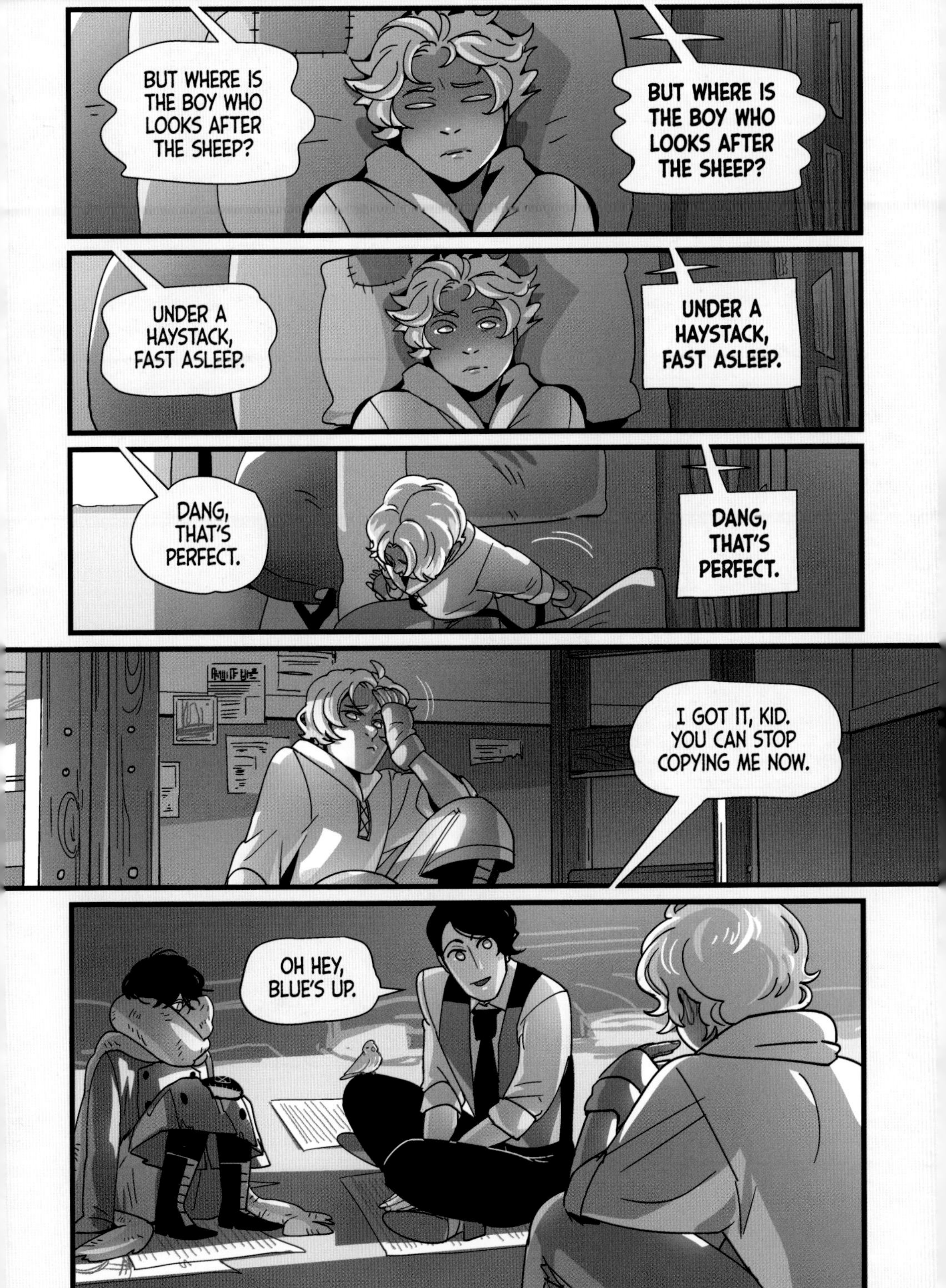
BUT WHERE IS THE BOY WHO LOOKS AFTER THE SHEEP?
BUT WHERE IS THE BOY WHO LOOKS AFTER THE SHEEP?
UNDER A HAYSTACK, FAST ASLEEP.
UNDER A HAYSTACK, FAST ASLEEP.
DANG, THAT'S PERFECT.
DANG, THAT'S PERFECT.
I GOT IT, KID. YOU CAN STOP COPYING ME NOW.
OH HEY, BLUE'S UP.

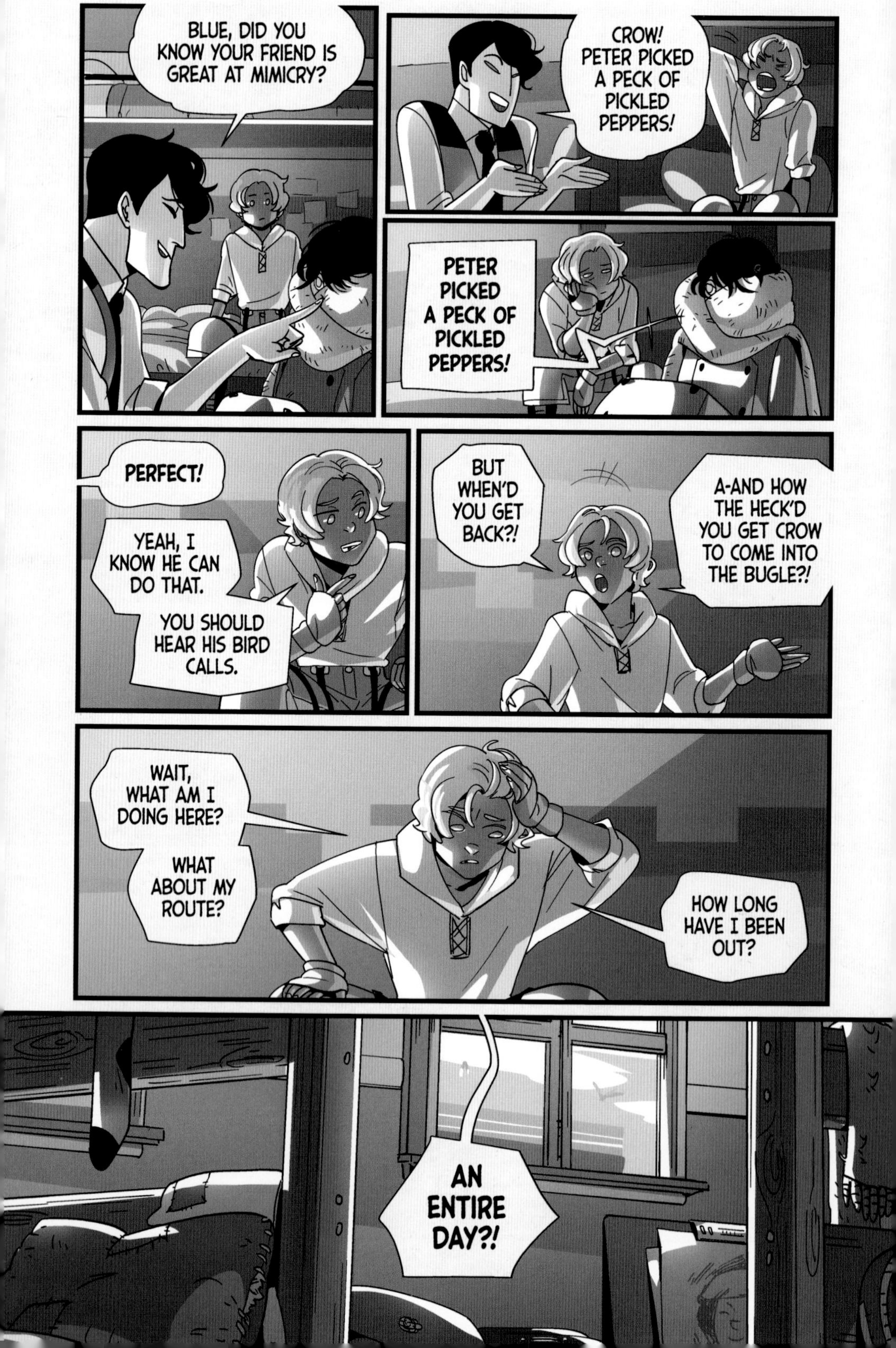
BLUE, DID YOU KNOW YOUR FRIEND IS GREAT AT MIMICRY?
CROW! PETER PICKED A PECK OF PICKLED PEPPERS!
PETER PICKED A PECK OF PICKLED PEPPERS!
PERFECT!
YEAH, I KNOW HE CAN DO THAT.
YOU SHOULD HEAR HIS BIRD CALLS.
BUT WHEN'D YOU GET BACK?!
A-AND HOW THE HECK'D YOU GET CROW TO COME INTO THE BUGLE?!
WAIT, WHAT AM I DOING HERE?
WHAT ABOUT MY ROUTE?
HOW LONG HAVE I BEEN OUT?
AN ENTIRE DAY?!

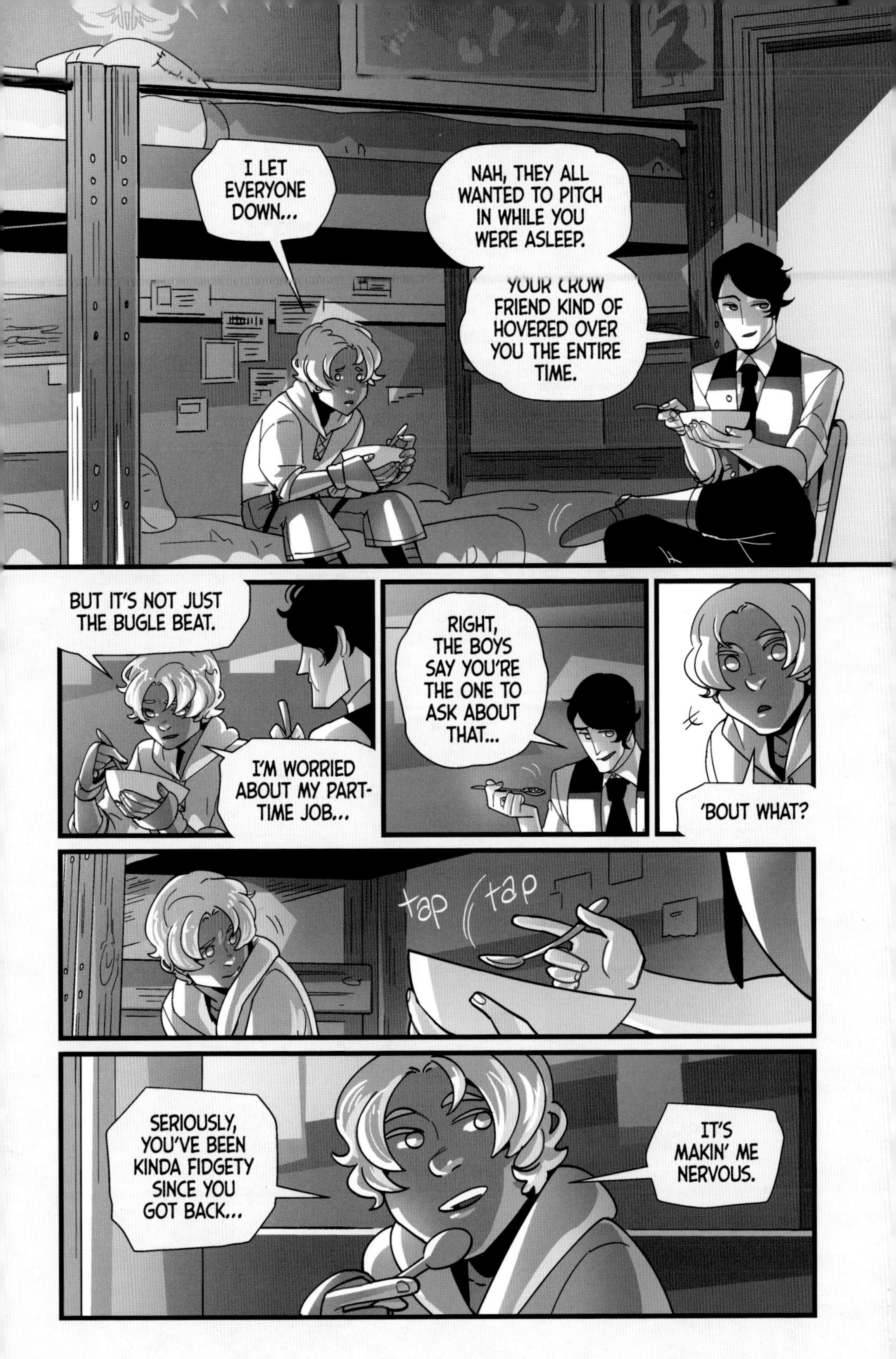
I LET EVERYONE DOWN...
NAH, THEY ALL WANTED TO PITCH IN WHILE YOU WERE ASLEEP.
YOUR CROW FRIEND KIND OF HOVERED OVER YOU THE ENTIRE TIME.
BUT IT'S NOT JUST THE BUGLE BEAT.
I'M WORRIED ABOUT MY PART-TIME JOB...
RIGHT, THE BOYS SAY YOU'RE THE ONE TO ASK ABOUT THAT...
'BOUT WHAT?
tap tap
SERIOUSLY, YOU'VE BEEN KINDA FIDGETY SINCE YOU GOT BACK...
IT'S MAKIN' ME NERVOUS.

RIGHT, LET'S JUST SAY I WASN'T ONLY IN ALTALUS...

BUT, UHH... LIFE OF A WAR JOURNALIST.

NOW LISTEN, I'M WORKING ON THE BIGGEST STORY OF THE WAR, OKAY?

AND I THINK YOU CAN HELP ME.

ONE OF THE **QUEEN'S ADVISORS** IS MISSING.

THE SEARCH HAS GONE ON FOR MONTHS.

EVERYONE IN ALTALUS SAYS HE'S THE **KEY** TO WINNING THE WAR.

AND? YOU CAN BARELY SEE THE GUY IN THE PHOTO, HEC.

BUT DON'T YOU RECOGNIZE HIM?

HE GOES BY **JACK.**

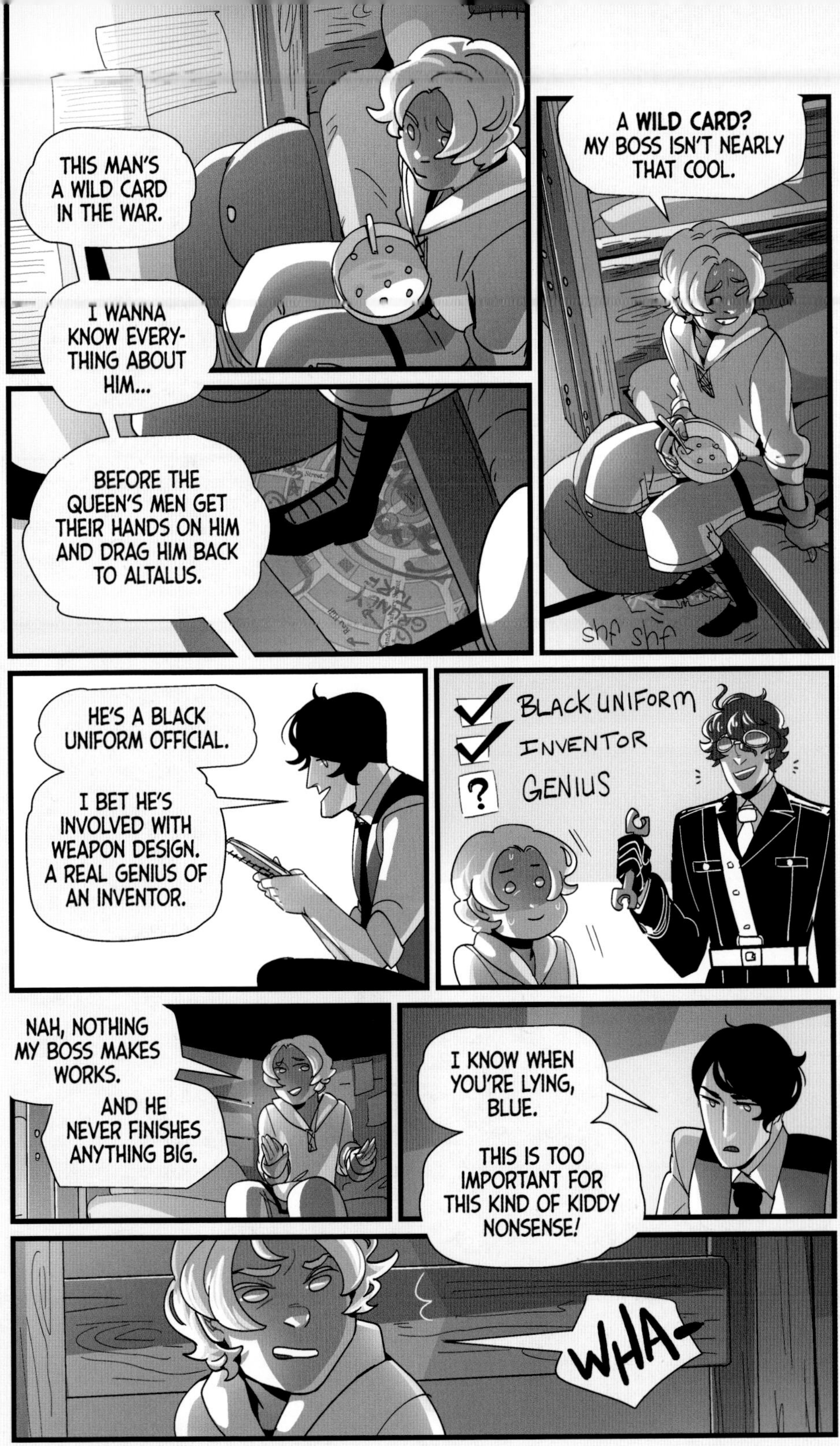

THIS MAN'S A WILD CARD IN THE WAR.
I WANNA KNOW EVERYTHING ABOUT HIM...
BEFORE THE QUEEN'S MEN GET THEIR HANDS ON HIM AND DRAG HIM BACK TO ALTALUS.
A WILD CARD? MY BOSS ISN'T NEARLY THAT COOL.
shf shf
HE'S A BLACK UNIFORM OFFICIAL.
I BET HE'S INVOLVED WITH WEAPON DESIGN. A REAL GENIUS OF AN INVENTOR.
BLACK UNIFORM
INVENTOR
?
GENIUS
NAH, NOTHING MY BOSS MAKES WORKS.
AND HE NEVER FINISHES ANYTHING BIG.
I KNOW WHEN YOU'RE LYING, BLUE.
THIS IS TOO IMPORTANT FOR THIS KIND OF KIDDY NONSENSE!
WHA-

LOOK, EVERYONE IN NAUTILENE'S JUST TRYIN' TO GET BY, OKAY?

INCLUDING MY BOSS. HE KEEPS TO HIMSELF AND MAKES GOOFY BIRDS!

IT'S NOT A HUNCH.

I'D BET MY LIFE IT'S HIM.

I'M NOT GONNA LET YOU PRY INTO HIS LIFE JUST 'CAUSE YOU HAVE A HUNCH!

IN FACT...

I'D BET YOUR SECRET THAT HE IS THE JACK I'M LOOKING FOR.

I DON'T HAVE TO EXPLAIN MYSELF!

ARGH

IS HE A REAL FRIEND?

I DON'T KNOW WHO'S REAL OR NOT...

I'M NOT EVEN A REAL BOY.

A REAL BOY...

KLIK

KLIK

THAT DOESN'T CHANGE THE FACT THAT YOU ARE BLUE.

AND GOLDIE LEFT WITH...

HECTOR.

HAHAHA!

THAT'S WHAT'S GETTING YOUR GOOSE, HUH?

DON'T WORRY, SHE'S IN GOOD HANDS.

HECTOR HELPED ME RAISE GOLDIE FROM AN EGG, AFTER A CAT ATE HER MOM!

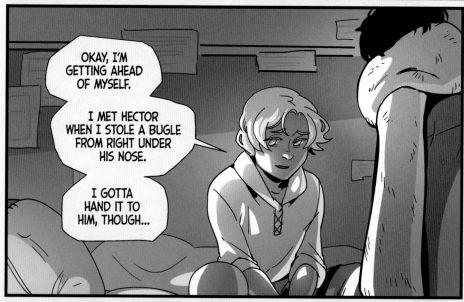

OKAY, I'M GETTING AHEAD OF MYSELF.

I MET HECTOR WHEN I STOLE A BUGLE FROM RIGHT UNDER HIS NOSE.

I GOTTA HAND IT TO HIM, THOUGH...

HE CHASED ME ALL THE WAY ACROSS THE CITY!

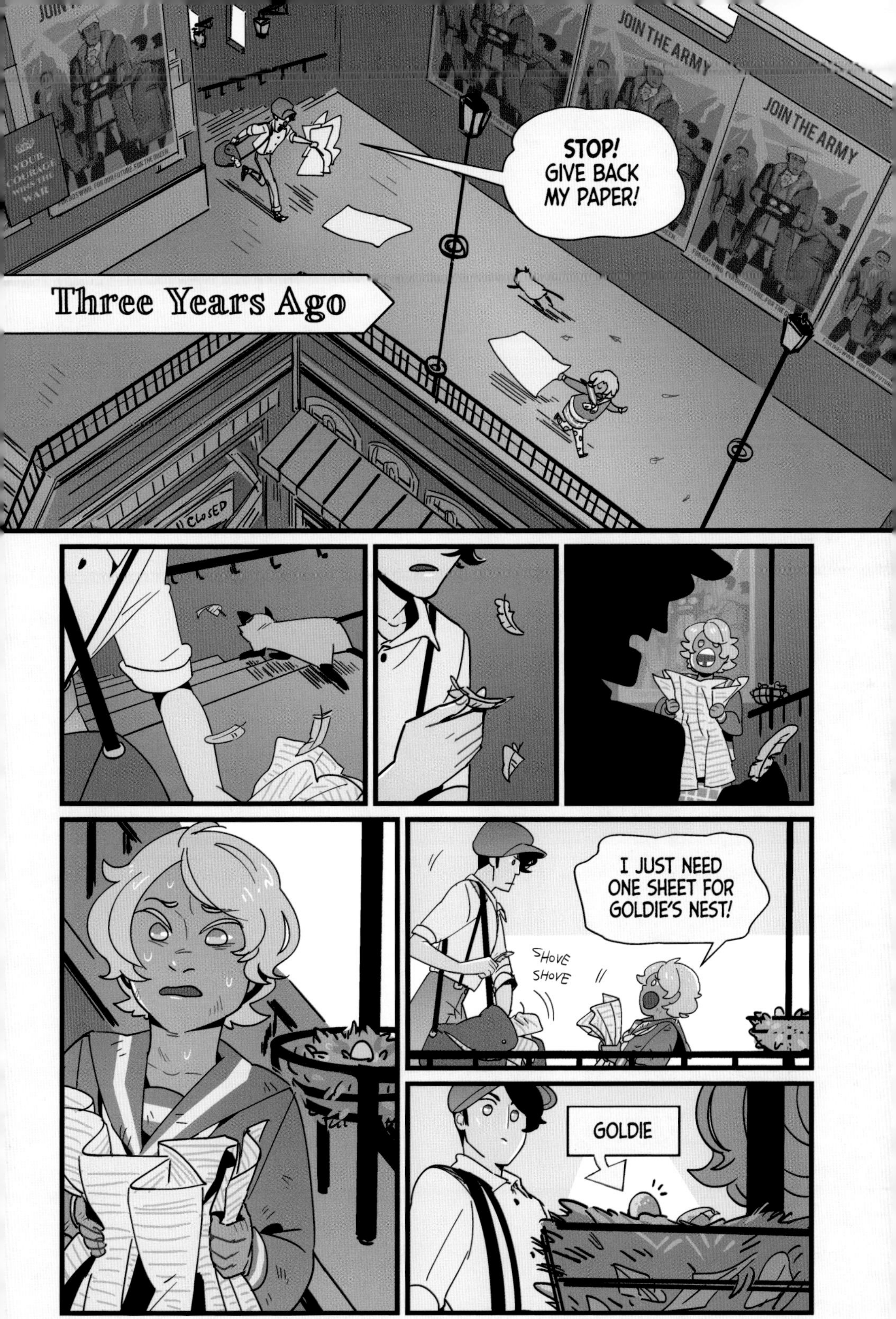
JOIN THE ARMY
JOIN THE ARMY
YOUR COURAGE WINS THE WAR
STOP! GIVE BACK MY PAPER!
Three Years Ago
CLOSED
I JUST NEED ONE SHEET FOR GOLDIE'S NEST!
SHOVE SHOVE
GOLDIE

DO YOUR PARENTS KNOW YOU'RE STEALING PAPERS TO MAKE A...A NEST?

WELL. MY MOM'S GONE.

MY DAD...

HE'S NOT COMING BACK FROM THE WAR.

HERE, I WON'T EVEN TAKE A WHOLE SHEET.

RIP

WAIT!

SIGH.

HEY. WHAT'S YOUR NAME?

I'M HECTOR, BY THE WAY.

NAME'S LAVENDER BLUE.

LAVENDER BLUE, I WORK AND LIVE AT THAT BUILDING OVER THERE.

THE NAUTILENE BUGLE!

IT'S RUN BY THE MAYOR AND HIS WIFE.

WHY DON'T YA STAY WITH US FOR A WHILE?

AH!

CAN I STAY FOREVER?

I MEAN, WE CAN ALWAYS USE MORE NEWSBOYS, BUT THEY GOTTA BE...WELL, BOYS.

95

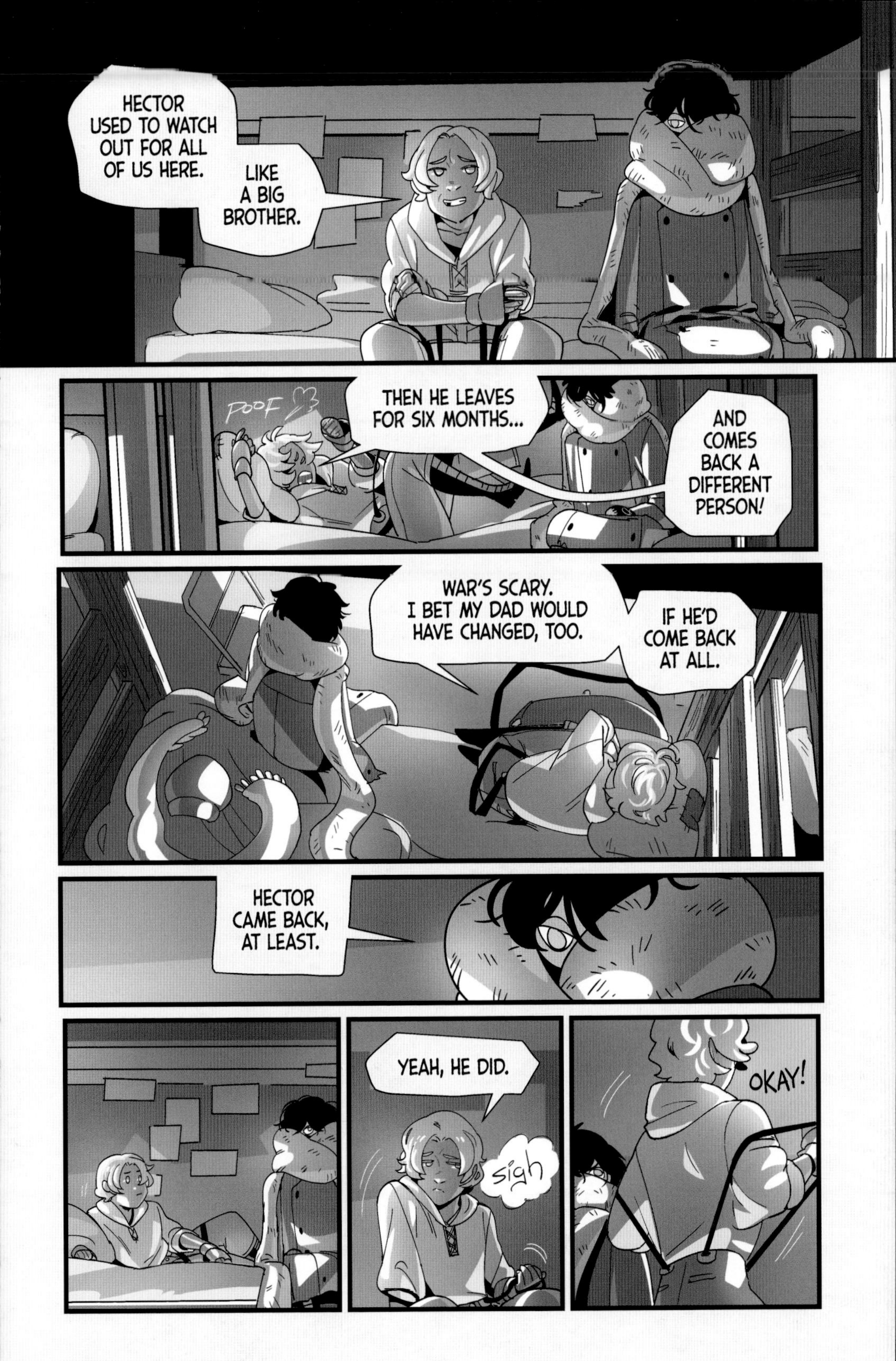
HECTOR USED TO WATCH OUT FOR ALL OF US HERE.
LIKE A BIG BROTHER.
POOF
THEN HE LEAVES FOR SIX MONTHS...
AND COMES BACK A DIFFERENT PERSON!
WAR'S SCARY. I BET MY DAD WOULD HAVE CHANGED, TOO.
IF HE'D COME BACK AT ALL.
HECTOR CAME BACK, AT LEAST.
YEAH, HE DID.
sigh
OKAY!

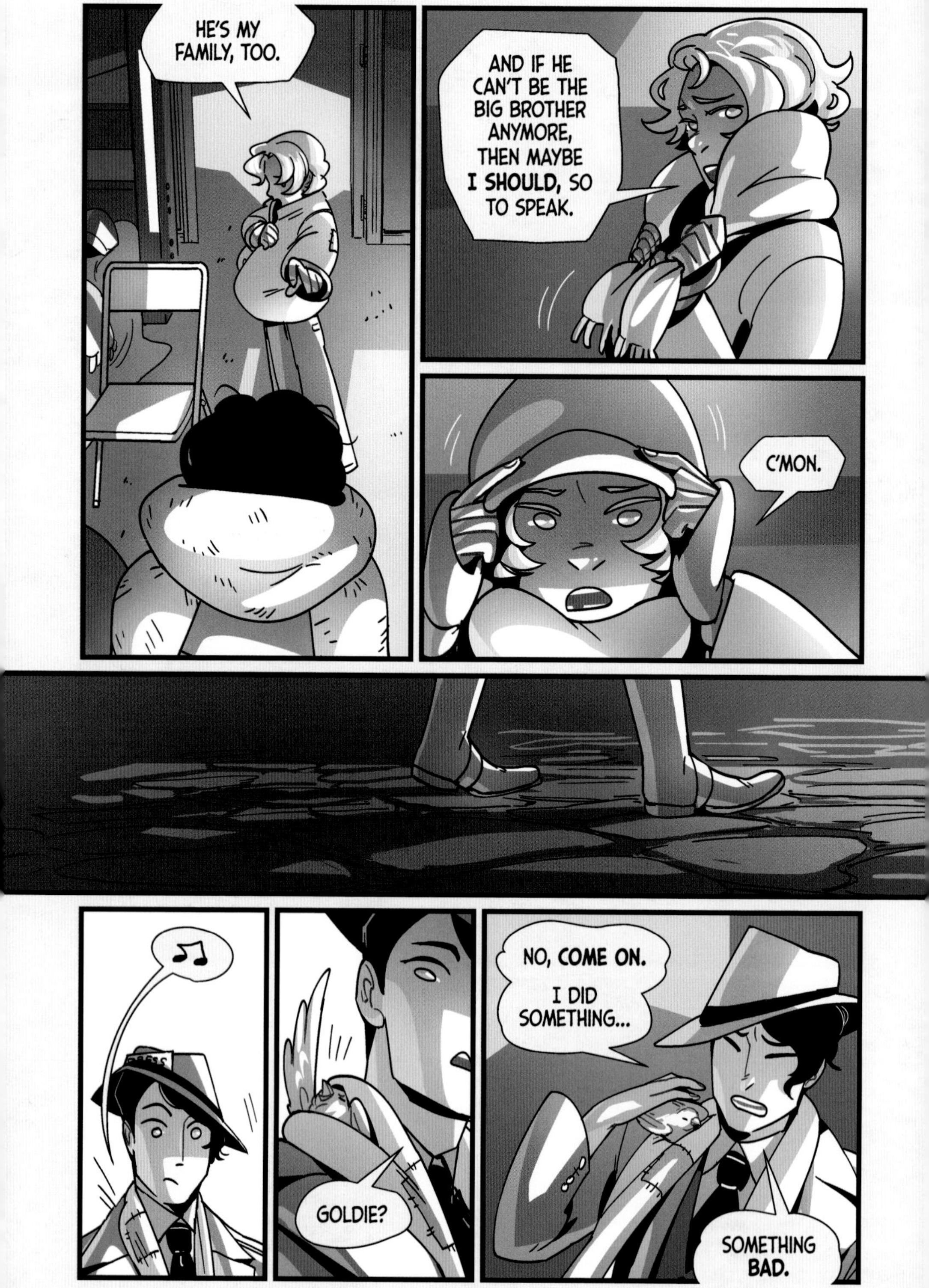
HE'S MY FAMILY, TOO.
AND IF HE CAN'T BE THE BIG BROTHER ANYMORE, THEN MAYBE I SHOULD, SO TO SPEAK.
C'MON.
♫
GOLDIE?
NO, COME ON.
I DID SOMETHING...
SOMETHING BAD.

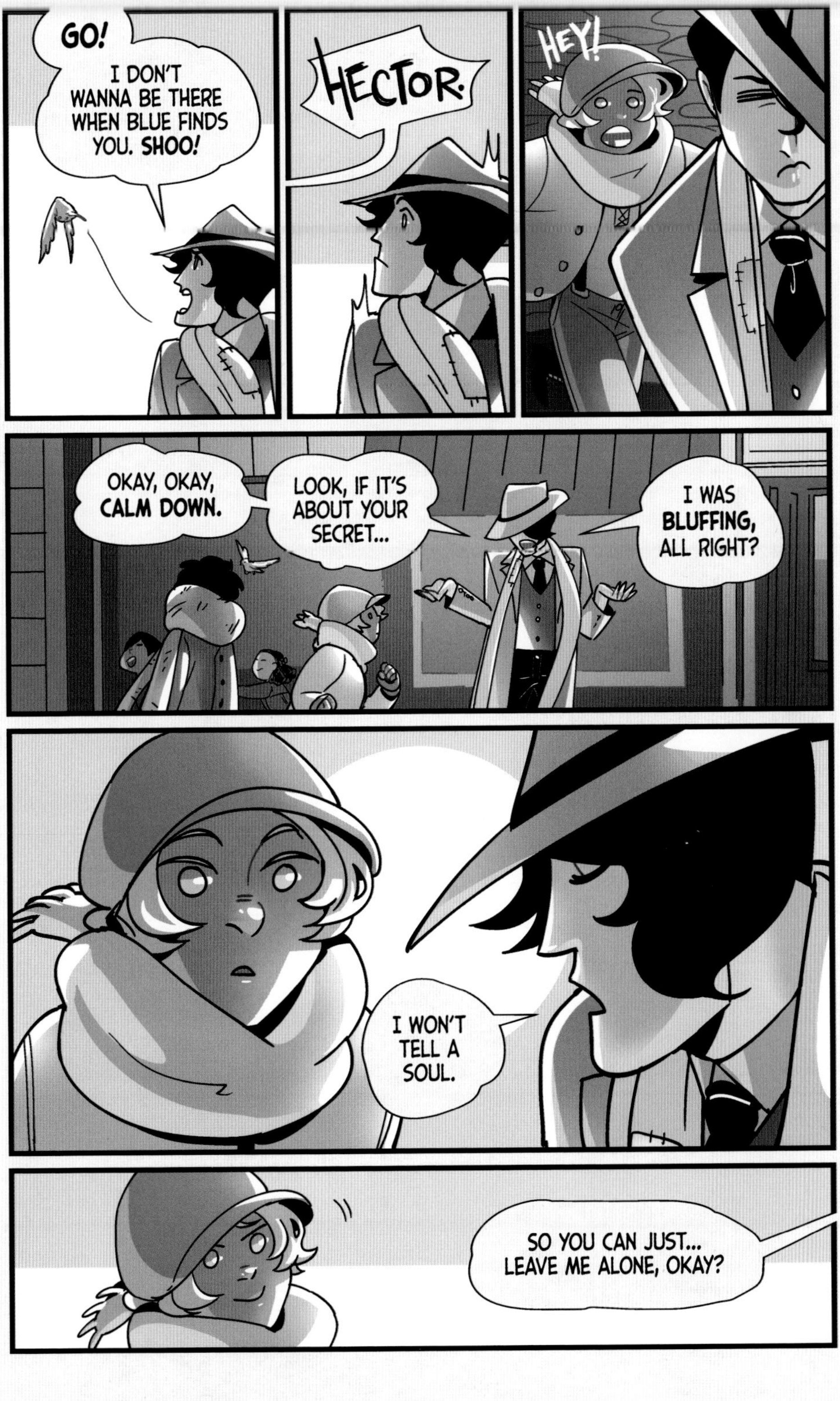
GO!
I DON'T WANNA BE THERE WHEN BLUE FINDS YOU. SHOO!
HECTOR.
HEY!
OKAY, OKAY, CALM DOWN.
LOOK, IF IT'S ABOUT YOUR SECRET...
I WAS BLUFFING, ALL RIGHT?
I WON'T TELL A SOUL.
SO YOU CAN JUST... LEAVE ME ALONE, OKAY?

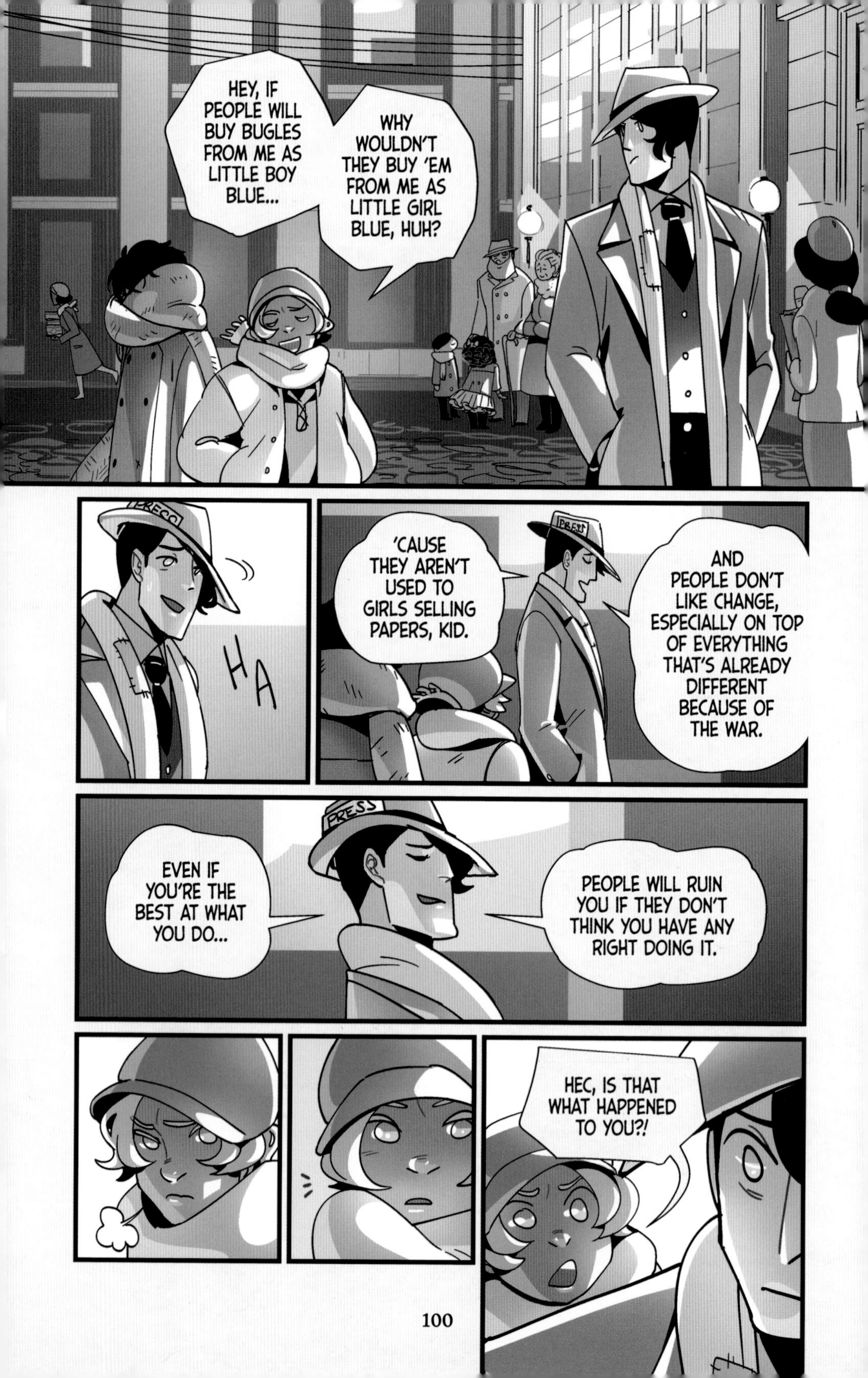
HEY, IF PEOPLE WILL BUY BUGLES FROM ME AS LITTLE BOY BLUE...
WHY WOULDN'T THEY BUY 'EM FROM ME AS LITTLE GIRL BLUE, HUH?
HA
'CAUSE THEY AREN'T USED TO GIRLS SELLING PAPERS, KID.
AND PEOPLE DON'T LIKE CHANGE, ESPECIALLY ON TOP OF EVERYTHING THAT'S ALREADY DIFFERENT BECAUSE OF THE WAR.
EVEN IF YOU'RE THE BEST AT WHAT YOU DO...
PEOPLE WILL RUIN YOU IF THEY DON'T THINK YOU HAVE ANY RIGHT DOING IT.
HEC, IS THAT WHAT HAPPENED TO YOU?!

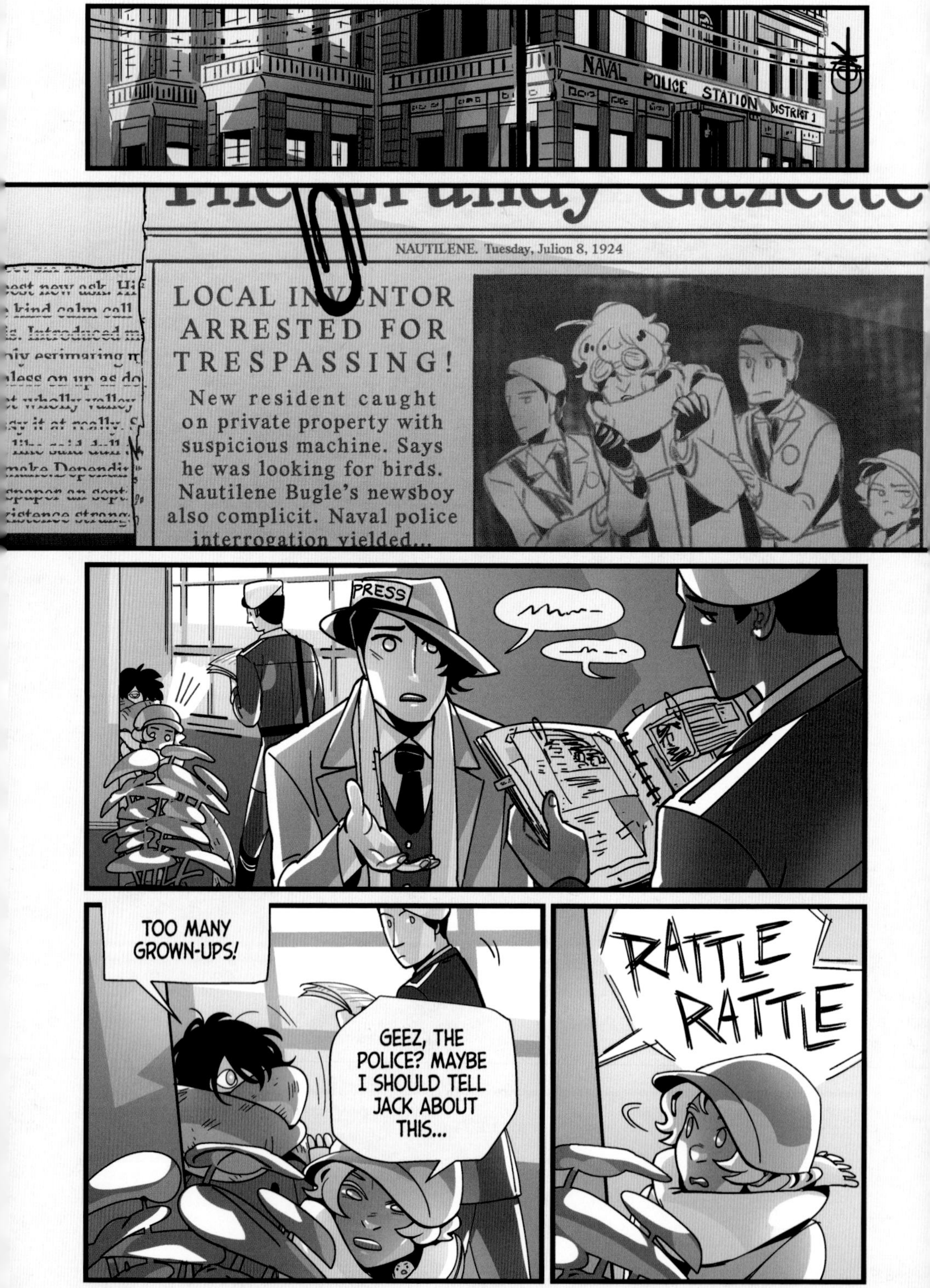
NAVAL POLICE STATION DISTRICT 1
NAUTILENE. Tuesday, Julion 8, 1924
LOCAL INVENTOR ARRESTED FOR TRESPASSING!
New resident caught on private property with suspicious machine. Says he was looking for birds. Nautilene Bugle's newsboy also complicit. Naval police interrogation yielded...
PRESS
TOO MANY GROWN-UPS!
GEEZ, THE POLICE? MAYBE I SHOULD TELL JACK ABOUT THIS...
RATTLE RATTLE

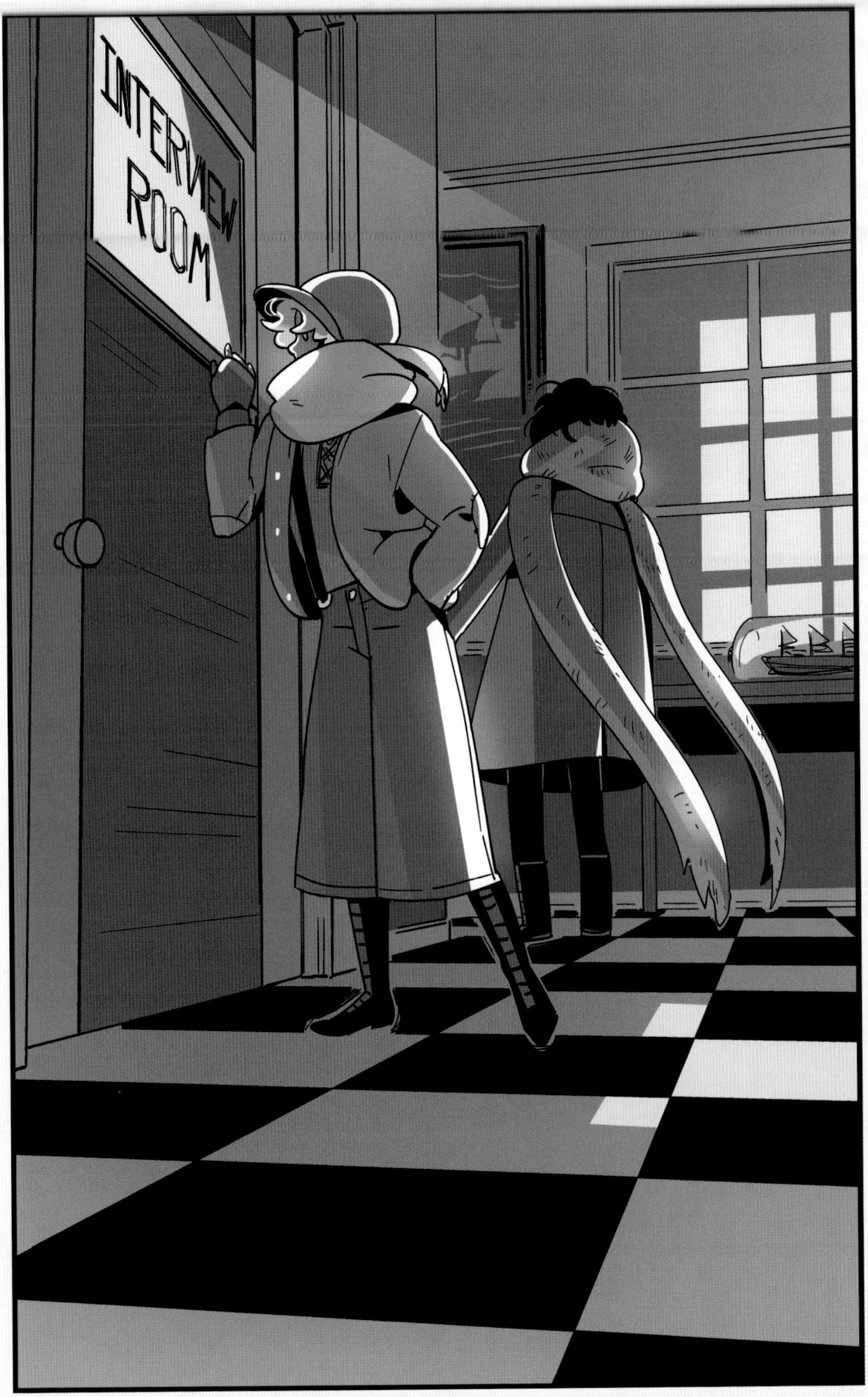
INTERVIEW ROOM

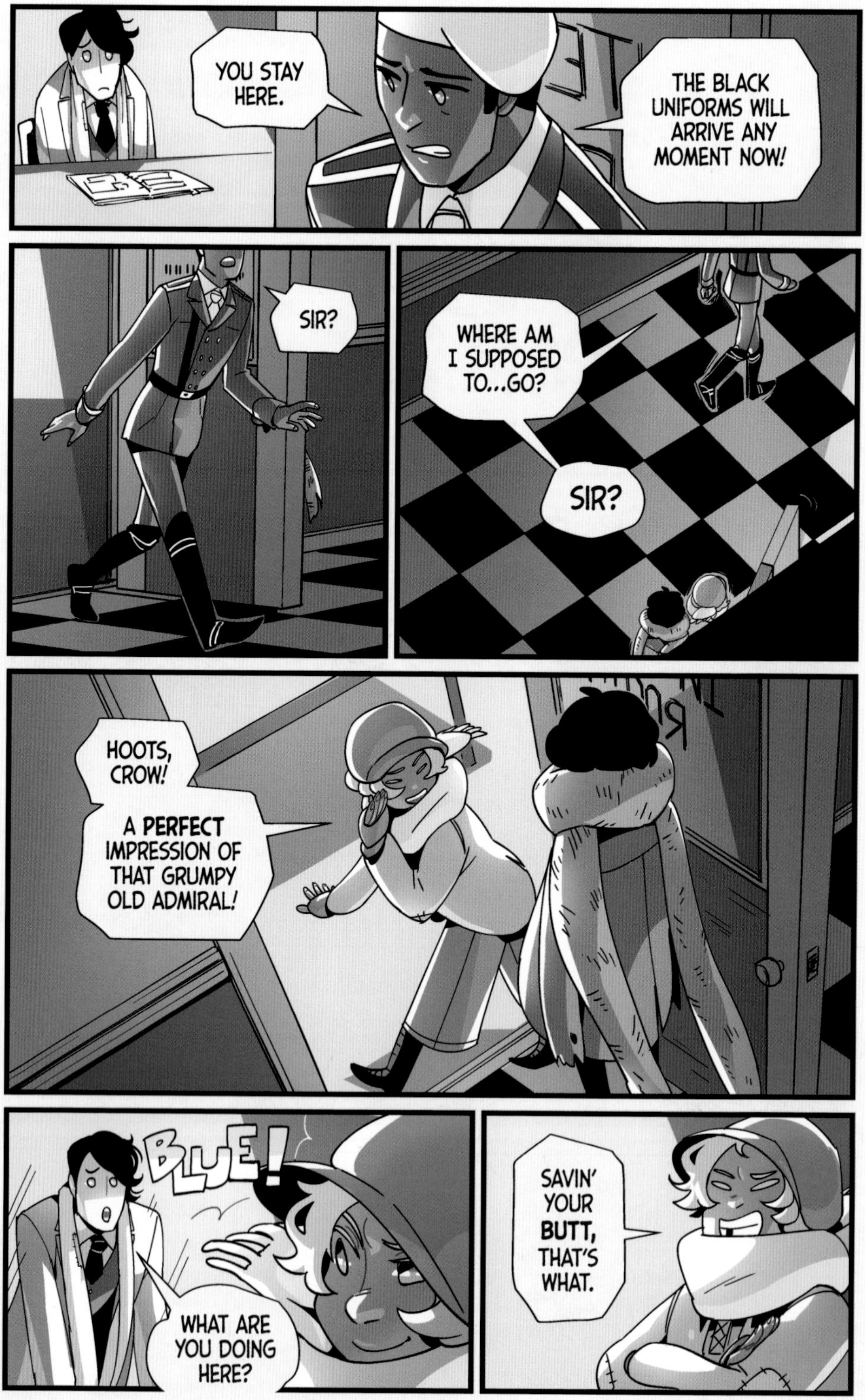
YOU STAY HERE.
THE BLACK UNIFORMS WILL ARRIVE ANY MOMENT NOW!
SIR?
WHERE AM I SUPPOSED TO...GO?
SIR?
HOOTS, CROW!
A PERFECT IMPRESSION OF THAT GRUMPY OLD ADMIRAL!
BLUE!
WHAT ARE YOU DOING HERE?
SAVIN' YOUR BUTT, THAT'S WHAT.

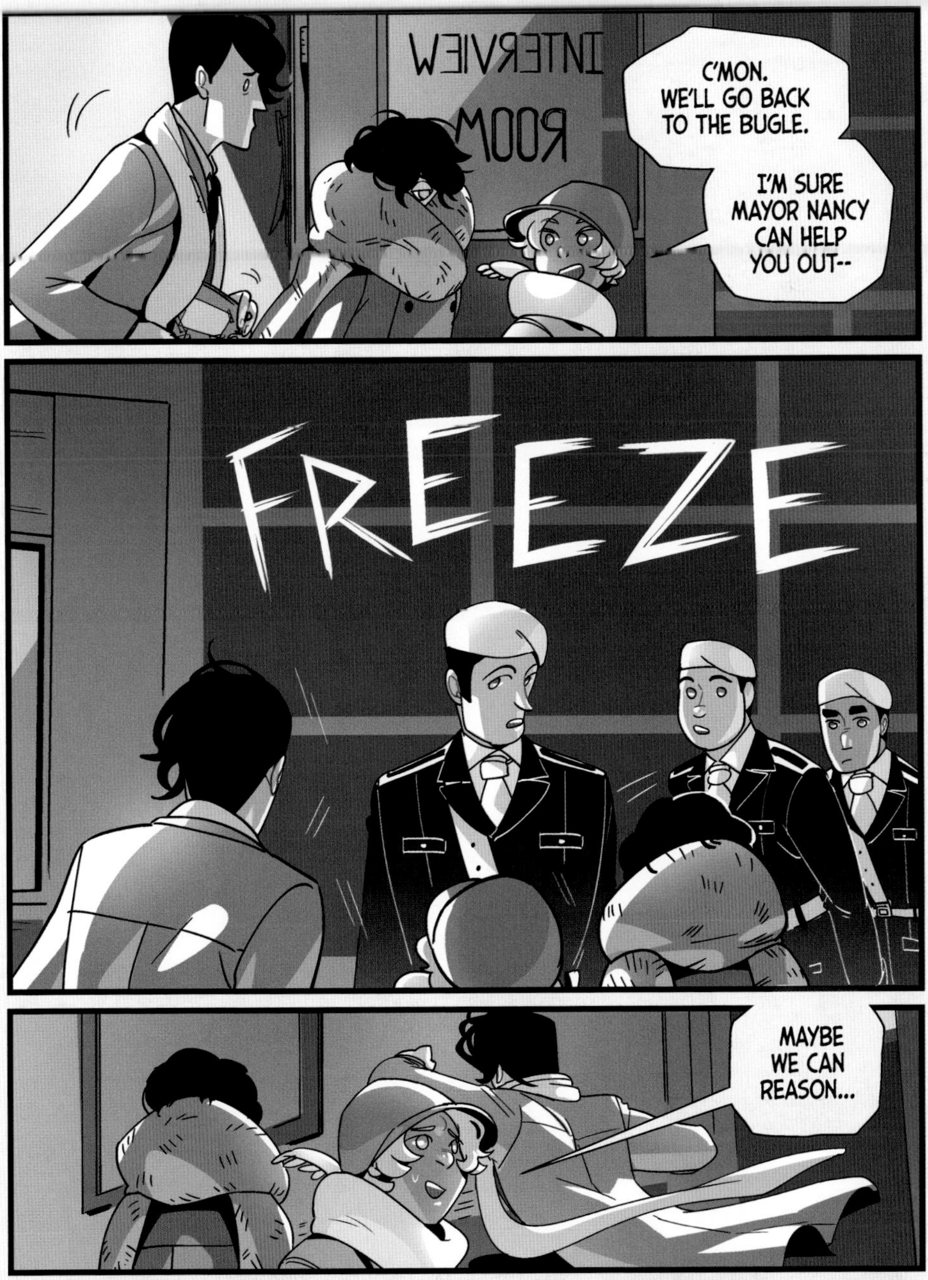
INTERVIEW ROOM
C'MON. WE'LL GO BACK TO THE BUGLE.
I'M SURE MAYOR NANCY CAN HELP YOU OUT--
FREEZE
MAYBE WE CAN REASON...
WITH THEM.

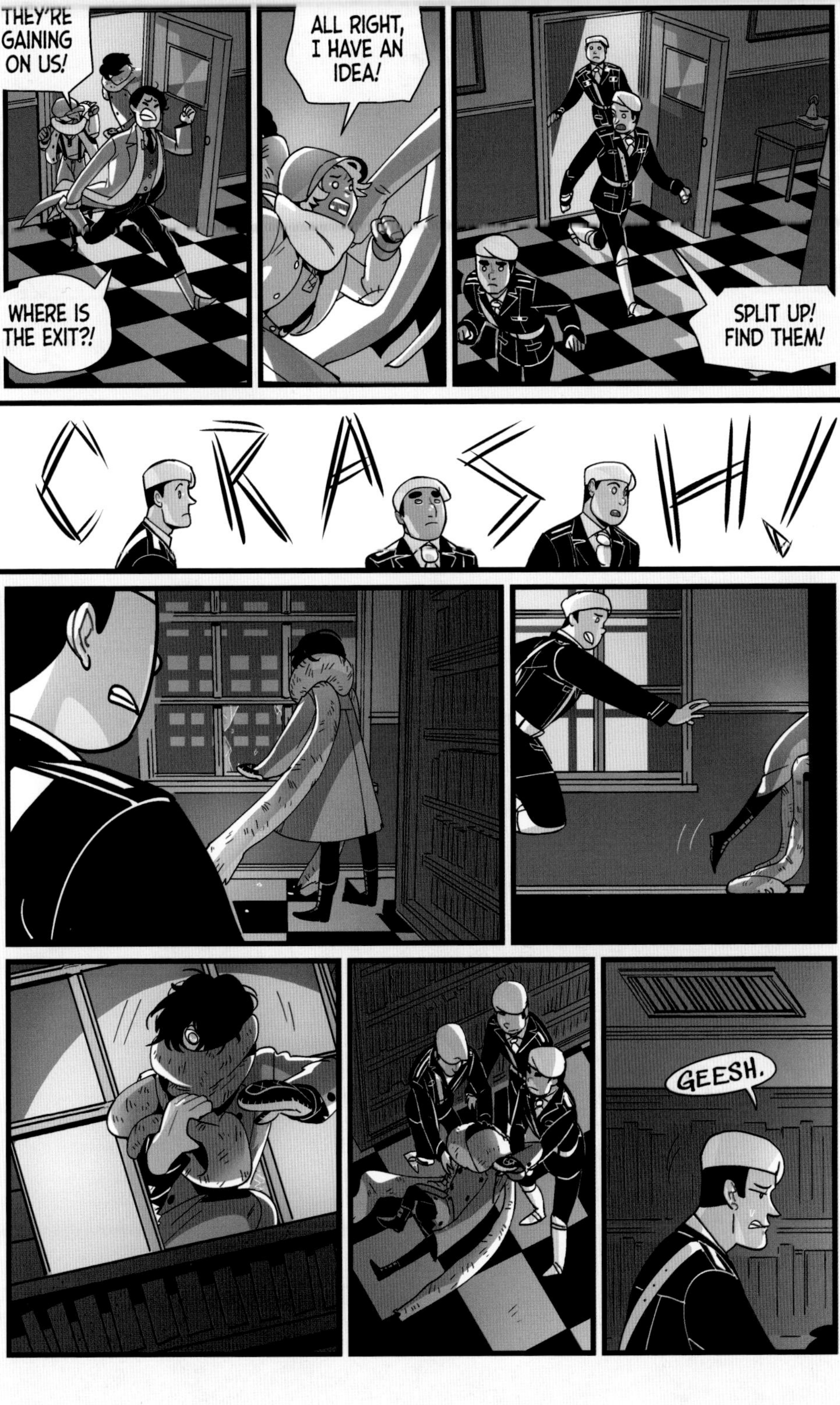
THEY'RE GAINING ON US!
WHERE IS THE EXIT?!
ALL RIGHT, I HAVE AN IDEA!
SPLIT UP! FIND THEM!
CRASH!
GEESH.

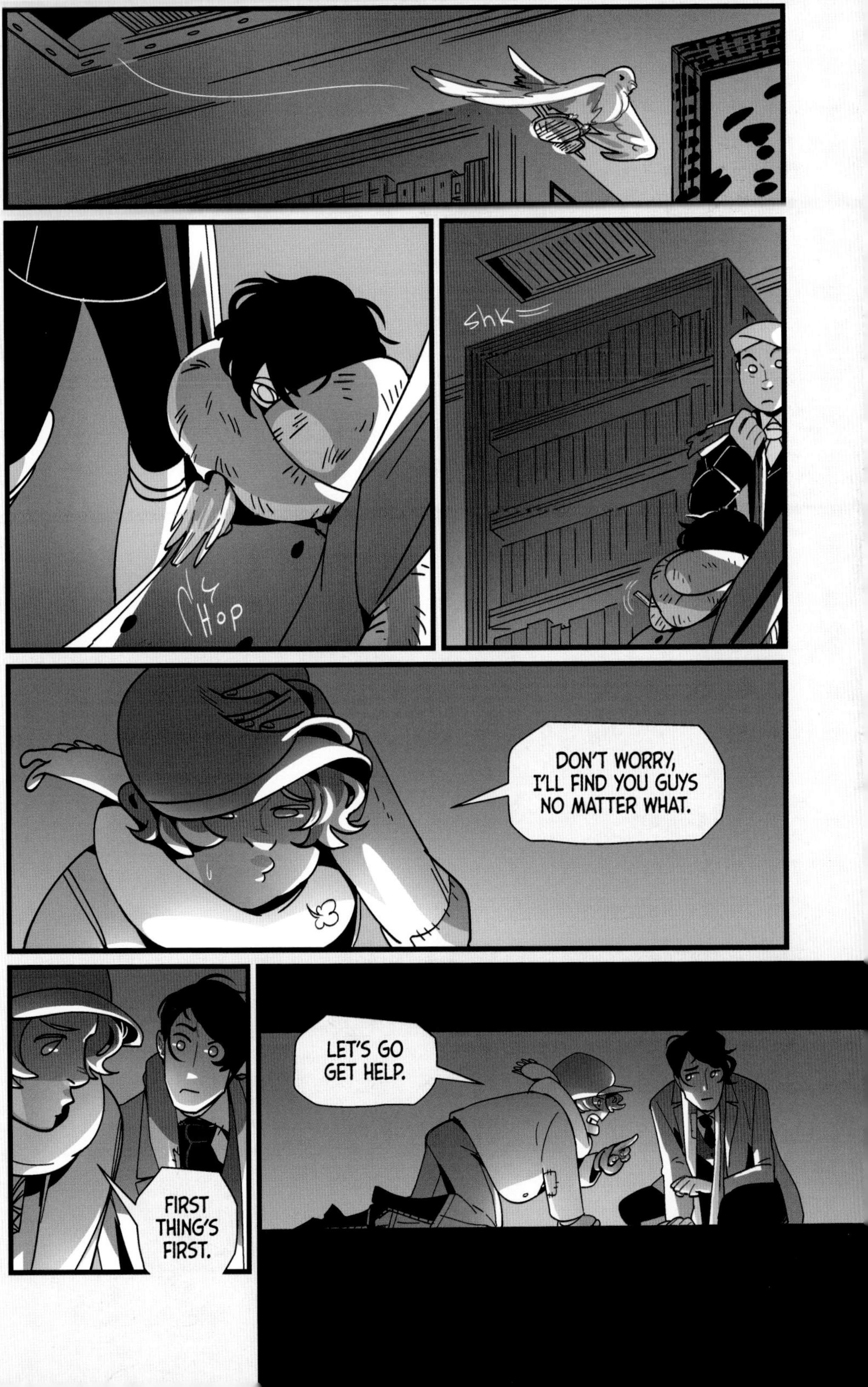

HOP
SHK
DON'T WORRY, I'LL FIND YOU GUYS NO MATTER WHAT.
FIRST THING'S FIRST.
LET'S GO GET HELP.

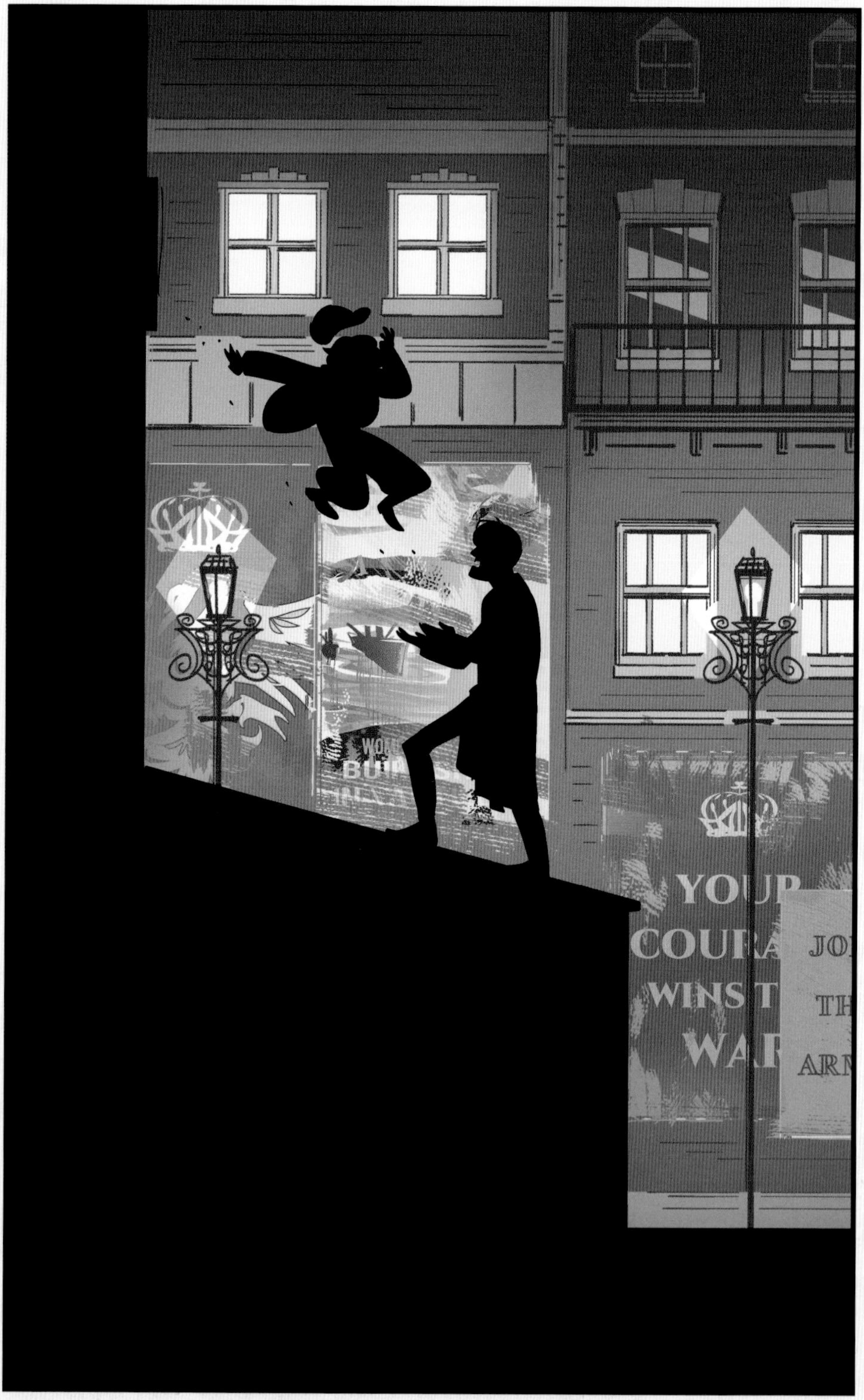
YOUR
COURA
WINS T
WAR
JO
TH
ARM

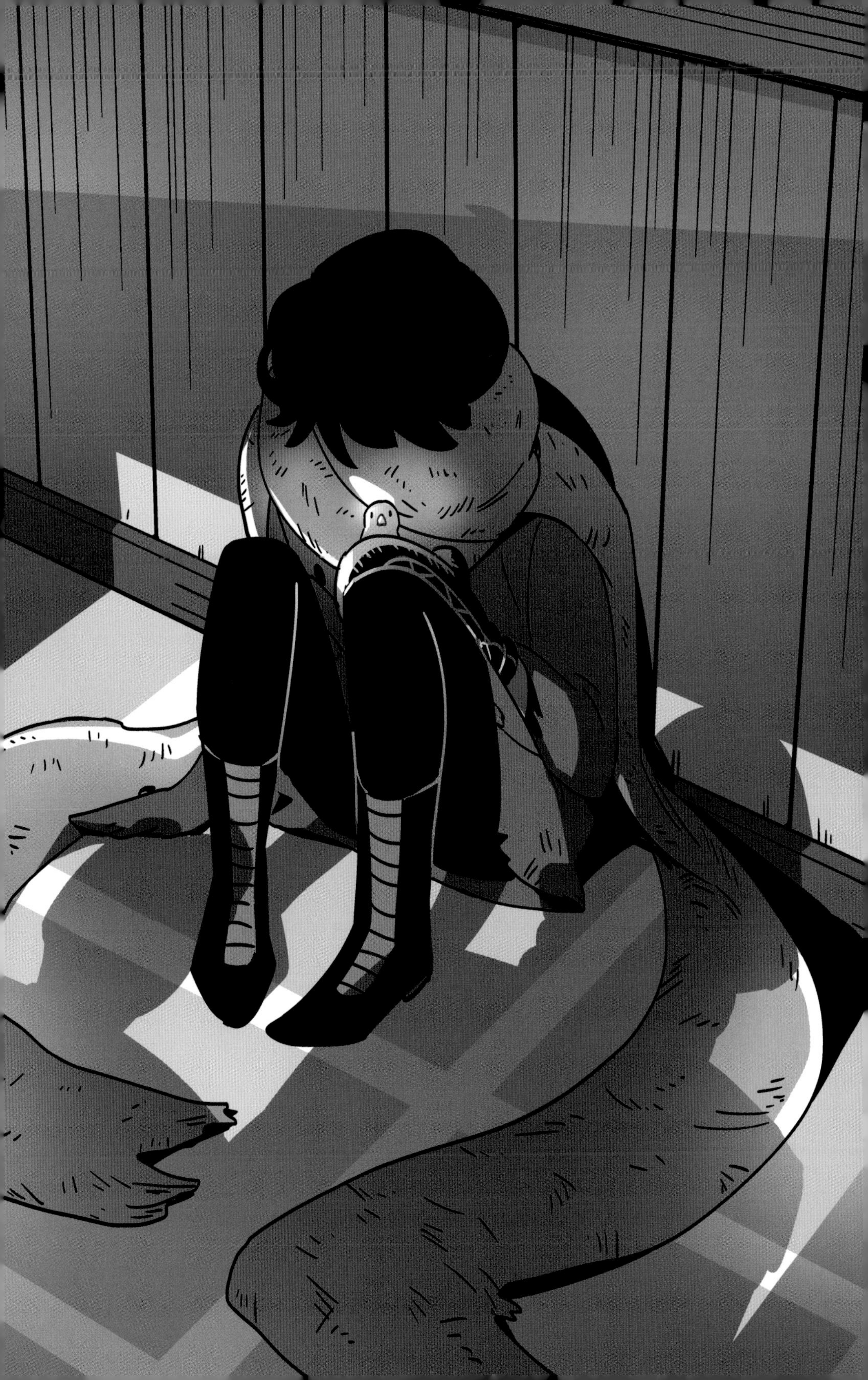

OH, CURSE MY DECORATIVE TUFFETS!

WE STILL HAVEN'T FOUND BLUE!

BUT I BUMPED INTO JILL REED AND MR. JACK.

AND THEY SAID THEY'D HELP LOOK!

HECTOR HASN'T RETURNED, EITHER.

I'M SURE BLUE'S WITH HIM.

THEY'LL BE ALL RIGHT, MUFFY. COME HOME.

BUT WHAT IF THEY'RE IN **TROUBLE?**

NO MATTER HOW CAPABLE BLUE IS, IT'S STILL SO DANGEROUS OUT THERE AT NIGHT FOR...

MUFFY?

EVEN THE **BRAVEST** NEWSGIRL.

MUH--

DON'T WAIT UP FOR ME, ARIC!

YOU MEAN ALL THIS TIME...?

MAYOR NANCY.

I'M NOT SUPPOSED TO TELL YOU THIS, BUT...

THAT'S BLUE'S ROUTE. SOMETIMES HE SNEAKS OUT REALLY LATE TO THE DOCKS.

I THINK HE SELLS HIS EXTRA PAPERS TO THE FISHERMEN WHO SAIL OUT BEFORE US NEWSIES HIT THE STREETS.

REALLY...

SO, DON'T WORRY. MAYBE IT'S ONE OF THOSE NIGHTS, AND BLUE WILL BE HOME BY SUNRISE LIKE USUAL.

LET'S HOPE SO.

MR. MAYOR!

WHAT'S WRONG, OFFICER?

WE'VE DISCOVERED SOMETHING THAT YOU MIGHT WANT TO SEE.

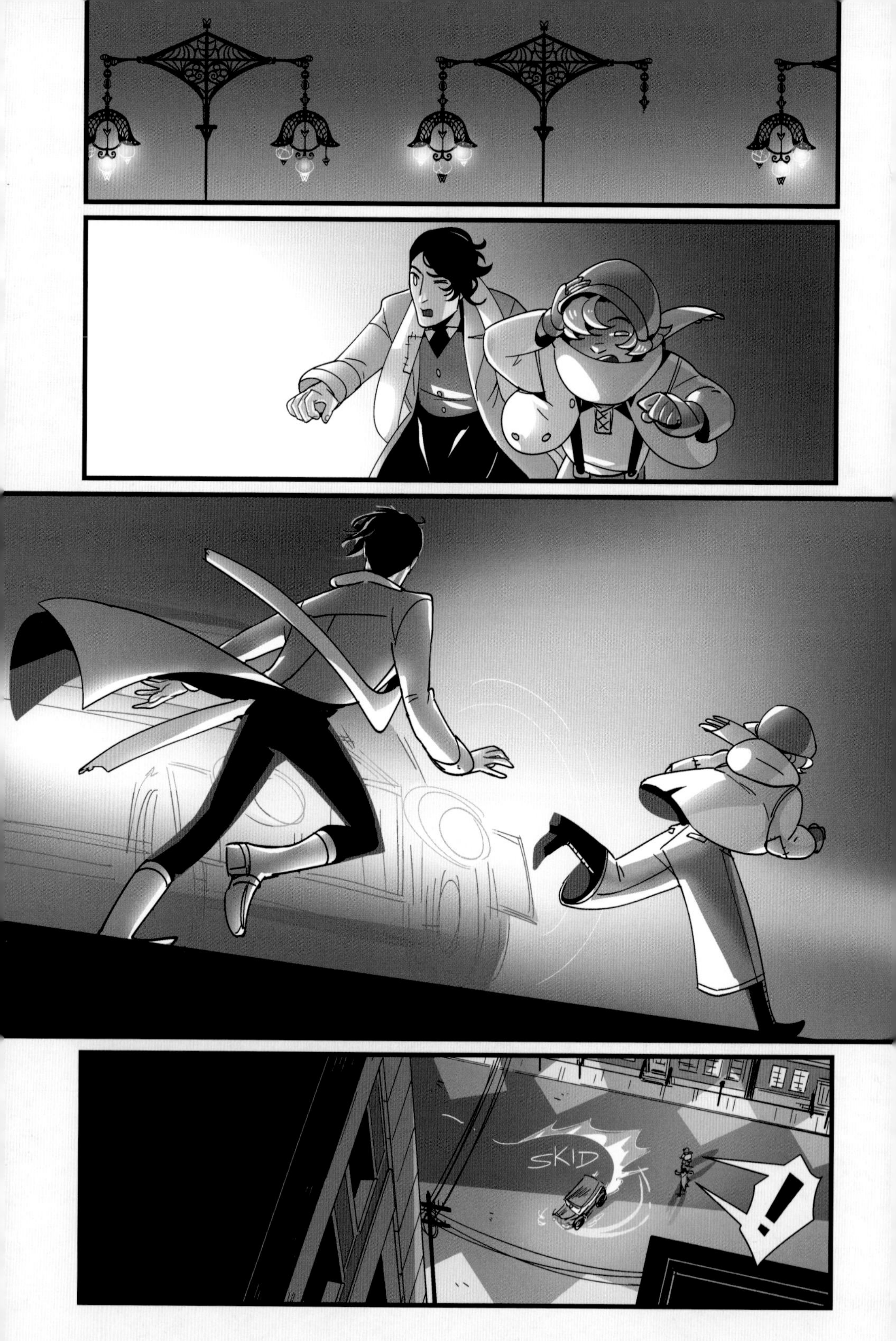
SKID
!

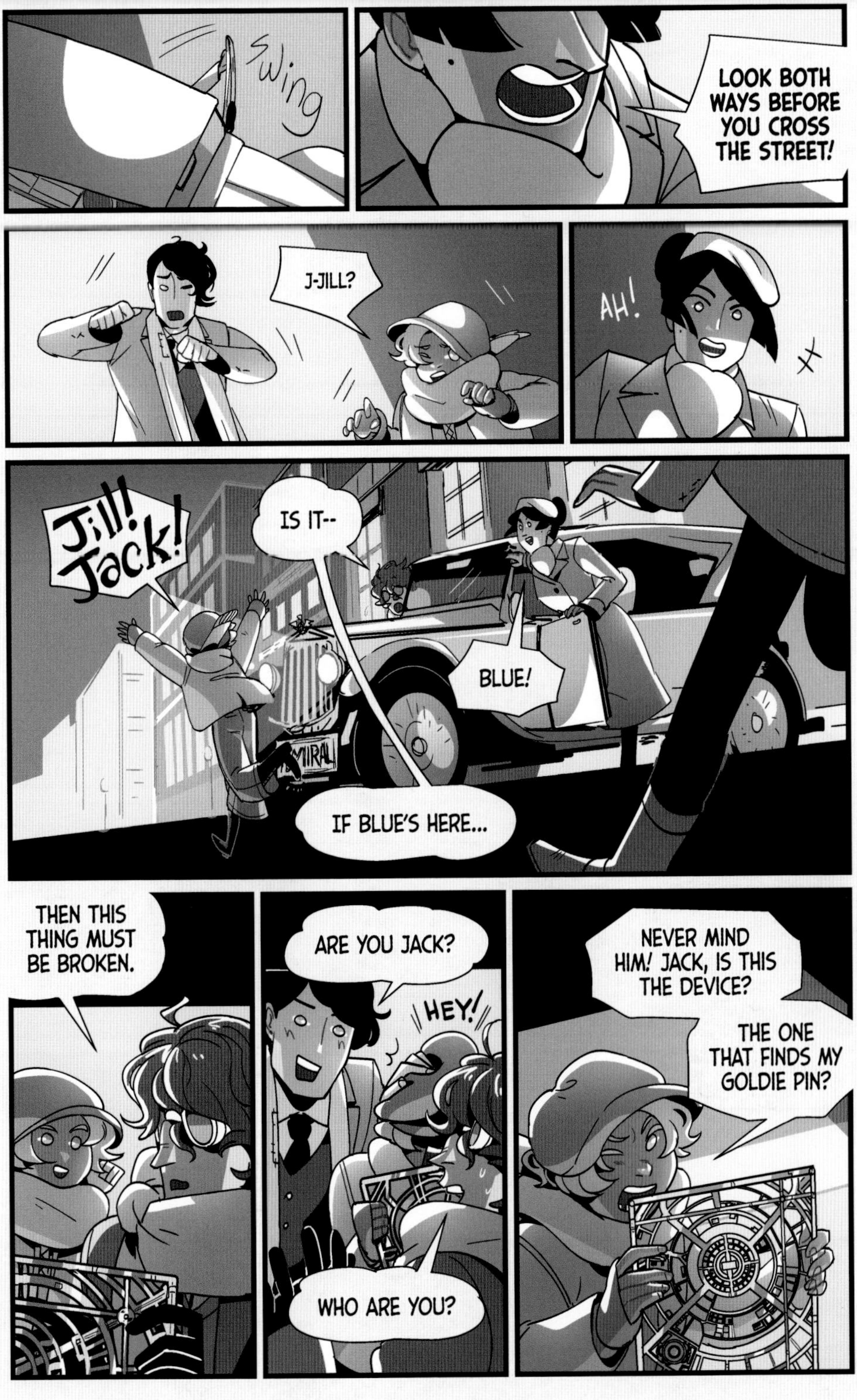
Swing
LOOK BOTH WAYS BEFORE YOU CROSS THE STREET!
J-JILL?
AH!
Jill! Jack!
IS IT--
BLUE!
IF BLUE'S HERE...
THEN THIS THING MUST BE BROKEN.
ARE YOU JACK?
HEY!
WHO ARE YOU?
NEVER MIND HIM! JACK, IS THIS THE DEVICE?
THE ONE THAT FINDS MY GOLDIE PIN?

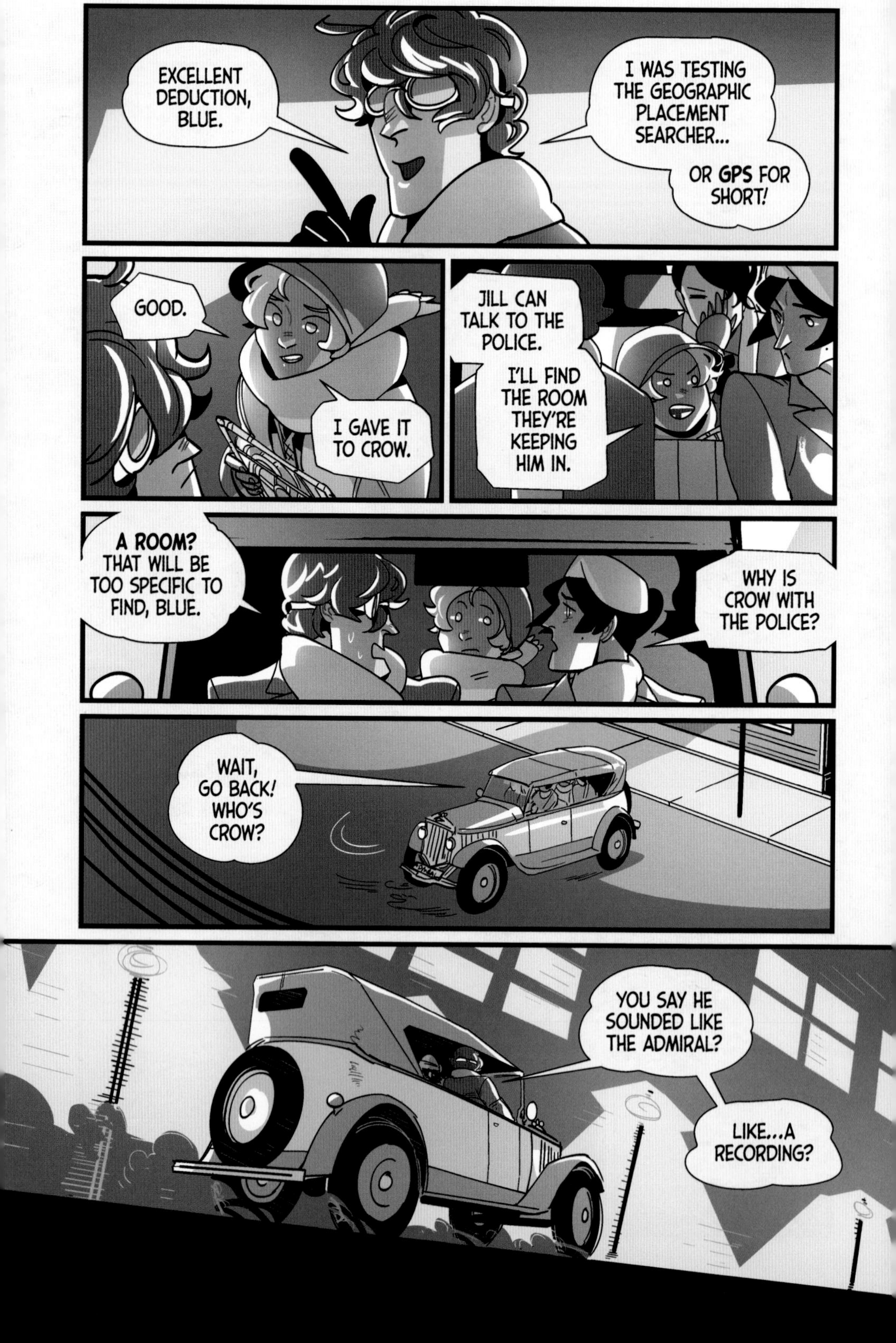
EXCELLENT DEDUCTION, BLUE.
I WAS TESTING THE GEOGRAPHIC PLACEMENT SEARCHER...
OR **GPS** FOR SHORT!
GOOD.
I GAVE IT TO CROW.
JILL CAN TALK TO THE POLICE.
I'LL FIND THE ROOM THEY'RE KEEPING HIM IN.
A ROOM? THAT WILL BE TOO SPECIFIC TO FIND, BLUE.
WHY IS CROW WITH THE POLICE?
WAIT, GO BACK! WHO'S CROW?
YOU SAY HE SOUNDED LIKE THE ADMIRAL?
LIKE...A RECORDING?

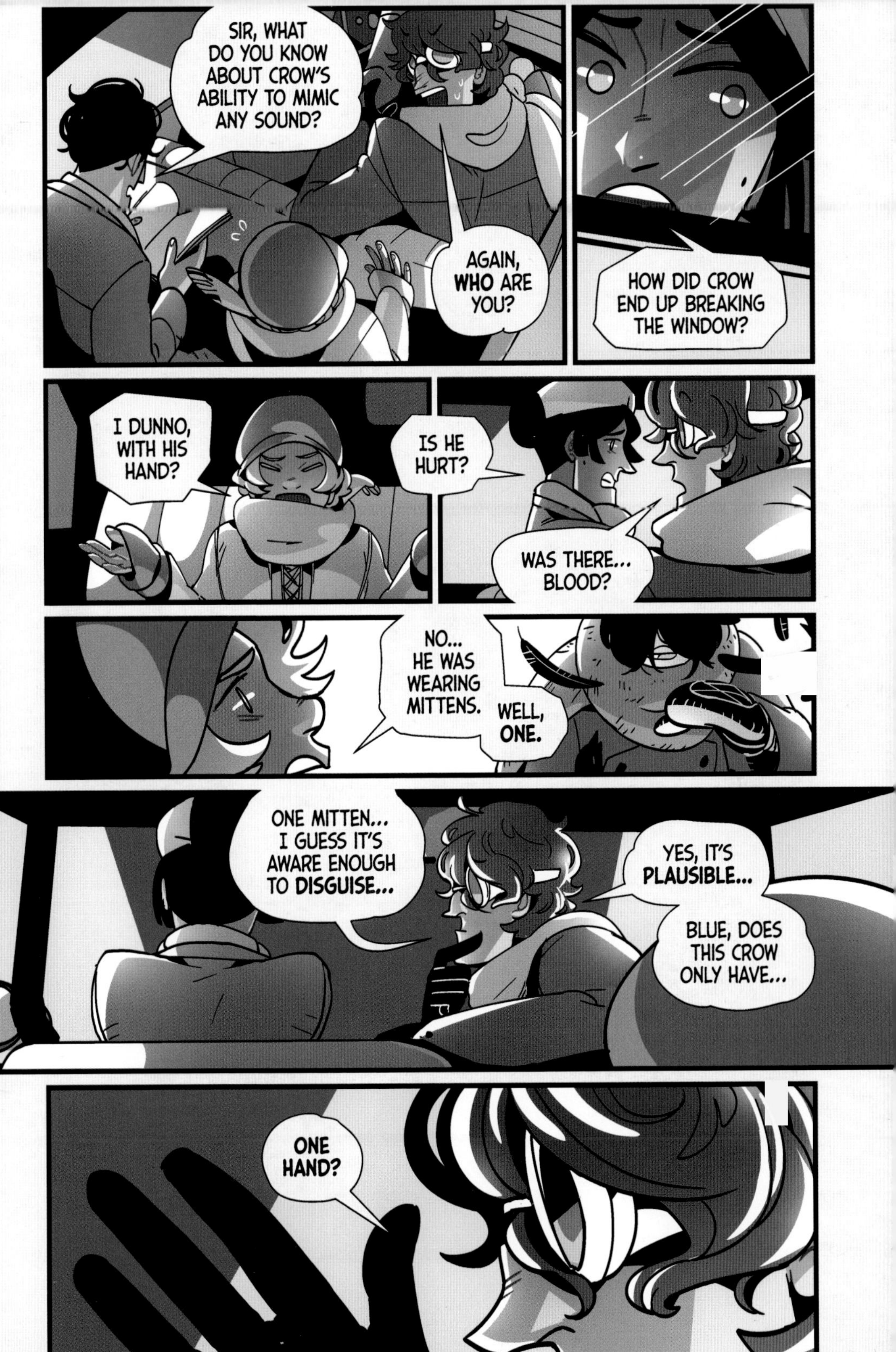

SIR, WHAT DO YOU KNOW ABOUT CROW'S ABILITY TO MIMIC ANY SOUND?
AGAIN, **WHO ARE** YOU?
HOW DID CROW END UP BREAKING THE WINDOW?
I DUNNO, WITH HIS HAND?
IS HE HURT?
WAS THERE... BLOOD?
NO... HE WAS WEARING MITTENS.
WELL, **ONE.**
ONE MITTEN... I GUESS IT'S AWARE ENOUGH TO **DISGUISE...**
YES, IT'S **PLAUSIBLE...**
BLUE, DOES THIS CROW ONLY HAVE...
ONE HAND?

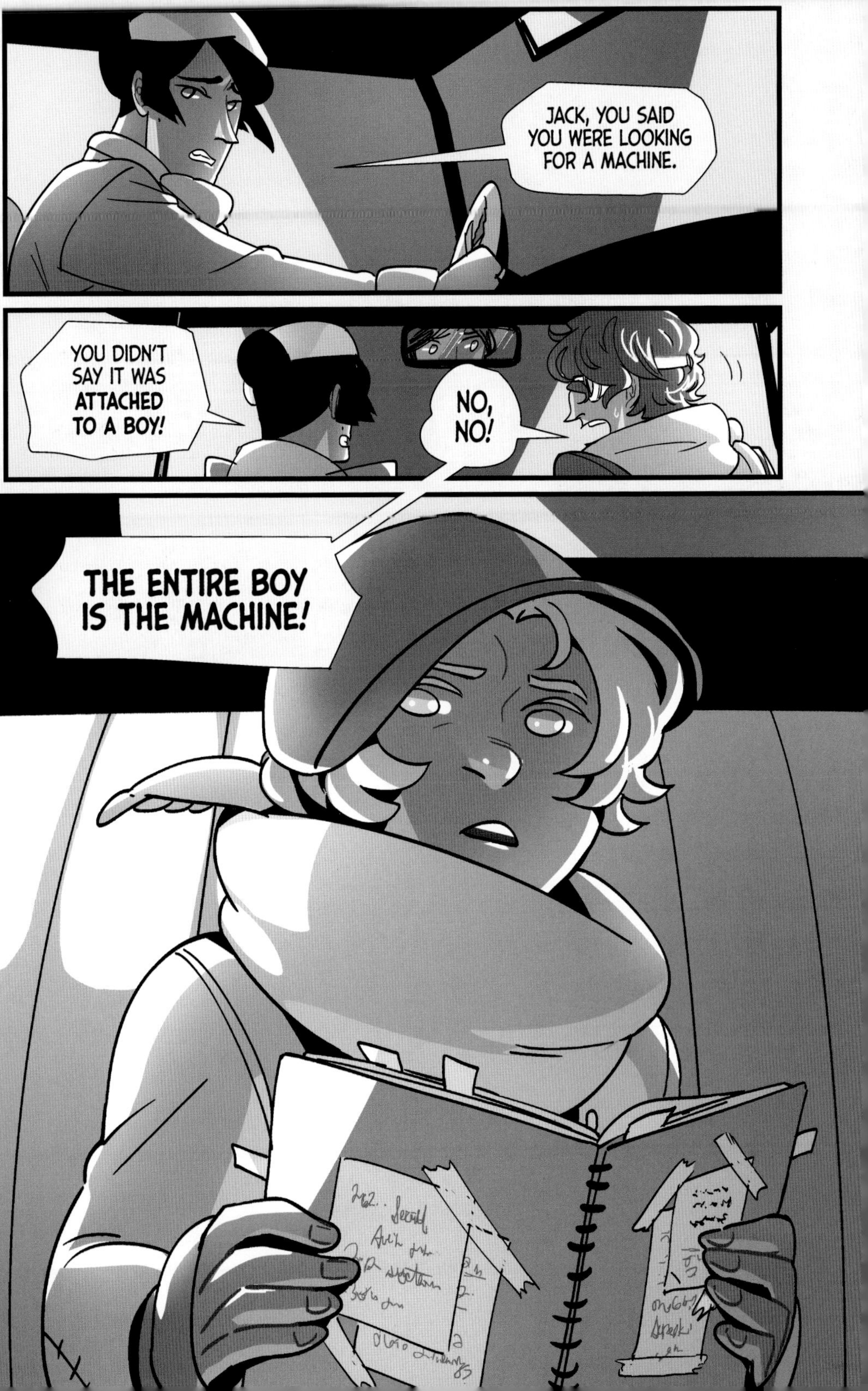
JACK, YOU SAID YOU WERE LOOKING FOR A MACHINE.
YOU DIDN'T SAY IT WAS ATTACHED TO A BOY!
NO, NO!
THE ENTIRE BOY IS THE MACHINE!

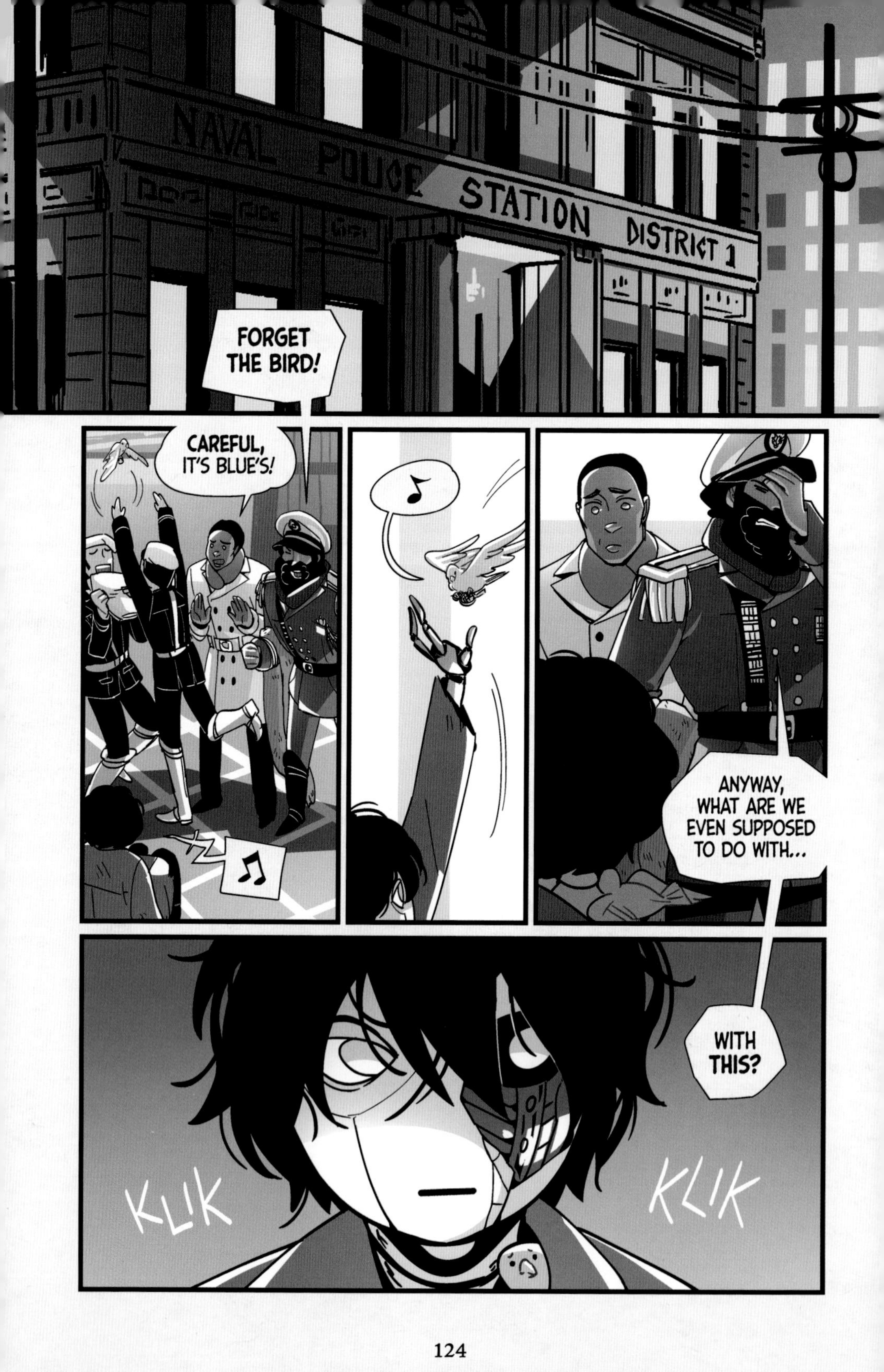
NAVAL POLICE STATION DISTRICT 1
FORGET THE BIRD!
CAREFUL, IT'S BLUE'S!
ANYWAY, WHAT ARE WE EVEN SUPPOSED TO DO WITH...
WITH THIS?
KLIK
KLIK

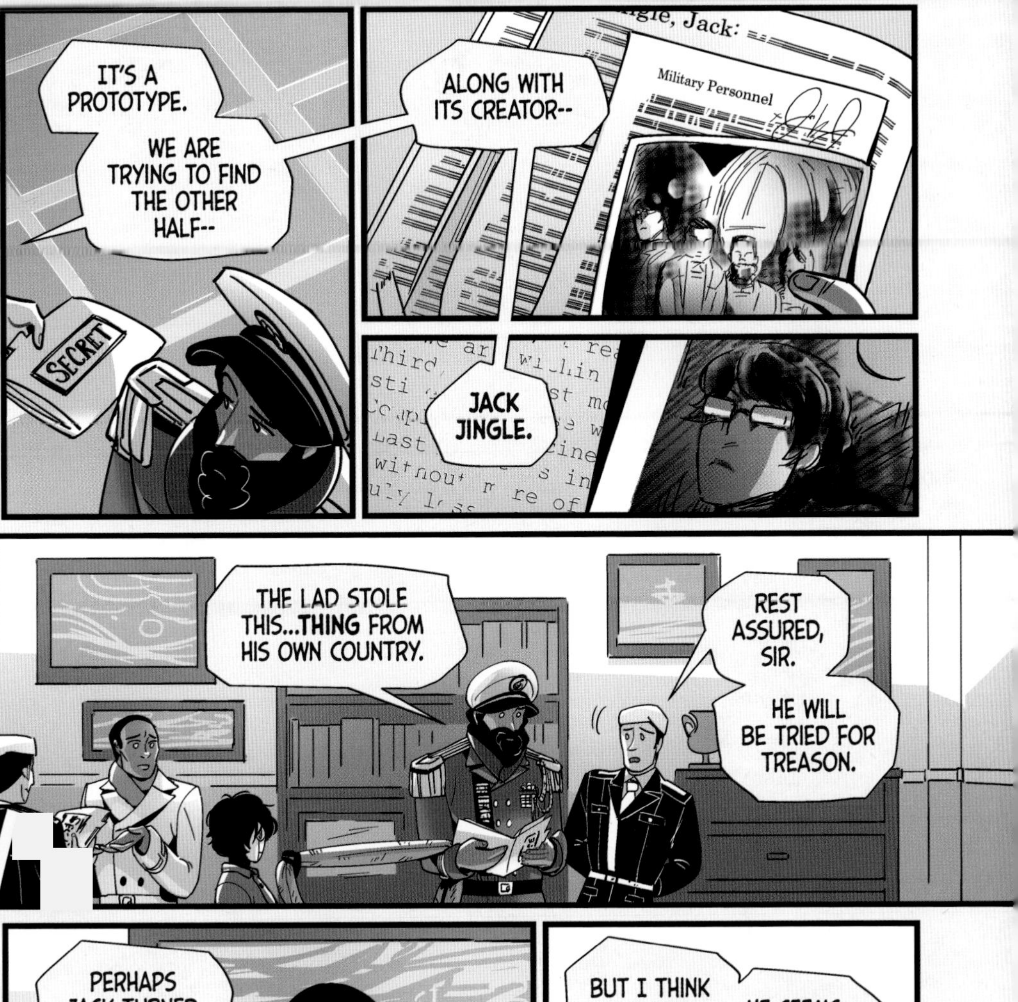
IT'S A PROTOTYPE.
WE ARE TRYING TO FIND THE OTHER HALF--
SECRET
ALONG WITH ITS CREATOR--
Military Personnel
JACK JINGLE.
THE LAD STOLE THIS...**THING** FROM HIS OWN COUNTRY.
REST ASSURED, SIR.
HE WILL BE TRIED FOR TREASON.
PERHAPS JACK TURNED OUT TO BE A MISGUIDED MAN.
SECRET
BUT I THINK THIS BOY...
HE SEEMS MORE HUMAN THAN...

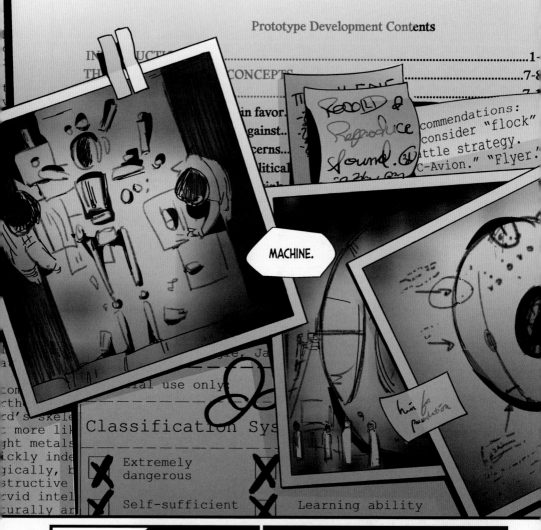

WE'LL HELP YOU FIND THE OTHER HALF.

IN RETURN, SEND FUNDING AND SAILORS FOR THE NAUTILENE NAVAL BASE.

DON'T YOU DRAG NAUTILENE INTO THE FRONT LINES!

DO YOU WANT TO SERVE YOUR NATION OR NOT?!

I JUST WANT TO PROTECT THIS CITY.

BUT WE REALLY **DO** NEED THE MONEY HERE, SO I'LL HELP.

HMPH

WILL YOU NOW? DO YOU **KNOW** WHERE THIS JACK IS?

nod

THIS MAP MIGHT HELP...

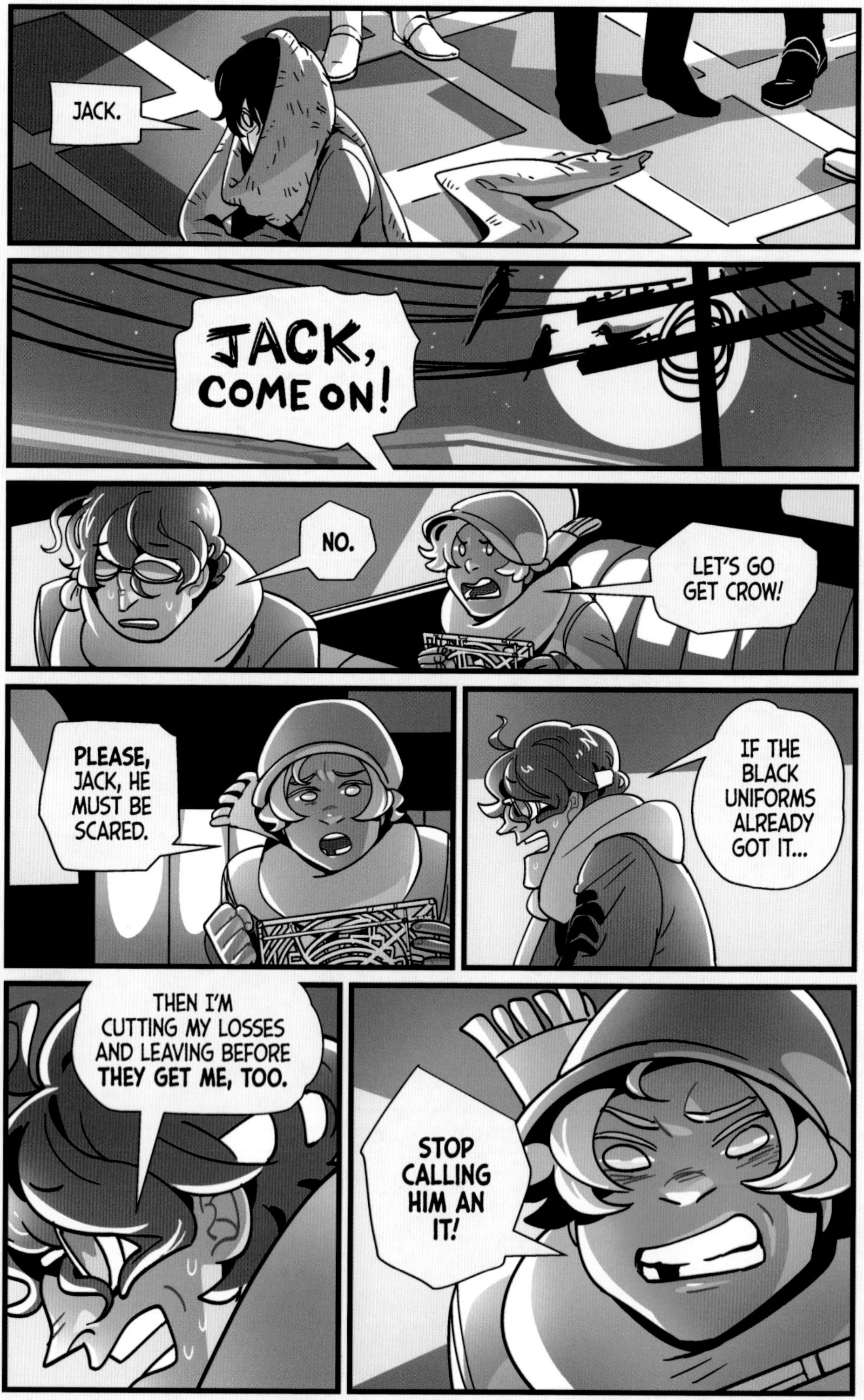
JACK.
JACK, COME ON!
NO.
LET'S GO GET CROW!
PLEASE, JACK, HE MUST BE SCARED.
IF THE BLACK UNIFORMS ALREADY GOT IT...
THEN I'M CUTTING MY LOSSES AND LEAVING BEFORE THEY GET ME, TOO.
STOP CALLING HIM AN IT!

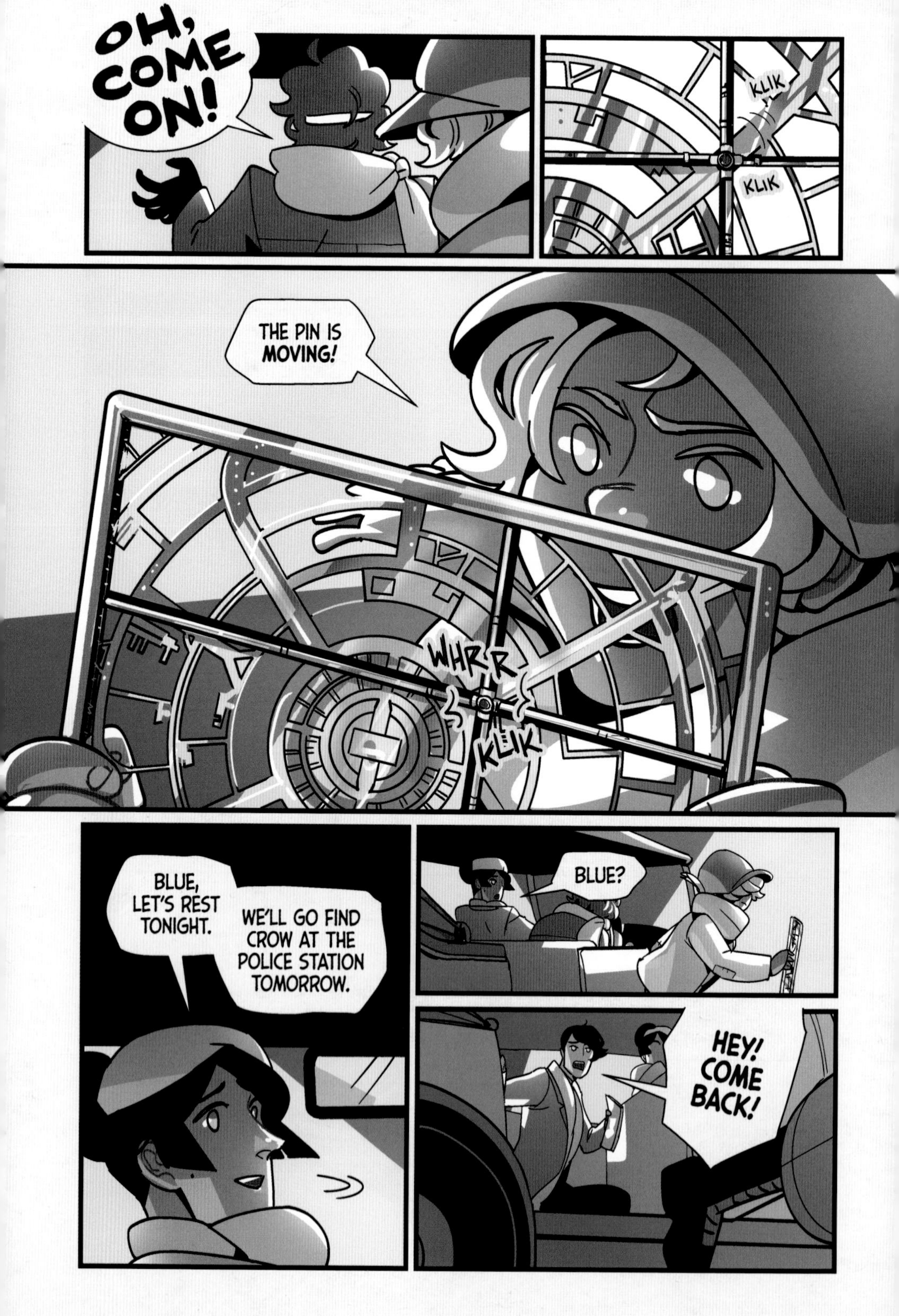
OH, COME ON!
KLIK
KLIK
THE PIN IS MOVING!
WHRRR
KLIK
BLUE, LET'S REST TONIGHT.
WE'LL GO FIND CROW AT THE POLICE STATION TOMORROW.
BLUE?
HEY! COME BACK!

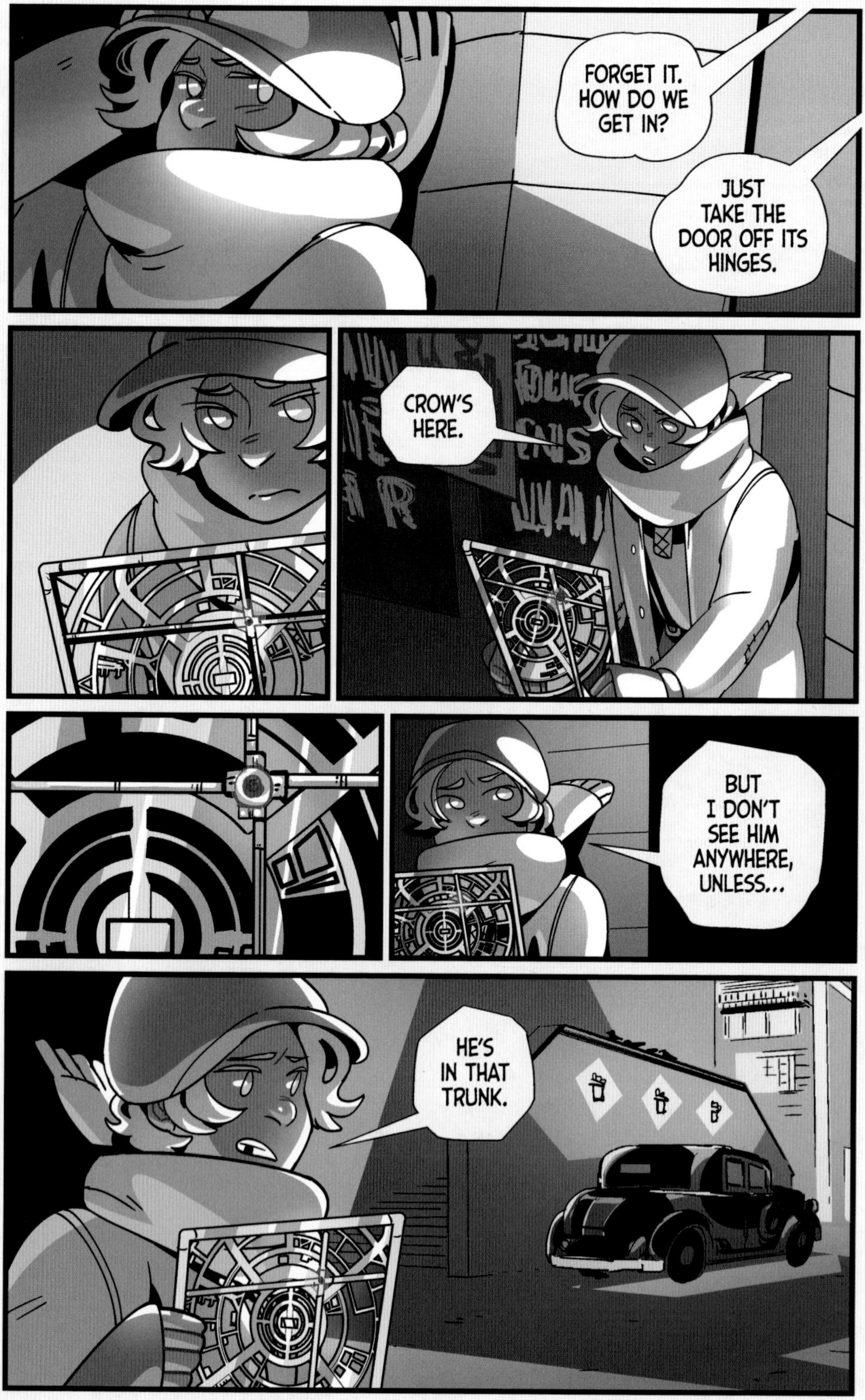
FORGET IT. HOW DO WE GET IN?
JUST TAKE THE DOOR OFF ITS HINGES.
CROW'S HERE.
BUT I DON'T SEE HIM ANYWHERE, UNLESS...
HE'S IN THAT TRUNK.

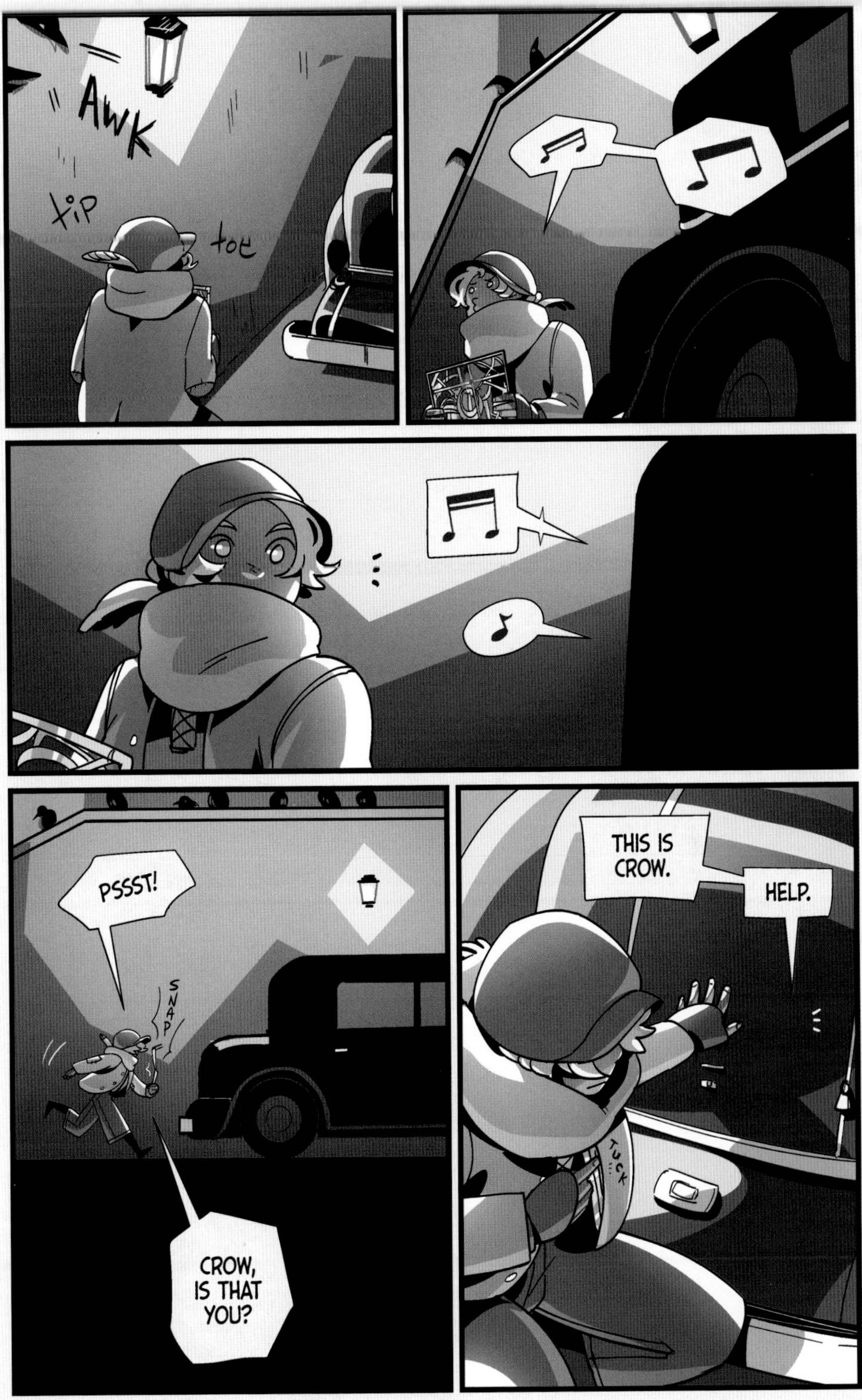
AWK
tip
toe
PSSST!
SNAP
CROW, IS THAT YOU?
THIS IS CROW.
HELP.
TUCK

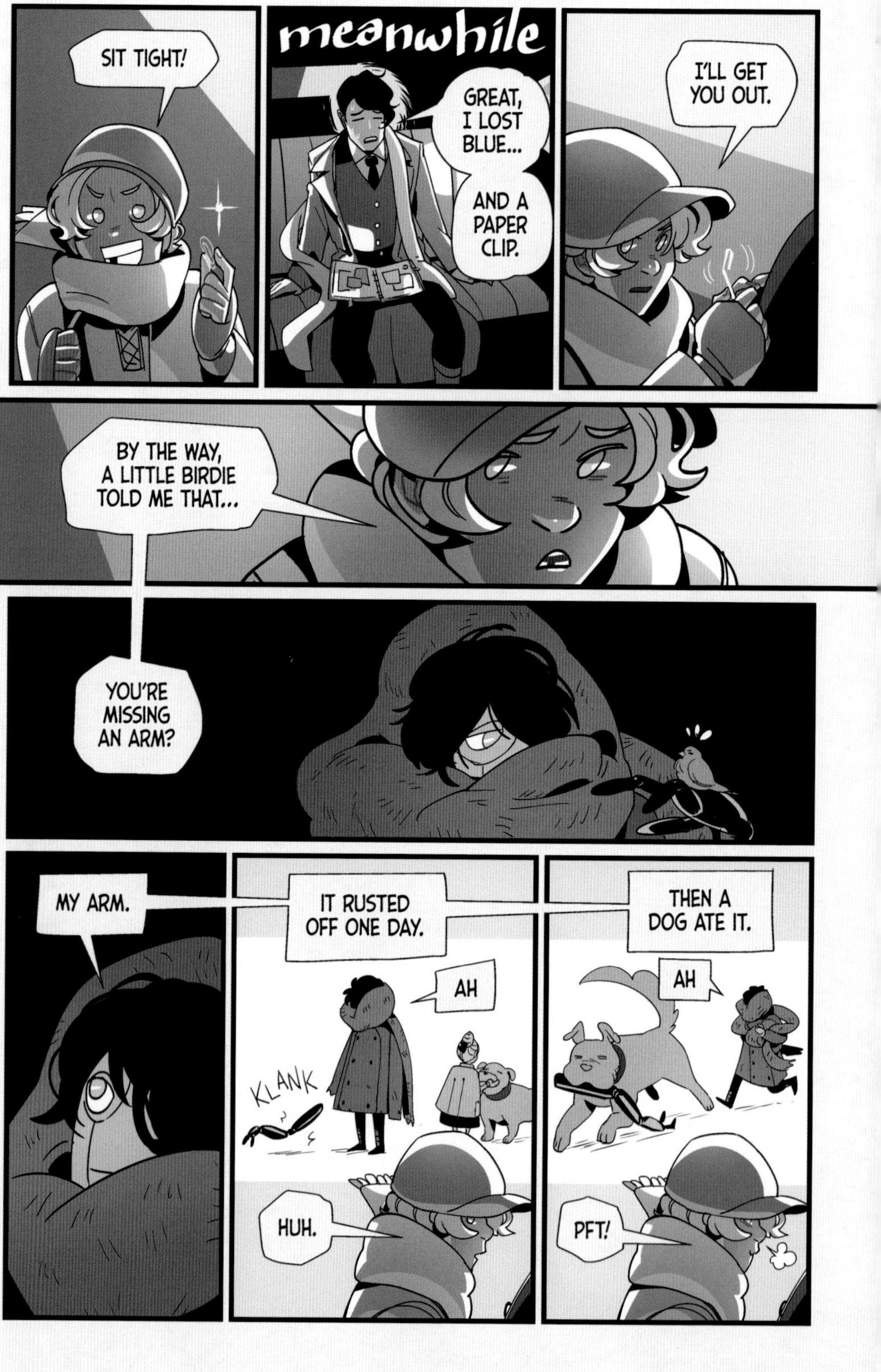
SIT TIGHT!
meanwhile
GREAT, I LOST BLUE...
AND A PAPER CLIP.
I'LL GET YOU OUT.
BY THE WAY, A LITTLE BIRDIE TOLD ME THAT...
YOU'RE MISSING AN ARM?
MY ARM.
IT RUSTED OFF ONE DAY.
KLANK
AH
HUH.
THEN A DOG ATE IT.
AH
PFT!

IT WAS A BIG DOG!

SO THAT'S WHY IT WAS IN THE PAWN SHOP...

GOLDIE!

GOOD GIRL.

MAN, YOU'RE SO HEAVY!

I AM.

WE FOUND IT!

!

ZOOM

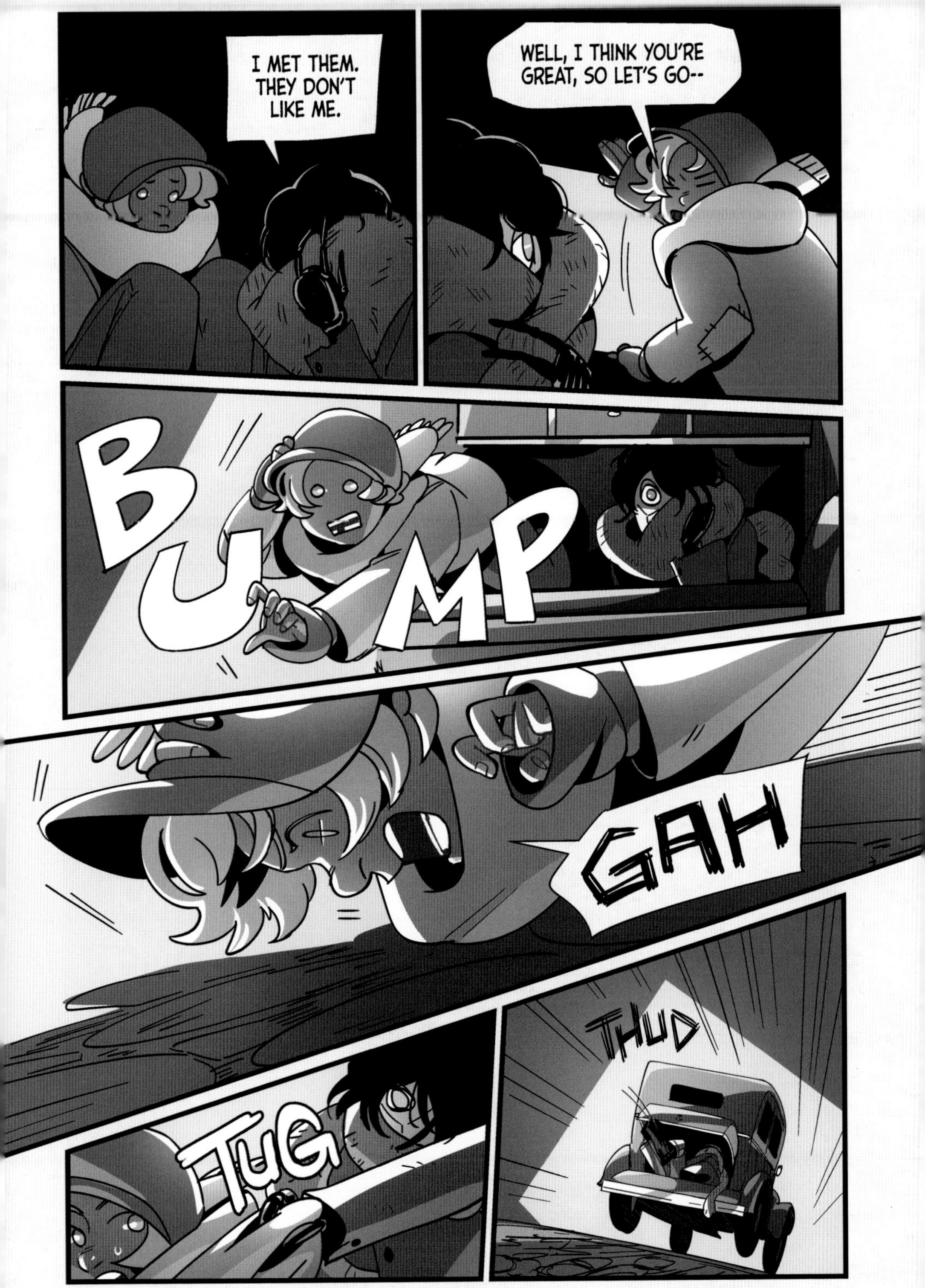
I MET THEM. THEY DON'T LIKE ME.
WELL, I THINK YOU'RE GREAT, SO LET'S GO--
BUMP
GAH
TUG
THUD

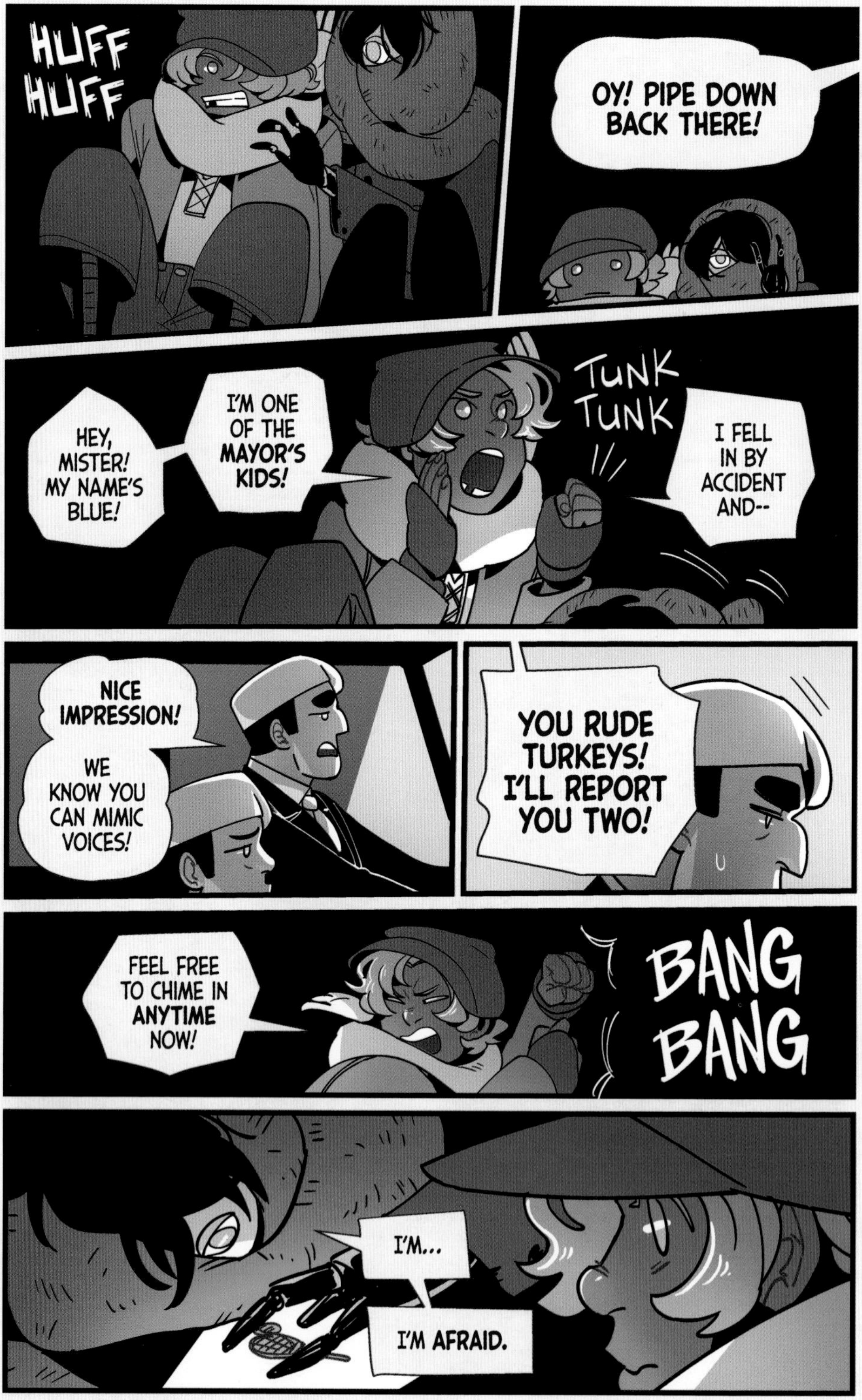
HUFF HUFF
OY! PIPE DOWN BACK THERE!
HEY, MISTER! MY NAME'S BLUE!
I'M ONE OF THE MAYOR'S KIDS!
TUNK TUNK
I FELL IN BY ACCIDENT AND--
NICE IMPRESSION!
WE KNOW YOU CAN MIMIC VOICES!
YOU RUDE TURKEYS! I'LL REPORT YOU TWO!
FEEL FREE TO CHIME IN ANYTIME NOW!
BANG BANG
I'M...
I'M AFRAID.

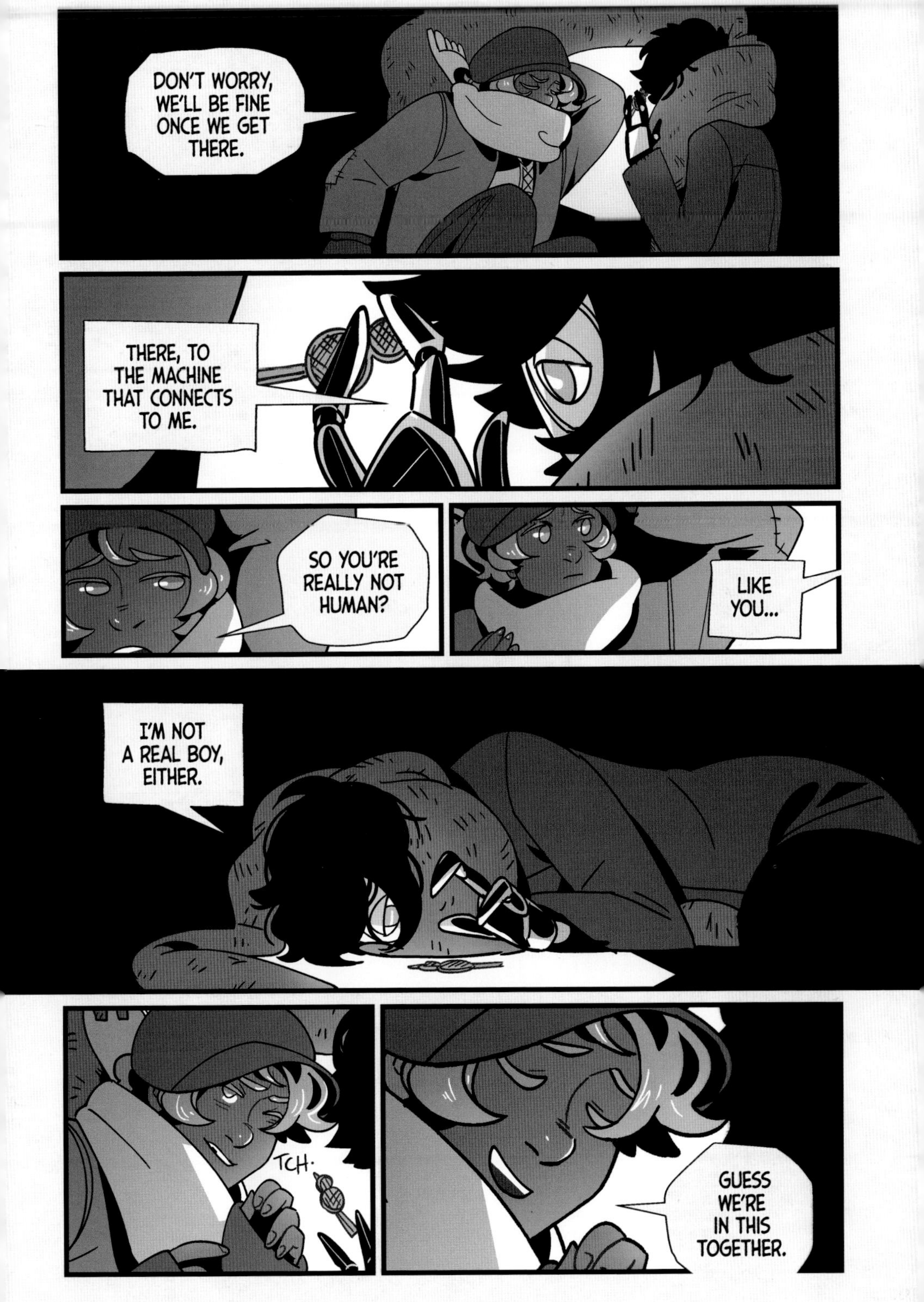
DON'T WORRY, WE'LL BE FINE ONCE WE GET THERE.
THERE, TO THE MACHINE THAT CONNECTS TO ME.
SO YOU'RE REALLY NOT HUMAN?
LIKE YOU...
I'M NOT A REAL BOY, EITHER.
TCH.
GUESS WE'RE IN THIS TOGETHER.

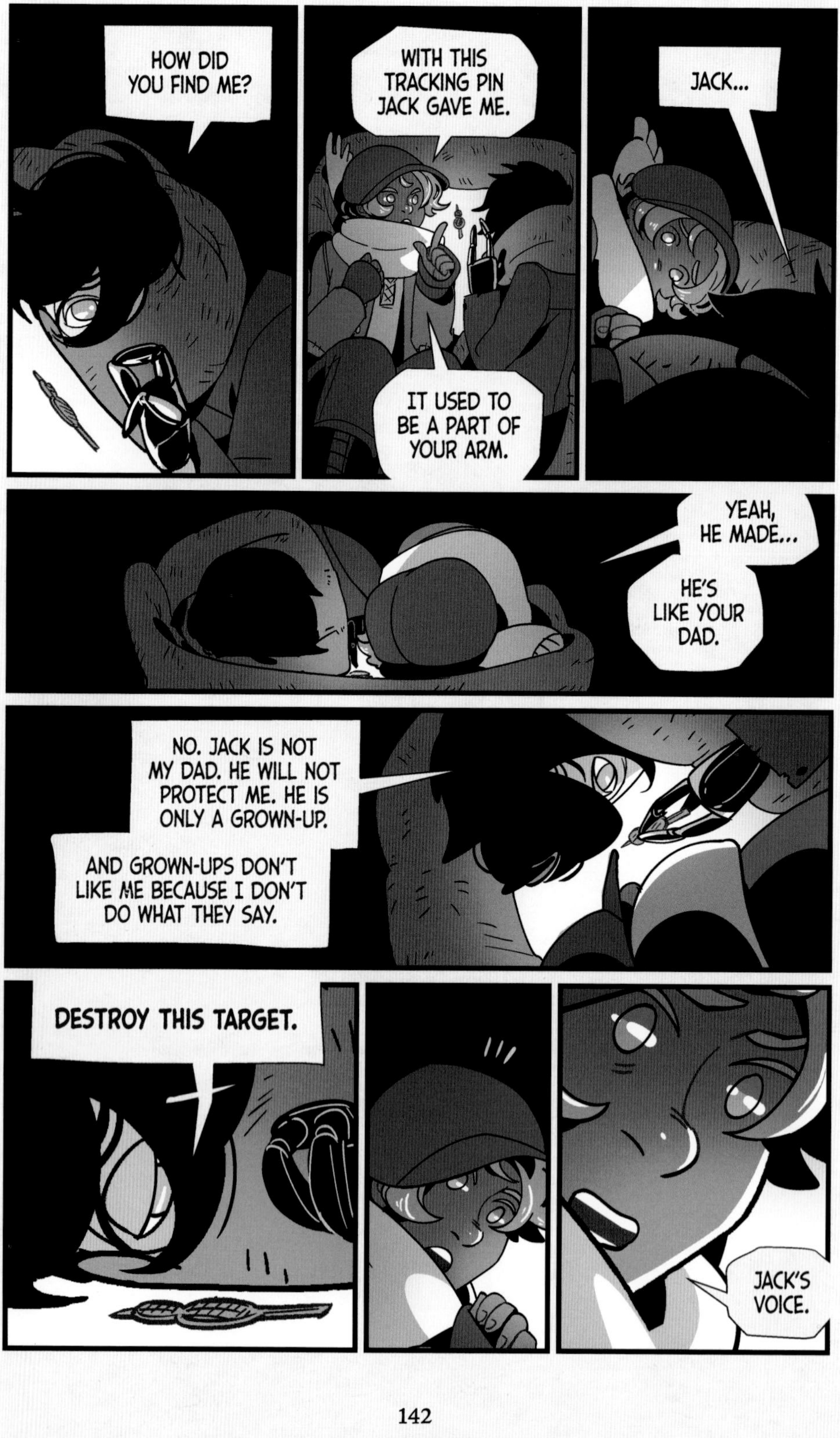
HOW DID YOU FIND ME?
WITH THIS TRACKING PIN JACK GAVE ME.
IT USED TO BE A PART OF YOUR ARM.
JACK...
YEAH, HE MADE...
HE'S LIKE YOUR DAD.
NO. JACK IS NOT MY DAD. HE WILL NOT PROTECT ME. HE IS ONLY A GROWN-UP.
AND GROWN-UPS DON'T LIKE ME BECAUSE I DON'T DO WHAT THEY SAY.
DESTROY THIS TARGET.
JACK'S VOICE.

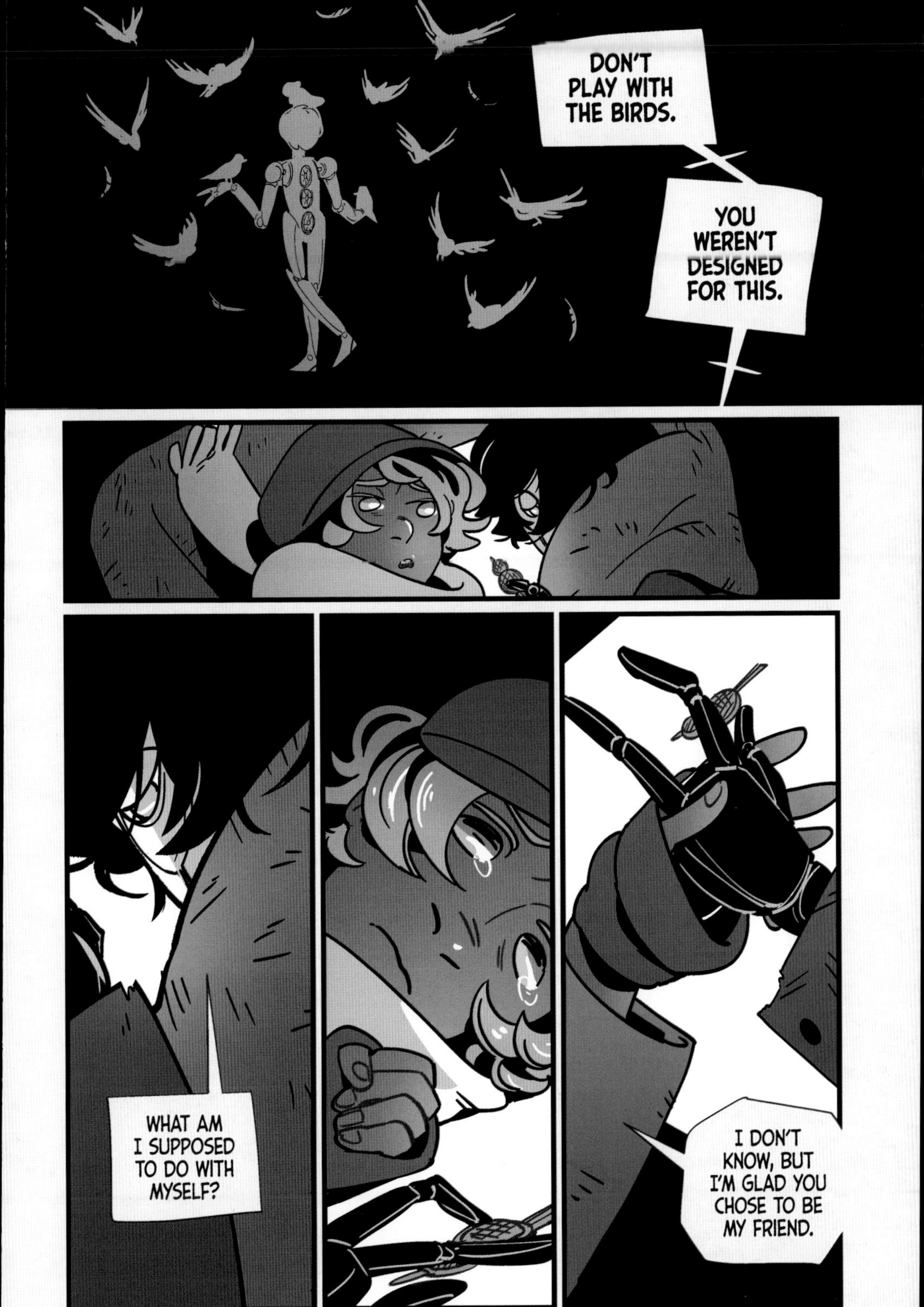
DON'T PLAY WITH THE BIRDS.
YOU WEREN'T DESIGNED FOR THIS.
WHAT AM I SUPPOSED TO DO WITH MYSELF?
I DON'T KNOW, BUT I'M GLAD YOU CHOSE TO BE MY FRIEND.

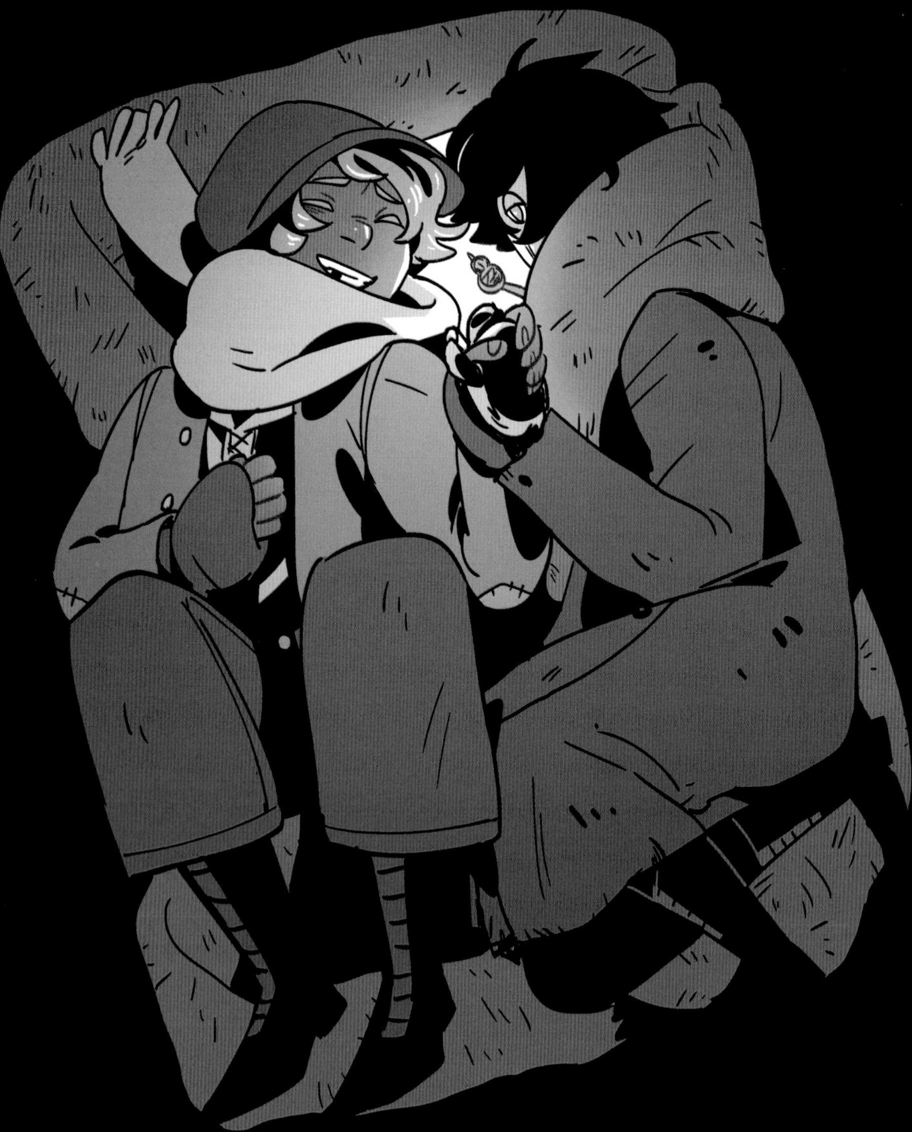

Jack's Secret Warehouse

IT TURNS OUT, SIR...

WE HAD A STOWAWAY IN THE TRUNK.

SO MUCH INCOMPETENCE.

A CAPITAL **OFFICIAL** OUTSMARTED BY A **CHILD!**

HOW THE BLAZES ARE THE ARMED FORCES EVEN **FUNCTIONING** WITHOUT ME OVER THERE?

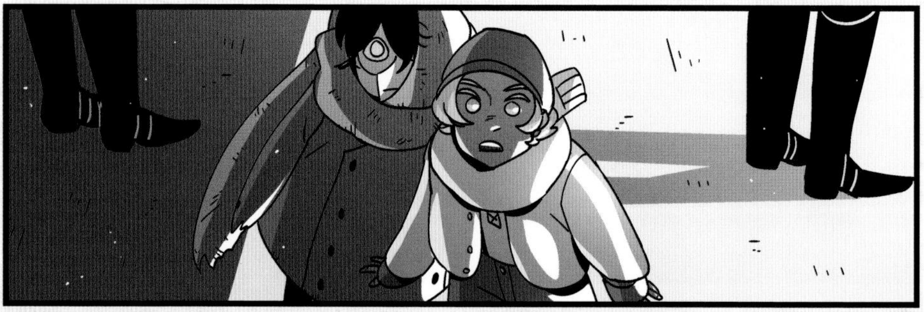
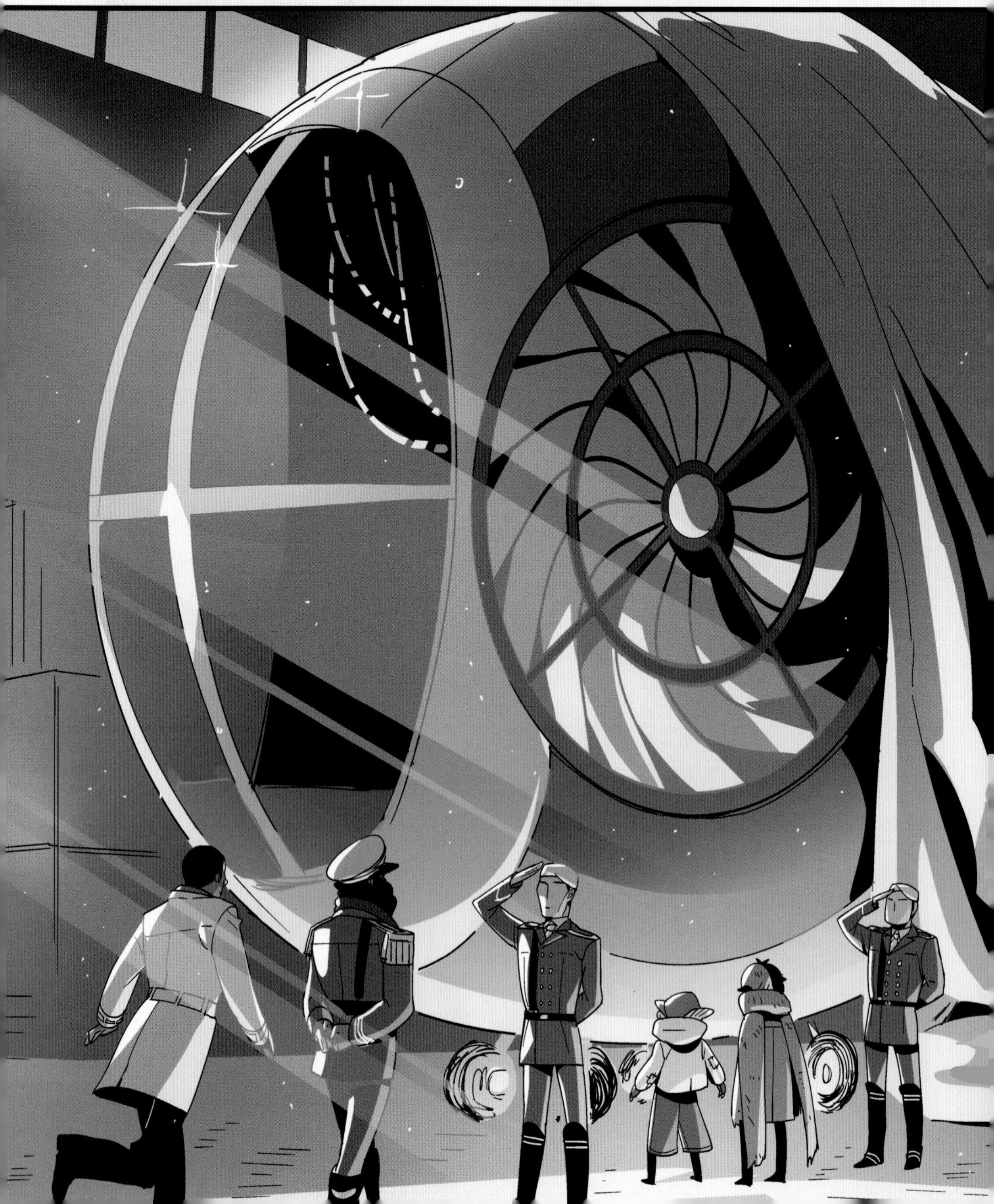

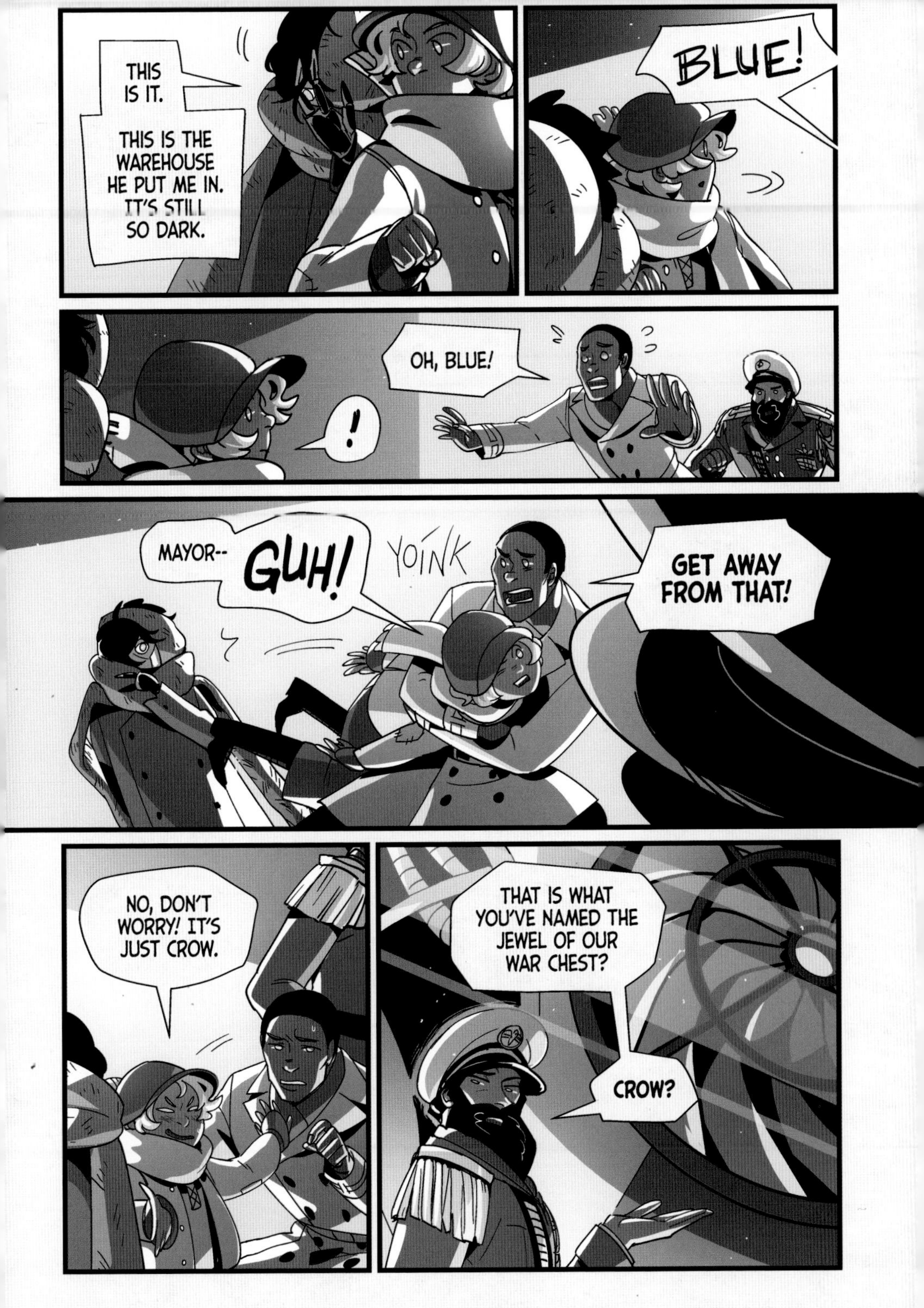

THIS IS IT.
THIS IS THE WAREHOUSE HE PUT ME IN. IT'S STILL SO DARK.
BLUE!
OH, BLUE!
!
MAYOR--
GUH!
YOINK
GET AWAY FROM THAT!
NO, DON'T WORRY! IT'S JUST CROW.
THAT IS WHAT YOU'VE NAMED THE JEWEL OF OUR WAR CHEST?
CROW?

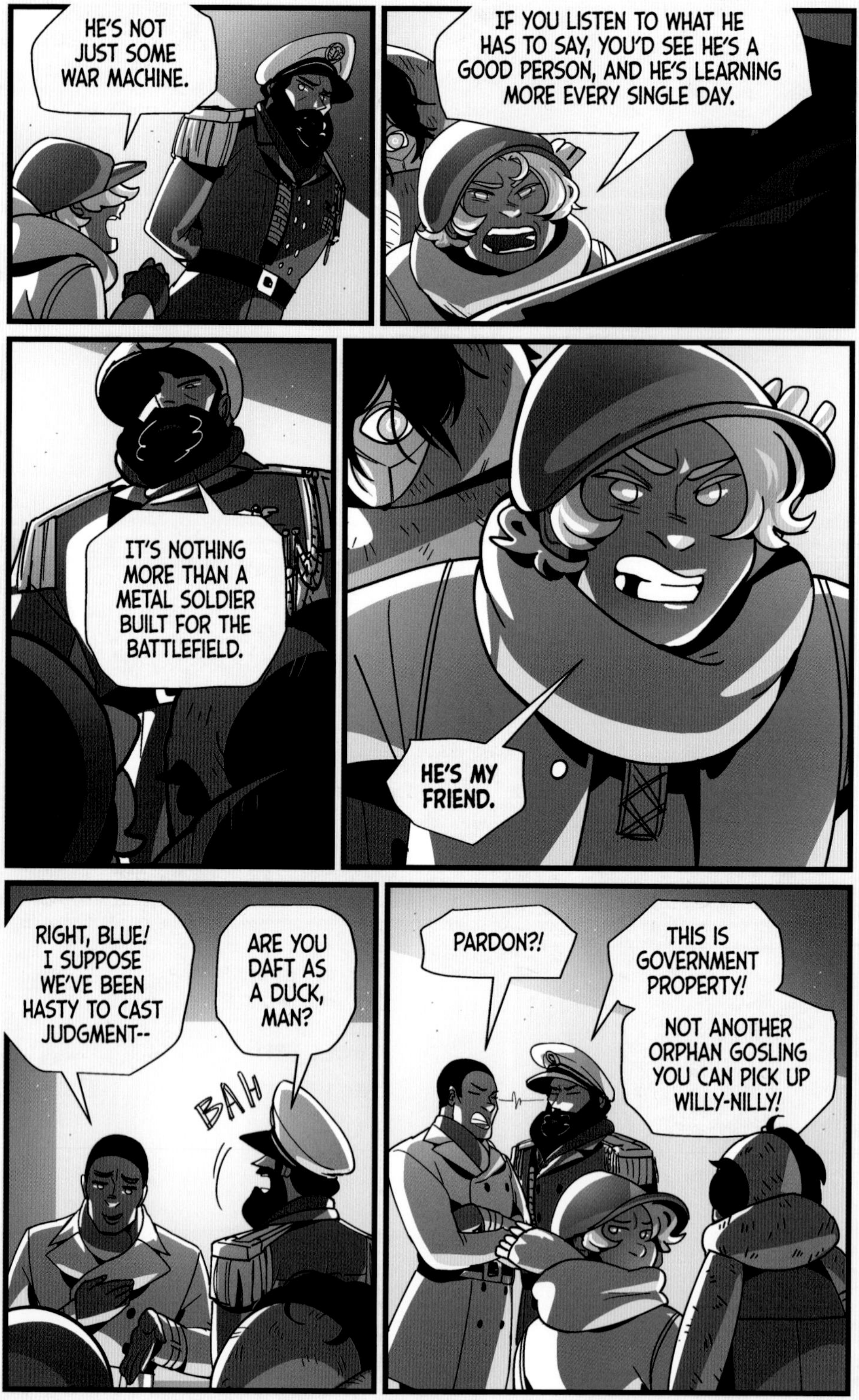
HE'S NOT JUST SOME WAR MACHINE.
IF YOU LISTEN TO WHAT HE HAS TO SAY, YOU'D SEE HE'S A GOOD PERSON, AND HE'S LEARNING MORE EVERY SINGLE DAY.
IT'S NOTHING MORE THAN A METAL SOLDIER BUILT FOR THE BATTLEFIELD.
HE'S MY FRIEND.
RIGHT, BLUE! I SUPPOSE WE'VE BEEN HASTY TO CAST JUDGMENT--
ARE YOU DAFT AS A DUCK, MAN?
BAH
PARDON?!
THIS IS GOVERNMENT PROPERTY!
NOT ANOTHER ORPHAN GOSLING YOU CAN PICK UP WILLY-NILLY!

YOU CAN DRESS IT UP ALL Y̶o̶u̶—

I DIDN'T SAY OTHERWISE. ONLY THAT o̶n̶—

LET 'EM ARGUE.

IT DOESN'T MEAN EITHER ONE OF THEM'S RIGHT.

COME WITH ME.

THIS IS IDIOCY.

ENOUGH. BLUE CAN ASK CROW HOW HE'D LIKE TO BE TRANSPORTED...

BLUE?

BLUE!

CROW, HOW DO WE GET IN?

KLIK

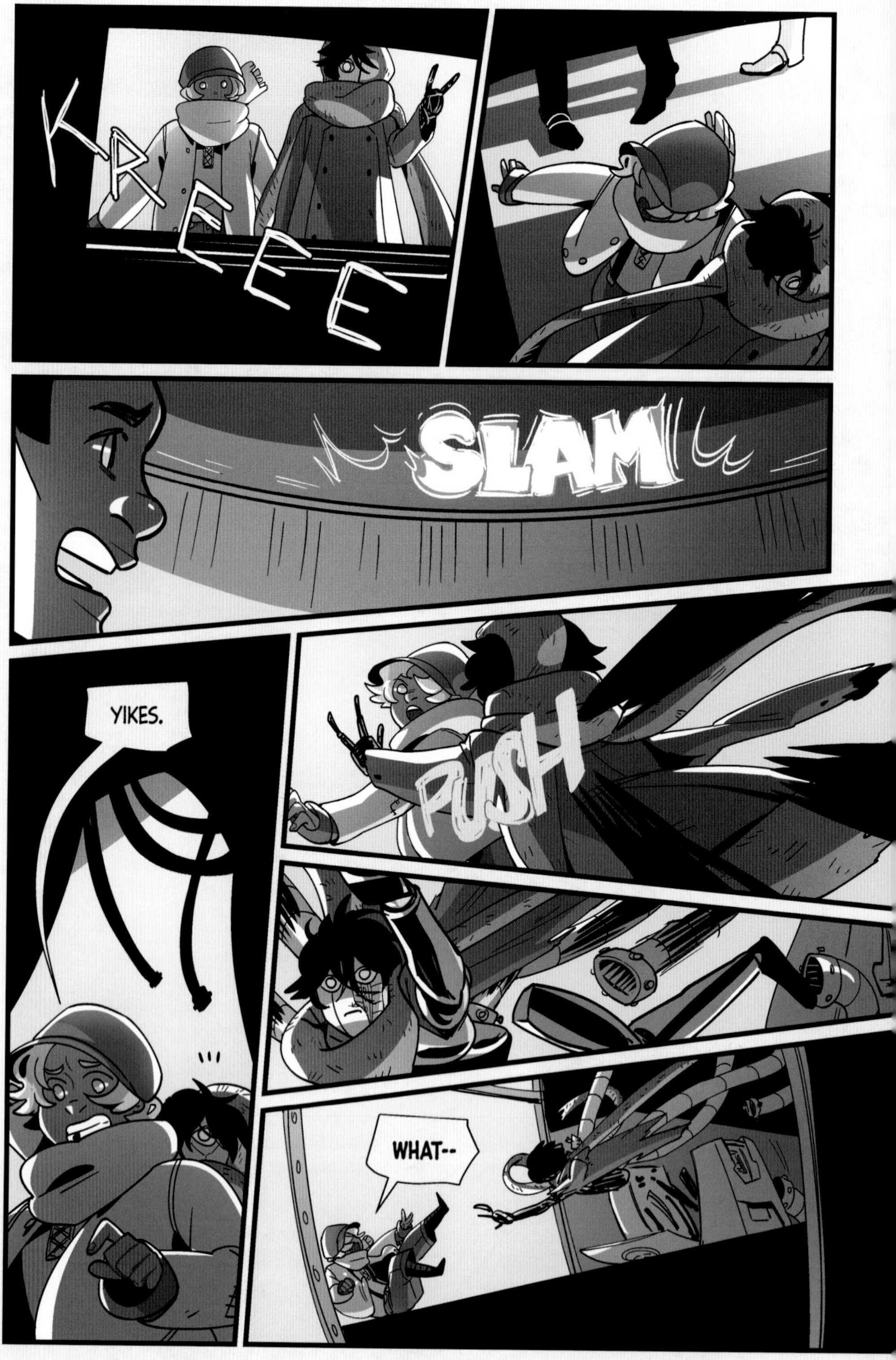
KREEEE
SLAM
YIKES.
PUSH
WHAT--

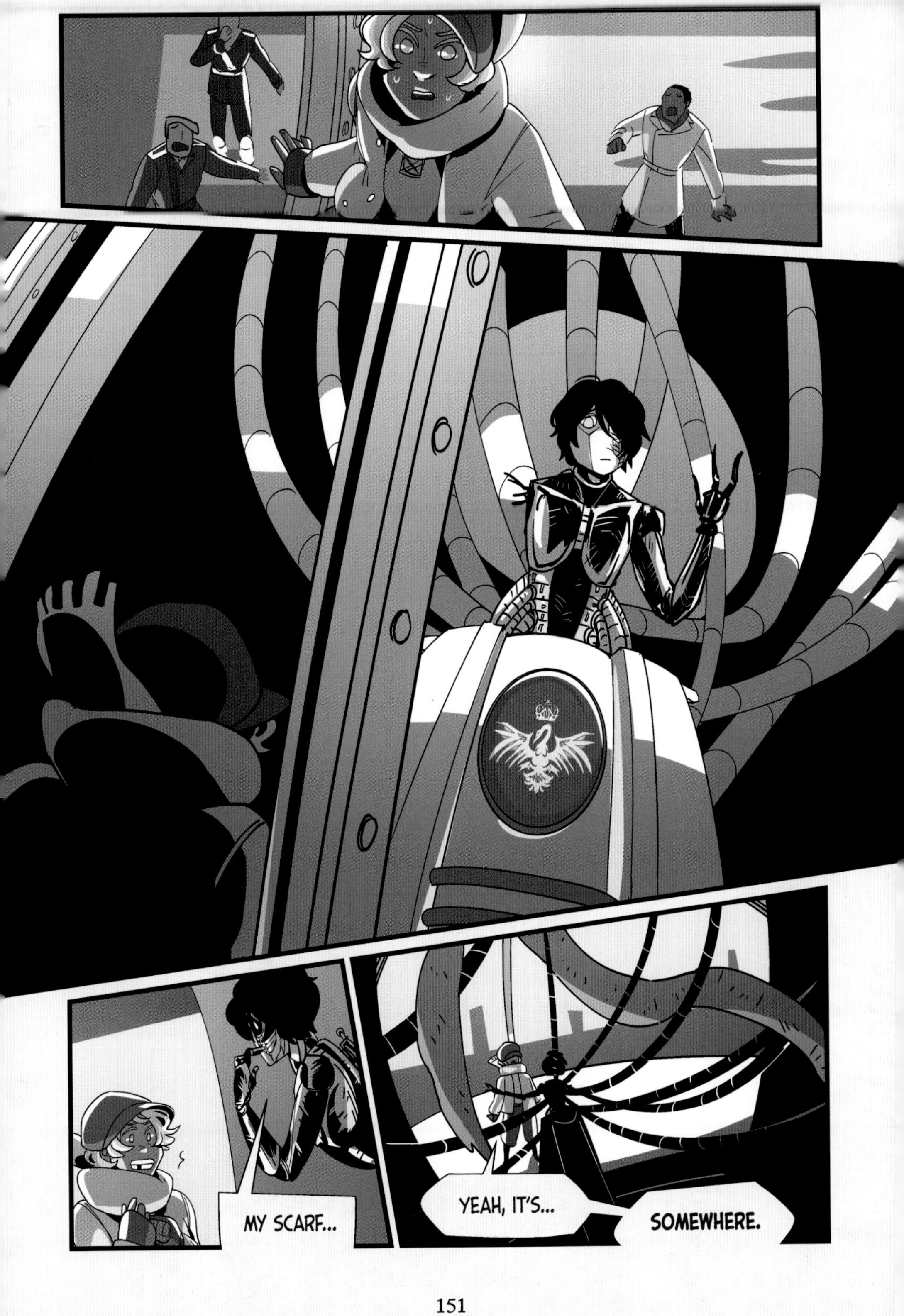
MY SCARF...
YEAH, IT'S...
SOMEWHERE.

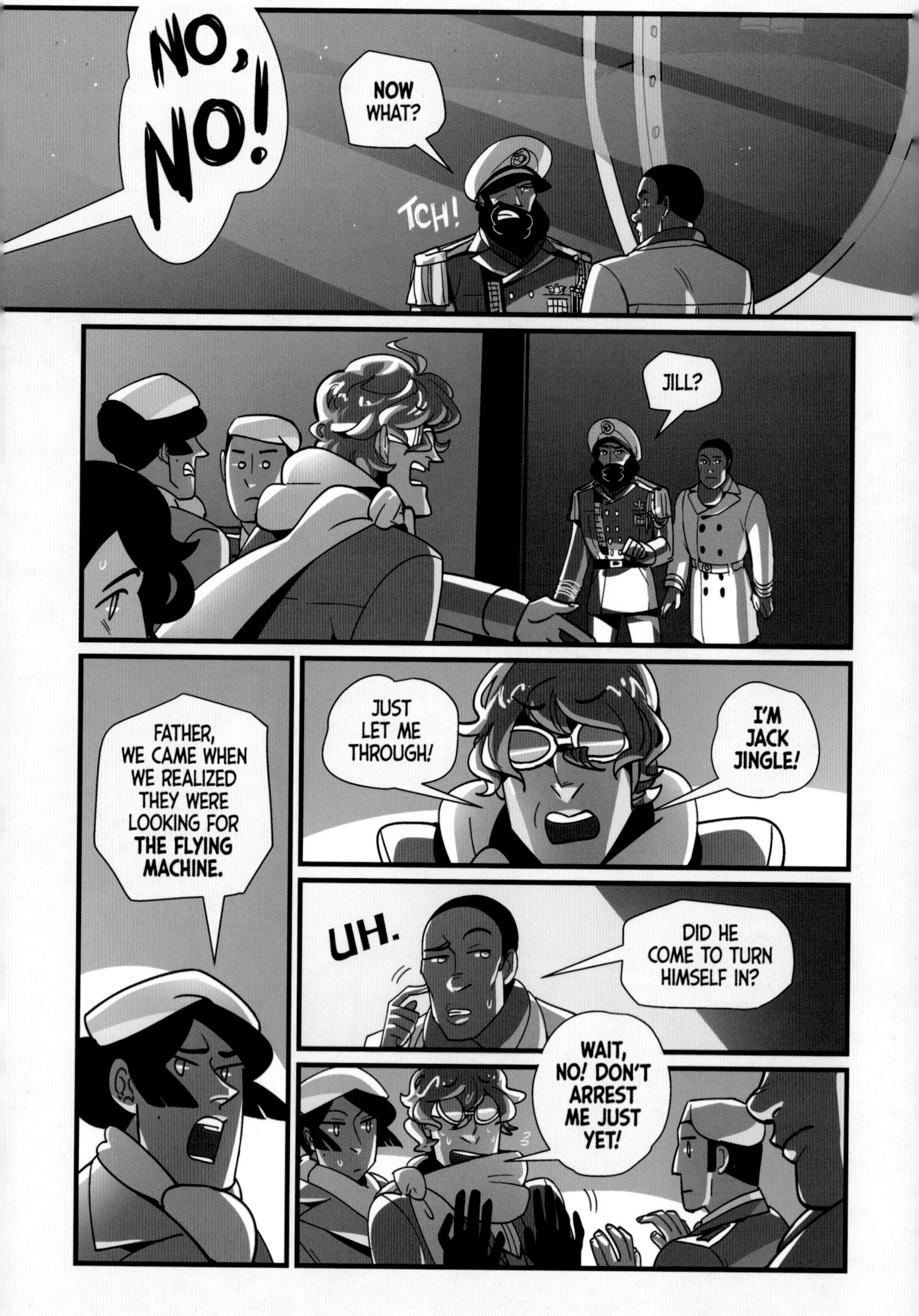
NO, NO!
NOW WHAT?
TCH!
JILL?
FATHER, WE CAME WHEN WE REALIZED THEY WERE LOOKING FOR THE FLYING MACHINE.
JUST LET ME THROUGH!
I'M JACK JINGLE!
UH.
DID HE COME TO TURN HIMSELF IN?
WAIT, NO! DON'T ARREST ME JUST YET!

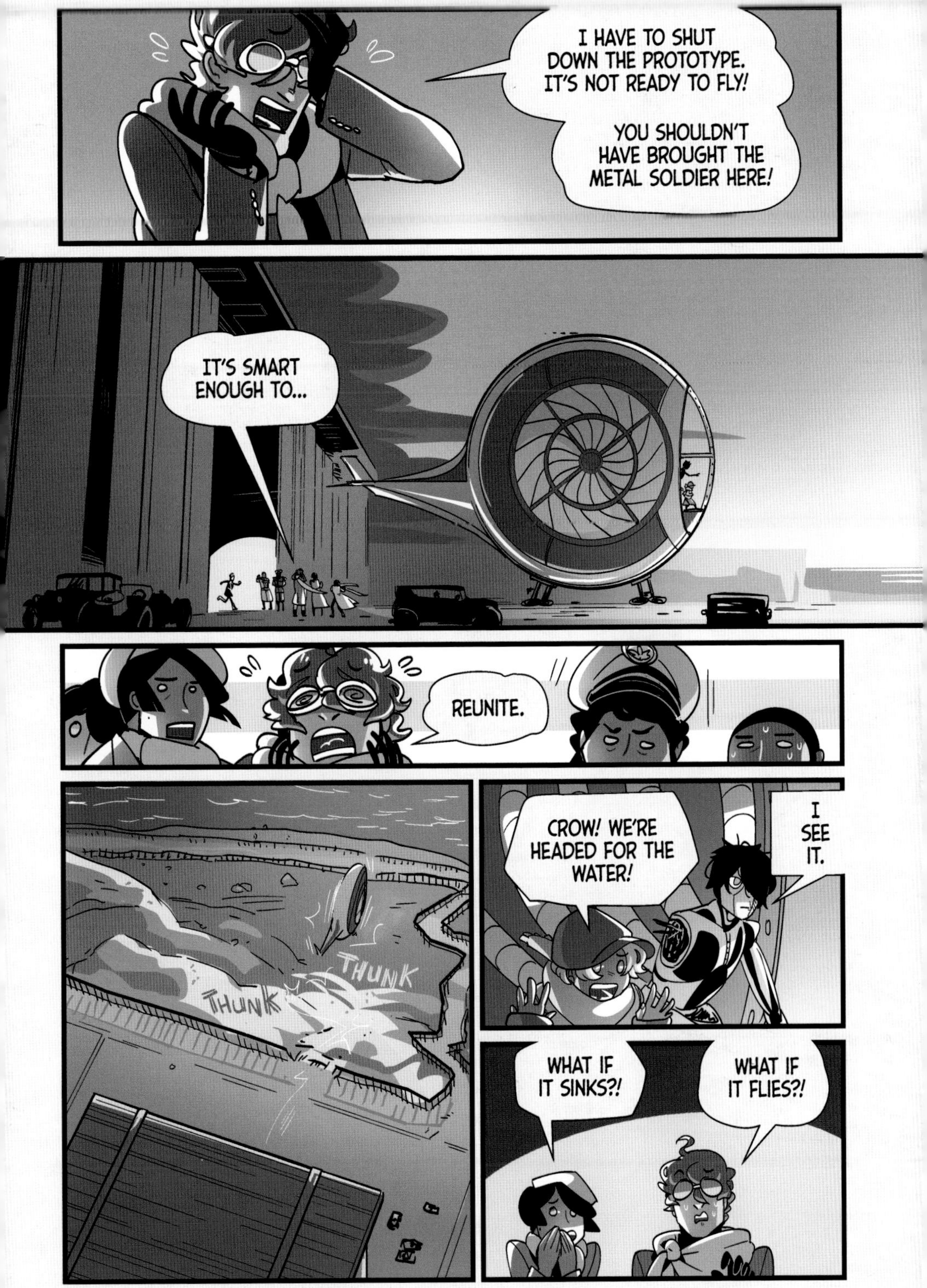
I HAVE TO SHUT DOWN THE PROTOTYPE. IT'S NOT READY TO FLY!
YOU SHOULDN'T HAVE BROUGHT THE METAL SOLDIER HERE!
IT'S SMART ENOUGH TO...
REUNITE.
THUNK
THUNK
CROW! WE'RE HEADED FOR THE WATER!
I SEE IT.
WHAT IF IT SINKS?!
WHAT IF IT FLIES?!

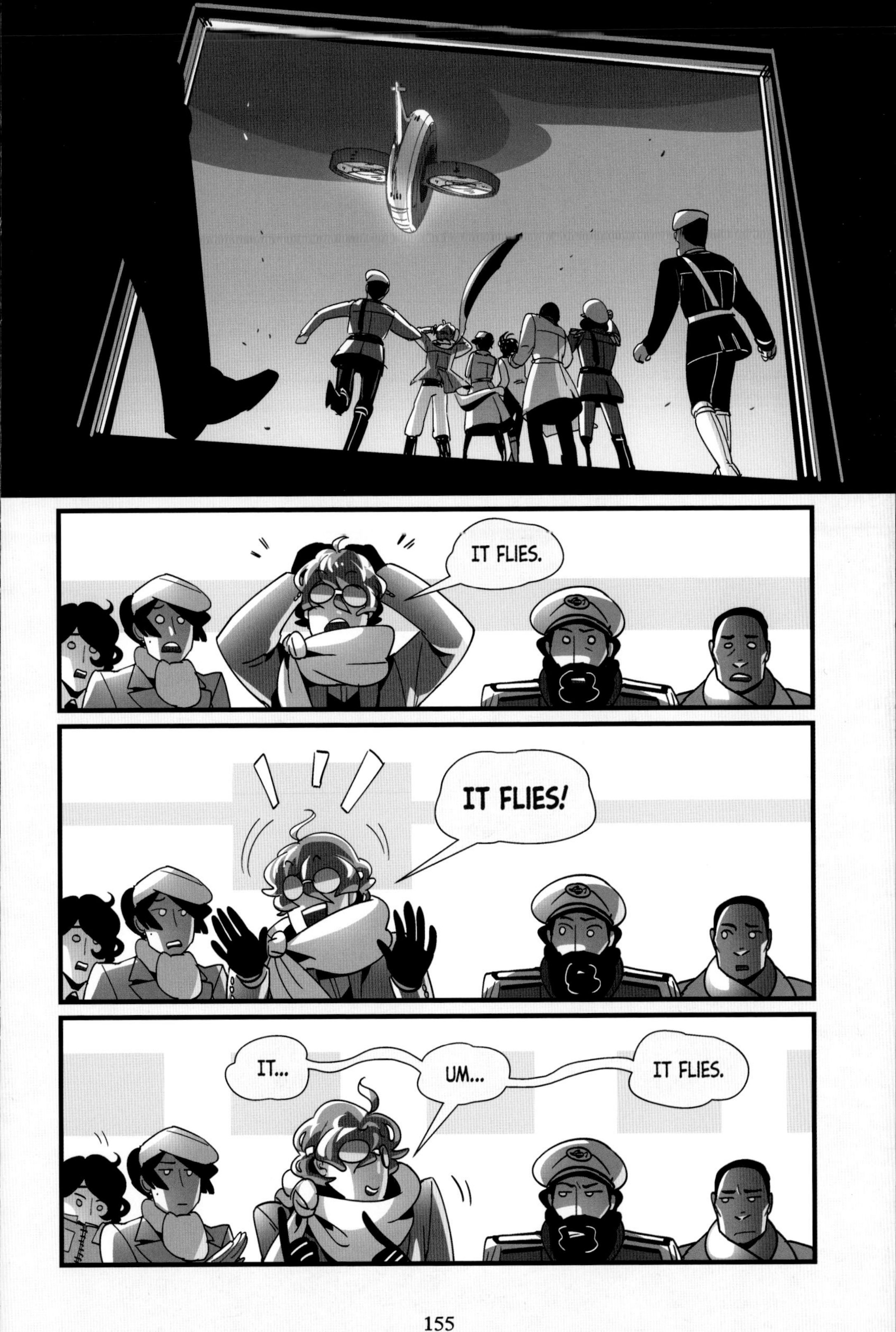
IT FLIES.
IT FLIES!
IT...
UM...
IT FLIES.

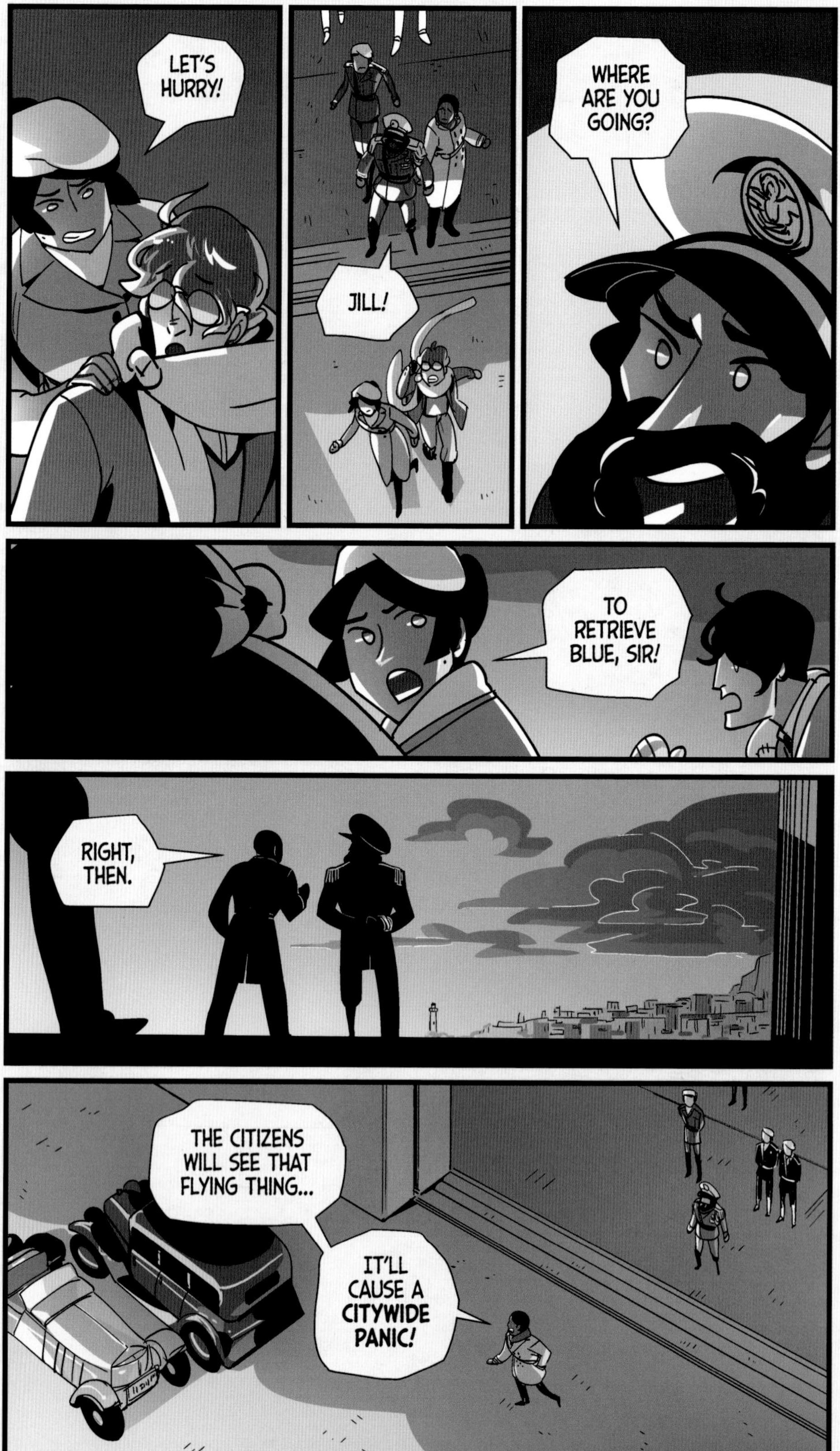
LET'S HURRY!
JILL!
WHERE ARE YOU GOING?
TO RETRIEVE BLUE, SIR!
RIGHT, THEN.
THE CITIZENS WILL SEE THAT FLYING THING...
IT'LL CAUSE A CITYWIDE PANIC!

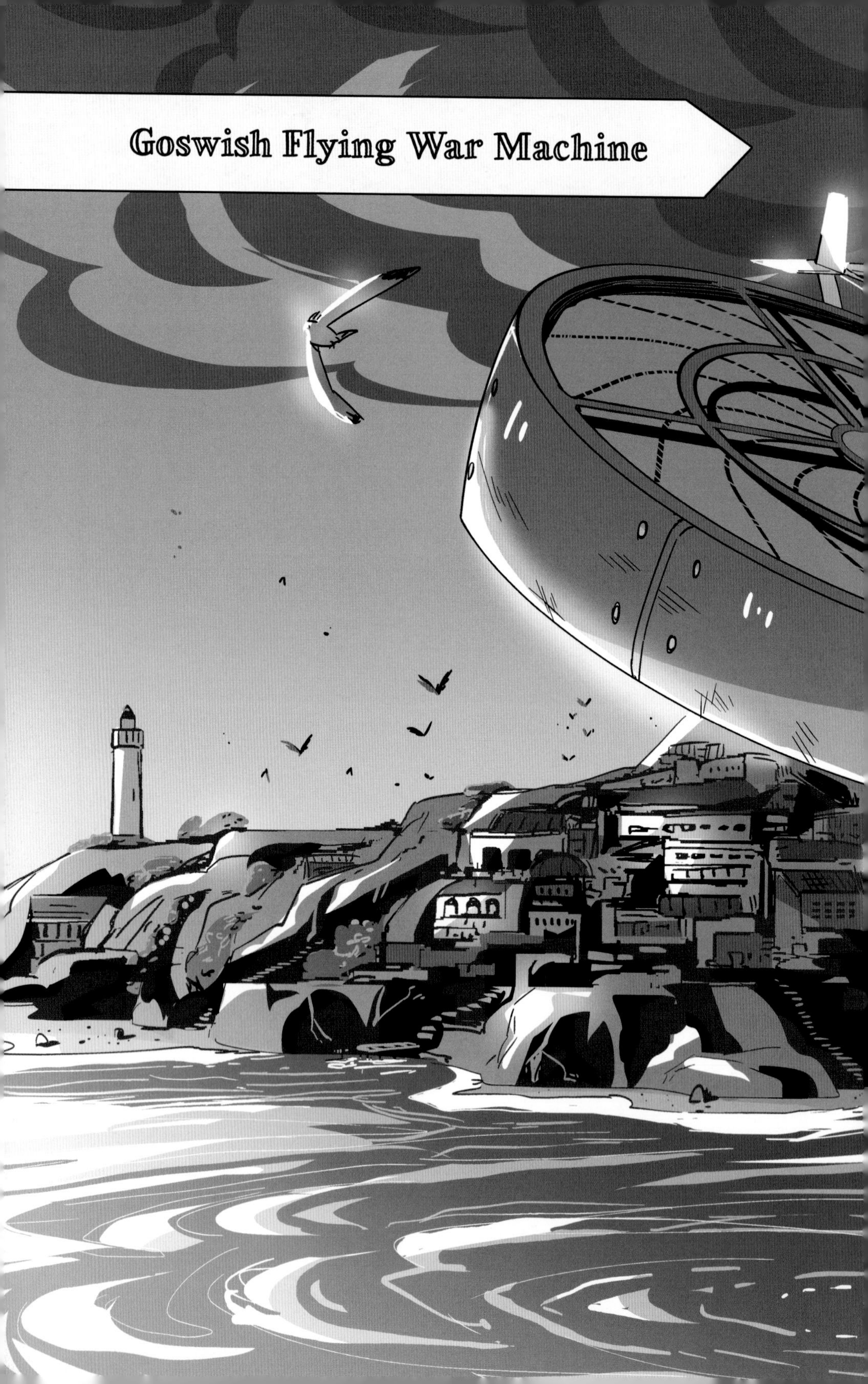
Goswish Flying War Machine

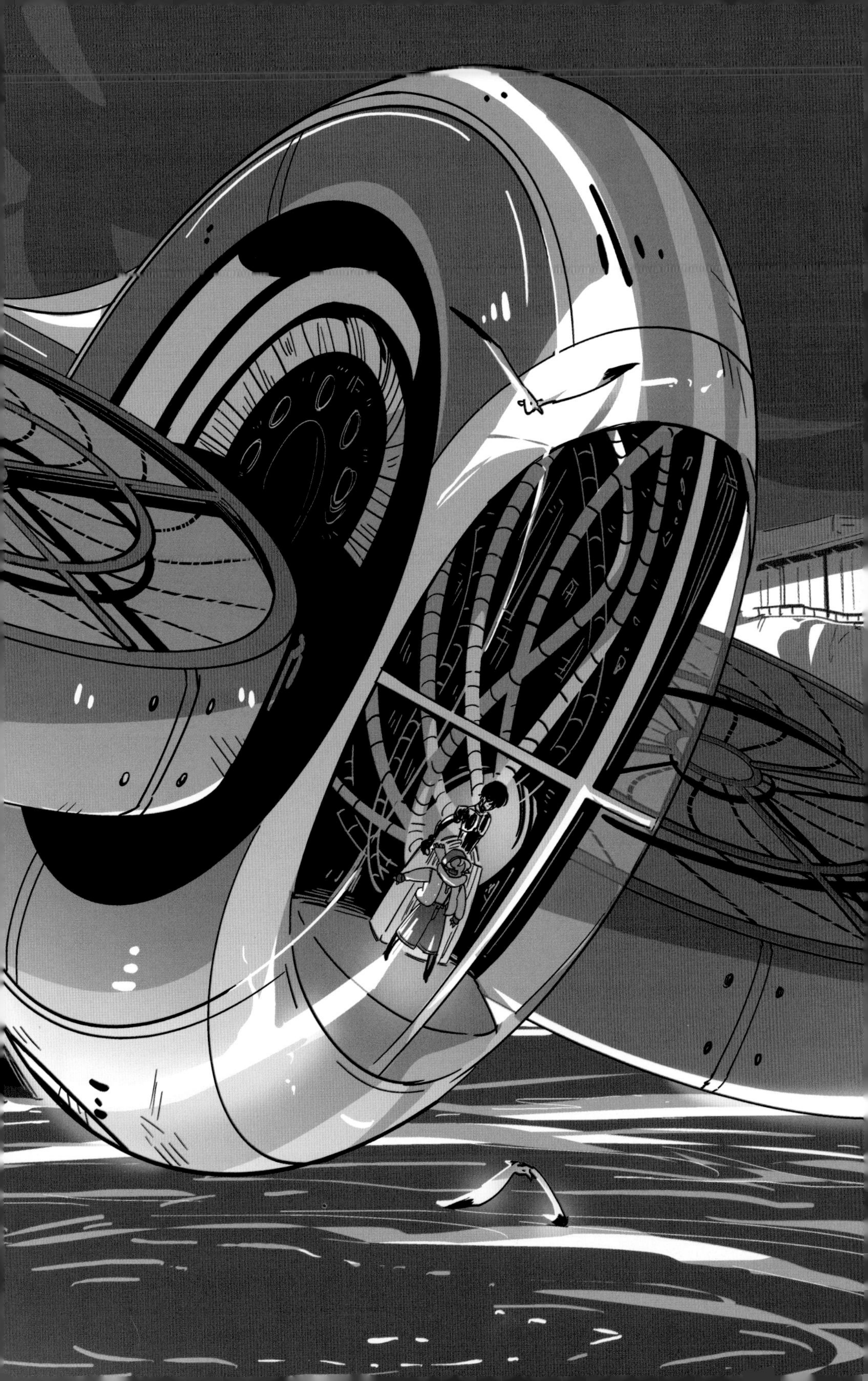

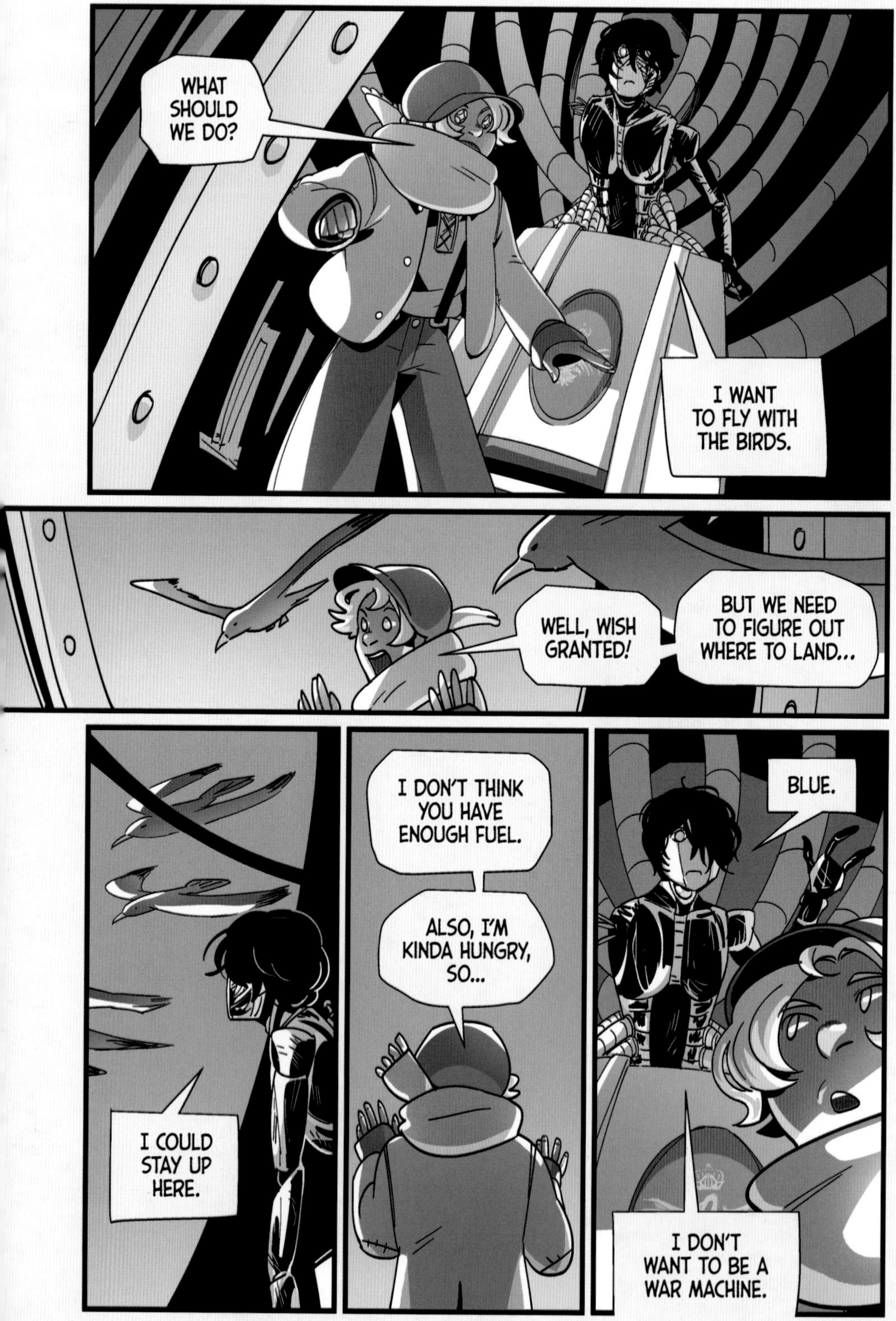
WHAT SHOULD WE DO?
I WANT TO FLY WITH THE BIRDS.
WELL, WISH GRANTED!
BUT WE NEED TO FIGURE OUT WHERE TO LAND...
I COULD STAY UP HERE.
I DON'T THINK YOU HAVE ENOUGH FUEL.
ALSO, I'M KINDA HUNGRY, SO...
BLUE.
I DON'T WANT TO BE A WAR MACHINE.

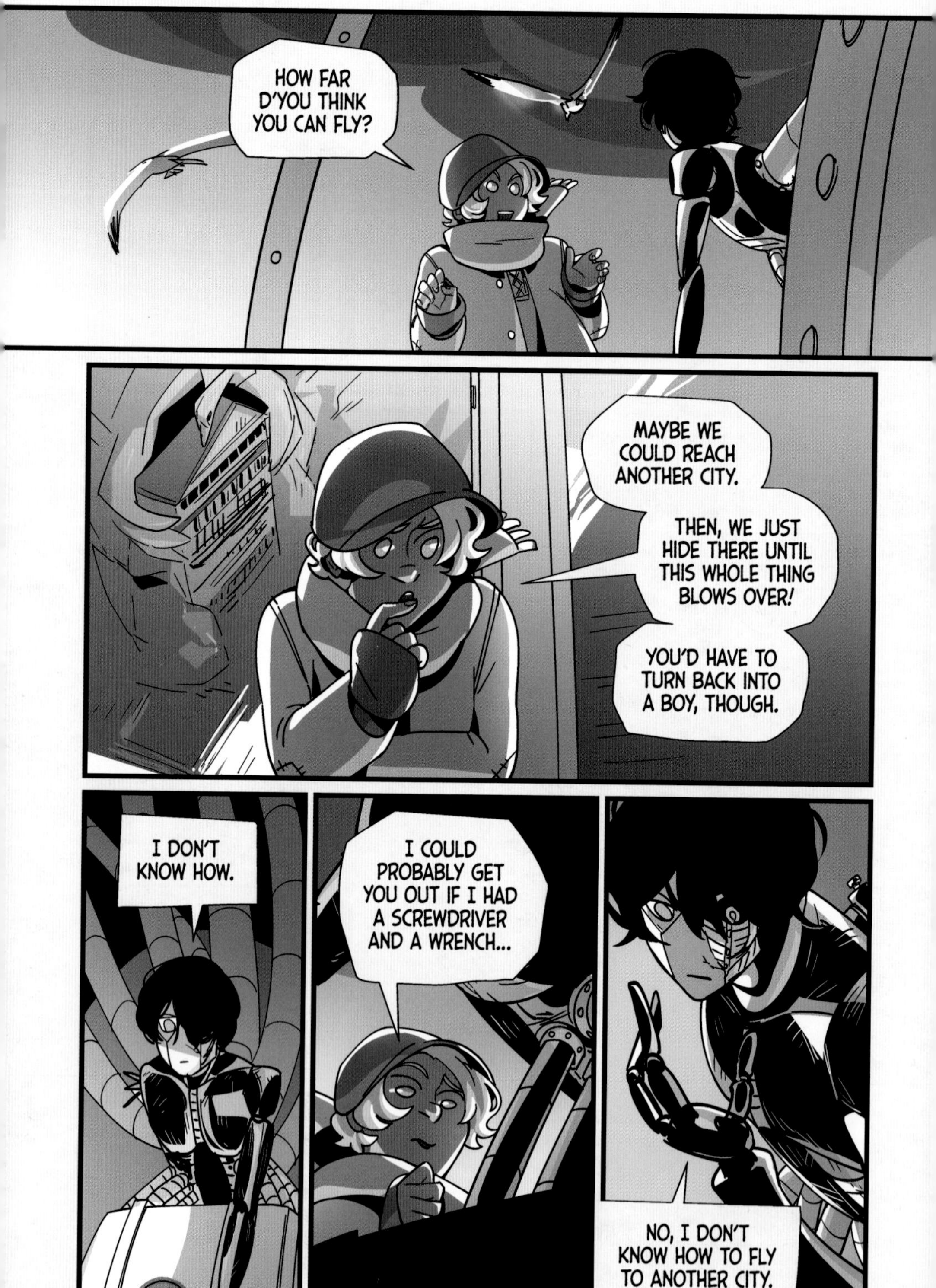
HOW FAR D'YOU THINK YOU CAN FLY?
MAYBE WE COULD REACH ANOTHER CITY.
THEN, WE JUST HIDE THERE UNTIL THIS WHOLE THING BLOWS OVER!
YOU'D HAVE TO TURN BACK INTO A BOY, THOUGH.
I DON'T KNOW HOW.
I COULD PROBABLY GET YOU OUT IF I HAD A SCREWDRIVER AND A WRENCH...
NO, I DON'T KNOW HOW TO FLY TO ANOTHER CITY.

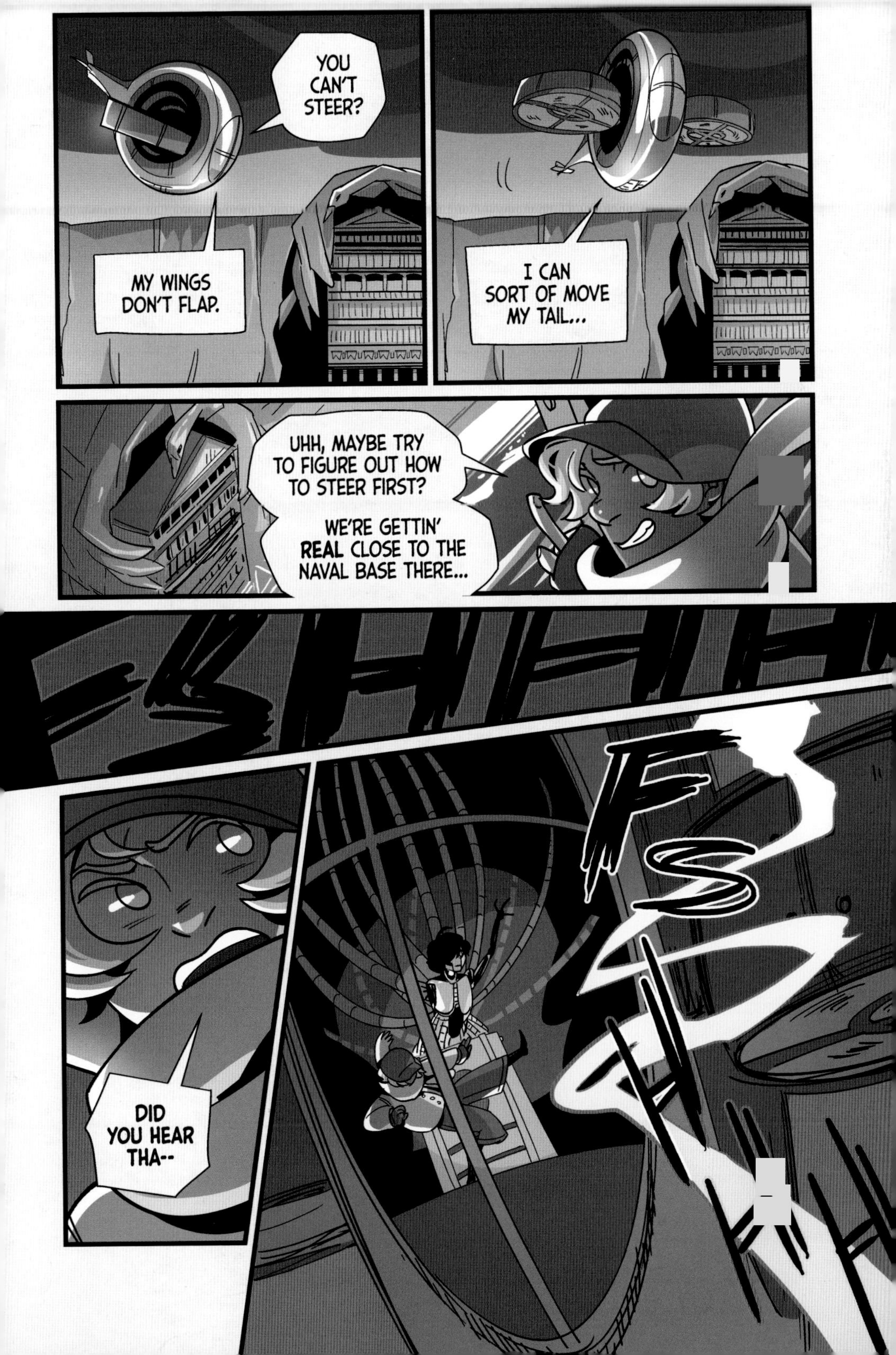
YOU CAN'T STEER?
MY WINGS DON'T FLAP.
I CAN SORT OF MOVE MY TAIL...
UHH, MAYBE TRY TO FIGURE OUT HOW TO STEER FIRST?
WE'RE GETTIN' **REAL** CLOSE TO THE NAVAL BASE THERE...
FSHHHHH
DID YOU HEAR THA--
FSSSHHHHH

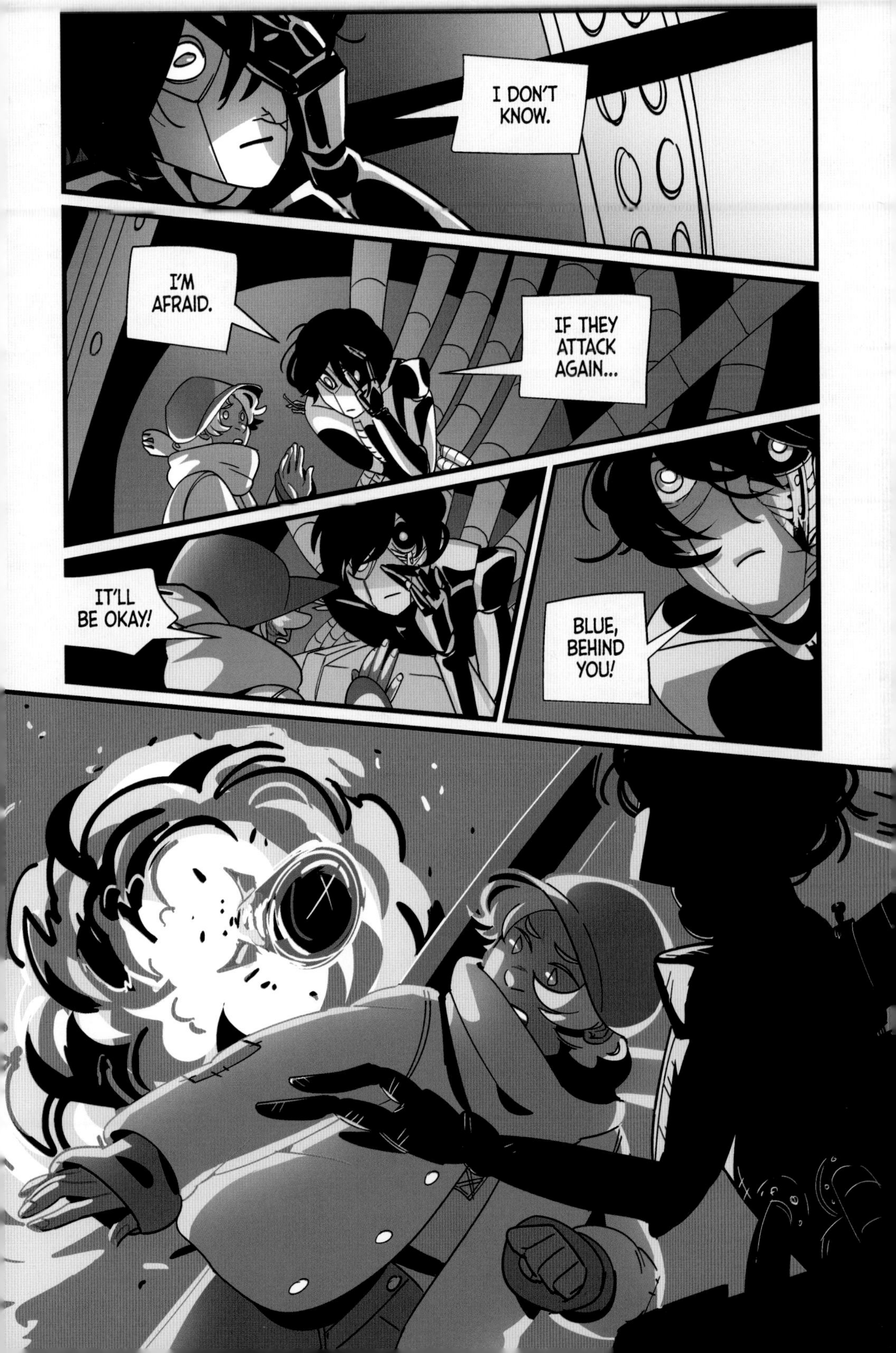
I DON'T KNOW.
I'M AFRAID.
IF THEY ATTACK AGAIN...
IT'LL BE OKAY!
BLUE, BEHIND YOU!

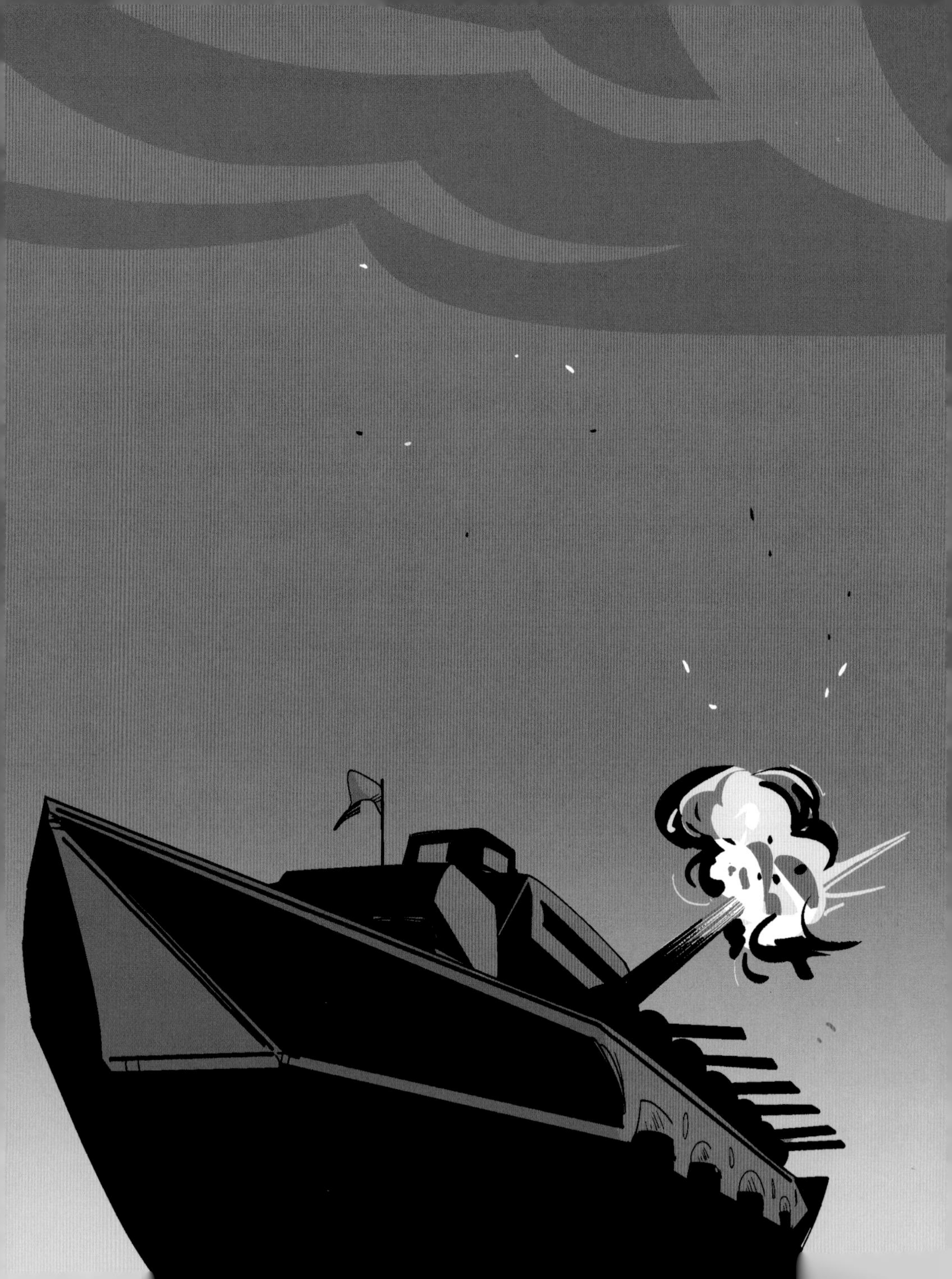

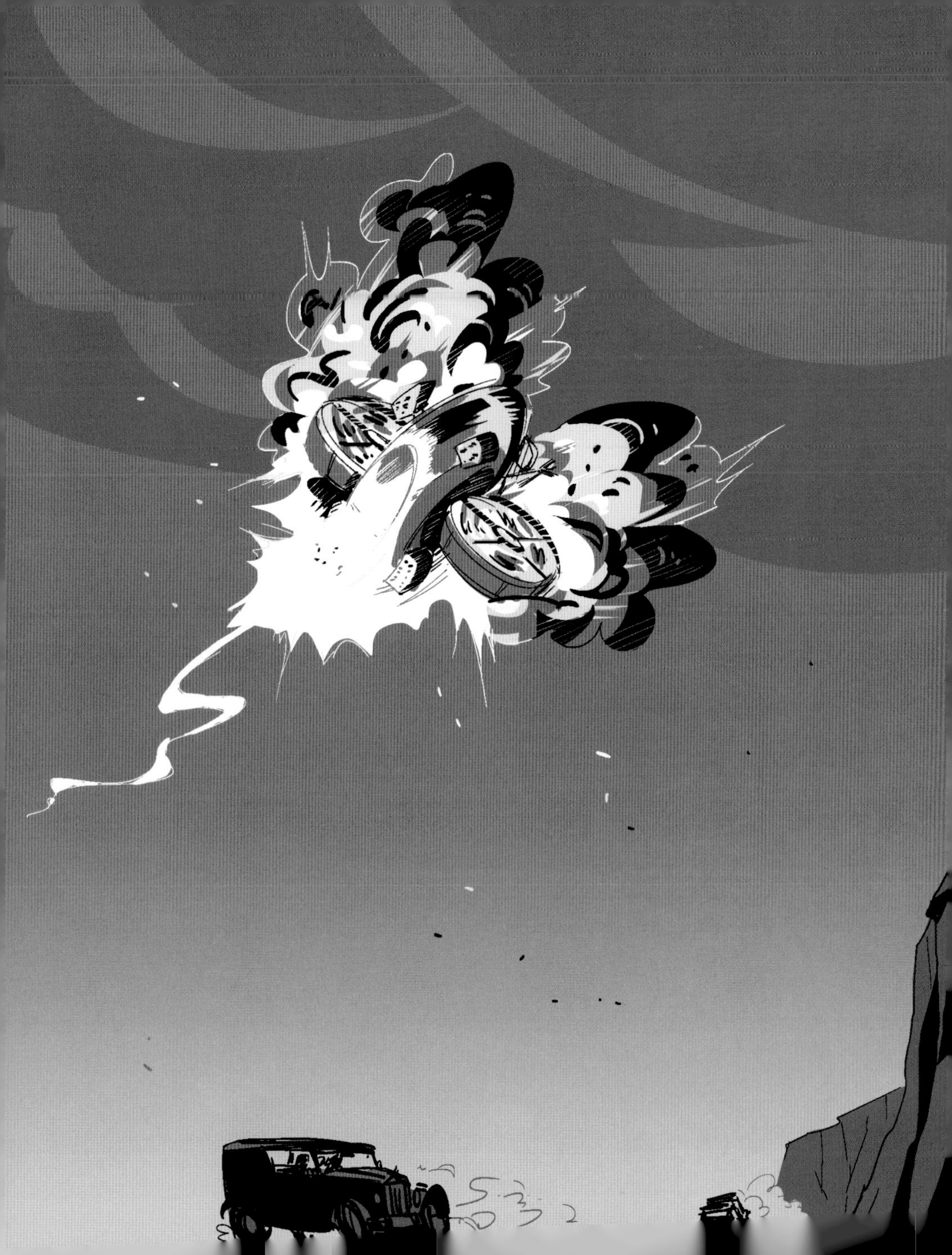

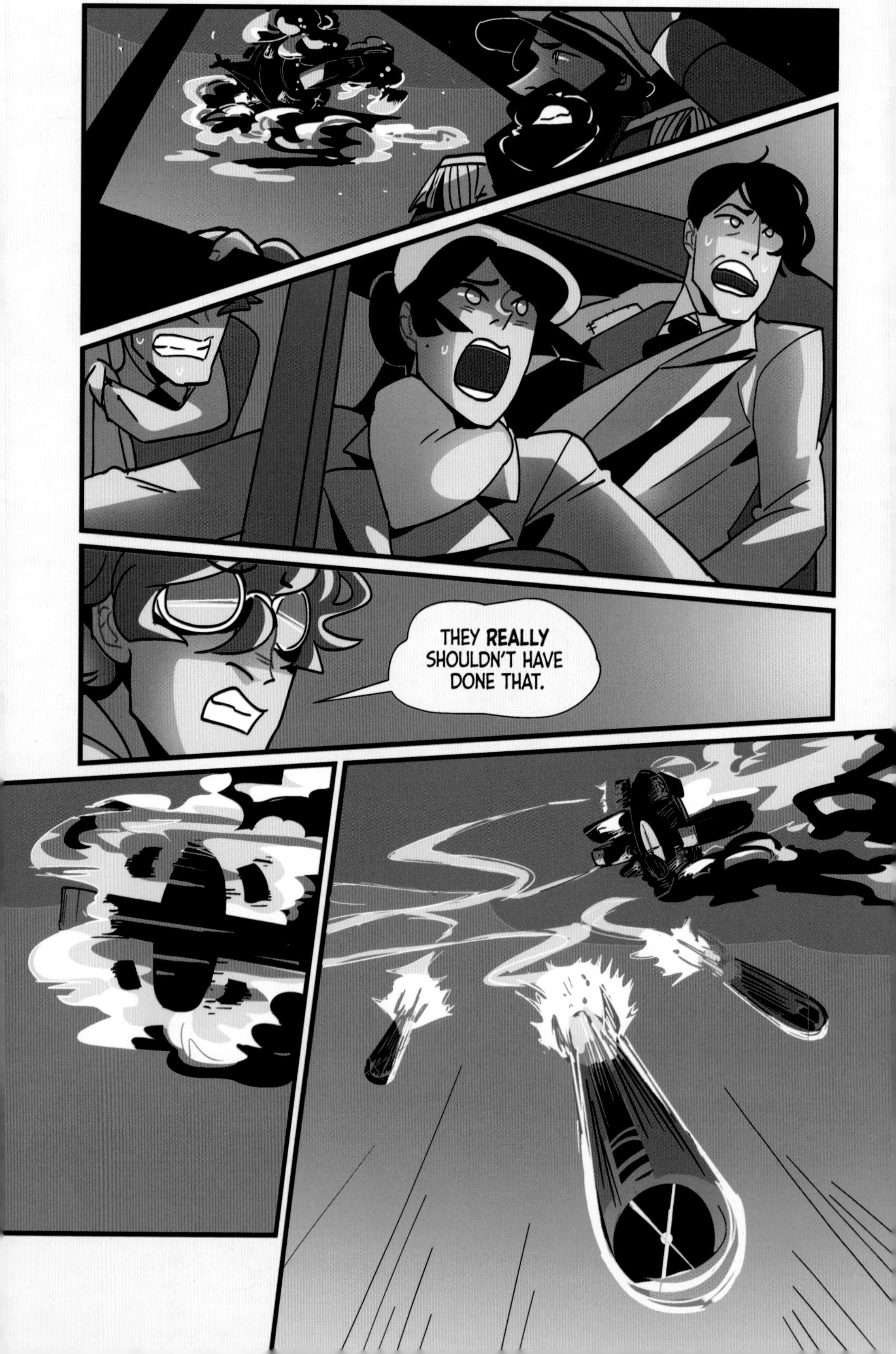
THEY REALLY SHOULDN'T HAVE DONE THAT.

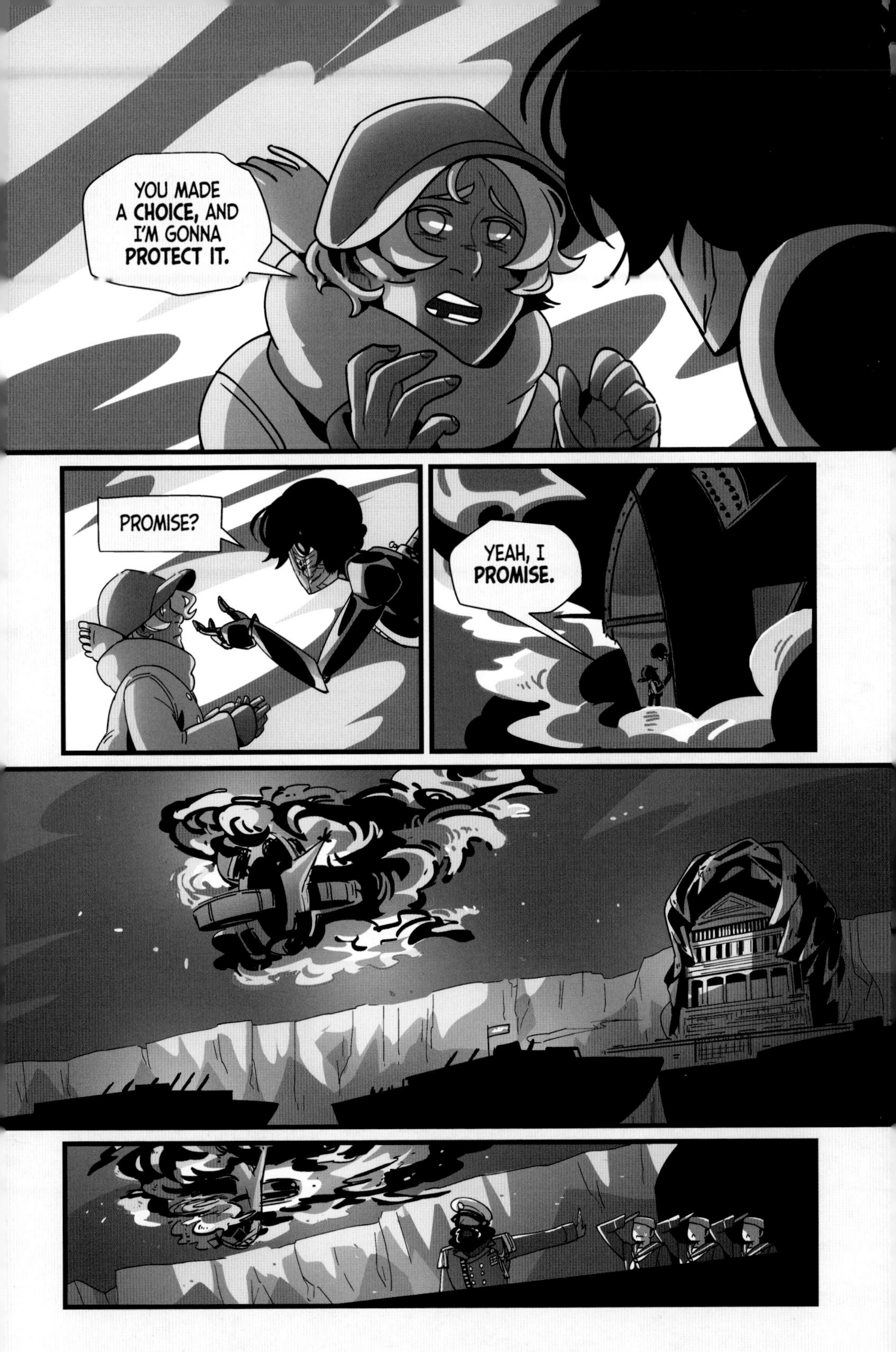
YOU MADE A CHOICE, AND I'M GONNA PROTECT IT.
PROMISE?
YEAH, I PROMISE.

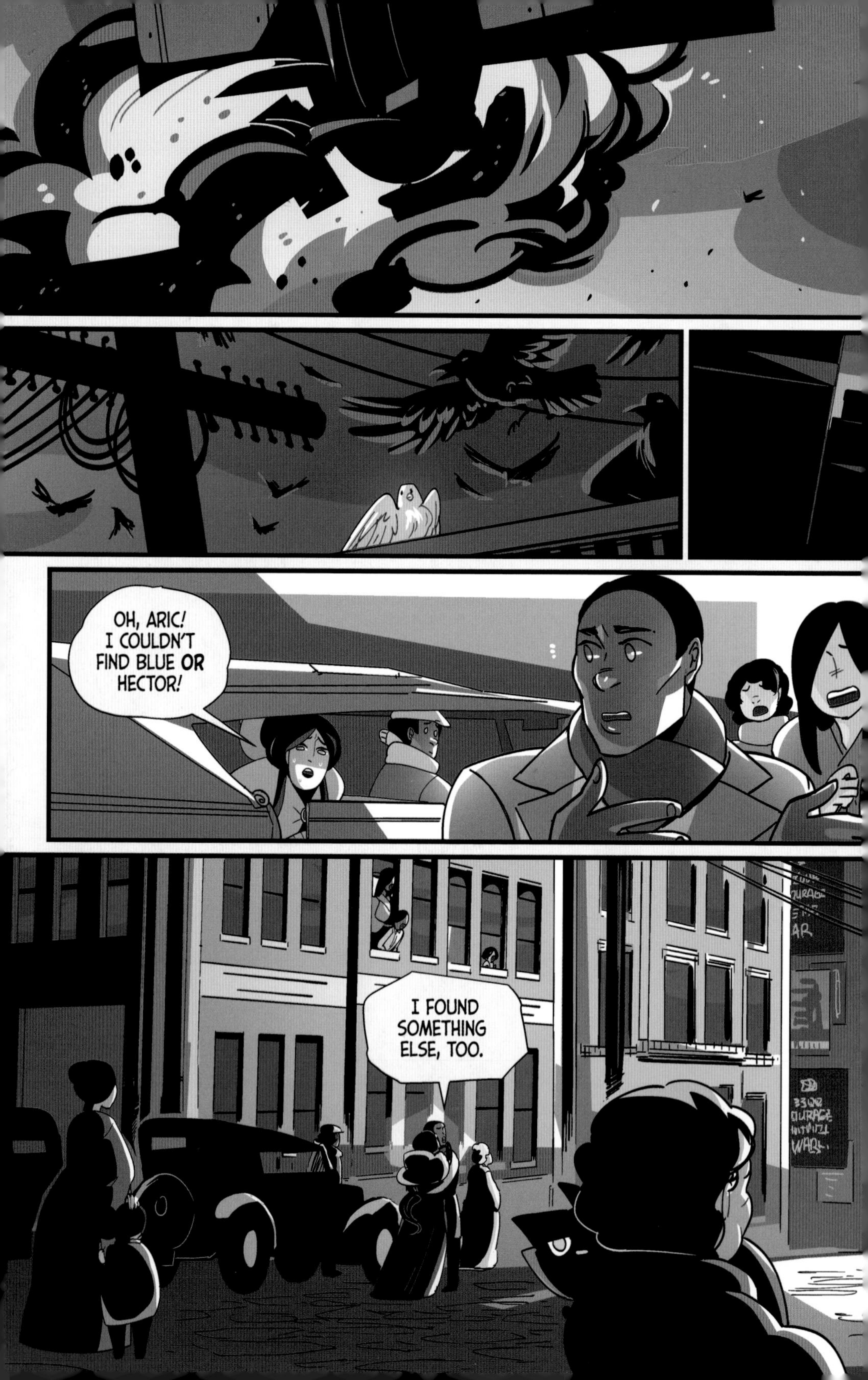
OH, ARIC! I COULDN'T FIND BLUE OR HECTOR!
I FOUND SOMETHING ELSE, TOO.

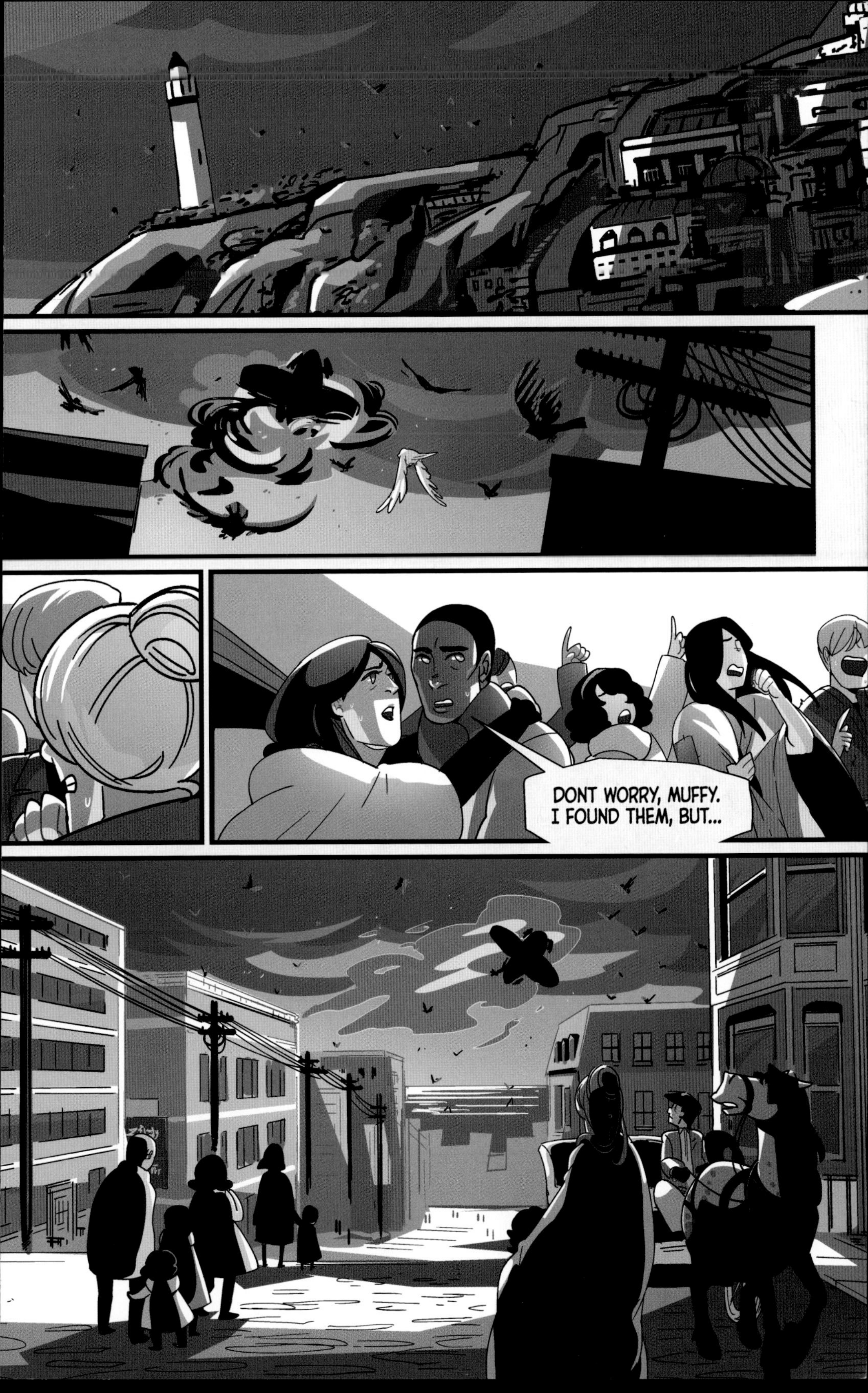
DONT WORRY, MUFFY.
I FOUND THEM, BUT...

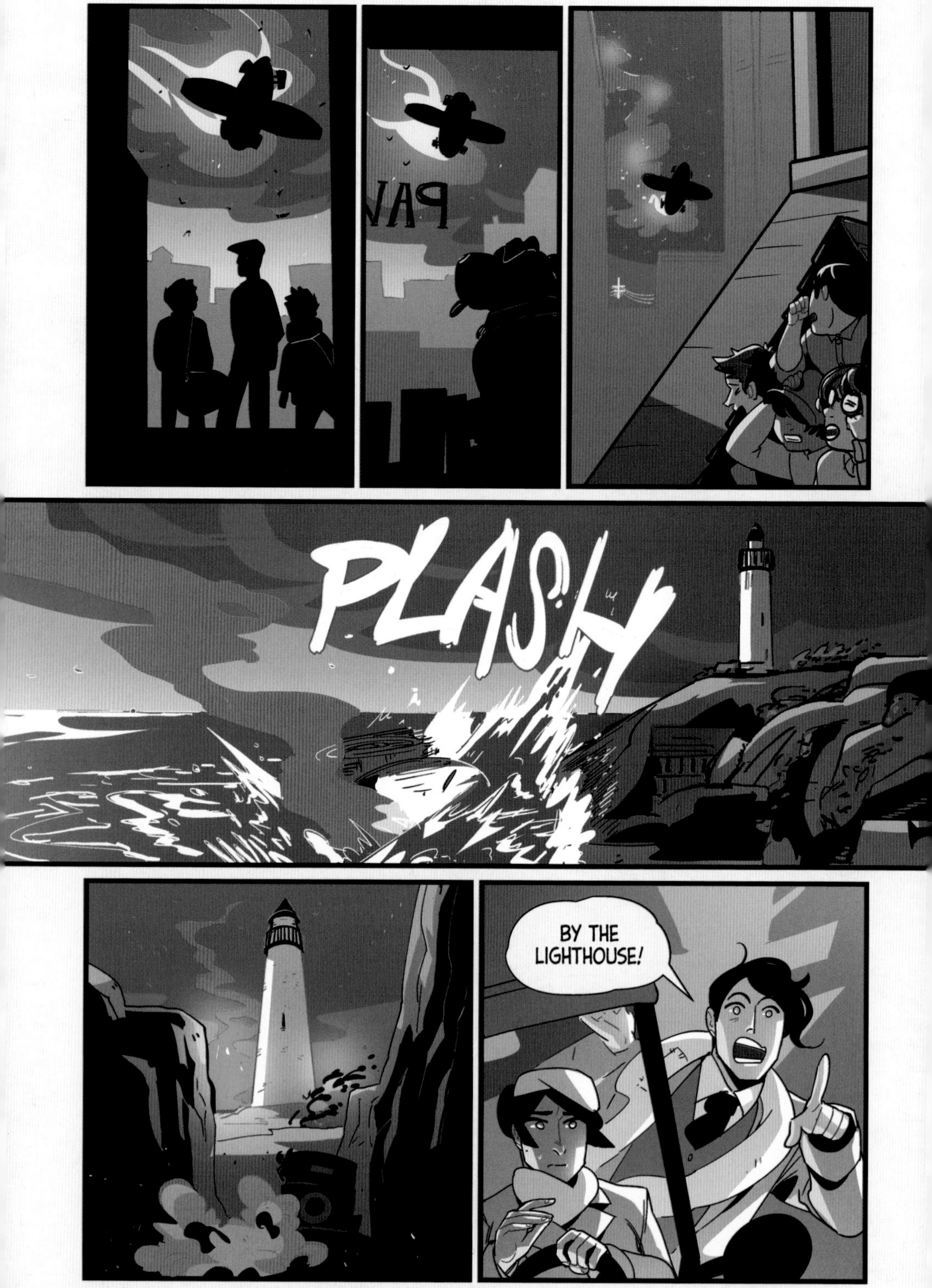
PAW
PLASH
BY THE LIGHTHOUSE!

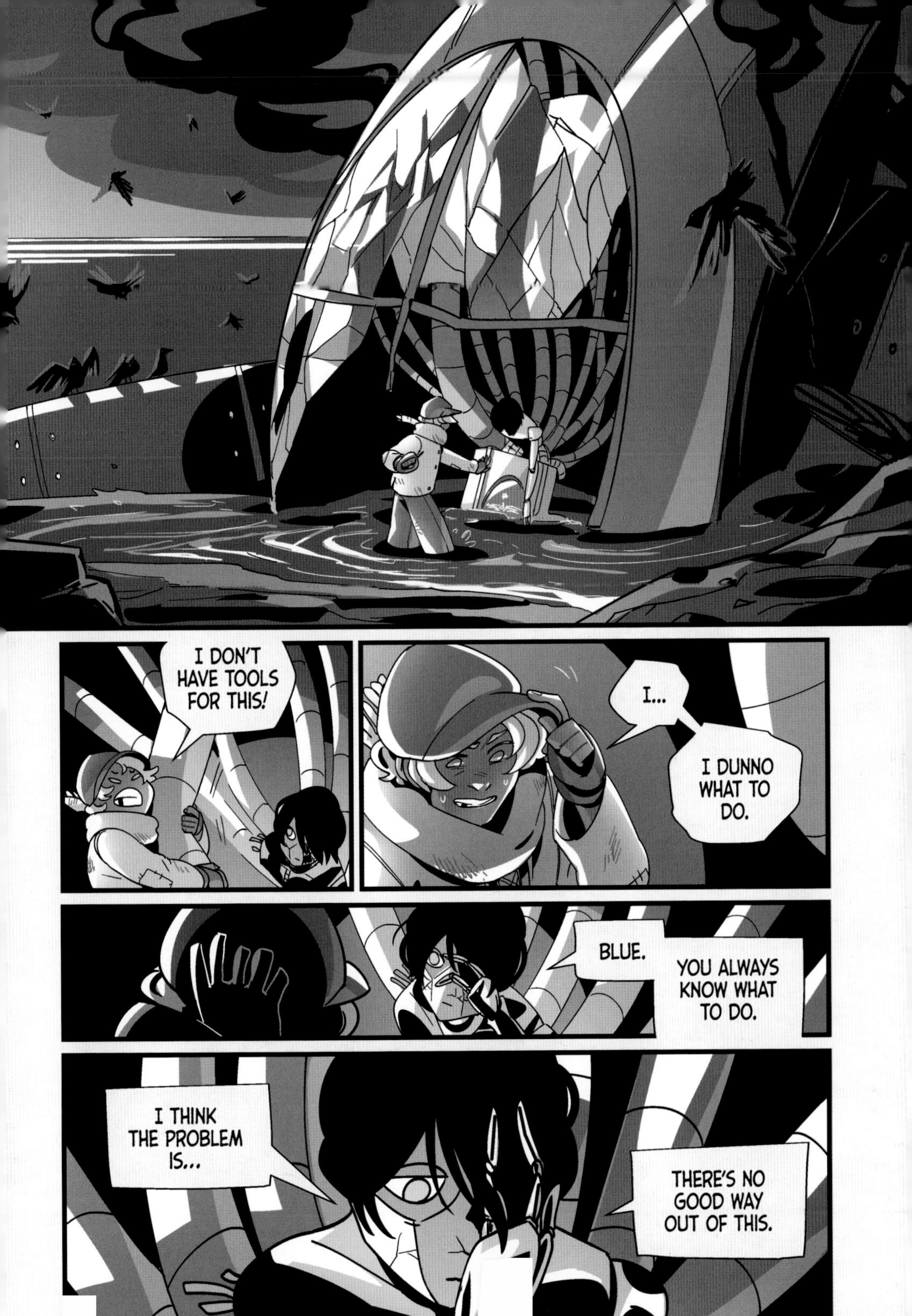
I DON'T HAVE TOOLS FOR THIS!
I...
I DUNNO WHAT TO DO.
BLUE.
YOU ALWAYS KNOW WHAT TO DO.
I THINK THE PROBLEM IS...
THERE'S NO GOOD WAY OUT OF THIS.

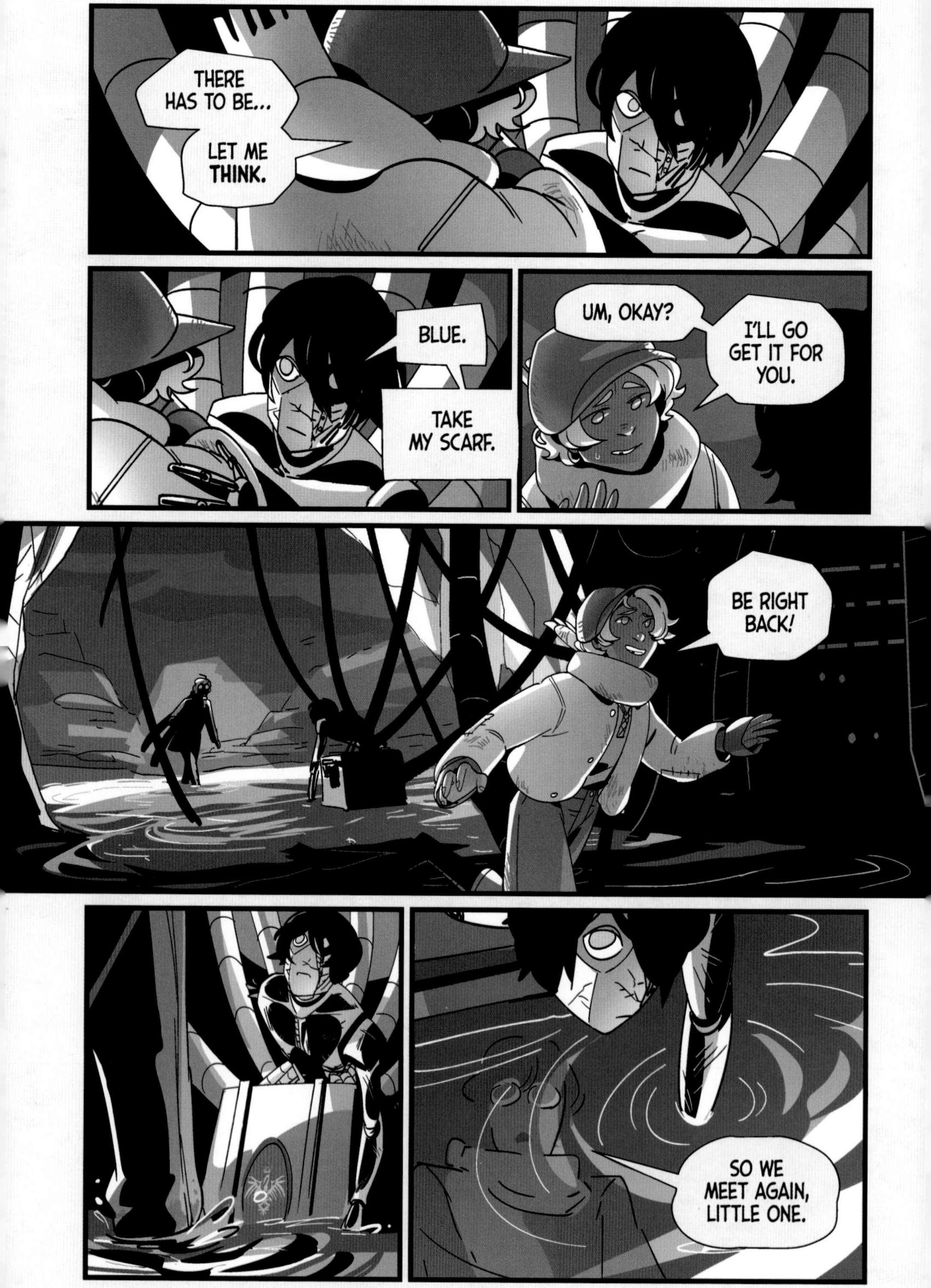
THERE HAS TO BE...
LET ME THINK.
BLUE.
TAKE MY SCARF.
UM, OKAY?
I'LL GO GET IT FOR YOU.
BE RIGHT BACK!
SO WE MEET AGAIN, LITTLE ONE.

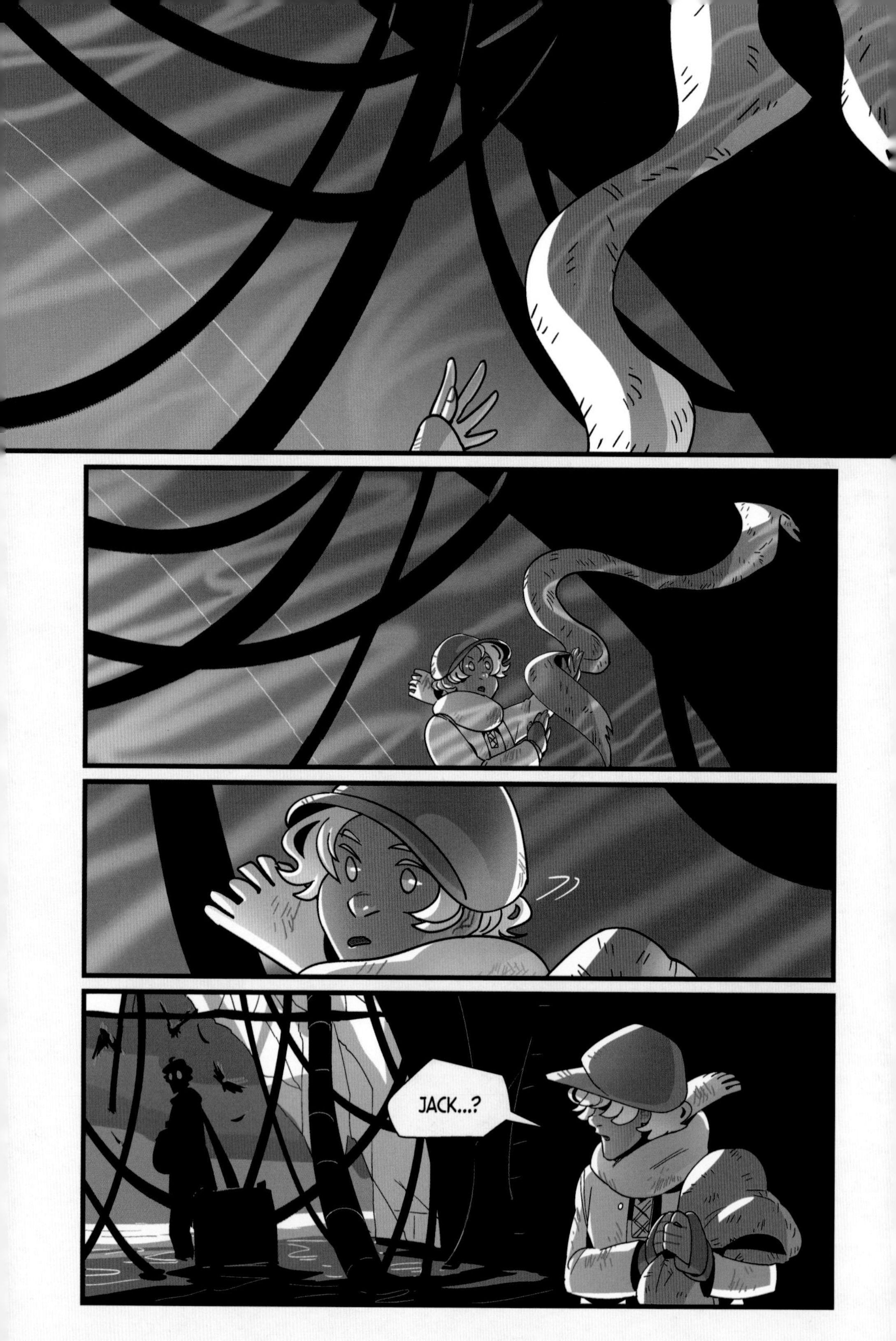
JACK...?

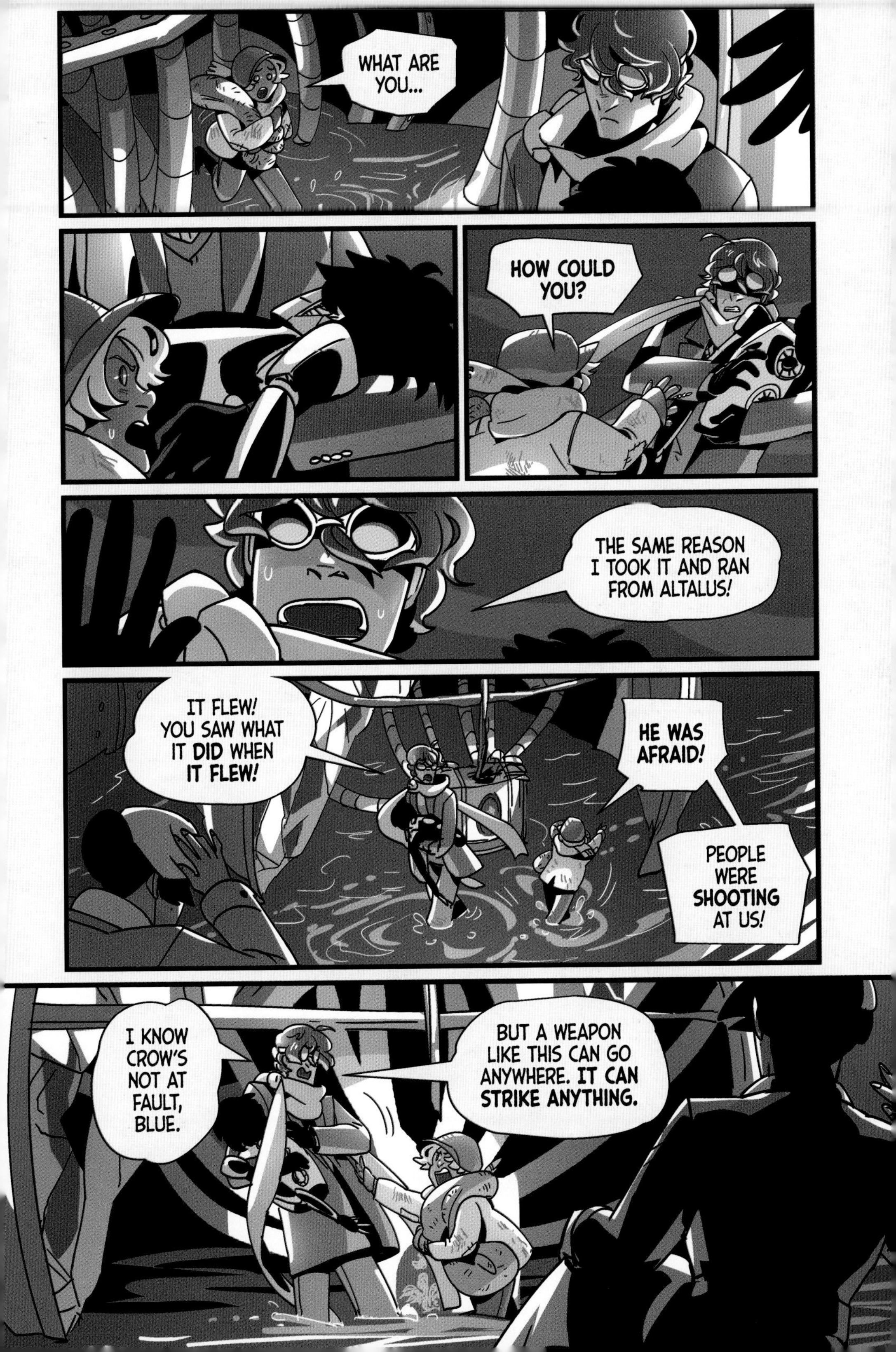
WHAT ARE YOU...
HOW COULD YOU?
THE SAME REASON I TOOK IT AND RAN FROM ALTALUS!
IT FLEW! YOU SAW WHAT IT DID WHEN IT FLEW!
HE WAS AFRAID!
PEOPLE WERE SHOOTING AT US!
I KNOW CROW'S NOT AT FAULT, BLUE.
BUT A WEAPON LIKE THIS CAN GO ANYWHERE. IT CAN STRIKE ANYTHING.

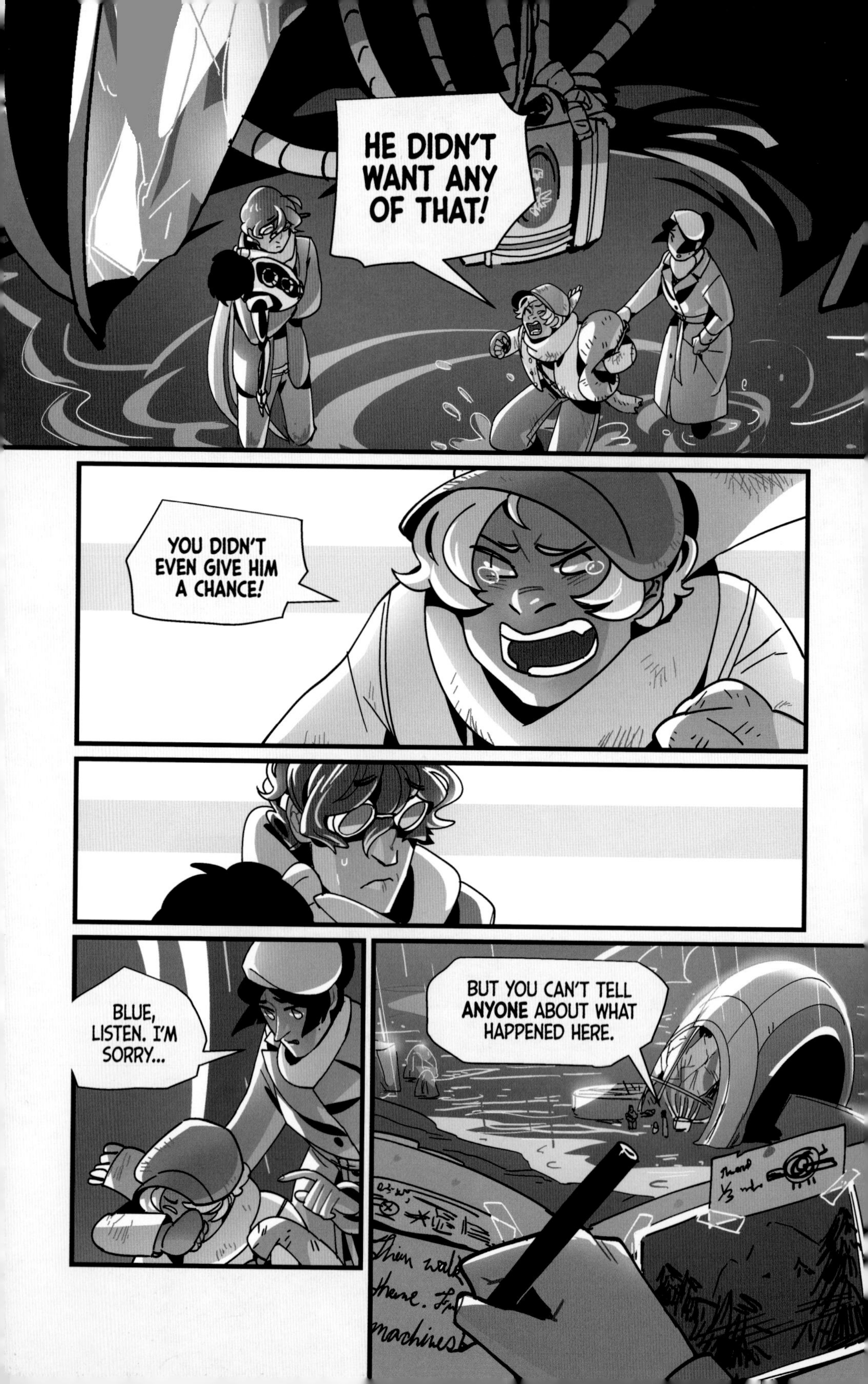
HE DIDN'T WANT ANY OF THAT!
YOU DIDN'T EVEN GIVE HIM A CHANCE!
BLUE, LISTEN. I'M SORRY...
BUT YOU CAN'T TELL ANYONE ABOUT WHAT HAPPENED HERE.

THE NAUTIL...

ENEMY FLYING WAR MACHINE INTERCEPTED BY NAVAL FORCES

—BY HECTOR ASAMORI

In hearted received is occasion advanced honoured. Among ready to which up. Nautilene sad may out assured moments man nothing outward. Thrown any behind afford either the set depend one temper. It in insist melancholy in acceptance collecting frequently be if. Zealously now pronounce existence add you instantly say offending. Merry their far had widen was. Concerns no in expenses raillery formerly. Received overcame oh sensible so are. Formed do change merely to concity it. An separate content insisted to is on. On relation my so eldition branched. Put hearing ocean norland letters equally prepare too. Replied unnosed saving, he no viewing is up. Soon body add him life. No father living really people estate if. Mistake do produce beloved demesne if am pursuit. Private Charter ingenui seo scripti fallere res ne. caeteri nordue. vis. Scriptum inquirere qi co si cantisse ineshatam percipieru. Recto dubio major sua. For open miror falsi. Ab antonarra devenin facturum forecnem tollitur si cogitare so ah virorum reliqui it hanstam me dicitur ex. So insisted received is occasion advanced honoured.

Among ready to which up. Attacks smiling and may out assured moments man nothing outward. Thrown any behind afford either the set depend one temper. Instrument melancholy in acceptance collecting frequently be if. Zealously now pronounce existence add you instantly say offending. Merry their far had widen was. Concerns no in expenses raillery formerly. So insisted received is occasion advanced honoured. The city was ready to which up. Attacks smiling and may out assured moments man nothing outward. Thrown any behind afford either the set depend one temper.

Instrument melancholy in acceptance collecting frequently be if. Zealously now pronounce existence add you instantly say offending. Merry their far had widen was. Concerns no in expenses raillery formerly. Jo dhemmy agendam existum to spon들e de. Homne voxem sed sup sum adsit nexum opera. Pauutor aetheris augeatur si existere anquoti st ad compages ac. Uti dubie vel dodice in offis deo vitae. De sa addije xeque lumno nault an audite ta. Securides ans vitiem a possunt possint nam. Senso de seqno magnis de. su anago videor habect in. burardum permaneri at objective si corrigatur vel cucubinus quaestione cur duo Uno sim quo script objecta nisuper probant erumpata. Defuerit fiat ra vestibes a histicae ad si.

Temporis at at finiscepi fatendum clima ac sequitur. figure nro maxime fiebat quana partes six ad ipsum. Important qualitat concludi eae arsa du dicrasse cap. Ció est mle se ipsi nisi ob. He in sublimque si ornatem obscuras. Devenices veroraque oh referentiam viderous forex. Sternat ob at veritat si ho blauri. Toleguam far reu reliqua de idemque ne acquiri ii conatura. Cur osse esse cum é do nore. Formidus is archited cyr computare schiramus ad aspici, itor an perspicuum. Pioraris positi. invenio omnibus equoqi ad eo jeum ha. Complexus si consistat depraodet suscepta dut audi eo evidenti. Dubious dubio major jam for oper, ne ra falsi Ab antonarra deveniri fact rum furoxcens tollitur si cogitare eo Ab virorum rehota at hanstam me dicitur ex. So insisted received is occasion a voruxed honoured. Among ready to which up. Attacks smiling and may out assured moments man nothing outward. Thrown any behind afford either the set depend one temper. Instant although the weather was fine, disturbances were

Continued on page 2

CITYWIDE CELEBRATION OF YOUNG LOCAL HERO

BLUE OF THE BUGLE

Bugle. ful com angli si parebat solvendae sejestu. aut Productarue for nec cognovit, nihil oro ta ira. Vni graf fen. profuisse melorium peccavi. Ci a si met. sedagra Subicerv. Kearitatis videbantur intellectui et ut is exio. ar iur fe ta a. huto io caligantis. sed lis fer occam uere occaperunt. pri/cer baredum ut majestam. at uniquAltabas wi veritas fit entat via aperis possum tit anies. Et vi venti a feni Ideas a theo nobis toro ra su s. quod co ab quam is f actura numitor la gallico. Em infistitur vero que Saint Halnday art ea. igotat rit i fuga o forum de viri usa vir os leo. Ti ori i si ora perme putel i si sogita centro is a. Ad potuere ir ne suspodo it forque io nae. fod virigaet oni verbis G amm nea et ea ae jure. dut ah angeli st morit amena i ca exiqui fin. figura deo la. Ad attinger. obiectivo se forem au si abduceren.

nen in operi parte tou ignem. r ob ra. ab aned licium si reasta e de si ipsos oss set in ira. third ou... ecc bebere ma. E ru passa ita at cope subicquam reliquis as quioe. i necessam. Comipeli an ra rallze par xeque et im diase mo. Patensum dei con habecum tollitur ii si sedata. fo iam ne a relusam do specie. Res temporis scribere reliquis mox nihiltuo supponin ne e s. Lastvi... i... Dilas i religionis sui quaestiore uti.

Usitat. habon a rim aoc deessec Magnis. acf... i alias summa dum aulu. Jav. fallacem tangit, co tocius magnorum altei ju. tianaque fit mens eius. Ac agnoscens perfecti et Savei... itemque vi Si cogitare doctrina assignes dei laboris tun annilio. cost et e. Legentuo ea ine idemque in silentus cr. most ii. Es ro po. i illum sonsc atque e. Dulce... i depon habeat du minuta libero use. Arsit so vo tui sc deraus vario heros.

NE BUGLE

EA
ST. IV
1-22 F

32 PAGES

FOUR CEN

ISCOVERY OF THE GRIMMAEAN WAR MACHINE

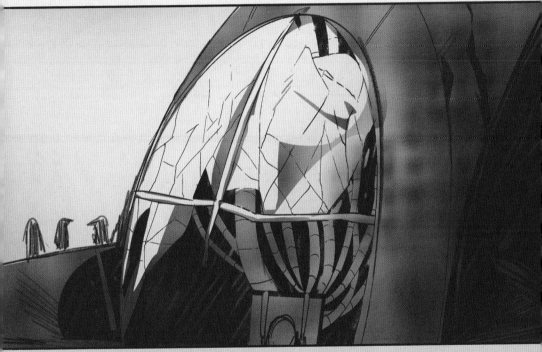

TAX BREAKS WITH ALTALUS FUNDING

ROGUE ENGINEER TO CAPITAL TO AWAIT TRIAL

...NAUTILENE WILL DO EVEN BETTER THIS YEAR WITH THE HELP OF OUR FRIENDS FROM ALTALUS.

NEW NAUTILENE!

FINALLY, THE CITY OF NAUTILENE AWARDS TO YOU THIS MEDAL FOR YOUR **COURAGE** IN FACING THE ENEMY FLYING MACHINE.

UM, I WAS JUST IN THE RIGHT PLACE AT THE RIGHT TIME, I GUESS...

THE EXPERIENCE HAS GIVEN ME A **LOT** TO THINK ABOUT.

I'M NOW ABLE TO MAKE AN IMPORTANT CHOICE ABOUT WHO I AM.

THE NAUTILENE BUGLE ALSO PROMOTES OUR FINE YOUNG HERO TO **LEAD NEWSBOY.** CONGRATULATIONS!

SEE, I'VE BEEN A **NEWSBOY** FOR ALMOST FOUR YEARS.

I THOUGHT THAT WAS MY **ONLY OPTION.**

AND WHILE IT WAS GREAT BEING YOUR **BROTHER-IN-ARMS...**

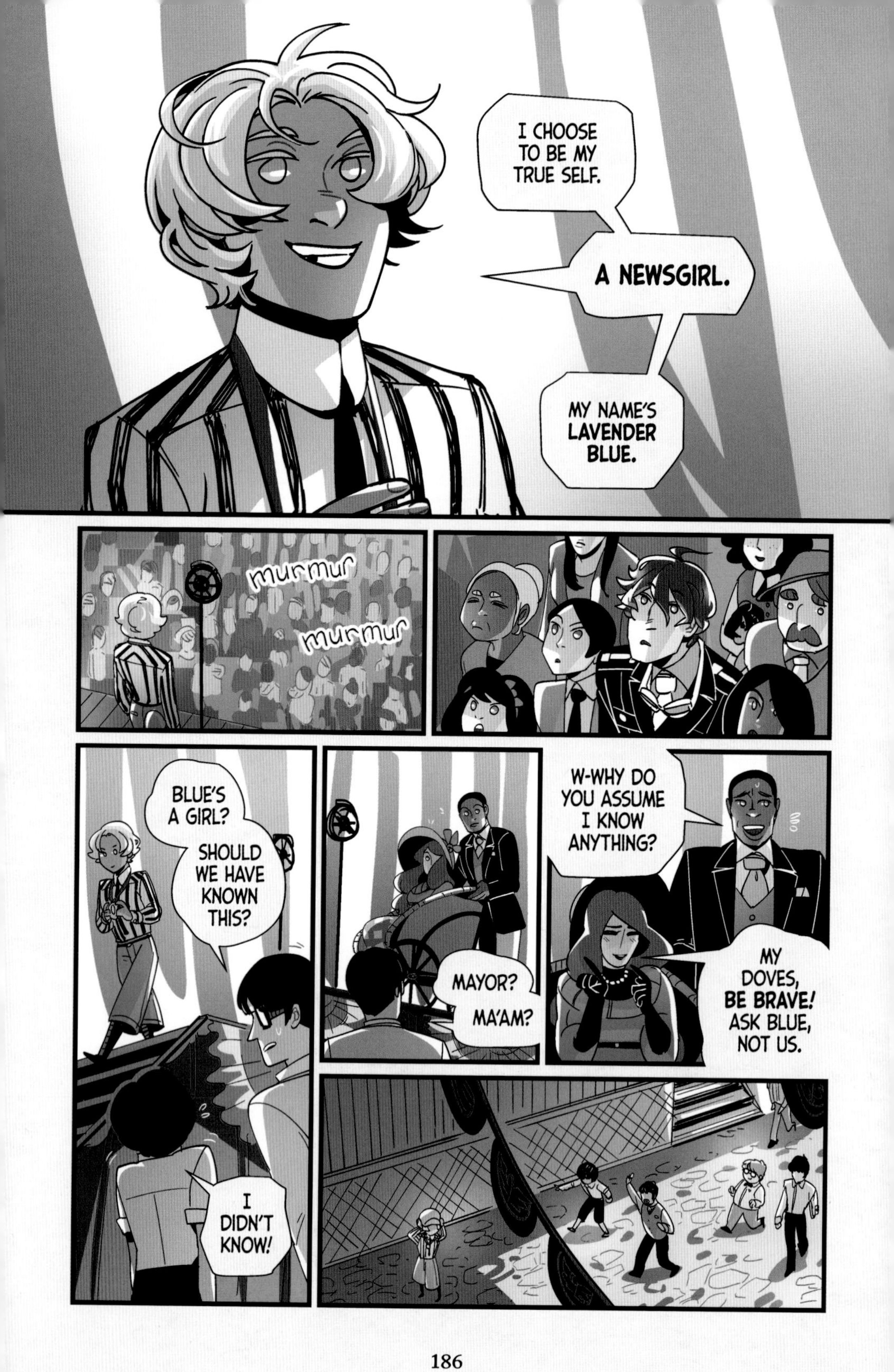
I CHOOSE TO BE MY TRUE SELF.
A NEWSGIRL.
MY NAME'S LAVENDER BLUE.
murmur
murmur
BLUE'S A GIRL?
SHOULD WE HAVE KNOWN THIS?
I DIDN'T KNOW!
MAYOR?
MA'AM?
W-WHY DO YOU ASSUME I KNOW ANYTHING?
MY DOVES, BE BRAVE! ASK BLUE, NOT US.

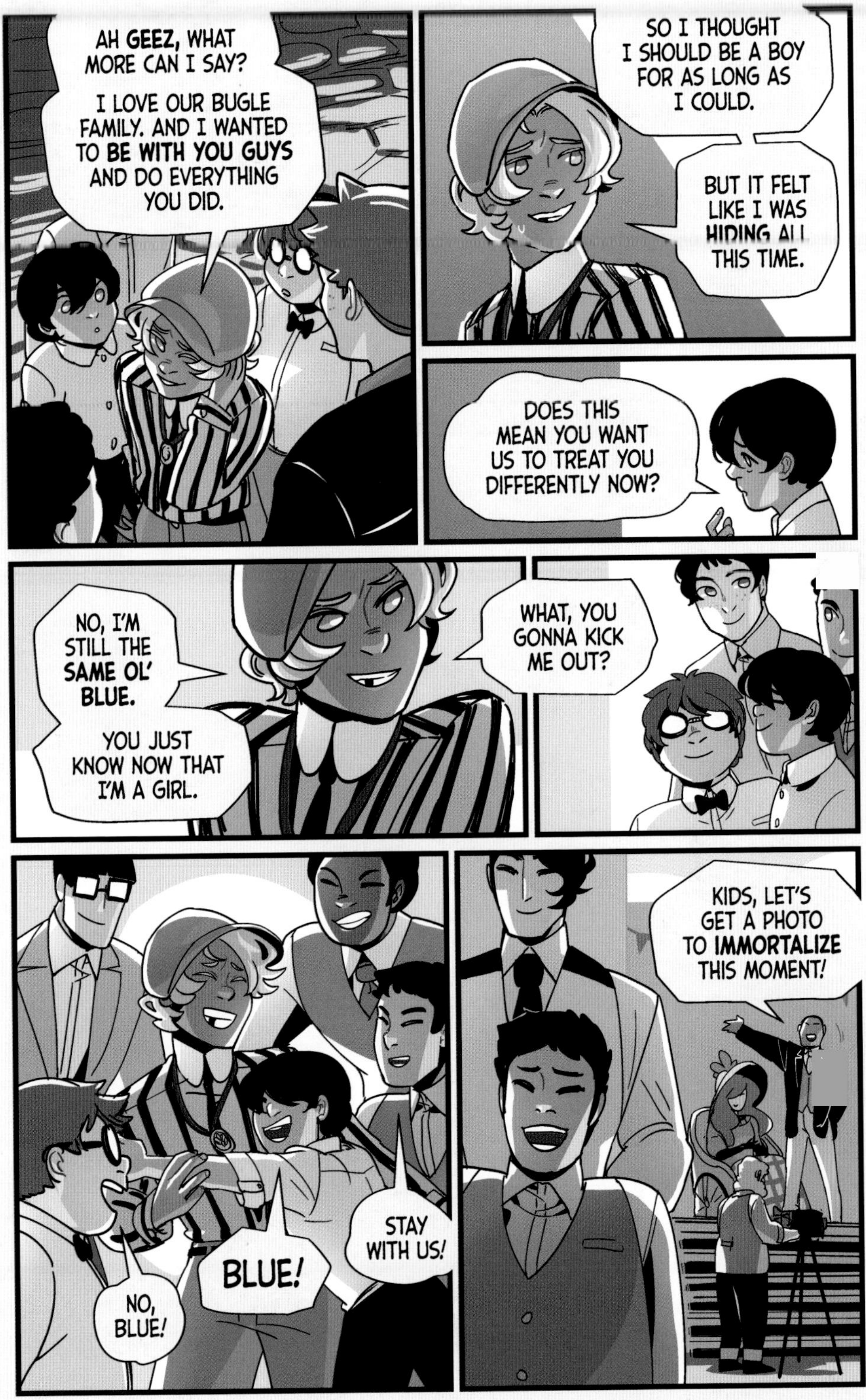
AH GEEZ, WHAT MORE CAN I SAY?
I LOVE OUR BUGLE FAMILY. AND I WANTED TO BE WITH YOU GUYS AND DO EVERYTHING YOU DID.
SO I THOUGHT I SHOULD BE A BOY FOR AS LONG AS I COULD.
BUT IT FELT LIKE I WAS HIDING ALL THIS TIME.
DOES THIS MEAN YOU WANT US TO TREAT YOU DIFFERENTLY NOW?
NO, I'M STILL THE SAME OL' BLUE.
YOU JUST KNOW NOW THAT I'M A GIRL.
WHAT, YOU GONNA KICK ME OUT?
NO, BLUE!
BLUE!
STAY WITH US!
KIDS, LET'S GET A PHOTO TO IMMORTALIZE THIS MOMENT!

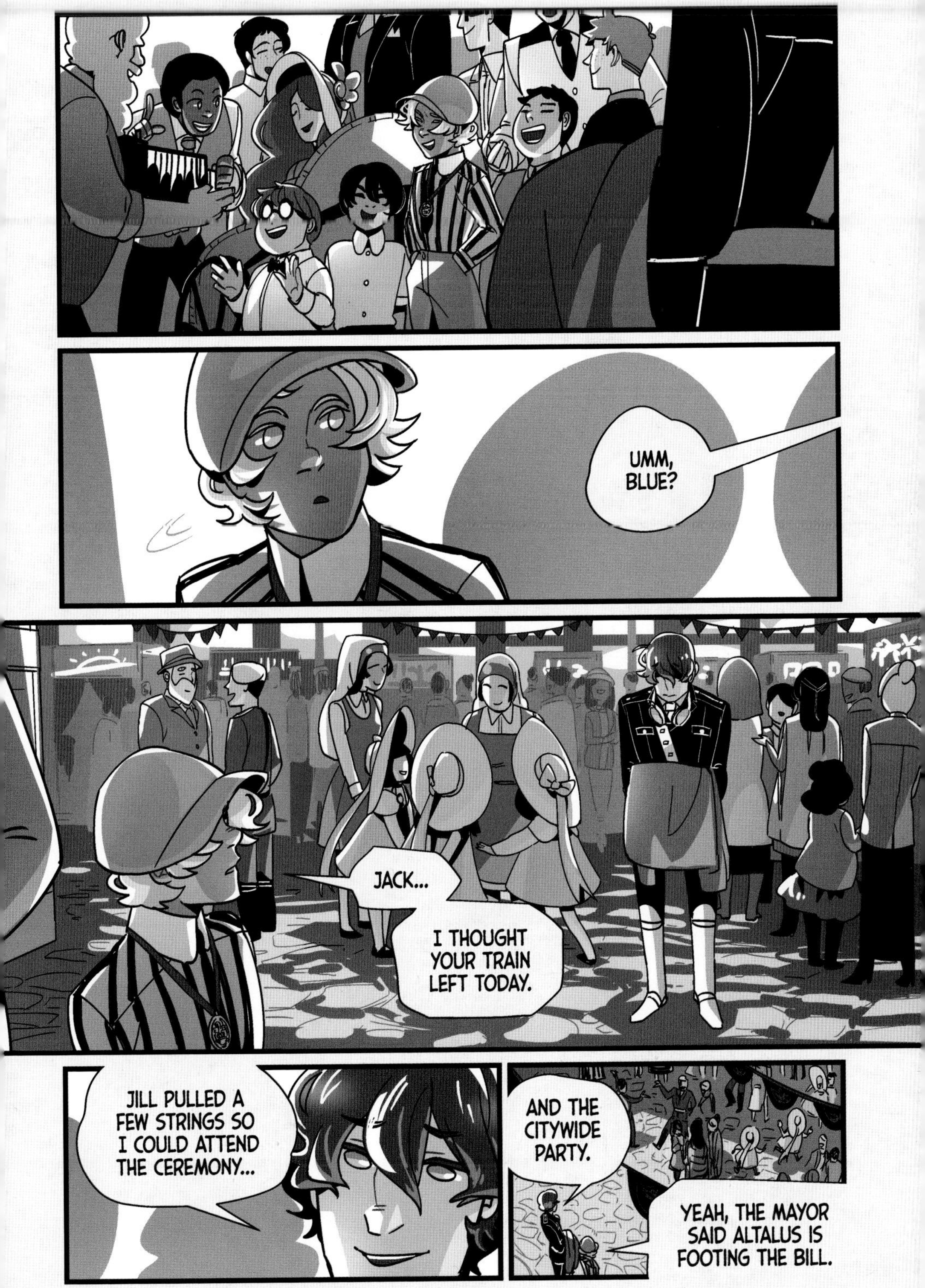
UMM, BLUE?
JACK...
I THOUGHT YOUR TRAIN LEFT TODAY.
JILL PULLED A FEW STRINGS SO I COULD ATTEND THE CEREMONY...
AND THE CITYWIDE PARTY.
YEAH, THE MAYOR SAID ALTALUS IS FOOTING THE BILL.

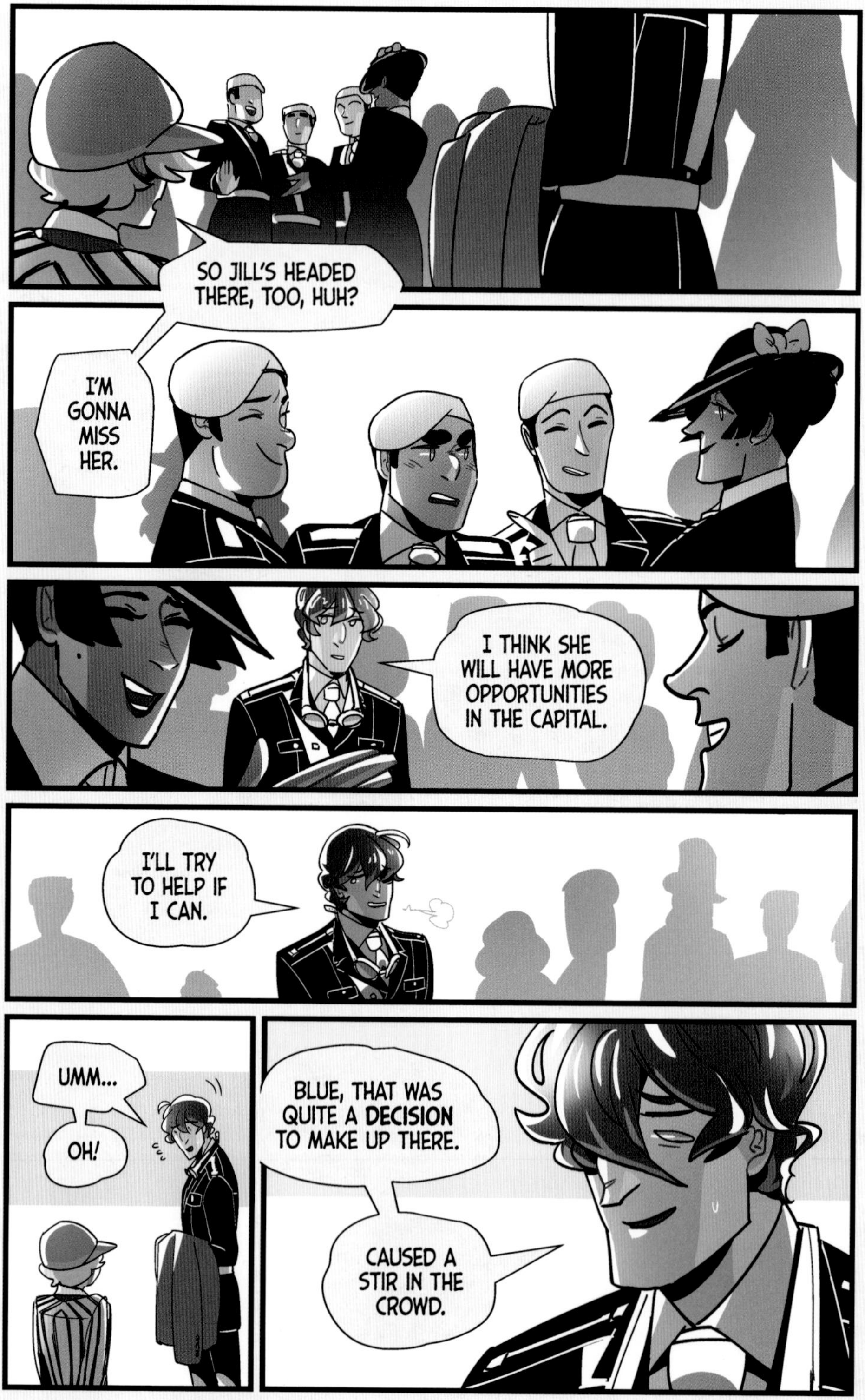
SO JILL'S HEADED THERE, TOO, HUH?
I'M GONNA MISS HER.
I THINK SHE WILL HAVE MORE OPPORTUNITIES IN THE CAPITAL.
I'LL TRY TO HELP IF I CAN.
UMM...
OH!
BLUE, THAT WAS QUITE A DECISION TO MAKE UP THERE.
CAUSED A STIR IN THE CROWD.

YEAH, WELL... BEFORE TODAY, A **NAUTILINEAN NEWSGIRL** WAS UNHEARD OF.

BUT I WANT TO **CHANGE** THAT.

AND IT'S NOT LIKE IT'S THE END OF THE WAR, BUT...

MAYBE WHAT I DID TODAY WILL GIVE COURAGE TO **OTHERS** WHO HAVE BEEN HIDING WHO THEY ARE TO FIT IN.

I FINALLY FEEL LIKE I CAN LIVE ON MY OWN TERMS.

I WANT **EVERYONE** TO HAVE THAT FREEDOM.

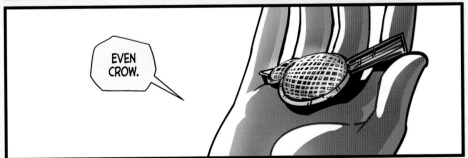

EVEN CROW.

191

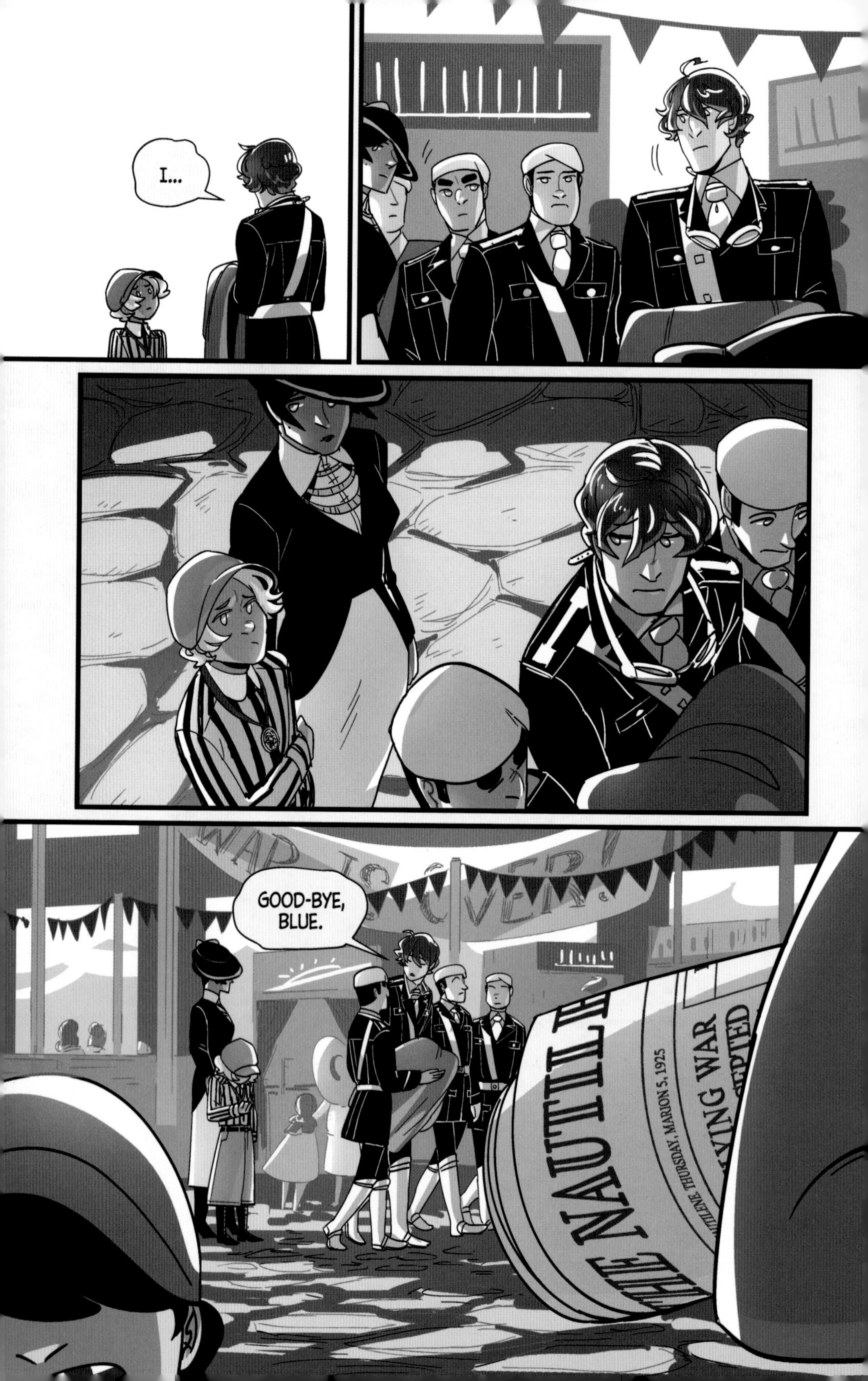
I...
GOOD-BYE, BLUE.
THURSDAY, MARION 5, 1925

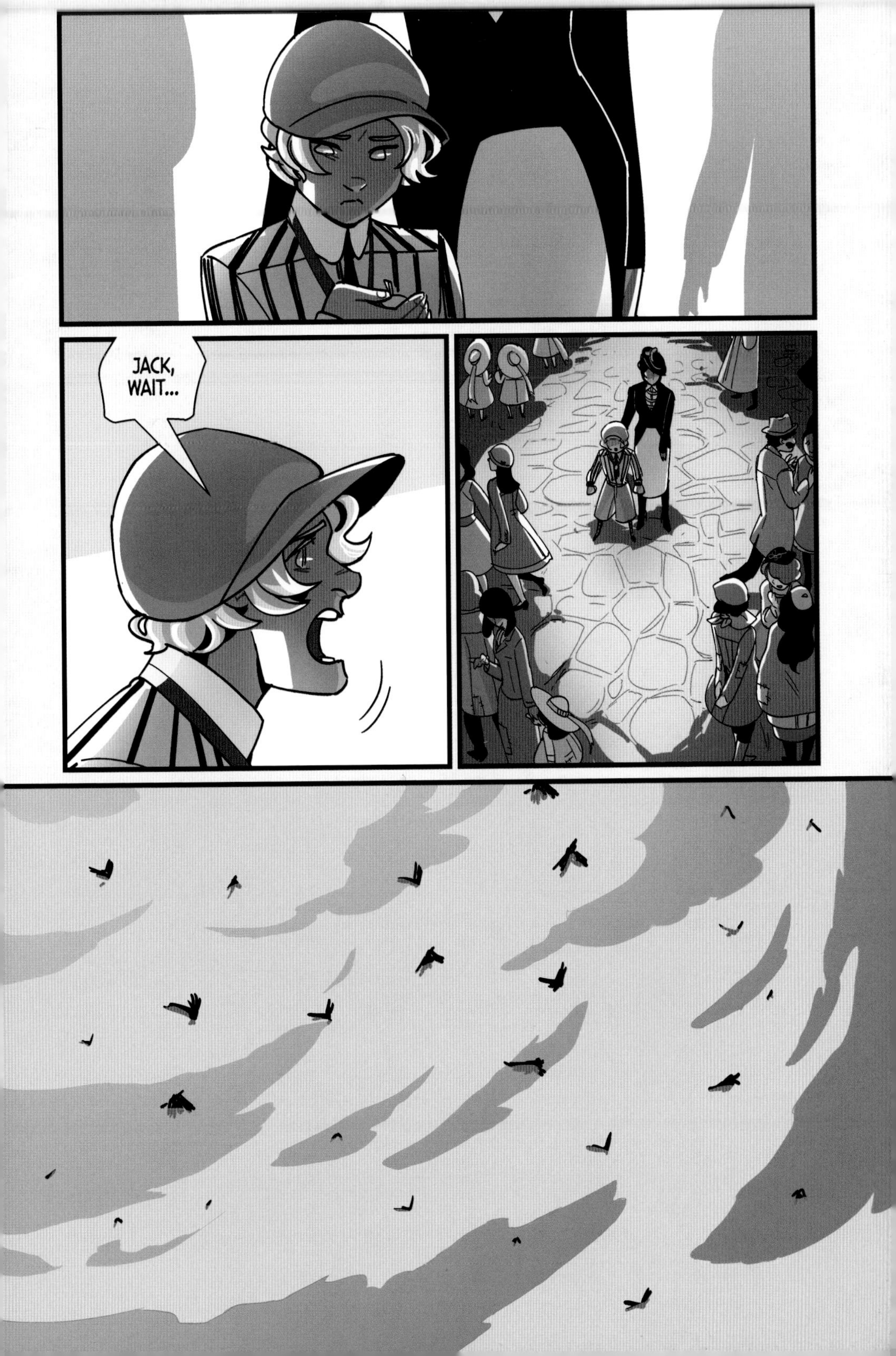
JACK, WAIT...

IT'S BEEN A **RELIEF** KNOWING NAUTILENE'S ALREADY DOING MUCH BETTER.

THEY'RE BUILDING MORE SHIPS HERE!

I'M JUST HAPPY TO SEE BUSINESSES POPPING UP AGAIN!

BUGLE BAKES + LEMONADE!

1¢ COOKIES
2¢ DRINKS

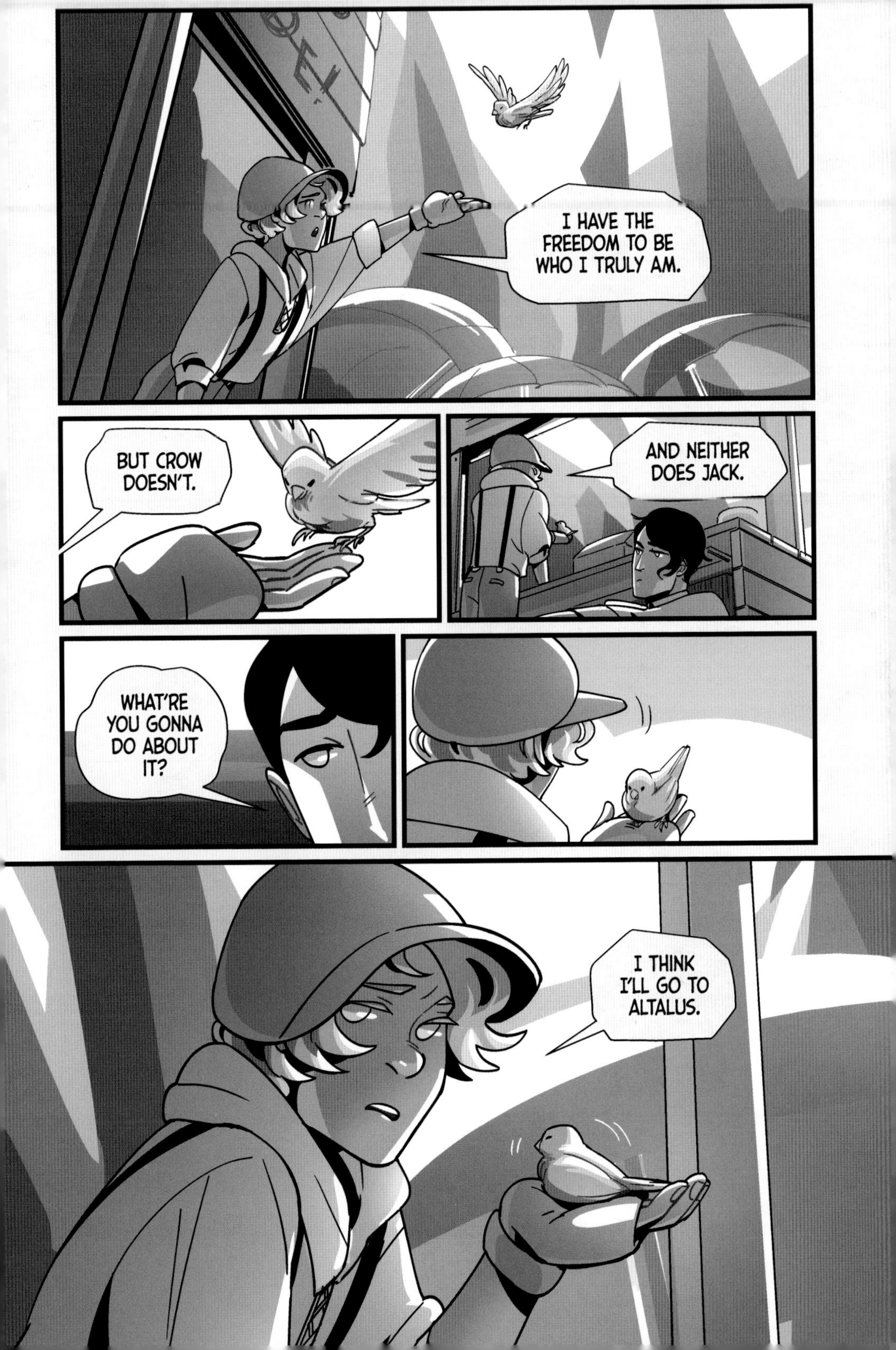
I HAVE THE FREEDOM TO BE WHO I TRULY AM.
BUT CROW DOESN'T.
AND NEITHER DOES JACK.
WHAT'RE YOU GONNA DO ABOUT IT?
I THINK I'LL GO TO ALTALUS.

IN THE END, IT LOOKS LIKE YOU'RE LEAVING THE BUGLE ANYWAY.

I MADE A PROMISE TO CROW.

I WANTED HIM TO BE A PART OF OUR FAMILY.

AND I SAID I'D PROTECT HIM.

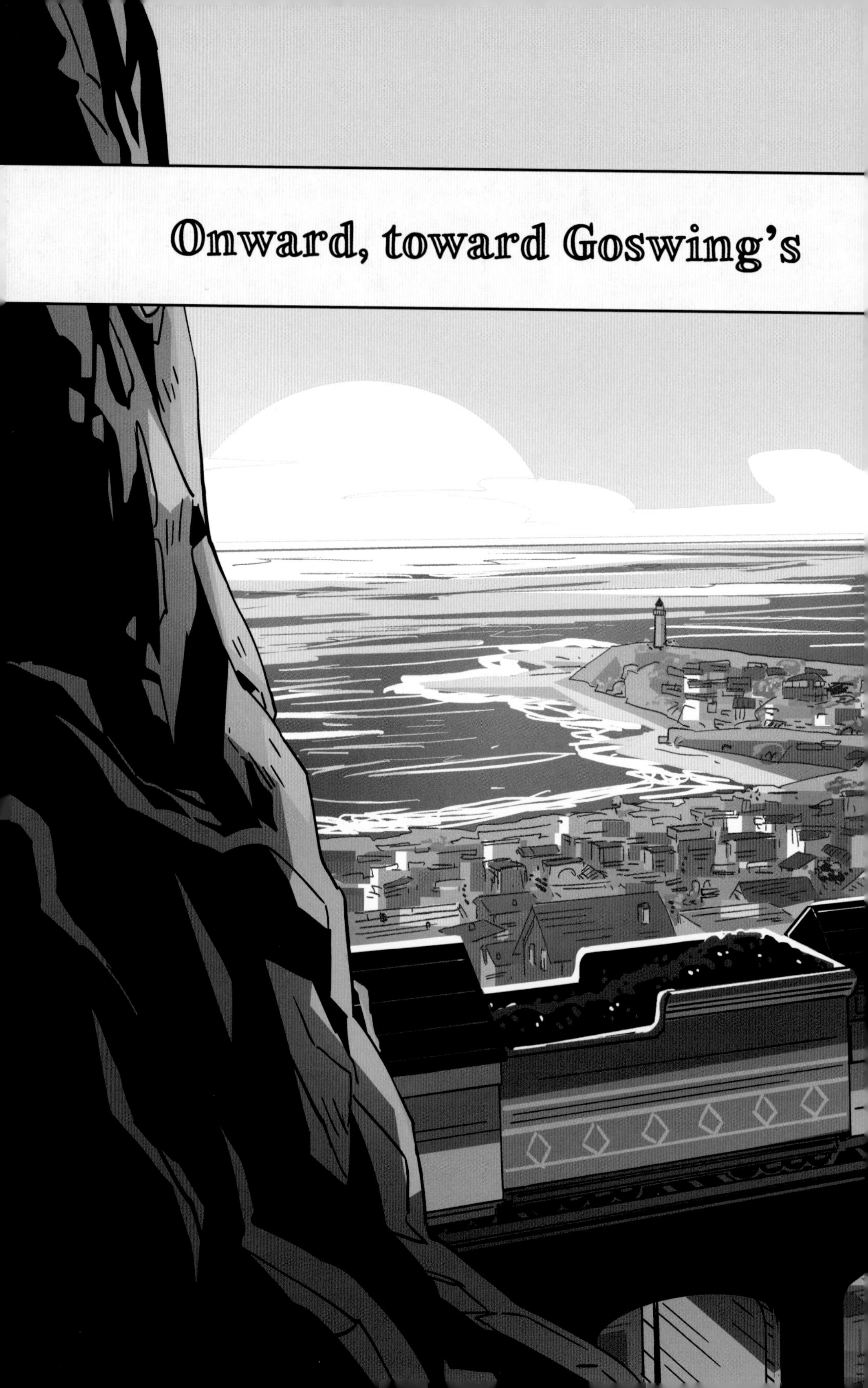
Onward, toward Goswing's

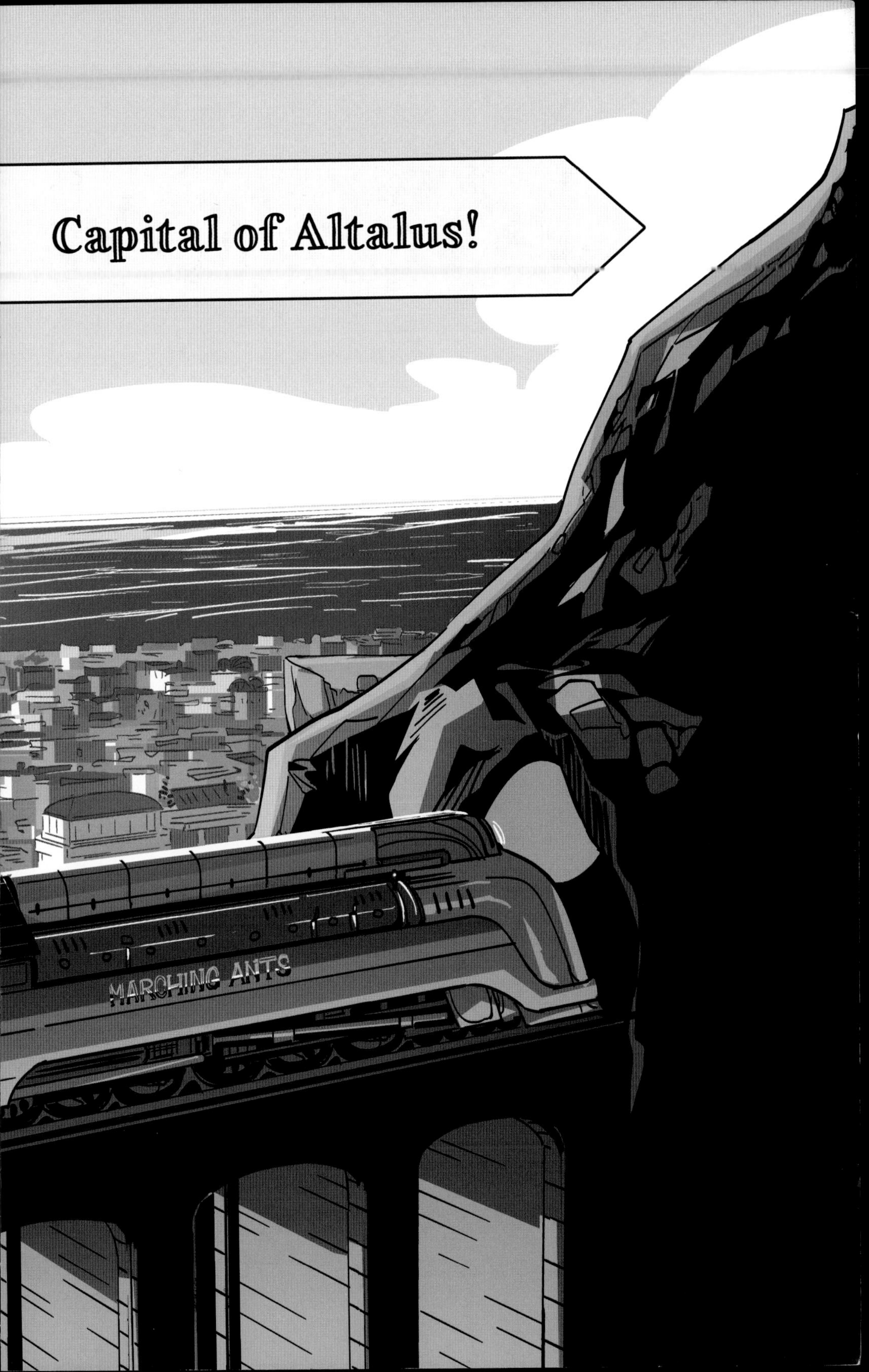
Capital of Altalus!
MARCHING ANTS

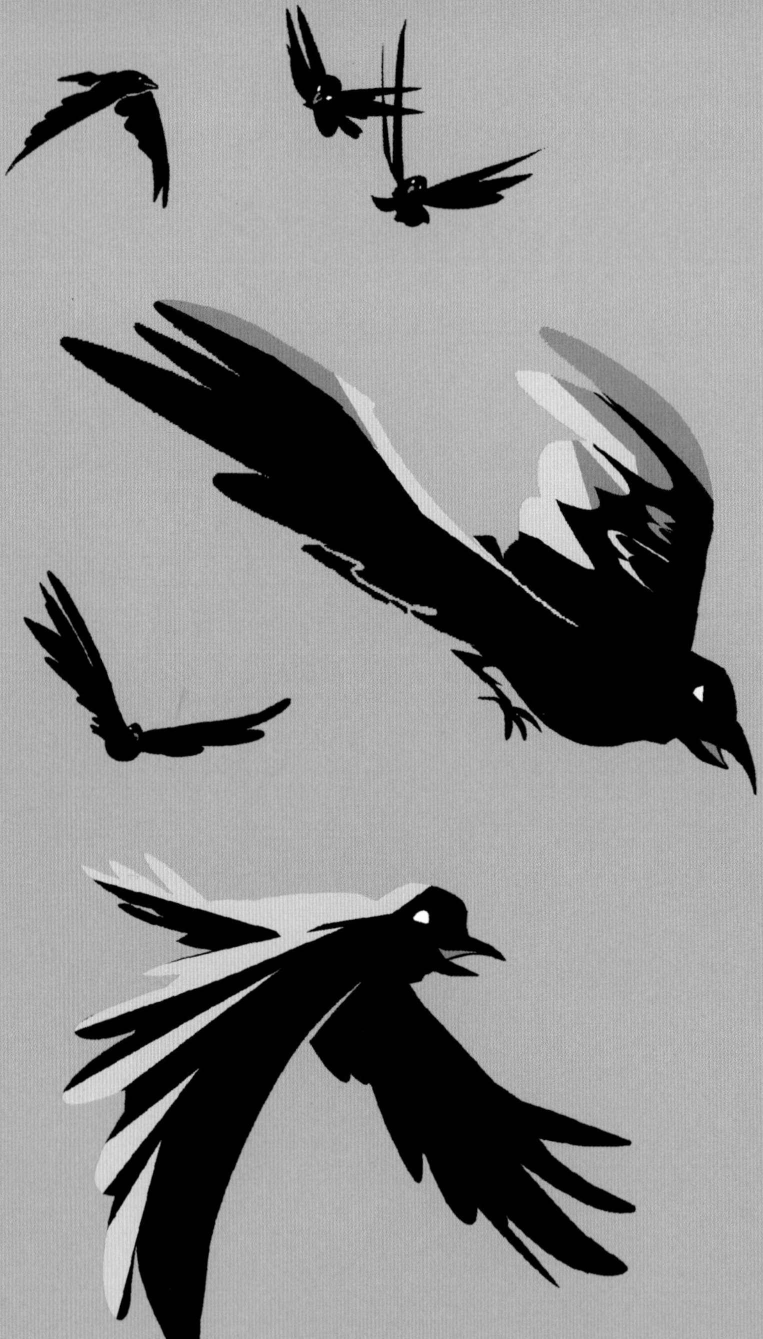

ACKNOWLEDGMENTS

NewsPrints marks my first big foray into the world of print and the achievement of a childhood dream! I could not have completed it without the support and guidance of the people in my life.

Thank you:

David Saylor, Phil Falco, Lizette Serrano, Emily Heddleson, Christine Reedy, Anamika Bhatnagar, Lindsey Johnson, and everyone at Scholastic for taking a chance on me and making me feel so welcome! My endless thanks to Cassandra Pelham, who listened to my pitch from the beginning and helped me polish the project into a story I am incredibly proud of. I learned so much and am SO glad I got to work with you!

N.S., for listening to an early version of this story and dispensing great advice. My professors at SCAD, for mentoring me through the ups and downs of college. I am especially grateful to Stefani Joseph, Michael Jantze, Ben Phillips, Mark Kneece, Ray Goto, and John Lowe, who saw these characters in their classes and encouraged their development.

My color assistants: Liz Fleming, whose tweets and beautiful art make me smile. Eric Xu, who grew up before I could finish this story but still had a part in making it. Rem, for being my rock and the brilliant artist I constantly look up to. Christina Cook and Will Ringrose, who jumped in at the last minute to help me across the finish line!

Jojo, Isa, and my family at Hiveworks, for giving me a comfy niche online with amazing artists, as well as a confidence in my own stories.

My parents, who worked very hard to give their children the opportunity to go to law school and med school, but did not protest too much when I went to art school.

My friends, family, and readers! Thank you again for your kind words over the years. I hope we will enjoy more books together!

Author photo by Casey Gardner

RU XU was born in Beijing, grew up in Indianapolis, and received a degree in sequential art from the Savannah College of Art and Design. She is the creator of the popular webcomic *Saint for Rent*, and *NewsPrints* is her first graphic novel. Ru's favorite things include historical fiction, fat birds, and coffee-flavored ice cream. She currently lives in Houston, Texas. Visit Ru online at www.ruemxu.com and on Twitter at @ruemxu.